SAVAGE TEXAS
REBEL YELL

SAVAGE TEXAS
REBEL YELL

William W. Johnstone
with J. A. Johnstone

PINNACLE BOOKS
Kensington Publishing Corp.
www.kensingtonbooks.com

PINNACLE BOOKS are published by

Kensington Publishing Corp.
119 West 40th Street
New York, NY 10018

PUBLISHER'S NOTE
Following the death of William W. Johnstone, the Johnstone family is working with a carefully selected writer to organize and complete Mr. Johnstone's outlines and many unfinished manuscripts to create additional novels in all of his series like The Last Gunfighter, Mountain Man, and Eagles, among others. This novel was inspired by Mr. Johnstone's superb storytelling.

All Kensington titles, imprints, and distributed lines are available at special quantity discounts for bulk purchases for sales promotions, premiums, fund-raising, educational, or institutional use. Special book excerpts or customized printings can also be created to fit specific needs. For details, write or phone the office of the Kensington special sales manager: Kensington Publishing Corp., 119 West 40th Street, New York, NY 10018, attn: Special Sales Department; phone 1-800-221-2647.

ISBN-13: 978-0-7860-3362-1
ISBN-10: 0-7860-3362-2

First printing: November 2014

10 9 8 7 6 5 4 3 2 1

Printed in the United States of America

First electronic edition: November 2014

ISBN-13: 978-0-7860-3363-8
ISBN-10: 0-7860-3363-0

GONE TO TEXAS
—Note posted on property abandoned by those
who left Dixie for points west after the war

ONE

"Trust! That's the heart and soul of the gunrunner's trade," Honest Bob Longford said. His statement was subject to doubt if the reaction of his listeners was any gauge.

Sully bridled, stiffening as if insulted. Hunch-backed Hump Colway sneered, muttering under his breath. Lank looked surprised. Fitch choked on his whiskey. He was drinking from a brown bottle, head tilted back, throat working as he guzzled.

Honest Bob's remark sank in, throwing Fitch off his rhythm. He coughed and sputtered. The whiskey was raw, pungent. It went down the wrong pipe, burning like fire.

Fitch's head felt like it was exploding. Brown liquid spewed from his mouth and nostrils. He staggered, wheezing, gasping, eyes tearing. He was careful not to drop the bottle, though.

Some of the outlaw gang laughed at him.

Fitch would have cursed them, but he lacked the breath. He sat down hard in the dirt, still mindful to hold the bottle upright.

"You made me choke on my redeye, Bob," Fitch said, wiping tears from his eyes.

"Reckon his remarks was a bit hard for you to swallow, eh, Fitch?" Half-Shot said slyly, working the needle.

"I'm gonna have a little fun with Fitch," Lank said, nudging Half-Shot in the ribs with an elbow. "Watch this."

"Uh-oh," Hump Colway said.

Lank went to Fitch and snatched the bottle from him. "Gimme that before you waste any more, hombre."

"Hey! Gimme that back," Fitch wheezed.

Lank raised the bottle to his mouth and started drinking.

Fitch struggled to his feet. "Gimme that, you! I ain't playing—" He lurched toward Lank, groping for the bottle.

Lank warded off Fitch's fumbling attempts with his free hand.

"Don't be like that," Fitch growled.

"Better break this up before it gets out of hand." But Hump made no move to interfere. He knew better.

Fitch lunged, grabbing for the bottle. Lank side-stepped, evading. Fitch stumbled. He nearly fell but recovered.

Lank upturned the bottle. He gulped, gurgling and draining the last of the whiskey.

Fitch crouched, breathing hard. "I'm ain't funning, damn you."

"Give him the bottle," Hump said.

Lank lowered the bottle, his face red and flushed.

"Sure. Catch!" He tossed the bottle underhand at Fitch.

Moving with surprising speed, Fitch grabbed it out of the air. He held it upside down, a last scant few drops dribbling from the bottle. "Empty!"

Lank's shrug said, *What of it?*

"You drunk it all to spite me," Fitch accused.

"I drunk it because I was thirsty," Lank said. "Besides, you had enough—"

Fitch threw the bottle at him. Lank dodged in time to keep from getting hit in the head.

Fitch charged, barreling into him and knocking him off balance. He launched a looping roundhouse right, slamming Lank's jaw with an audible thud. Lank went down, taking a pratfall.

Some of the outlaw gang laughed, mainly those standing where Lank couldn't see them. He was a bad man to cross. They all were.

Lank sat up, dazed. Fitch stood ready, fists upraised.

"You hit me!" Lank said wonderingly, rubbing the side of his swollen jaw. His eyes shone with a wild light. He grabbed for his gun.

"Don't!" somebody cried, but it was too late. It was always too late.

Fitch drew first, firing before Lank's gun cleared the holster. He pumped a couple quick shots into Lank.

The reports were loud in the oven-like air, the smell of burnt gunpowder heavy.

"Damn!" Half-Shot whispered, awed.

A hush came over the gang.

Lank flopped back down in the dirt, raising a small cloud of dust. His chest was shattered by three bullet holes. Blood pooled from them, so dark it was more brown than red, soaking his shirtfront.

His eyes were open, unseeing. He looked puzzled, abstracted, as if trying to work some complicated sum in his head. His right leg kicked a couple times and then was still.

"That tears it," Honest Bob said. "He's done."

"Ya reckon?" Sully said sarcastically, because he was that kind of hombre. Never an encouraging word.

Fred Sullivan was his real name. Sullen Fred Sullivan, they called him. Sully.

Fitch stood still, motionless, a line of gun smoke curling from the barrel of the gun in his fist. He shook his head as if trying to clear it.

He turned, facing the rest of the gang. The gun turned with him, pointing at the outlaws but not at anyone in particular. Those in his line of fire were careful to keep their hands away from their guns and avoid making sudden moves. Or any moves at all.

"You all seed it. Lank went for his gun first . . ."

"We saw it, Fitch. Now put down the gun before anybody else gets hurt," Honest Bob said.

Drunk though he was, Fitch couldn't help but see the humor in the sweet talk. He giggled. "Hurt? Hell, he's daid!"

"Easy does it, bo," said a voice behind Fitch. "You don't want to kill nobody else. You don't want to get killed yourself."

It was the voice of Sefton, standing with a gun to Fitch's head. Fitch's eyes widened when he felt the muzzle of the gun against the back of his skull.

"Nothing personal, Fitch, but I surely will blow your head clean off if you don't drop that gun. And I mean right now," Sefton said calmly. He could afford to be calm—he had the drop on Fitch.

Fitch swallowed hard, letting the gun slip from his fingers. It fell into the soft sandy soil without going off.

Sefton swung the gun barrel hard against Fitch's head. It hit with a *thunk*.

Fitch staggered, going wobbly in the knees. He stayed on his feet, though. Sefton hit him harder, frowning. Fitch went down. Sefton's frown smoothed out.

Bending down, Sefton picked up Fitch's gun. "He did enough damage with this already. Too much."

"Hang on to that gun. Fitch is gonna want it later," Honest Bob cautioned.

"So what? Who gives a damn what he wants?"

"We're gonna need every gun we've got when the Comanches show. Drunk or sober, Fitch can shoot."

"He sure proved that!" Half-Shot said.

"We'd be in a fine fix if them savages showed now," Honest Bob added. "They'd sure 'nuff catch us with our pants down!"

That struck home with the others, because it was true. They looked around, scanning for Comanches, finding none. But that didn't mean they weren't somewhere near, hiding.

A couple outlaws stood over Lank, eyeing him. Honest Bob went down on one knee beside the body for a closer look.

"Dead?" somebody asked casually.

"Dead as they come," Honest Bob said.

A harsh metallic smell of fresh-spilled blood came off the corpse. The bullet holes in Lank's chest were closely spaced together.

"Nice target grouping," Honest Bob murmured admiringly.

"I said that boy could shoot!" Half-Shot cackled.

"Yeah, if he gets any better, we won't have any men left," Sully said sourly.

"Can't say I cared too much for Lank. He was always trying to get at a fellow, like a burr under the saddle." Half-Shot said.

"Him and you both," Hump Colway cracked.

Half-Shot gave him a dirty look, but Hump ignored it.

"Lank won't play no more of his sly tricks," Half-Shot mused.

"He tried them on the wrong man this time, that's for sure," Hump agreed.

Honest Bob rose, brushing dust off the knees of his pants. "Got to get that body out of sight. Can't let the Comanches see that. Dead white man's liable to give them ideas."

"They don't need to see Lank for that. They already got plenty of ideas on that score," Sully said.

"Some of you men get some shovels and bury him," Honest Bob ordered. He was the leader of the gang, at least out on the plains where the day's mission was concerned.

Hump Colway drifted away, making himself scarce, a habit of his when hard work was involved.

Honest Bob's beady-eyed gaze fell on Half-Shot and Sully. Although there were plenty of men in the gang, they were the nearest to hand. And their gun-handling skills were only fair to middling compared to some of the others, an important consideration.

"Get to it, you two," Honest Bob snapped. "Don't plant him near the water or the horses."

Half-Shot and Sully stayed in place, not moving.

"What's the problem? You deaf or something?" Honest Bob demanded.

Half-Shot held his hat in his hands, turning it around by the brim, fidgeting. "It's too damn hot for any grave digging," he said at last. Sully nodded in sullen agreement.

Honest Bob thought it over and decided not to push it. There'd already been one senseless killing. "What do you suggest?" he asked, throwing it back to them, trying in vain to keep the harshness out of his voice.

"Dump him behind some rocks out of sight," Sully said.

Half-Shot looked like he was thinking it over. "That'll do for a start, but pile some rocks on top of him so wild animals can't get at him."

"Want to hold services over him, too?"

"Hell, Sully, that's the least we can do. After all, Lank was one of us."

"Didn't you just get done saying you didn't like him?"

"Haul him out of sight and pile some rocks on him," Honest Bob said. "Get two more men to help you out. Tell them I said so."

That seemed reasonable. Half-Shot and Sully dragooned two of the gang's smaller fry, lesser even than they, into helping. Each took hold of a limb by ankle or wrist, lifted Lank off the ground, and lugged him a stone's throw away, behind some boulders.

There was no shortage of boulders at the secret meeting place under the cliffs on the Texas plains. Numerous rockfalls and landslides had peeled off from the scarp. The burial detail picked up rocks from the ground, covering up Lank.

Fitch lay sprawled flat on the ground, stunned, groaning. Honest Bob and Sefton carried him to the wagon and rolled him under it, out of the sun. Half-Shot joined them. They stood for a moment looking down at Fitch, who lay twitching and breathing heavily through his mouth.

They turned, looking east across the wide open plains. Sefton pushed back his hat brim, wiping the sweat from his forehead on his shirtsleeve.

"What was that you was saying before about trust, Bob?" Half-Shot asked slyly, starting up. He was a needler. He liked to pick at people if he thought he could get away with it. He was not unlike Lank on that score. "Something about trust and gunrunning, I do believe?" he pressed.

Honest Bob cut him a sharp side glance but then condescended to reply. "I was about to make some remarks on that subject, now that you mention it."

"Looks like your proposition got shot down along with Lank."

"How so?"

"Lord knows Lank wasn't the easiest person in the world to get along with, but he and Fitch seemed to get on all right. Yet Fitch burned him down quick as winking!"

Sefton spat. "What choice did he have? Lank was reaching. What the hell!"

Half-Shot flinched, fearing he might have irked Sefton. He wasn't one you wanted to rile. He was moody, unpredictable. He stalked off, to Half-Shot's evident relief.

Honest Bob caught the play, chuckling. The other's

momentary fright put him in a good mood. "Fitch gunning Lank proves my point."

"Which is?" Half-Shot asked.

"Trust *is* the basis of the gunrunner's trade."

"You're loco, Bob," Sully said, walking up. "What a damn fool thing to say!"

"What's got you in an uproar, Sull?" Honest Bob asked mildly. "It sure ain't Lank getting killed. You never had any use for him."

"Lank was an idjit, pulling a damn-fool stunt like that on Fitch. But at least Fitch had a skinful of hooch," Sully said, spitting out words like a snapping turtle going after live bait. "What's your excuse?"

Greatly amused, Honest Bob gave Half-Shot a wink that only he could see.

"Trust?" Sully said. "*Trust*? Maybe you forget who we're dealing with!"

"I ain't forgetting nothing, Sull."

"Comanches, that's who! Them red devils would cut all our throats given half a chance, and you talk about *trust*!" Sully went on, warming to his theme. "Never mind about them heathens, though. Take a look closer to home. Look at Fitch killing Lank over a bottle of rotgut whiskey . . . and not even a full bottle, neither! Trust? Hell, we don't even trust each other!"

"Speak for yourself. Personally, I trust all the boys. Trust them with my life. Otherwise, I wouldn't be here now." Honest Bob smiled.

"Sometimes you talk like a politician," Sully sneered.

"There's no call for that kind of abuse," Honest Bob said sharply.

"That was out of line, I admit," Sully said, backing down.

"See that it don't happen again."

"Sorry."

Two more of the gang, Melbourne and Chait, drifted over to see what all the jawing was about, as did Santa Fe Comancheros Felipe Mercurio and his pistolero bodyguard Rio.

Honest Bob was mindful that he was drawing an audience and began playing to them. "You know what your trouble is, Sully?"

"I'm sure you're gonna tell me, Bob."

"You're a man of little faith. Me, I trust the Comanches!"

That provoked a lot of loud protests from the others, dirty laughs, groans, eye-rolling expressions of disgust.

Honest Bob held up his hands to quell the noise. "Let me explain, let me explain. You'll all admit that the Comanche wants guns. That's plain to see. We wouldn't be here if it wasn't true. Them red rascals want guns and ammunition. Want them bad. And that's good, by Heaven, because we've got them!"

"Damn straight," somebody shouted.

"I'm talking about the real goods here, the quality. We ain't foisting no castoffs on our Indian friends— no rusty out-of-date smoothbore muskets, no pieces with broke firing pins, jammed actions, and bent barrels. No, sir." Honest Bob went on. "We got new guns . . . and like-new guns," he conceded. "Like new I said. Barely used, in good condition. We got long guns and carbines, famous name brands like Winchester, Sharps, and Henry! Repeaters! Repeating rifles! We've got them.

"Why, most of the cavalry out West ain't even outfitted with repeating rifles yet! Mostly, they've got outdated single-shot jobs."

"They got repeaters at Fort Pardee," Chait said pointedly.

"Sure, and look at all the trouble they had getting them," Honest Bob countered. "Their first shipment was hijacked out from under their noses before they ever took delivery. They had a devil of a time getting them back."

"They got 'em now," Chait pressed, his buddy Melbourne at his side, urging him on. They were a pair of professional guns, gunslicks hired for the protection their skills could bring. They weren't beholden to Honest Bob or any of his Hog Ranch crowd. Like the man said, they didn't give a damn whether school kept or not, and they didn't care who knew it.

"Look at all the trouble they have holding onto them! Troopers are always deserting, going over the hill with a repeater and a good horse," Honest Bob said. "But never mind about them Fort Pardee bluebellies nohow. They're at less than half-strength and stretched mighty thin, too.

"From what I've heard tell, they ain't gonna be a problem for much longer," he added darkly in an aside. Those who knew what he meant didn't react to it.

"Here's my point. When it comes to guns, Mr. Comanche can't get a better gun nowhere," Honest Bob went on quickly.

He noticed Mercurio standing nearby, listening intently. "Now before I go on, let's give credit where credit is due. Fact is, we wouldn't have these fine guns if not for Señor Mercurio here and our good friends in Santa Fe."

Mercurio was a stocky middle-aged man with thick black hair and a bushy mustache. He was a member of the Santa Fe Ring, longest established and most powerful Comancheros in the territory. He nodded, acknowledging the other's words.

"To continue," Honest Bob said, "here's a question. What do Comanches like more than guns?"

The outlaws shouted various answers.

"Horses!"

"Horse stealing!"

"Women!"

"White women!"

"No, no, amigos," Rio said, standing at Mercurio's elbow. He was Mexican American, one of a group of Hispanics associated with the Hog Ranch gang. Rio was a dangerous man. "What does the Comanche love best of all? *Killing.*"

"That's it! Killing is what those heathens love best!" Sully cried. "They'd like nothing better than to take our scalps."

"If they could," Melbourne said meaningfully, patting his holstered gun to show what he meant. He fancied himself quite the gunman.

Honest Bob nodded agreement. "That's it! Eagle Feather and his bucks would like nothing better than roasting any and all of us over a slow fire. Sure, they'd kill us if they could, but not before putting us through an almighty hard time first. Never mind that that would kill off the best source of guns they've got or will ever have.

"Or take our late friend Lank. Now you just don't go stealing a man's redeye. Everybody knows that. It ain't done. But Lank couldn't help himself. He just naturally liked getting folks riled up. That was his nature.

"That's the bedrock truth of my calculations. *People are gonna do anything you can't stop them from doing.* I trust in that and act accordingly. I trust the Comanches to kill us if we don't outgun them and outsmart them.

"That's why I say trust is the basis of our business," Honest Bob concluded.

"I don't know about that, Bob, but there is one thing that you've proved beyond a shadow of a doubt."

"What's that, Half-Shot?"

"That you sure 'nuff like the sound of your own voice!"

Half-Shot's crack got a laugh from some of the men.

"Of that there can be no doubt," Honest Bob said, laughing along with the others to show that he was a good sport. He wasn't, not really. But he could fake it when he had to. It was all part of being a leader of men, he told himself.

The group started to break up into smaller knots, going about their chores.

"Keep your eyes open and your guns handy, boys. Eagle Feather will be along directly," was Honest Bob's parting comment.

Sully didn't much care for company, not even his own. Still, he wanted to be off by himself. Not too far off, though. It wasn't safe. Comanches were beyond masters at taking stragglers and making them disappear.

Sully's path took him past a freight wagon nestled at the foot of a cliff. It was the wagon under which Fitch lay in a moaning stupor.

The gun wagon.

Guns and ammunition were in wooden crates in the hopper. The wagon team had been unyoked and corralled with the rest of the horses to prevent the Comanches from stampeding a harnessed team and running away with the wagon and its precious cargo of firearms.

Ricketts sat up on the front box seat, pale-eyed and swarthy with bristly beard stubble like steel wool. He flicked the edge of a thumbnail against the phosphorus-coated tip of a wooden matchstick. A lucifer type incandescent match, self-igniting. The tip sputtered, hissing into flame.

Sully recoiled, thunderstruck. "The hell you doing, Ricketts?"

"What does it look like?" Ricketts asked mildly.

"Like you're fixing to get yourself blowed up and me along with you!"

Ricketts waved away his concern. "I'm lighting my cigar, Sully, ya danged fool." He spoke as if talking to a child, a slow child.

The hot plains air was very still in the lee of the cliff. Ricketts had no need to cup a hand around the flame to protect it. He held the fire to the tip of a fresh cigar clenched between his teeth and puffed away, setting the cigar alight.

"Don't you know not to play with matches around gunpowder?" Sully demanded. "You'll blast us all sky-high!"

"I know what I'm doing," Ricketts said chuckling. "That's why they got me playing nursemaid to this here gun wagon and its combustible insurance policy."

The "insurance" was a desperate last resort against

Comanche treachery. In the wagon behind the seat stood a big keg of gunpowder lashed in place, a length of quick-burning fuse cord coiling out of a hole in the barrel lid.

Ricketts's job was to light the fuse to blow up the wagon and its contents if the Comanches tried a cross and jumped the gunrunners.

"Quit your fussing, Sully. Danged if I'm gonna lay off cigars just cause you're fussing like an old woman." Ricketts touched a fingertip to the match. It was cold. He broke the matchstick in two, tossing the fragments at Sully. Sully scuttled away, cursing.

Ricketts laughed. But he stopped laughing when he glimpsed a dust cloud in the east.

The site was on a flat. Ricketts was raised up higher than the others by virtue of being perched up on the wagon box seat. "Hey! Hey, you all. Looky there!" he shouted, rising up, pointing at the dust cloud in the distance. "It's *them*! Here they come!"

The outlaws turned to see what Ricketts was pointing at, studying on the dust cloud some miles away. It wasn't much. Just a thin brown smudge floating in the air a few degrees above the horizon. A dirty fingerprint on the rim of the upside-down, yellow-white bowl of sky.

The gunrunners were stung into action. They scrambled, grabbing up rifles and gathering closer together. There was a lot of peering, craning, and neck-stretching. A couple men climbed up on boulders to improve their vantage point.

They looked . . . and wondered.

"Is it them?"

"Don't look like much."

"Don't take much to kick up dust out there."

Honest Bob moved among them. "Look sharp, boys, and step lively. The scalp you save may be your own. Or even better, mine."

They were gunrunners and Comancheros—Honest Bob and Sully, Mercurio and Rio, Fitch, Hump, Half-Shot, and all the rest. They numbered a baker's dozen in all, unlucky thirteen, a gang of whites and Mexicans who sold guns and ammunition to the Comanches. A dangerous trade.

They were gathered in the barren wastelands of the North Central Texas plains on a hot afternoon in the fall of 1866 for a meet with a Comanche raiding party.

The War Between the States had been over for a year and a half. Yet that titanic conflict between North and South was but a brief moment in time compared to the centuries-long struggle for the frontier.

The War for the West was an epic clash between Indians and Caucasians for dominance of that part of the planet.

Paramount among all mounted Plains Indian tribes were the Comanches. They were Lords of the Great Plains, masters of a vast prairie expanse in the center of the American heartland bounded on the east by the Mississippi River and the west by the Rocky Mountains.

The Comanche broke the back of the Spaniards' northward thrust out of Mexico, limiting their Great Plains holdings to a few scattered fortress towns— Santa Fe, San Antonio, and a handful of others.

Next came the Anglos, English-speaking Texas settlers the Comanches called *Tejanos*. An irksome folk, they were numerous and land-hungry.

For long years, tribesmen kept the Texans bottled up east of the ninety-eighth meridian, a longitudinal line running north-south through such settlements as Dallas and San Antonio. They tormented the Tejanos with relentless raids of rape, robbery, torture, and murder. The ninety-eighth parallel marked the limiting line of westward American expansionism.

Yet the Texans were stubborn. Worse from the Comanche point of view, the Texans were adaptable. Slowly but surely, they learned the ways of making war on horseback, Indian style. The frontier conflict, always fought with bitterness and cruelty on both sides, was fast becoming a war of extermination.

Then came secession and the war between the Union and the Confederacy. Frontier expansion was halted for the duration. The whites were so busy trying to kill each other that their war against the Indians was neglected.

The War was finally over and American westward migration was once more in full flood, greater than ever. Comanches once more felt the pressure as hordes of returning whites nibbled locust-like westward, crowding past the ninety-eighth parallel to the hundredth parallel.

Longitude 100 degrees west now marked the frontier. It was the dividing line between civilization and wilderness.

Part of the line ran north-south through Hangtree County, Texas.

The gunrunners' meeting place was some fifty miles west of the line, where the bounds of Hangtree County blurred with the beginnings of the Llano Estacado. The Llano, "Staked Plains" to the Spaniards, was a vast wilderness misnamed by some early American mapmaker as "The Great American Desert."

It wasn't, not really. Subsequent events would

soon prove the contrary. But its endless expanse of emptiness sprawling under the big sky tended to have an unnerving effect on travelers. There was a sense that here was the rim of the abyss, the edge of darkness.

The Llano was prairie flatland, hundreds of square miles in area. It had water and grass enough to support the buffalo in all their teeming masses. In time, it would prove equally capable of supporting great cattle herds and then the great land rush would be on.

But not yet. Not while the Comanche still held sway over the region.

The meeting place was set at Bison Creek under Boneyard Bench.

The Llano, though flat, was not without distinctive landforms—cuts, rises, folds, rock spurs, outcroppings, ridges, hills, and more.

The Bench was a limestone plateau rising out of the flat, a shelf-like scarp whose eastern edge featured a sharp twenty-five-foot drop. Its eastern face of cliffs ran north-south for dozens of miles.

A solid, impenetrable wall, there were no gaps and passes. Riders went around it. On a horse, there was no way to climb the cliffs. They formed a giant wall or bench set amid the flat.

Gravity is a useful thing. The Comanche set it to work by stampeding buffalo herds eastward across the plateau and over the edge, causing them to fall to their deaths. Descending to the flat, the braves would harvest the carcasses.

Long years of such practices had littered the foot of the cliffs with the skeletal remains of hundreds, if not thousands, of buffalo. Heaps and mounds of clean-picked bones glared whitely under the midday sun where the gunrunners waited.

Thus the name given to the site by whites—Boneyard Bench.

Cracks in the cliffs held springs, which issued streams of water. Buffalo routinely drank their fill during wanderings.

The largest such watercourse was Bison Creek. It was an ideal spot for those wishing to conduct their business far from prying eyes. It was well-watered. Sheer, unscalable cliffs shielded against attack from the west. Rockslides, boulders, and fans provided plenty of cover.

The gunrunners were massed in a shallow basin at the foot of the cliffs south of Bison Creek.

A cleft in the cliffs served as a makeshift corral, its open end roped off. Guards were posted to keep watch over it.

Comanches were passionate horse thieves. If they could steal the gunrunners' horses, they would, and damn the consequences!

The unhorsed gun wagon stood in the center of the basin. Men were grouped around it in a half-circle facing east, the cliffs protecting its rear from the west. The gang was well-armed with repeating long guns and six-shooters.

The Comanches appeared not in the east where the dust cloud had first been sighted but in the south near the cliffs.

"Looky there!" Half-Shot cried, indicating a second dust cloud to the south. It showed near the cliffs several miles away, much closer than the dust to the east.

The south cloud moved north toward them while the east cloud stayed where it was. Strong sunlight streamed down from overhead, gilding the southern dust plume. At its base rode a knot of mounted men, ten in number. They came on at a steady walk.

"That's them all right," Melbourne said. "Dirty stinking redskins!"

"They're not so bad," Hump Colway said.

"The hell you say!"

"Not as bad as some white folks. At least they don't try to rub my hump for luck."

"Is that lucky?" Chait asked, genuinely curious.

"Not for them," the hunchback said. "The last few who tried, I shot them to pieces. Lucky for me, though," he added. "Must be."

"How do you figure?"

"I'm still here," Hump said.

"Is that so great?" Melbourne said, snickering.

"To me it is. Beats being dead," the hunchback said.

The Comanche riders narrowed the distance, closing on Bison Creek hollow.

"Huh! They don't look like much," Sully said, disdainful.

"Reckon you don't look like much to them," Hump said. "You don't look like much to me."

Sully knew better than to mess with Hump and kept his mouth shut. He was worried about the Comanches, not Hump's slighting remark.

The Comanche riders were short stocky men riding small scruffy horses. But they were killers, horseback warriors. The horses were Indian ponies born of a long line of wild mustangs with endurance far beyond their more domesticated cousins.

The braves were Quesadas, most aloof of all Comanche tribes, making their home deep in the Llano.

They generally shunned not only whites and their works but their fellow red men as well. Their stand-offishness served them well, protecting them from catching the whites' diseases such as smallpox.

Somewhere in the Llano's trackless wastes lay their homeland, its whereabouts unknown to whites. It was hidden somewhere in the expanse but where, no living white man could say.

The brave at the point sported a lone feather rising vertically from the back of his head, held in place by a headband. He was Eagle Feather, leader of the band. He raised a hand, signaling a halt. The Comanches reined in, watchful and waiting.

Honest Bob motioned for them to advance and they rode in.

The braves showed wide faces, high cheekbones, dark watchful eyes. Thick, greasy, shoulder-length black hair was worn loose or in braids. Most of them wore white men's shirts—plaid or patterned, open and unbuttoned—and knee-high moccasin boots. Some wore breeches, others loincloths.

A few bows and arrows, war hatchets, and a lance or two were seen among them, but were far out-numbered by firearms. Firearms were the weapon of choice. Some were armed with long guns, rifles, and carbines. A few had pistols tucked into their belts.

The gunrunners were wary, restive.

"Easy, boys, easy," Honest Bob said. "This ain't the first time we've been to the fair. Don't get trigger-happy and we'll get through this fine just like we've done before." He readied himself to start forward. "Stand ready, Ricketts!" he called.

"I'm ready!" Ricketts sat perched on the wagon's

box seat puffing a cigar. His hand was closed around a line of fuse cord, its end curling out the top of his fist.

Honest Bob gave him a two-fingered half-salute. He turned, facing the Comanches. "Sefton, you come with me. I'm gonna meet Eagle Feather halfway."

"All right, Bob." Sefton was a fast draw and a cool-nerved customer.

"You men cover us," Honest Bob told some of the others.

"Right!"

Honest Bob and Sefton started forward. Honest Bob was empty-handed, carrying no rifle. He wore twinned belt guns and could get at them fast if he had to.

Sefton held a rifle cradled against his chest, muzzle pointed skyward. He could get it into action quick enough. That went double for the gun holstered at his side. Others were faster—Melbourne and Chait, for sure—but Sefton had better judgment.

The Comanches sat their horses, watching the duo approach. The braves were motionless, stock-still. Masklike faces were cut deep with hard lines. They were stoics with good poker faces.

Their horses were well-trained, but the nearness of Bison Creek water made them restless. Their long faces and snouts were powdered with dust. No doubt they'd been ridden a long way between waterings.

Honest Bob halted a few man-lengths from the Comanches, Sefton stopping alongside him. Honest Bob held up his right hand palm out in the I-come-in-peace gesture. "Howdy, Eagle Feather!"

Eagle Feather nodded, some of his men grunting

as if to themselves, the lines in their faces deepening into scowls.

That was all right with Honest Bob. He didn't give a damn if they liked him or not. Not that there was much chance of them liking any white man unless he was on the business end of a scalping knife. But they liked the guns he sold well enough, and that was what counted.

"You got guns, Honest Bob?" Eagle Feather asked. He always called the gun dealer by his full moniker of "Honest Bob," whether in mockery or not was known only to himself. Comanches held little faith in the honesty of whites, period.

"Got gold?" Honest Bob countered.

"Ugh." Eagle Feather nodded. *Yes.*

"You can see the wagon for yourself. We're ready for business, so let's get to it." Honest Bob indicated the dust cloud in the east. "Your friends out there can come in, too. We're not afraid. We'll give them a warm welcome."

"You trade horses for guns?" Eagle Feather asked, thrusting his hatchet-faced head forward. "They good horses. Fast, strong."

Honest Bob shook his head no. "You know my policy, Eagle Feather. I only trade for gold or cash money. Gold, silver, or jewelry."

"Eagle Feather know. We catch plenty horses, by damn! Good horses!"

Stolen horses, Honest Bob knew. Presumably the eastern dust cloud was made by them and the braves tending them. Maybe. Or maybe it was the rest of a war party standing by waiting for the signal to attack.

"Eagle Feather tell braves stand off. Honest Bob

no want horses," the Comanche said, indicating the eastern dust cloud.

"That's the way of it," Honest Bob said.

"When you go, we water horses here at Bison Creek, yes."

"When we go, you can do what you damn well please for all I care."

"No want horses, good horses?" Eagle Feather pressed.

"No stolen horses, thanks," Honest Bob said, shaking his head. "I don't want to hang."

"You look good that way, by damn!" Eagle Feather's eyes gleamed and the corners of his wide mouth quirked upward in grim amusement. A rare show of emotion for him.

"You'd like to see me hang, wouldn't you, Eagle Feather," Honest Bob said. It was not a question.

"Eagle Feather want see all gunrunners hang,"

"Then who'd sell you guns?"

"Always greedy white men sell Comanches guns."

"Not good guns like I got."

"Mebbe so, Honest Bob. Mebbe so. Eagle Feather want all Comancheros hang. You cheats."

"That ain't so, Eagle Feather. You know that. I never cheated you."

"You cheat but not so bad as other white men," Eagle Feather grudgingly allowed.

"The truth of it is, you'd like to see all white folks hang," Honest Bob said, grinning.

"Mebbe so, mebbe so."

"Well, let's get to business." Honest Bob turned and walked away, Sefton following.

The Comanches came afterward, walking their horses at a slow pace.

Two

"The gang's all here," Sam Heller said to himself. "Gunrunners, Comanches—and me. The uninvited guest." He was in a covert, a kind of shooting blind. A sharpshooter's nest.

It was in a cleft at the top of the rock walls of the eastern face of the bench overlooking Bison Creek. A V-shaped crack dropped vertically from the edge of the cliff. It was six feet wide and ten feet long, tapering downward.

It was five feet wide up on the cliff top, forming a kind of cup-shaped hollow or basin. The cup was roomy enough for Sam to curl inside. Its floor consisted of loose rocks and dirt, which filled the cleft from its base to cup. Scrub brush, weeds, and vines grew from the surface of the dirt at the top of the cup.

The cliff top rim was thick with brush. Shrubs and bushes covered Sam, screening him from view of any of those below who might casually glance upward at the scarp.

It was a tight fit in the sharpshooter's nest, sharing it as he did with his rifle and supplies. Sam lay on his

side in the nest, legs together and bent at the knees.
He propped himself up on an elbow.

He was a big man, six-foot-four, 210 pounds, full-grown, and in the prime of life. He wanted to stay that way, a condition that would require some deft maneuvering and more than a little bit of luck in the next twenty-four hours or so. He had yellow hair and a same-colored beard, looking like a blond Viking. He hailed from Minnesota but had spent most of his youth in the West. A committed Unionist, he had fought for the North throughout the war.

Sam wore a dark, battered slouch hat, buckskin vest, brown denims, and moccasin boots. The boots were knee-high and worn under the denims. Beside him in the nest was a knapsack and canteen.

He was armed with a Winchester rifle, a .36 Navy Colt worn on his left hip in a cross-belly draw, and a bowie-style Green River knife sheathed on his right side. Twin bandoliers crossed chest and shoulders, their loops holding rifle cartridges.

The rifle was one of the new Winchester 1866 models, Sam's piece having been one of the first to come off the production line. It was one of the most effective and up-to-date weapons on the frontier—in the world, for that matter.

A keen-eyed viewer would have noticed that the rifle displayed several unique modifications. Special socket rings and fittings showed at the front stock and butt. Sam had chopped the rifle, sawing off most of the barrel and butt stock to create a mule's leg, as sawed-off repeating rifles were popularly called. It was generally worn in a custom-made holster on Sam's right hip, though not at the moment.

Sam was a born outdoorsman, and his trade required him to spend a good amount of time on narrow streets and in crowded saloons, gambling dens, meeting halls, cafés, and such in frontier towns and settlements. Easier to sport a mule's leg in those places than tote a long rifle.

It could be put into action quicker, too, a vital attribute in deadly encounters where a matter of split seconds might spell the difference between life and death. He could unlimber the mule's leg faster than most triggermen could shuck a handgun from a holster.

There were times, though, when a man preferred to work at a distance rather than up close. For such times, a long gun was necessary.

Thus the special fittings on the mule's leg, allowing different-length barrels to be attached to the muzzle, with similar arrangements at the rear allowing for the add-on of wooden stocks in place of the standard curved pistol-grip handle. The piece had all the modifications as Sam lay curved in the hollow, awaiting the moment of truth.

He'd waited a long time, weeks of solitary prowls through plains, badlands, and back trails, searching for signs that would lead to his quarry. He was a special agent with a presidential warrant. His mission was to break up the gangs supplying weapons to the Comanches of the Texas frontier.

The hundredth meridian *was* the Texas frontier, so Sam had set up his base of operations in the town of Hangtree in Hangtree County. What began as a mission had become a quest. He'd seen what the Comanches could do when it came to turning the frontier into a living hell.

There were many Comancheros of the rank-and-file

variety, foot soldiers of the gunrunners' trade, who dealt directly with the Indians. They were renegades, enemies of humanity, and Sam killed them when he could.

But they weren't his real target. He was after the big fish, not the small fry. He wanted the ones at the top of the pyramid, the ringleaders, the organizers who supplied the contraband in bulk.

A long dark trail had led him to Bison Creek under Boneyard Bench. Honest Bob Longford and the rest of the bunch were far from unknown to Sam Heller. He'd long been aware they were Comancheros, part of the Hog Ranch outfit.

The Hog Ranch was a low dive, a deadfall that lay near Fort Pardee. It was a thieves' den, a magnet for saddle tramps, drifters, and outlaws. It featured cheap whiskey, saloon girls, and gambling. It was a great favorite with the cavalry troopers of the fort, despite having been posted off-limits by their commanding officer.

Sam had had his eye on the Hog Ranch for some time, but it was only in the last few weeks that his suspicions had taken shape regarding the expedition to the Llano. He had trailed the gunrunners to Bison Creek, always keeping out of sight.

Under Boneyard Bench, Honest Bob's bunch had tied in with the next rung of the ladder, Felipe Mercurio, who would lead to the Comanchero bigs. With his sidemen, he had supplied Honest Bob with a wagonload of weapons. Mercurio was the Santa Fe Ring's man. The Ring were known Comancheros, biggest in the territory.

Mercurio's presence was the first link to directly tie the Ring to gunrunning on the Llano. He and his men had met Honest Bob and company at the creek the previous day at dusk, delivering the wagon full of guns. They'd stayed the night, sitting around the campfire with the Hog Ranch crew, eating and drinking while Sam made cheerless camp hidden on the cliff top above.

He guessed they were sticking close to the site until the Comanches took possession of the weapons. Maybe Mercurio wanted to make sure the transaction was completed in full and Honest Bob didn't make off with some of the guns to resell them on his own. Mercurio might also be dogging Honest Bob for his share of the proceeds.

Whatever the reason, Sam meant to find out. He was no lawman, though he could have been called a law enforcer in the loosest sense of the term. He was a man on a mission, authorized by the highest law in the land, the President of the United States.

He was not bound by the rules of evidence and legal protocol. He didn't have to prove a case against his quarry in court or even bring them back alive. In fact, it was often preferable to leave as many dead as a warning to others.

He was a troubleshooter, and it was his job to shoot trouble

It had been a long hard hunt. As he watched the negotiations below him, he thought back to the past few days.

Alone, he had dogged Honest Bob's crew from the Hog Ranch to the Llano, trailing them just at the edge of vision, following them into the badlands. Their southwesterly course took them toward Boneyard Bench.

Sam knew the way. In the months since first arriving in Hangtree County, he'd ridden trail in the territory, criss-crossing it a number of times. He wished to live, so he'd learned where the water was. The twenty-five miles of the bench's eastern front was the source of three different dependable watercourses. Bison Creek was the most abundant of the three.

Sam guessed the gunrunners would make for it. Breaking off direct pursuit, he detoured northwest, taking a course that would bring him to the north end of the bench. He knew there was no way through the scarp, only around it. He rounded the gentle slope where the north edge of the bench joined the flat and rode up on top of the plateau, heading south.

The landscape was all earth tones—a dust-muted blur of grays, yellows, and browns—speckled here and there with patches of dark green. On the plains, the winds blew mostly from the west, sometimes from the north. They could whip up a hellbender of a gale, but the air was hot and still, though from time to time, a welcome breath of a breeze lifted. It barely stirred up a scrum of dust, whipping it a few inches above the ground for several dozen yards, only to let it fall, exhausted.

The plateau summit was flat tableland that came to an abrupt end in the east. Sam was careful to ride far enough into the interior to avoid skylining in the east and being spotted by anyone in the Boneyard. In the other three directions it showed empty plains as far as the eye could see. If Comanche raiders spied him, he would be in a tight spot. There was nowhere to hide, not when once seen.

What seemed unyielding monotony of landscape proved to present a variety of terrain. Seemingly featureless plains were broken by rises and dips, rocks, trees, and brush.

The prairie unrolled as Sam rode south. If he'd guessed wrong, if Honest Bob had altered his southwesterly course toward the bench for points unknown, Sam would have lost him. It was highly unlikely that he could pick up the gunrunners' trail again.

But if he was right, if Honest Bob planned to set up shop somewhere in the Boneyard, the detour could save Sam many hours of hard riding. The Boneyard offered water and cover, things generally unavailable farther out on the plains.

High overhead, black V shapes circled. Vultures searching for carrion.

Several hours later, a ring of green brush took shape in the distance. It bordered a shallow basin about eight feet wide and three feet deep. A waterhole. A small spring lay beneath the basin, filling it with several inches of muddy brown water.

Sam halted, stepping down from the saddle. Small game trails arrowed in and out of the basin rim, indicating that local wildlife drank from the spring.

Good. That means the water isn't poisoned, he thought. Sometimes waterholes were contaminated by trace elements of corrosive minerals.

Sam cupped a hand, scooping out some water and tasting it. It was not warm but hot from the sun, brackish and muddy. It tasted good to him, whose water supply was so tightly rationed.

He filled his canteens, then let Dusty, his horse, drink. The animal was a gray Steel Dust, part mustang, short and scrappy. After watering the horse, Sam let it browse on the greenery ringing the waterhole, then he saddled up and moved on, reaching what he judged to be the midpoint of the plateau. Ahead lay a small cone-shaped hill, looking like an overgrown ant mound. A stand of thin straggly trees grew at its base. The cone was a landmark, a signpost pointing to Bison Creek below.

Sam halted at the mound about a hundred yards away from the cliff edge. He stepped down and tied the horse's reins to a tree branch.

Tree? Little more than scrub brush, really, but no less welcome for all of that. A man without a horse on the plains was for all intents and purposes a dead man. That's why horse theft was a capital crime on the frontier. Stealing a man's horse was pretty much the same as condemning him to death. The frontier was no country for a man afoot.

Dusty began nibbling on the green leaves. He wasn't the type of horse who ran away. He'd stay in place when his reins were free with their ends dangling on the ground. But Sam wasn't a man to leave things to chance. No telling when the unexpected would rear its ugly head and let chaos loose.

Sam heard noise—voices, shouts, horses neighing, movement. The sounds made his skin tingle, quivering like a struck drumhead.

He prowled the edge of the cliff, screened by thick bushes. The rim was not a straight line, solid and unbroken, but was saw-toothed with seams and fissures. One in particular looked promising, a V-shaped vertical cut topped by a dirt-filled hollow cup.

Nearing the edge, Sam ducked down and lay flat on the ground. He crawled to the cliff's edge, staying low. He parted the brush, looking down.

Rock walls dropped straight down to the flat twenty-five feet below.

Yes, gunrunners were making camp at Bison Creek.

A cut in the cliff wall below had been pressed into service as a makeshift corral. Sticks and branches were used for a palisade type fence and gate. A thin trickling vein of Bison Creek ran through it. There was green grass for grazing. Two guards were posted outside the gate, armed with repeating rifles.

There was not much work to be done by the gunrunners. Their tasks were finished and they busied themselves with eating, drinking, smoking, and loafing.

Sometimes a trick of the air currents brought a taste of tobacco smoke to Sam's nostrils. He thought of his own tobacco pouch and sighed. No smoking now, not for him. He couldn't risk having the smoke seen by the foe.

He sternly put the thought of it out of his mind, but the craving kept sneaking back.

He had a hat to keep the sun off his bare head, a canteen full of water, and beef jerky to chew. Nothing for him to do but watch and wait.

Late afternoon shadows were falling and the sun was lowering in the west when the next round of newcomers arrived.

Felipe Mercurio and the Comancheros rode in with the gun wagon. Two men sat up front on the box seat. Five men rode escort alongside. Honest Bob's bunch acted glad to see them.

Sam knew the man in the passenger seat beside the wagon driver. Mercurio was a well-known figure along the owlhoot trail on both sides of the Rio Grande. A killer, slaver, dealer in contraband, he was henchman to Quatro Matanzas, driving wheel of the Santa Fe Ring.

That was a surprise. Sam hadn't known the Ring reached so far east.

While Mercurio and Honest Bob conferred, the newcomers squared away their mounts in the corral. The gun wagon was placed at the foot of the cliff. Half-Shot showed the new arrivals to the cooking pots so they could chow down and drink up, not necessarily in that order.

Sam's empty stomach rumbled. No hot meal for him. He dared not risk lighting a fire. He used his blade to cut off a chunk of beef jerky, jammed it between his jaws, and went to work on it. Strong white teeth slowly ground it to pulp. It had to be chewed slowly if he wanted to keep those teeth intact and unbroken. He washed it down with sips of muddy water from his canteen.

One of many such cheerless meals he'd had on the trail, but that was how he managed to stay alive.

The sun set, a cool breeze whipping a snaky line of dust eastward. Venus twinkled low in the west, stars brightening in a blackening sky.

Sam rose, shaking out the kinks of knotted muscles from his long vigil. He went to his horse, stroking its muzzle. He took some dried parched corn from his saddlebag and munched it, washing it down with several mouthfuls of water. He made camp nearby, a simple camp with no fire. He spread his bedroll on the ground and used his saddle for a pillow. He lay on his back and went to sleep with the Navy Colt in his hand under the blanket.

Sam awoke sometime during the night. He sat up, blankets falling around his waist, Navy Colt held steady in his hand. What woke him? Natural body rhythms or something afoot in the night? He looked around, eyes accustomed to the dark. Dusty stirred nearby, aware he was up.

A half moon hung in the sky. Fitful night breezes rose out of the west and northwest. Somewhere out on the plateau a coyote howled, a lonesome sound that never failed to send a chill along Sam's spine.

It sent the same reaction, but for different reasons. Was it a coyote? Or a Comanche imitating a coyote, signaling to his fellows, maybe giving the signal to move in for the final assault?

The night cries were not repeated. Sam sank back down, pulling the blankets up, and went back to sleep, gun in hand.

When he woke again, the sky was lightening in the east. He stretched, then got up. "Going to be a big day!"

It was a cold cheerless breakfast he fixed for himself. No coffee. A fire was needed to make coffee. He consoled himself with a slug of whiskey gulped from a pocket flask he carried. "For medicinal purposes only," he told himself. It was no time to go on a tear, but a drink wouldn't do him any harm. Might do a bit of good.

He took a generous swallow of the stuff, a line of fire plunging down his throat, blossoming into welcome heat in his belly. Welcome recompense for his dog's breakfast of pemmican and parched corn washed down with tepid murky water.

Another belt of the whizz would sure go down good, but he capped the flask and put it away. Only half-joking, he said, "Satan, get thee gone . . ."

It was light enough for him to get about his business, so he picked his way along the cliff rim, returning to the spot he had chosen for his sharpshooter's nest. The brush screened him from those on the flat below. Through spaces in the foliage, he could spy on the gunrunners' camp without being seen.

Sam set to work shaping up his shooting platform and readying his weapon. It was a good feeling, knowing the showdown was nigh.

He'd been on the trail for days . . . weeks. Weeks of burning days and chilly nights. Even the steadiest nerves became taut and worn from relentless stress.

However long the wait, he could stand it, especially with the end in sight. The nearness of his quarry was a tonic.

It was more than a bit provocative, that nearness. He had to fight the urge to start lining up the gunrunners in his sights and opening up on them, burning them down. He was seized with an almost overwhelming desire to get an early start on the cleanup but fought it down.

The long day wore on. Sam told himself he should have known that the Comanches would wait till the last before showing.

They did it deliberately, of course. It was a stalling tactic designed to prey on the nerves of the gunrunners, wearing them down. Comanches were always looking to maximize their advantage at the expense of their foes—or friends; the role could change in a moment according to want and whim. If they saw an edge they'd take it; if not, they'd make it.

Sam readied. "The gang's all here," he muttered again.

THREE

Tension was thick among the gunrunners. They lacked the Comanches' mask of stolid indifference and were no good at hiding their emotions. Inside their heads, fear and anxiety warred with greed.

It wasn't that the Comanches didn't give a damn whether they lived or died. They did. In a shooting scrape, they were careful not to risk themselves pointlessly. They were known for breaking off attacks they thought they couldn't win, showing that they valued their lives no less than the whites.

The numbers between the two groups seemed about even, with the gunrunners having a slight advantage.

That was not so good for the whites perhaps, since each Comanche warrior reckoned himself to be the match of two or three *taibohs*—whites. It was how the Comanches saw themselves.

Was it true? That remained to be seen. But that confidence bordering on arrogance might give them an edge.

Grouped in a loose semicircle whose ends were anchored to the cliffs, the gunrunners had their backs to the rock walls and stood between the Comanches, the corralled horses, and the gun wagon. The outlaws' postures were stiff with tension, most of them sharp, angular. A few affected nonchalance and might even have meant it. But in the main, no matter how calm and uncaring a man looked on the outside, it was hard to remain cool and unruffled in the presence of hostiles whose fondest wish was to hang them head down over a small fire . . . just for starters.

The gunrunners were heavily armed. Rifles were held pointed down or away from the braves. Not too far away, though.

Sam recognized the band's Quesada markings. They knew something of him, too, or would have had they known of his shadowy presence, for the Comanches well knew of the one they called *El Solitario*, the lone rider with the long gun who dogged their war parties, killing them from a distance.

El Solitario who rides alone. The Man with the Devil Gun.

Comanche braves were born hunters, successful predators in a hard and unforgiving environment. It was rare that the hunter became the hunted, rarer still when the hunted were the Comanches themselves. But in recent moons, their bravest and boldest had fallen victim to the Taiboh with the long gun.

Whoever he was, El Solitario threw a wide loop, roaming most of Comancheria deep into the panhandle country between the Arkansas and Red rivers. He prowled west into New Mexico, south to the Rio Grande, even venturing into the remote vastness of

the western Llano wilderness they proudly claimed for
their own.

As they saw it, the phantom killer struck without
warning, not for gain or plunder, which they could
understand, but simply for the killing. They could
understand that, for they often fought merely for
prestige and glory, but it was not a trait they generally
attributed to white men. El Solitario opened fire on
warriors in camp or on the trail day and night, and
when he struck, bodies piled up.

More than one campfire conclave had concluded
in blood and slaughter as the unseen rifleman lurked
in the darkness beyond the flickering circle of firelight. But of the nearness of Man With the Devil Gun
lurking on the cliff top above, Quesada braves and
outlaw gunrunners alike were blissfully unaware.

Wiry and long-limbed, Eagle Feather was at the
fore leading his braves to the gun wagon. He was
sided by henchman Han-Tay, his second in command.
Han-Tay was deeper in the chest, thicker in the
arms. The notorious Maldito rode abreast of but
apart from the other two in the leading wave.

"Maldito? That little fellow?" Gunslick Melbourne
scoffed. "He ain't big enough to carry that name considering all I've heard about him. What a killer he's
s'posed to be—"

"He lives up to his rep," Hump Colway said curtly.

Maldito was short even for a Comanche, almost
dwarfish, being some inches short of five feet tall. His
upper body development was powerful, impressive.

"Look at the size of them arms, them hands," Half-
Shot marveled. "Strangler's hands if ever I seen them.

He gets them hands on you, he could tear your head off without half-trying!"

"Well he ain't gonna get a hand on me. I'll shoot him first," Melbourne said. "Now what do you think of that?"

Maldito's head was wider than it was long. A triangle of muscle descended from ears to his shoulders, making it look like he had no neck. His eyes seemed on the verge of popping from their sockets. They were the fierce rolling eyes of a wild horse. The rest of his visage was stony, blank-faced.

The band of braves were loosely bunched together, except for a rider or two bringing up the rear. Among them was Barbero, the scalp hunter. The reins of his horse were decorated with scalps of all types and colors.

"Looky there! One of them scalps come off a yellow-headed woman," Half-Shot husked breathlessly.

"A couple look like they come off kids. They're smaller," Sully said.

"Seeing that makes my blood boil," Melbourne muttered. "It ain't right. He's flaunting it. Might as well be waving it in our faces!"

"That's why he does it," Hump said matter-of-factly.

Chait's elbow nudged Melbourne in the ribs. "Careful you don't get yourself a halo to go along with that sermon you're preaching, Mel."

"How do you mean?" Melbourne asked.

"Way you're carrying on, you'd think you're in the wrong line of work," Chait said. "What do you think the Comanches are doing with those guns Honest Bob sells them?"

"I dunno. I never gave it much thought before now," Melbourne said.

"Well, don't. Let it go, Mel. Let it go. This is just another job for us, a job of work. It don't bear too much thinking," Chait said.

"That's right. We came here to trade, not to fight," Sully agreed.

"Who asked you?" Chait said, turning on him.

Sully shut up.

More Comanches neared the gun wagon, gathering around. Dog Fat, an oily fellow with a big belly, brutish Spotted Calf, and lofty Tizane, almost a head taller than his fellows, Thieving Crow, Wolf Track, and others.

Shepherding the gun wagon as the Comanches grouped around it, Ricketts puffed away at his cigar. His closed fist was sweaty where he gripped the fuse cord attached to the gunpowder bomb.

"You know you can trust me, Eagle Feather," Honest Bob said with bluff heartiness, beginning his pitch.

"You no trust Comanche. You trust Dynamite Man," Eagle Feather said, indicating Ricketts perched on the gun wagon.

Unhappy at being singled out by Eagle Feather, Ricketts started, the cigar almost falling from his mouth. The result was to make him look even more guilty and self-conscious.

Honest Bob smiled, unabashed. "That's for safety's sake, Eagle Feather. Yours and mine. Any hothead tries to steal the guns gets them blown up in his face. A simple precaution, that's all."

In the blind above, Sam heard it all. "Ol' Bob's got the soul of a natural-born horse trader," he whispered.

Eagle Feather spat to show what he thought of Honest Bob's line of reasoning. He turned toward

Ricketts. "You, Dynamite Man! Blow up wagon, you blow up, too!" Eagle Feather paused to let it sink in. "How you like that, eh? Damn you!"

Ricketts was dumbfounded, at a loss for words.

"He likes it fine," Honest Bob said airily, doing the talking. "He knows that everything's gonna go fine today with no trouble at all."

"You lie. Him scared," Eagle Feather insisted.

"Ricketts just ain't used to meeting a famous war chief of the Comanches like you, Eagle Feather. He's overcome by your greatness."

"You think you pretty damned smart, Honest Bob!"

"I can't deny it. But now to business."

"Honest Bob—businessman."

"That's me, Eagle Feather."

"Do not brag of it. All businessman liars," Eagle Feather said.

Such testing and taunting on the part of Comanche clients was nothing new or unexpected to Honest Bob. It came with the territory. It happened each and every time. They'd come on a lot more threatening and frightening than Eagle Feather. He just kept his eye on the main chance, pushing the deal through. That's why he was still alive, as well as being one of the best in his line.

"You bad friend," Eagle Feather said, going off on another tack. "We ride long, far. We Comanches thirsty, but you give us nothing to drink."

"Why, there's plenty of water all around!" Honest Bob said, pretending to misunderstand. "The creek's over there. Help yourself!"

"Water, *phaugh*!" Eagle Feather's expression of disgust was a cross between a choking cough and a throat-clearing. "Honest Bob funny man," he said, unamused. "Eagle Feather want whiskey—whiskey! What you drink!"

"No firewater here, Chief. No redeye hooch or whiskey. It's for your own good, for my good, for the good of us all. I ain't like them other fellows, crooks I call them, who pose as a friend of the Comanche. Honest Bob is a *real* friend. I don't get you all liquored up drunk with bad whiskey so's I can cheat you. You keep a clear head, you know what you're buying."

Some gunrunners did give the braves liquor to sweeten them up, Honest Bob knew. There was a word for such traders—*dead*. When a Comanche got liquored up, he went crazy drunk, indulging every mad murderous whim or notion he got in his head. Once he got a skinful of redeye, there was no stopping him . . . short of killing him.

"Remember, you know what you're buying from Honest Bob," he reminded Eagle Feather.

"You cheap crook and bad friend. That's why you no give whiskey to Eagle Feather."

"Wasn't there something about guns, Eagle Feather?" Honest Bob prompted, trying to get the deal back on track. "You want guns, don't you? That's why you're here. You want guns and Honest Bob's got them. Good guns!"

"Show me," Eagle Feather said, arrogant and demanding—his usual mode of address to white and red men alike.

"Show me the gold," Honest Bob said.

Eagle Feather nodded to Han-Tay. The warrior untied a pouch hanging from his neck by a rawhide thong. He gave the pouch to Eagle Feather, who opened it, pouring some of its contents into an open palm.

Fragments of yellow metal glinted in the blue-shadowed gloom below the cliffs. The glint of gold was sharp and bright even to Sam up in his perch on the cliff top.

The take represented a heap of scavenging. Mexican and American gold coins, gold pocket watches, wedding bands, chains, lockets, and bracelets—all of them gold. There were even a few raw golden nuggets in the mix.

Gold was in short supply for the vast majority of settlers and emigrants on the frontier. Most of those who actually had gold stayed the hell off the frontier. Sam wondered, *How many wagon trains were waylaid, stagecoaches robbed and plundered, and ranches and farms raided and pillaged to collect the take?*

Honest Bob breathed hard, his heartbeat quickening. His face lit up at the sight, underlit by golden highlights reflected off the handful of loot. "I think we can do business," he allowed, sounding out of breath.

"Gold—white man's firewater," Eagle Feather said, sneering. "You loco for yellow stone."

For once Honest Bob had no reply. He turned to face the outlaw gang. "Bring the crate with the star on the lid!"

The starred crate stood at the rear of the wagon's flatbed hopper, edging the extended tailgate. It looked the same as the others except for a palm-sized red star hand-painted on the upper right corner of the lid.

Fitch had his gun back but was still in the doghouse for killing Lank. He had a hangdog look. He was still pretty well hungover. He kept his head down, walked soft, and did what he was told without complaint. He and Sully hauled the crate across the wagon tailgate, wrestling with it.

"It's heavy!" Sully hissed through gritted teeth.

"Help 'em out, Half-Shot," Hump Colway said.

"Why me? Why do I have to do it?"

"Because I said so and I'm ramrodding this chore."

Half-Shot pitched in, joining the other two. Huffing and puffing, the three of them managed to manhandle the crate off the wagon and across the ground to Honest Bob and Eagle Feather. The haulers set the crate down on the ground with a crash.

"Open it," Honest Bob said.

Hump handed Fitch a crowbar, and he went to work, wedging the prying end of the bar between the lid and the top of the crate. Squeals and screeches sounded as he levered up the cover and nails gave way.

The lid splintered, cracked, and broke. Fitch pried the pieces loose. Inside the crate were new guns—rifles.

Eagle Feather was no fool. Before he was done, he'd have every crate opened to ensure that they held the guns and ammunition he wanted and weren't filled with rocks. But the first crate had his full attention.

His mask of aloof indifference slipped. The unveiling of the armaments interested him intensely and he showed it. He crowded in, looming over the crate. Han-Tay stood close beside him. Wild-eyed and stony-faced, Maldito moved in alongside them for a better look.

More braves gathered round, dark eyes glittering in leathery faces.

Honest Bob pulled a rifle out of the crate, holding it in his arms, cradling it. "Winchester Model 1866, just like the pony soldiers have at Fort Pardee. My gift to the mighty war chief Eagle Feather!" He handed the rifle to Eagle Feather, who snatched it up greedily in both hands.

"The redskin's sure loving that piece," Melbourne snickered, low-voiced.

"He looks about as happy as he's ever gonna be," Chait agreed.

Eagle Feather frowned fiercely, a study in furious concentration as he hefted the rifle, weighing it first in one hand, then the other, then with both hands. Lovingly he ran caressing fingers along the machined cold metal barrel and the fine-grained wooden stock.

A thoughtful look flickered across his face as he worked the lever, then turned the rifle so that it was leveled on Honest Bob.

"It's not loaded," the gunrunner said.

Eagle Feather bared stained yellow teeth in a snarl. He shouldered the rifle, pointing it at a distant vulture flying high overhead. A metallic click sounded as he pulled the trigger and the hammer came down on an empty chamber. "Empty gun no good," he said, scowling. "Maybe shoot straight, maybe not. Who knows?"

Honest Bob was ready for that one. He handed Eagle Feather one bullet. Just one.

"Bob's taking a long chance," Half-Shot said, worried.

"Not so long," Hump Colway said. "If Eagle Feather cuts up, he'll be cut down fast. Look at Melbourne and Chait itching to throw down on him."

"Fat lot of good that'll do Bob."

"Bigger shares for the rest of us."

"Always looking on the bright side, ain't you? Shares depend on who's left standing, Hump."

"I'll be there," the hunchback said. "Hell, the Comanches ain't so dumb as to start a fight they can't win. They like living just like we do.

"But if something jumps off, don't forget to duck."

"Thanks. That's a big help," Half-Shot said. "But a shoot-out's like a prairie fire. Once it gets started, it eats up everything fast."

Eagle Feather fed the long bullet into the breech and changed his grip on the rifle.

A shot sounded.

Honest Bob lurched as if hit by a hammer. He was violently thrown down to the ground. He lay there inert, unmoving, showing not so much as a twitch of motion.

A breathless pause hung shimmering in the air as everyone held their breath, not knowing what would happen next, yet knowing the inevitable consequences of the fatal shot.

No one looked more surprised than Eagle Feather, who stood stupidly staring at the rifle, turning it over in his hands. He hadn't fired it. It hadn't shot, but a man was dead.

"You killed him," Sefton said to Eagle Feather, drawing his gun.

Again, a shot sounded.

It tagged Eagle Feather with a *thwack*. Like a wooden mallet slamming into a side of beef. He crumpled in the middle and went down.

Blood splattered on Han-Tay and Maldito, who were standing on either side of Eagle Feather, striking their faces and necks with stinging force, speckling them with ruby-red dots like scarlet teardrops.

It was Sefton's turn to look surprised. The gun in his hand was leveled and pointing at Eagle Feather, and yet he knew he hadn't fired it. No gunpowder smell, no smoke was curling from the barrel.

Both shots had come from Sam Heller's Winchester 66. His move put a thumb on the scales and tipped the balance back to hate—hate and fear. He paused to watch the party start. He did not have long to wait.

Sefton's gun had cleared the holster when the second shot struck, making it look like he'd shot the Comanche war chief. Maldito was the first to react, stepping inside Sefton's guard and clamping one hand down on the wrist of the outlaw's gun hand. His grip of iron immobilized Sefton's arm, numbing it where those thick strangler's fingers clutched it.

Maldito's free hand pulled a knife from a belt sheath at his hip. He thrust the blade deep in Sefton's belly, ripping it open, disemboweling him.

Maldito jumped back to get out of the way as gray loops of viscera spilled from Sefton's split belly.

The fight was on!

That's all the belligerents knew. For critical instants, both sides had been taken aback, neither side believing that the other would make a dumb play so disastrous, so fatal to the hopes and lives of all.

So of course it happened, or so they understood it. After the heart-stopping pause, they got to it with no holds barred.

Fitch drew and shot two braves standing opposite him on the other side of the crate. Dog Fat was next in line but proved slippery and elusive as his namesake. He threw himself to the side, ducking behind a rock. He dove, came up rolling, and ran to his horse, jumping up on its back.

Fitch ran after him, chasing and shooting. Dog Fat kept zigging when Fitch thought he was going to zag, causing Fitch to keep missing. He pegged another round, missing the Indian but creasing the horse's rump. With a shriek, it upreared on its hind legs.

Dog Fat grabbed his rifle from where it was tied to the saddle, taking it with him as he fell off the horse. He lay prone on the ground, shooting at Fitch, whose gun was empty. He hit Fitch in the middle, mortally wounding him.

Fitch staggered but kept on going, mechanically working the trigger of his empty gun.

Dog Fat shot again and Fitch fell down.

On hands and knees, the brave started to get up, but his fear-crazed horse stepped on him, trampling him under. Dog Fat screamed, trying to get out from under flailing razor-edged hooves.

Frightened all the more, the horse began dancing on him, pounding him flat. Finally breaking loose, it ran away. Dog Fat lay in place, writhing like a half-squashed bug.

Still standing by the crate, Maldito was next on Sam's list. He was a bad one. Sam knew his history, knew the world would be well improved by his removal from it. But Sefton, though dead, was blocking Sam's clear shot on the dwarfish brave.

Sam shifted gears, swinging the rifle in line with another target—one of the outlaws guarding the corral. Sam's shot slammed him to the ground.

Thinking his partner had been downed by Comanches, the other guard cut loose at the nearest knot of braves, levering his rifle as he pumped lead. Shrieks rang out as braves went down.

Similar scenes were being enacted all over the

place. Comanches and gun sellers were blasting at each other. Blood, noise, and death were everywhere.

Horses in the corral panicked. They crowded near the gate, pressing against it, shying, sidling, and shouldering. The gate flew open, slamming back against the fence, tearing loose from the rope hinges. The animals bolted from the corral, fanning out, racing for open spaces. Woe to anyone luckless enough to be in their way!

They ran down white and red men alike, plowing them under. Trampling was not necessarily fatal but it didn't help. When the last horse had escaped the mangled victims were in pretty bad shape. They wouldn't be getting up in a hurry.

The fugitive horses kicked up a lot of dust, further obscuring the scene.

Ricketts's jaw had dropped in open-mouthed astonishment when the shooting started, causing the lit cigar to fall. It dropped into the trough of the boot beneath the box seat. He ducked down and fumbled for the cigar, dropping it several times before getting a good grip on it.

He had a mission to carry out—blow up the wagon if the Comanches tried to take it. Well, if they didn't take it, it wouldn't be for lack of trying. They were sure enough on the warpath.

With trembling hands, Ricketts pressed the lit end of the cigar to the tip of the fuse, whose curling cord-like length terminated in a wooden keg filled with black gunpowder. The fuse sputtered into life, burning like a Fourth of July sparkler.

A bullet tore into his upper body, knocking him off balance. It threw him for a loop, and he let go of the fuse. A canny Comanche had shot him to forestall lighting the fuse, but he was too late. The fuse was lit and burning.

Ricketts pitched forward and to the side, falling in front of the wagon. He rose to his knees. A shot drilled him through the chest. He went down again, not getting up.

A Comanche brave rushed the wagon, knife in hand, intending to cut the fuse before it touched off the gunpowder. He clambered up the front seat of the wagon just in time to catch a bullet from Chait's gun. He pitched backward into the dirt.

The sputtering fuse burned lower, way low. Maldito started toward the wagon but shifted course fast when he saw the brave who was climbing the wagon get cut down. He flung himself to one side, saving himself from the bullet Sam pegged at him. Sam wanted Maldito dead and that gunpowder bomb blowing the gun wagon to kingdom come.

Maldito scrambled behind some rocks, crawling on hands and knees, too low for Sam to hit.

Sam breathed a silent curse. *Maldito is lucky, damn him!*

He stayed out of Sam's line of fire, preventing Sam from taking him down with a follow-up shot.

A couple of braves leveled rifles to cut loose on Melbourne and Chait. Rifles traded fire with six-guns. Chait dodged for cover, catching a bullet for his trouble. Melbourne swung his gun around to cover Chait. A Comanche rifle tagged him, spilling him into the dust.

Grounded, they were prime targets for Comanche bullets, which riddled them. They writhed and spasmed as each fresh slug ripped them, but soon they lay still and unresponsive. They were dead.

Sam had fewer opportunities for clear shots, but he managed to pick off one or two shapes amid the dust and smoke. Comanches and gunrunners were doing a pretty good job of picking each other off without his help.

Bison Creek was aswirl with gun smoke and dust. Men became dim outlined forms, stumbling and staggering. Gunfire lanced the murk with bright red and yellow lines seeking targets. Outcries sounded when a shot speared a man.

Time had run out on the fast-burning fuse. Its last fractional length sparked and sizzled its way into the big keg of black powder. There was a chuffing sound, like the heavy outrush of breath of some great beast, as the gunpowder ignited. Detonating.

The wagon and its contents vanished in a flash of light. A glare bright as the sun filled the space where the wagon had been. The explosion was a vortex of blazing forces—heat, light, and noise.

Sam ducked down, curling up in the hollow of the shooter's nest. He flattened himself as best he could, keeping his head down, clutching his rifle, and hugging it to him.

The ground shook. A brief thought flashed through him. It would be a hell of a note if the blast tore loose the rim of the cliff top where he was perched, sending him crashing down amid tons of rubble to add his remains to the boneyard.

A pillar of smoke and fire thrust skyward from the flat below. A vortex sucked up wreckage, hurling it aloft. The blast was followed by a rain of debris.

Sam was temporarily deafened by the explosion. The earth had been hammered like a gong, making his ears ring. Sam was in none too much of a hurry to stick his head up, not with all the debris pelting down. Some of it was big enough to knock a man's brains out. The cliff top was peppered with the stuff.

The downfall lessened, playing out. Sam uncurled himself, sitting up. His body ached from head to toe, the result of the concussive blast. He felt beat up, like he'd been hammered with iron fists and feet.

Beaten up? A thought struck him, making him grin. "Think this is bad? You should see the other fellow!"

Things had worked out better than he'd expected thanks to the keg of black powder Honest Bob had rigged as a last-ditch defense against being plundered by Comanches. It might not have made a clean sweep below, but Sam reckoned there wouldn't be many survivors.

Standing up on shaky legs, he brushed himself off.

Finding out if dirt had gotten into the rifle barrel and inner workings was a top priority. He didn't dare fire the rifle until he'd given it a clean bill of health. At least the cliff side hadn't come tumbling down, taking him with it. He grinned again. *A lucky break!*

Sam peered through the brush at the flat below. There wasn't much to see—dirty air, dirty sky, all paled by dust and smoke, like a low-level sandstorm. Yellow-brown billows slowly rolled across the plains, stately as sailing ships. Strands of black smoke coiled serpent-like through earthbound yellow-brown clouds.

Sounds? All he could hear mostly was the ringing in his ears.

He didn't want to break cover yet in case there were any survivors below to see him. That wouldn't fit in with his long-range plans.

Let gunrunners and Comanches alike think that

the other side had betrayed them. Let the word go out to the bucket-of-blood saloons and deadfall dives, up into Comancheria, and south down the Comanche Trail deep into Mexico. Rumors of treachery would sow suspicion, causing discord and mistrust between gunrunners and Comanches and poisoning relations between the two.

Time passed. Dust settled though the yellow-brown haze that remained, deepened by long shadows of gathering dusk.

Bison Creek looked like what it was, a battlefield. Bodies of men and horses littered the flat. The gun wagon was gone, pulverized. A wide shallow crater still smoldered, marking where the wagon had stood. The crater walls were streaked by veins and rays of dark brown earth heaved up to the surface. A heavy gun-powder smell hung over all.

Stray horses that had fled the corral roamed the prairie. Of the two-legged survivors of the battle and blast, there were only a few. A handful of riders raced south. Another small group hurried north. Neither bunch had the heart to keep fighting. They were getting out while they could.

Easy enough to figure what had happened. The Co-manches who'd come out alive were the ones riding south, while the last gunrunners ran north.

The ordinarily horse-mad Comanches must've been pretty hard hit to pass up the chance to round up some of the many strays roaming the range. If they wanted to return to the Quesada homeland in the Llano, they'd have to get clear of the cliffs before striking west.

Sam had a pretty good idea where the gunrunners were bound. Their goal most likely was home base at the Hog Ranch near Fort Pardee. There they could lick their wounds while working up fresh new devilments.

Something must be done about the Hog Ranch soon, Sam resolved. *Something massive.* He grinned, satisfied. "Still, in all, a good day's work!"

FOUR

Dusty was a warhorse. He'd been in battle amid the cannon fire, blood, and smoke. The big blast had made him restless but not so much as to spook him into running. Dusty wasn't much for spooking.

Sam went to him. The horse nuzzled him, nudging him with its snout.

"Hey boy! Glad to see me? I'm glad to see you! Some blast, huh? Still it's not so much compared to some we've seen."

Dusty was lively, alert. Sam got his hands on the animal. The comforting hands reassured the horse, gentling him down. Not that he needed much gentling. He was a warhorse

Sam stroked the animal's snout and sleek powerful neck. He kept up a line of patter, nonsense really, but felt that Dusty took some comfort in the sound of his voice. He knew that he took comfort in talking to him. "You've got more sense than most people I know, horse."

He poured water from a canteen into his upturned

hat and held it under Dusty's mouth so the horse could drink. He gave him two hatfuls. Dusty could have gone for several more, but Sam was running low on water. After Dusty drank, Sam had some water from his canteen.

Strapped to the saddle so that it lay along Dusty's left side, its long axis horizontal, was a long, flat, wooden box. Sam unfastened it, taking it down. He sat on the ground cross-legged. "Indian style" folks called it, or sometimes "tailor style." Placing the long box on a folded blanket, he unlatched and lifted the lid. Inside, the box was lined with cushiony velour type fabric, with hollow areas shaped to hold gun parts.

He had examined the Winchester earlier and found that no dirt had fouled it and it was in good working order. It had completed a big job and was due for a thorough cleaning and oiling, but that must wait until later. He broke down the rifle, unscrewing the long barrel and add-on stock, restoring it to its basic proportions as a mule's leg.

He fitted barrel and stock extensions in the cushioning shaped spaces designed to receive them. Securing the gun parts, he closed the lid and fastened the box to its fittings on the saddle.

A saddlebag yielded the gun belt for the mule's leg, a custom leather rig with a long thigh-length holster. He holstered the mule's leg, fastening the leather strap at the top to keep the piece buttoned down tight until needed.

Sam took several empty canteens and slung them by the straps across his shoulders. He unfastened a lariat fixed to the right side of his saddle, slipped his arm through the center hole, and slung it over his shoulder.

He patted Dusty's muscular neck affectionately. "Be back soon, boy." He had a job to do. He wanted accurate information about the butcher's bill for today's fracas—who'd lived and who'd died—but riding to the end of the bench where the cliffs rejoined the flat, then riding to Bison Creek would be a big investment of time and energy. He needed a shortcut and he had one—straight down.

Sam went to the edge of the cliff. The twenty-five-foot drop from cliff top to Bison Creek was a barrier to a rider, but not to a climber. His rope was long enough to reach the bottom. He could climb down and back up.

He scanned the scene below. It seemed empty of all human presence.

Sam hitched one end of the rope to a bent but sturdy tree, testing his weight against it. It passed the test. He let the other end fall down the face of the cliff.

He double-checked the gear on his person, making sure it was all secure and squared away. He pulled on a pair of wrist-length, rawhide range gloves, flexing his fingers inside them for a snug fit, then took hold of the rope and started down. The hempen cord was made to withstand the efforts of a charging bull or runaway horse. It held his weight.

Down he went, using the irregular rock face as a stepping-stone.

He touched ground, taking cover behind a shoulder-high boulder, and loosened the holster strap on the mule's leg to get the piece into action fast. Crouched low, he began prowling the site.

Sam eyed his handiwork and found it good. The carnage was rough, but he'd seen—and done—worse. Always on the side of the angels, of course.

Debris from the explosion was spread over a wide uneven field.

First order of business was to make sure the dead were really dead. A mortally wounded man could still slay a perfectly healthy one. Beware the cunning enemy playing possum. He moved from body to body, Navy Colt in hand.

There were no ringers among the cadavers. The dead were well and truly dead. Some had escaped the reckoning to ride away, he knew. He'd seen them. He wanted a better idea of who had cheated the Grim Reaper and who hadn't.

Some of the bodies were mutilated beyond recognition, others were badly burned. Several had perished not by blast, gunfire, or blade but by explosive-powered shrapnel. Wooden shards and staves had been turned into high-speed lightning-like flying daggers.

A stir of motion behind Sam sent him spinning around, gun ready.

A brave who lay nearby, half-buried under a heap of rubble, was propped up on an elbow, raising his upper body. His arm was upraised and in motion, hand holding a knife ready for throwing. The blade leaped into the air, whirling, glittering.

Sam fired without thinking, shooting the knife out of the air. The brave flinched, eyes wide, hands thrown up in front of his face to protect against shrapnel.

If Sam had had time to think about it, he'd never have made that shot.

Lucky shot! A close one, he thought.

The brave groaned, sinking back down flat to the ground. The secret of the Comanche's survival showed on his twisted form. His lower body was crushed below the waist, buried under several hundred pounds of rocky debris. His upper body was relatively undamaged, save for swelling and mortification caused by the maiming of his lower half.

He'd been awake and aware when Sam started nosing around the scene. Opportunity presented itself when Sam had turned his back to examine a nearby victim. The brave gambled on a toss of the knife. Sam couldn't help but admire his single-minded dedication to slay a last foeman en route to the Great Dark.

Sam approached him warily. Standing over him, he held his gun along his side, pointing down. He was ready to use it if the warrior had any more surprises.

The Comanche's gaze was steady, his expression set in grim lines of silent suffering. He would fight to the last to keep from showing how great his pain was. "Good shot," the brave said in English, forming his words with difficulty, his voice weak. "Your gods with you today . . ."

Nothing to say to that. Sam shrugged.

"You—Tejano?" the brave asked, meaning Texan.

"American," Sam said. "*Yanqui.*" A Yankee.

"Good . . . hate Tejanos." The brave looked pointedly at Sam's gun, raising his gaze to meet Sam's eyes. "You kill, eh?"

Sam hesitated.

The brave looked down at his body beneath the waist, twisted, mangled, and buried under several hundred pounds of rocks and dirt. "No good." He shook his head no. "You kill . . . kill quick . . ."

Sam nodded, lifting the gun. The brave nodded encouragingly. Sam pointed the gun at him. He fired once, delivering the coup de grâce of a bullet in the head.

Sometimes the greatest act of mercy was providing a quick neat exit.

The gunshot startled some nearby buzzards feasting on a choice carcass. One buzzard flew away with a great flapping of wings. The others remained earthbound at their places at the feast, returning to their feeding before the last echoes of the gunshot had faded.

Sam resumed making the circuit, going from body to body. When he had examined the last, he totaled up the score.

Most of the top men were dead—Honest Bob Longford and Felipe Mercurio, Eagle Feather and Han-Tay.

Some key players had escaped, most notably Hump Colway. No worries about mistaken identity there. No amount of damage could disguise that body with its distinctive humped back. Nature had compensated him for his deformity by giving him a cunning brain, steel nerves, and plenty of guts. His escape from the killing ground showed he was lucky, too. A formidable combination and a dangerous man.

Hump Colway would be heard from again, sooner probably rather than later.

Maldito, too, that imp of Satan, had postponed his

day of reckoning. Sam had very much wanted to bag him, but Maldito had had the Devil's own luck working for him and had escaped. He was a vicious foe. The latest setback wouldn't improve his disposition any.

Rio, Mercurio's bodyguard, also seemed to have gotten clear, but Sam couldn't be sure. Several bodies loosely matched Rio's specifications, but they were too badly burned or blasted to verify their identity. Sam's gut feeling was that when a bad hombre like Rio was among the missing, chances were he was alive.

If so, Rio's future prospects were mixed at best. He was a bodyguard who had failed to guard the body that was paying him. Mercurio, Rio's patron, had been an important man with many powerful and influential contacts in business and criminal circles on both sides of the border. Some of them might take exception to Rio having outlived his master and be minded to correct that oversight.

In any case, Sam Heller's work at Bison Creek was done.

On to Hangtree!

FIVE

Mabel's Café faced north on the south side of Trail Street, Hangtree's main drag. It was a long narrow space with a dining room in front and kitchen in back. The place was small, modest, and unassuming. The food was good, the portions hearty.

There were nine tables in the dining room—four small square-topped tables for single diners or couples, five larger round-topped tables for groups of three or more. Two small tables bracketed the connecting door to the kitchen. Another two stood against the front wall under a row of windows.

The round tables were all filled. One of the small tables in the rear was unoccupied, as was one in the front.

Luke Pettigrew sat at the other front table. He was busy tucking into a plateful of steak and potatoes. In his early twenties, he was wiry, lean to the point of being gaunt. Lank brown hair reached down past his bony jawline. He was red-eyed from too much drinking. Prominent canine upper teeth gave him a wolfish look, a not unfriendly wolf.

He wore an open lightweight gray Confederate army tunic, lightweight red shirt, baggy brown pants, and boots. A short-brimmed gray forager's cap hung from the decorative knob on top of the back of the empty chair at his table.

He looked every inch the unreconstructed Johnny Reb he was. And damned proud of it!

Luke was a hometown boy born and raised on a ranch outside town. He had enlisted as soon as news of the firing on Ft. Sumter reached Hangtree. He'd served throughout the war years as one of John Bell Hood's Texans, seeing action in that celebrated unit's big battles east of the Mississippi.

In the last year of the war, a Union cannonball took off his left leg below the knee. It had taken him the better part of a year to get home after the surrender at Appomattox.

Luke wore a first-class combination artificial leg and foot strapped to what remained of his leg. The limb had adjustable sliding fastenings, allowing it to be locked extended straight for standing upright or bent at the knee at a ninety-degree angle for sitting.

The Randle brothers walked in off the street, coming through the front door like any other patron. Why not? It was lunchtime and the café served a pretty good lunch.

Most of the patrons were focused on their plates. A few diners took a casual interest in the newcomers. In a town like Hangtree, more than a few folks had reason to be wary of others who might be looking for them.

Casual glances at the duo prompted no flicker of recognition. Sighting no known foe, the curious, the guilty, and the just plain cautious turned their attention elsewhere.

Cort Randle held a rifle pointing down at his side, nothing out of the ordinary in Hangtree on the frontier. He stood to one side of the front door, back to the wall, showing a funny kind of smile as if amused by some private joke.

Devon Randle went down the center aisle toward the back of the dining room, where a set of swinging doors opened into the kitchen. An arm's length or so short of the doors, he'd turned hard on his heels, spinning, shucking a pair of six-guns out of the holsters and into his hands. He'd stepped to the side, out of the way of the swinging doors, so no one could surprise him from that direction.

A medium-sized man, he showed a quick graceful efficiency of movement. He held his guns level, aiming at everyone and no one, gaining the attention of all.

Cort Randle's rifle came up, held hip-high.

The dining room was suddenly quiet, hushed.

"Hell, the food ain't that bad," said some half-drunk souse.

"No holdup here, folks," Cort announced. "We don't want your money."

"As if these yokels have anything worth taking," Devon said, sneering.

"Now, now. No call to make small of these good people, brother Devon," Cort said, not really minding what his brother said, but amused.

Devon addressed the diners. "It's possible some of you folks might not know who we are. We're the Randle brothers. I'm Devon and that small excitable fellow with the hogleg is Cort. He's the quick-triggered type. It wouldn't take much to make him cut loose, so if any of you have the idea of playing hero, I'd advise you to think better of it.

"But set your minds at ease. We've got no quarrel with you folks."

"Not unless your name is Cross," Devon said laughing, a mean kind of laugh, nasty and lowdown.

Mention of the name *Cross* set off alarm bells in Luke Pettigrew's head. No way he could sit this one out. Not now.

Luke had heard of the Randle brothers. They hailed lately from the Dallas Black Earth region. They came from north Alabama, part of a long line of feudists, soldiers, gamblers—violent lawless men, all. Of late, they'd been based in nearby Parker County, where they ran with the Moran gang—which might mean gang chief Terry Moran and the rest of the bunch weren't too far away.

The brothers were in their mid-twenties. Devon was younger but looked older. He was the brains of the two. Sharp-featured with a hollow-cheeked face, he looked prematurely aged.

Cort, older of the two, was handsome, athletic, and said to be something of a favorite of the ladies when he wasn't off killing and robbing folks.

"I'm a fool for luck," Luke mumbled to himself. *But what kind of luck?*, he wondered. *Good, bad, or something in between?*

That remained to be seen. He reckoned he'd find out pretty soon, one way or another.

On the good luck side of the ledger, he just happened to be having lunch at Mabel's Café in Hangtree town, where a couple of bushwhackers were laying for his partner Johnny Cross.

On the bad side, Luke found himself in the same position as the rest of the café's patrons—covered by the guns of those would-be ambushers, the Randle brothers.

He was on the spot. There wasn't but one person named Cross in Hangtree that the Randles were liable to be gunning for. That was Johnny Cross, Luke's best friend and partner.

Funny . . . Luke couldn't think of any reason why the brothers would be after Johnny. As far as he knew, there was no bad blood between Johnny and the Randles or their gang boss Terry Moran. Not that some of the Texas fast guns needed any more reason than trying to build a reputation to put them on the hunt for another gunslick.

Could be it tracked back to Moran, the Randles' chief? "Terrible Terry" as he was known. An overbearing ambitious outlaw and gunhawk looking to make a name for himself.

No better way to shoot his name into fame than by burning down Johnny Cross. Even if it took a couple back shooters to do it.

No surprise, either, that the Randles dare not face Johnny out in the open—the yellowbellies! They lacked the sand to face him in a fair fight, them and their headman Moran.

"No point in wondering what it's all about," Luke told himself. The question was, what was he going to do about it?

The clock was working against him. Johnny had gone down the street to the Golden Spur for a few quick ones while Luke, a real chowhound, grabbed some lunch first. Any minute, Johnny was liable to come looking for him without knowing he was heading into a death trap.

One thing worked in Luke's favor. The Randles hadn't known him. They hadn't done their homework. Otherwise, they'd have known that Johnny Cross had an ally who always covered his back in a fight. He was a young, wolfish, one-legged Texas Reb named Luke Pettigrew. Either that or they hadn't spotted him yet.

The latter possibility was unlikely. Cort was standing little more than a man's length away from Luke at the front of the café. It seemed like he didn't know Luke from Adam. And Devon could see Luke sitting there with his crutch propped up in a corner nearby.

So they weren't on to him. That gave him something of an edge, no matter how slim.

The café showed a narrow end to the street. The entrance door was closed to keep out dust and flies. To the right of it, a row of three windows stretched across the upper half of the front wall. The windows were open. To protect against the hot Texas sun, their upper halves were covered with dark green pull-down shades and the lower halves were covered with thin blue-and-white checked curtains strung along a thin brass rod. Only a narrow strip of windowpanes was uncovered, affording passersby a minimal view into the café.

Outside, folks were about their business, going somewhere to eat their lunch, coming from having eaten it, using the lunch hour to run some errands, or just ambling along enjoying the fine fall weather. Their outlines could be seen flitting past the curtained, shaded windows. Their voices rang out as they hailed each other in casual conversation.

A person inside the café need merely call out to them for help—and catch a fatal bullet or two in swift recompense from the Randle brothers. So the captives within stayed silent, tight-lipped.

Luke was a good shot with a long gun but only fair with a handgun. That's why he toted around a sawed-off shotgun, usually slung over his shoulder by a leather carrying strap. Unfortunately, it was hanging by the strap over the round knob across from where his cap hung on the extra chair at his table. It hung muzzle-down.

The chair was tucked under the table; the table-top screened the weapon from the view of the Randle brothers. Or so Luke suspected; in any case they hadn't called him on it. The piece was within reach, but if he made a play, the Randles were sure to pick up on it and tag him before he could get the gun in play.

Cort Randle spoke to the diners. "Lest any of you get the wrong idea, I'd like to point out that this is a private matter that don't concern y'all. It would be a shame to get killed meddling in something that ain't none of your affair. Keep your hands where I can see them and keep on eating before your food gets cold."

"I'd best clear the kitchen," Devon said

Cort nodded. "Go ahead. I've got them covered." To the diners, he added, "You folks don't want to make a liar of me in front of my brother."

Devon turned and faced the kitchen doors, toeing one so that it swung inward. He stepped into the doorway, holding the door open with his booted foot.

On the other side of the threshold, the cook stood ready to attack. He was taken by surprise, caught in the act.

He was Brand McGurk, owner and proprietor of the café. He was a grizzled middle-aged man, balding and bearded. A hard item, he was almost as tough as the lean stringy cuts of meat he sent out of the kitchen to the dining room.

McGurk wore a dirty white bib-front apron over a green flannel shirt with the sleeves rolled up past the elbows, baring brawny, hairy forearms. One arm was held upraised, bent at the elbow, poised to strike with a meat cleaver whose handle was clutched in a raw-knuckled fist. The keen-edged cleaver was the only spot of brightness about the man.

Click! The hammer of a gun was thumbed into place, muzzle pointed at McGurk's potbelly. "Whoa, pardner," Devon drawled.

McGurk froze. Behind him, deeper in the kitchen, stood his kid helper Josh, a gangling pimply-faced adolescent.

"Planning on a little meat cutting?" Devon said sarcastically.

McGurk said nothing, staring down at Randle's guns.

Devon waved his gun. "Set the meat ax down on the counter. Gently, gently."

McGurk obeyed, laying the meat cleaver down on its side and stepping away from the counter. He held his hands up chest high.

"I ought to shoot you for that, but I've got bigger fish to fry," Devon said. "Go out front in the dining room with the others."

McGurk moved toward the doorway stiffly, like a man going to the gallows. Josh stood frozen in place, trembling, knock knees quaking.

"Anybody else back there?" Devon demanded.

Josh started to speak, but fear had left his mouth so cotton-dry that he had trouble speaking.

"Spit it out, sonny," Devon said impatiently.

"N-no, sir. Nobody but me," Josh said.

"You go out, too," Devon said, indicating the youngster.

Josh shuffled forward. McGurk sidled past the gunman and through the doorway into the dining room.

Suddenly, savagely, Devon lashed out with the gun, clouting McGurk behind the back of his skull.

A few diners winced in sympathy. A female patron cried out, abruptly stifling herself by bringing a fist to her mouth and gnawing on a knuckle.

McGurk groaned, staggering. His glazed eyes swam in and out of focus. He had a hard head, though, and stayed on his feet. Devon clouted him again.

McGurk's face scrunched up as if squeezed in a vise. His eyes crossed, then rolled up into the tops of the sockets, the whites of his eyeballs showing. He folded up at the knees, falling on the wood-planked floor.

"That's what he gets for trying to play hero." Devon wagged the gun, motioning along Josh, who'd stopped moving when the gunman laid out McGurk. "Into the dining room, junior."

The youth lurched forward, scuttling past Devon. Just when he thought he was safely clear of the gunman, he was the recipient of a well-planted boot to the rear. The kick lifted him off the floor into the air.

"Quit dawdling! No wonder the service here is so slow," Devon said with a mean grin.

Cort chuckled indulgently, as if to say, Who wouldn't be amused by the antics of such a loveable rogue?

The kid stumbled over McGurk's inert form, spilling his length on the floor with a loud outcry.

"Quit your squalling, brat," Devon said.

"You scum!" an elderly spinster lady spat, no longer able to restrain herself.

A middle-aged woman eating at the same table urged, "Stay out of it, Miss Phoebe—"

"You his ma?" Devon demanded of the older woman.

"No, I'm not," Miss Phoebe began, "but no decent woman would coutenance that kind of brutality toward a youngster, or anyone else for that matter!" She was trembling with indignation.

"Hush up now, ma'am," Cort said good-naturedly, amused.

"Yeah," Devon said, "don't get yourself into trouble over some punk kid who ain't no kin of yours, you old bat."

"Well!" Miss Phoebe clamped her mouth shut, white-lipped, rigid.

Josh got up on hands and knees, looking around. A few men sitting at a table nearby started up out of their chairs to help out.

Cort Randle swung the rifle to cover them, shaking his head no. "As you were, gents."

Burly ranch hands from the look of them, they were rough and ready and on the boil, but being under the gun, there was nothing for them to do but take it. They sat back down, eyes downcast, looking away.

Josh rose shakily and stood swaying on unsteady feet, his dark eyes popping in a drawn white face.

"Sit down at one of those tables and stay out of the

way," Devon said. "And the next time you're told to do something, hop to it."

"Yes, sir!" Josh's voice cracked in mid-phrase.

Devon laughed cruelly.

Josh lurched toward the nearest table with an empty chair. He was limping, hurt. He sat down, elbows on the table, head hanging down so low his chin touched his chest.

Devon Randle studied McGurk, still sprawled face-down on the floor, motionless. Blood trickled from a lumpy purple goose egg on the back of his head

"Y'all who was so eager to lend a hand to Sonny Boy can make yourselves useful now," Devon motioned with a gun, indicating McGurk. "Yeah, you," he said to the cowboys who'd started up to help Josh. "Move that side of beef out of the way. Somebody might trip over him and hurt themselves."

The cowboys stayed seated, not moving.

"Somebody's sure 'nuff going to get hurt if you don't haul ass out of those chairs and get to it," Devon said.

Chair legs scraped against floorboards as the cowboys pushed back from the table and stood up. They went to McGurk, walking soft like they were walking on eggs. They stood around McGurk, his face lead-colored, watching Devon out of the corners of their eyes, hating him.

"He don't look so good," one said.

"He still breathing?" asked another.

"Can't tell."

"He'll live, but some of you won't if you don't get to it," Devon snapped.

The cowboys reached down, taking hold of McGurk's limbs.

"All together now, boys."

Grunting exhalations of strain, they lifted McGurk off the floor by arms and legs, forcing a muffled groan from the unconscious man.

"Set him there against the wall," Devon said, indicating the long wall on the left-hand side of the room.

The cowboys tried to position McGurk in a kind of sitting position with his back against the wall and his legs stretched out on the floor, but he kept leaning to one side or the other and toppling over. After several attempts, they succeeded in wedging him upright so he wouldn't choke on his own blood.

"That'll do," Devon said. "Leave him there and sit down."

The cowboys returned to their table.

A thought struck Devon, something he had neglected. "I'm going to lock the back door, Cort."

"Okay, brother. I'll hold the fort." Cort motioned with his leveled rifle to emphasize his words.

Devon went into the kitchen, doors swinging shut behind him.

Cort stood with his back to the wall, positioned between the front door and the windows, screened from the view of passersby on sidewalk or street. "Keep your heads down, folks. Don't kick up a fuss and you won't get hurt."

The kitchen was small, hot, and steamy. Piles of dirty dishes lay heaped up in the sink and adjacent sideboard.

Devon holstered his right-hand gun and went down the aisle past the steam table and grill to the back door. It was open. He stuck his head outside and looked around. The view opened on the south side of town. Clumps of wooden frame buildings dotted a wide flat area. There were more vacant lots than structures, a lot more. Few people were out and about in that part of town; none seemed to be taking an interest in the café.

Devon closed the door, bolted it, and went back into the dining room. "Y'all wouldn't be so quick to shovel in that slop you call a meal, if you got a look at that kitchen. It's a pigsty!"

Nobody in the dining room was eating. Mounds of food sat cooling on their plates unattended. Being held under the gun tended to quash even the heartiest appetites.

"Anything happening out there?" Devon asked Cort, indicating the street.

"All quiet so far as I can tell. Mostly I've been keeping my eyes on the folks here."

Devon crossed to the unoccupied table bracketing the kitchen doors, pulled out a chair, and sat down facing front, his back to the wall. His hands rested on top of the table, a gun in each fist covering diners on both sides of the center aisle. "Take a look now, Cort."

"Right." Cort turned toward the window. He paused to give Luke a hard look, one that said, *Stay put and don't try anything funny.*

At least that's how Luke read it. He sure didn't want to be recognized. That could only change the situation for the worse by delivering a prime hostage into the hands of the foe.

Trust Johnny to make some damned fool self-sacrificing play to save Luke's neck. If it should come to that—No, Luke wouldn't let it come to that. He'd make a play that would force the Randles to shoot him and upset their whole applecart.

If they did for him—well, what of it? He was already half a man and it wouldn't be much of a sacrifice for him to go the whole route. No great loss to the world . . . or him, either.

So went the wild bubbling froth seething in Luke's brain. He had no worries for himself and that was an asset. The plain truth of it was, he just plain didn't give a good damn whether he lived or died.

It was important to win, to foil the enemy. Take the initiative and turn the tables on them. About that, he was unyielding, filled with the old die-hard Rebel spirit.

No sign, no hint of the inner turmoil showed on Luke's face. He kept a poker face, not making eye contact with Cort because that's the way a cowed citizen would react.

To show defiance would be a mistake. If Cort or Devon Randle thought he had fight in him, they'd watch him more closely, ready to call him out if he made trouble. It would lessen his chances when he finally did make his play.

That he would was a foregone conclusion. Of that, there could be no doubt.

The question was, When?

Pretty damned soon from the look of things. Time was running out.

Most of the diners were armed, the men anyhow. It might not be too far-fetched to suggest that more than one woman was packing a little low-caliber ladies' pistol in a purse or handbag. But the Randles hadn't bothered to disarm the patrons of the café. Too big a job, too burdensome, too many guns to handle at once. The brothers counted on keeping the crowd buffaloed.

From their point of view, it was better, easier and more practical to cover the diners en masse and ventilate any who reached for a weapon—or looked like they were reaching. The brothers were counting on the universal truth that sensible folks were not minded to risk their own necks to intervene in somebody else's private quarrel. Not when it was a killing matter.

Cort stood beside a window, holding his leveled rifle below the sill—an extra precaution against being seen by outsiders. Although the curtains screened him from the view of passersby, he avoided showing himself as much as possible. His rifle was pointed at Luke in a seemingly offhanded manner but that was deceptive. Those restless eyes of his didn't miss much.

He looked out the window, scanning the scene. Along Trail Street coursed a small but steady stream of traffic—horseback riders, singly or in groups, carts, and wagons. People on foot crossed to and fro, none giving the café a second glance—and why should they? From all outward appearances, nothing was unusual, nothing untoward going on there. More important were their own errands and private business.

Three men stood loitering in the street at the southeast corner of the Cattleman Hotel, "best in town," farther west on the north side of Trail Street. It was the place where the big buyers and wealthy ranchers stayed. Its private dining rooms served as meeting places for the gentry from near and far while its expansive bar served as their exclusive watering hole. On the veranda, rocking chairs and wicker couches were set out for the use of hotel clientele.

Three idlers were tough-looking hombres—very tough. They didn't look out of place. Hangtree was a town where hard men were the rule rather than the exception. The trio was well-armed with a formidable array of six-guns. They were intently looking east along the street, eyeing the café as if waiting for someone or something.

"Terry and the others are in place," Cort said, noting the threesome.

"Give them the high sign," said Devon.

Cort went to the front door, opening it partway and leaning outside. He held the rifle so it was hidden behind the door. He waved the trio on the corner in front of the hotel. One of them waved back. Cort ducked back inside, closing the door and bolting it shut. "They're ready to go."

"Now all we need is Johnny Cross," Devon said.

"He'll show when Moran calls him out."

"That'll be any minute now."

"You boys fixing to go up agin' Johnny Cross?" The speaker was Pete Conklin, a gray-bearded oldster who'd fought in the Texas War for Independence against Mexico's Santa Anna, the U.S War against Mexico in 1846.

More recently, he'd served in the Lone Star Home Guard militia during the War Between the States. He hadn't served in the regular Confederate army because the recruiting officers had said he was too old. They wouldn't budge on their decision, so for Conklin, the militia it was, where he rode as long and hard as men half his age.

A salty old character, Conklin sat at one of the round tables with a handful of likeminded old cronies. They'd been having lunch before the Brothers Randle came storming in. He knew Luke Pettigrew well, and Johnny Cross, too. He'd been a Hangtree resident for as long as Luke could remember.

As a crotchety middle-aged man he'd loosed more than one shotgun barrelful of rock salt at the fleeing backsides of Luke, Johnny, and some of their buddies when they'd made nighttime raids to steal fresh fruit from the apple trees in his orchard. Now he was a crotchety old man still full of piss and vinegar.

Luke listened carefully. He surely hoped that mouth of Conklin's wouldn't give away who he was.

"We're not going against Cross. Our pard is," Cort smiled.

"And who might that be?" Conklin challenged.

"Terry Moran—Terrible Terry Moran! I reckon you've heard of him."

"Nope," Conklin said flatly. Maybe it was true or maybe he didn't want to give the brothers the satisfaction.

"You're not fooling anybody, old-timer," Devon said, rising to the bait, irked. "You're not so far off from Weatherford and Parker County that you haven't heard of Terrible Terry and his gang. Nobody could be that ignorant."

"We got enough real fire-eaters out this way without having to keep track of a lot of Weatherford trash."

"You got a nasty mouth on you, old man."

"Truth hurts, huh?" Conklin said, emphasizing his words by elbowing one of his cronies in the ribs.

"Haw! That's a good one, Conk," cried one of his cronies at the table.

Devon rose from his chair. "That's enough out of you, you old fool—"

"Easy, brother. He's just trying to get your goat," Cort said, playing peacemaker.

Devon sat back down. "Sure, you're right, Cort. What else can you expect from a passel of backwards hayseeds?"

Cort shrugged. "Let them talk. They don't mean nothing by it. Even if they did, what could they do?"

"Fixin' to shoot Johnny Cross in the back, are ye?" Conklin asked.

"We're not fixing to shoot him at all," Cort said. "Terry Moran doesn't need us to do any back shooting. Not Terrible Terry, Fastest Gun in All Texas—"

"Think so, do ye? Heh, heh, heh!" Conklin gave him the horse laugh. "Maybe you got another think comin'! That Johnny Cross is a ring-tailed whizzer with the plow-handles and no mistake—"

"Not fast enough to beat Moran on the draw."

"Don't bull me, mister. I know a bushwhacking when I see one."

"I believe it! Bushwhacking and back shooting are what put Hangtown on the map," Cort said. "We're going to make sure it doesn't happen to Terry when he downs your boy."

"Hangtree don't work like that, mister. You must've got us confused with Weatherford."

"This is Cross's town, see? He's got lots of friends here," Cort went on. "We're here to make sure none of them interfere or side him at the showdown. It's going to be a fair draw between Terrible Terry and Cross, savvy?"

"Johnny Cross don't need nobody to fight his battles. He does for hisself," Conklin said, careful not to look in Luke's direction.

The old buzzard still has his wits about him! thought Luke.

Cort said, "We're also backing Moran's play against interfering lawmen."

"Huh! No worry about that with what passes for the law in this town!" Conklin cracked.

"Pretty soon, Terry's going to call Cross out and then we'll see who's who and what's what."

"We sure will!"

"Now hesh up and eat your soup," Devon snapped.

"It's gone cold," Conklin complained.

"Eat it anyway."

"Hold it! Something's happening outside," Cort said, a note of urgency in his voice.

Devon rose, guns in hand.

"This is it," Cort said.

Terry Moran strode east down the middle of Trail Street, flanked by his two sidemen Slug Haycox and Justin Kern. They halted facing the front entrance of the Golden Spur Saloon, which lay on the north side of Trail Street fronting south.

Terry Moran cupped a hand to his mouth to amplify his bellowing. *"Cross! Johnny Cross! Come on out!"*

SIX

A newly arrived coach stood in front of the Cattleman Hotel, offloading passengers. A onetime stagecoach—battered but serviceable—it had been converted to private use. It was drawn by a six-horse team yoked in tandem. The wheels' iron rims were hammered thin and fraying from traveling over endless miles of hard road. A thin coat of reddish brown paint covered the vehicle but could not disguise the peeling wooden panels beneath.

It showed the signs of a recent road trip. The coach was powdered with dust. Mixed with sweat, it formed a kind of paste on the hard-breathing horses. They seemed grateful for the rest; weary, they were slumping in the traces.

Two rough-and-ready-looking characters rode topside in the front box seat. A mature adult, the driver was narrow-eyed, grim-faced, and square-bodied. He climbed down from the box seat, something martial in his bearing. He seemed not a man to show fatigue no matter how long or far he had traveled. The shotgun messenger was an oversized hulking youngster—big, rawboned, and long-limbed. He wore a floppy hat with a high crown and wide brim worn cavalry style with the brim pinned up to the front of the crown.

He stowed the shotgun away in the scabbard in the coach boot and looked around. Wide-eyed, he marveled at what he saw, giving the impression he was a backwoods boy who hadn't seen too much in the way of big towns.

The coach's arrival attracted interest among the locals, active folk and idlers alike. Newcomers were always of interest on the edge of frontier civilization, especially those who could afford to travel by private coach.

Facing east in front of the Cattleman hotel, the side door opened and a well-dressed man wearing a gun belt got out. He seemed athletic and energetic, with a spring in his step. He had neatly trimmed black hair and a Vandyke mustache and goatee combination. He wore a wide-brimmed straw planter's hat, brown jacket with dark brown satin trim edging his lapels, and a ruffled white shirt. He looked something of a dandy but capable with a six-gun holstered low on his right hip.

He reached into the coach, pulled out a sturdy wooden footstool, and set it on the ground below the bottom of the open door, making sure it was securely settled. With an air of eager expectancy and showy cavalier courtesy, he extended a helping hand to an unseen passenger.

A decidedly feminine hand, slim, white, and elegant, reached out, taking hold of his proffered arm.

"This way if you please, Miss Ashley," he murmured.

"Thank you, Kale," a lilting honeyed female voice replied.

A rustling of skirts and petticoats sounded as an exquisite slender leg stepped out and down from inside the coach. Town gawkers, loafers, and the curious were rewarded with an alluring glimpse of a slender well-turned ankle and small booted foot.

An attractive young lady stepped down from the coach onto the footstool and then the street. No overstatement was involved to say she was beautiful—a tall, slim, high-breasted, leggy, fair-skinned blonde.

Those of her admiring viewers who'd drunk champagne had a standard by which to describe her hair color. She showed fine sculpted features, blue eyes, and a generous pink-lipped mouth. Her coloring was natural, without a trace of rouge or cosmetic powder. In that time and place, only loose women wore makeup.

Her hair was sensibly pinned up at the back of her head for convenience and comfort while traveling. A light fawn-colored dress hugged her enticing youthful curves in a nice ladylike way.

Her appearance created a stir among the gawkers, brightening eyes and drawing smiles and appreciative murmurs. Among the younger men, elbows nudged ribs.

One high-spirited youngster had licked his lips and was puckering them up to whistle when a long shadow fell across him. It belonged to the shotgun rider standing at his elbow and looming over him, a head taller and with cold unfriendly eyes.

The youth glanced up, pinned by the other's eyes glaring down at him. The youngster's mouth and throat went dry, the appreciative whistle he'd been about to make dying unsounded. Paling, he backed off and made himself scarce.

The rest of the porch-side good old boys got the message that here was a lady and one to be treated as such.

As if to underscore the lesson, the man named Kale let his hand significantly drop to his side to brush his coat flap away from his sidearm, resting his hand on the gun butt. "Be polite—gentlemen," he said, pleasant-seeming but with clenched teeth.

"Get the Squire's chair, Piney," the coach driver said.

"Okay, Top," replied the oversized backwoods helper. He clambered across the stagecoach's roof to the rear of the vehicle, where a tailgate flap secured various items of baggage, several steamer trunks, and a number of suitcases and traveling bags. They were all covered with a canvas tarp lashed into place by rope. He opened a jackknife, lovingly unfolding a long, sharp, gleaming blade, sunlight glinting on it. Stretched out flat on his belly across the roof, he cut the cords securing the tarp.

Piney climbed down to help Top unfurl the canvas tarp covering the baggage. Neatly stowed on top of the trunks and suitcases was what looked like a long piece of furniture or equipment. It was wrapped in blankets to cushion it from the rigors of the road.

"Set it down on the hotel porch, Piney."

"Right, Top."

Piney wrestled the bulky object across a broad shoulder, his stork-like legs bending at the knees under the weight.

"Need a hand?"

"I got it, Top." Piney carried the mysterious object up the wooden front stairs to the veranda, onlookers moving aside to make room for him. He set it down and began unwrapping it. The curious idlers leaned in to see what lay within the coverings.

The wrappings came off, revealing a wheelchair. It was a handsome specimen, high backed and hand tooled, well cushioned.

Piney went back to the open coach door. He and Top assisted another passenger, a pink-faced older man with white hair and a bushy white beard, carrying him outside. He wore a pair of spectacles with small dark green circular lenses, a big man in a baggy brown suit. There was something wrong with his legs. He couldn't stand up on them.

Piney scooped him up in both hands, and holding him like a child, carried the invalid up the front steps. Top hovered around them, fussing, while Kale and the young woman stood to one side watching.

Piney gently deposited the white-bearded man upright in the wheelchair. "There you are, Mr. Mallory."

"Thank you, Piney."

Top unfolded a blanket, covering Mallory from the waist down. Mallory thanked him. Top started adjusting the blanket around the other's legs, but the young woman interceded.

"I'll take care of that, Top."

"Very good, Miss Ashley." Top relinquished his place to her.

"Allow me, Father," Ashley said, arranging the blanket folds around Mallory's lower body, tucking them in neatly, taking great pains with them.

"Thank you my dear. You're so good to me," Mallory said, beaming benevolently.

Terrible Terry Moran started raising hell down the street outside the Golden Spur, calling out Johnny Cross. He cupped his hands and bellowed, *"Cross! Johnny Cross! Come on out. I know you're in there!"* Twenty-six, Moran had a long, oval, sheep-like face, his short fair curly hair curled like lamb's fleece. There was nothing sheep-like about his demeanor, though. He was hot-tempered, short-fused, and as vain as a matinee idol of the live stage theater.

Small, round, red eyes and a snaky-veined forehead dominated a fiery red face. His gangling long-limbed form quivered with indignation. A black hat with a stiff, flat, perfectly circular brim was worn tilted way back on his head like a black halo. Twin guns were worn holstered way down on his hips. The guns were worn butt-first in tied-down holsters.

A pair of hardcases, Haycox stood on his left, Kern on his right.

The Golden Spur, a stand-alone building with no adjoining structures, lay on a diagonal, opposite Mabel's Café. The Spur being a favorite watering hole of his, Johnny Cross was inside.

When Moran and company stepped out of the sidelines to stride boldly along the middle of Trail Street, those nearby hadn't needed to be told that trouble lay ahead. They knew the drill—Hangtree was a wild town.

Loafers and passersby made themselves scarce. They'd absented themselves from the scene even before Moran started shouting. Some had moved east, some had moved west, some had ducked into north and south cross streets, others into alleys or doorways. They all had scrambled for cover. More than a few got clear but not so far away that they'd miss the show.

"Woo-wee, see how they run!" Cort Randle had crowed.

"The fat's in the fire now," brother Devon had noted with approval.

Batwing double doors of the Golden Spur's entrance remained inert, unopened.

"Cross! John Cross! This is Moran speaking. Terry Moran!" He shouted with his left hand cupped to his mouth. "I'm calling you out, Cross!" Moran cut sidelong glances at Haycox and Kern.

Time passed with Johnny Cross a no-show and no one else in the saloon stupid enough to stick their head out to see what was happening.

"He ain't in no hurry to show himself," Haycox said, spitting.

"Can you blame him? I wouldn't be in no hurry to go up against Terry Moran neither," Moran said, preening.

"There's movement behind those windows," Kern noted.

"Hell, it's probably folks crowding to get a better look at me," Moran said.

"I got my eye on the window on this side," Haycox said. "I see anything that looks like a gun sticking out, I start blasting."

"You cover the window on your side, Kern," Moran said.

"That ain't Cross's way. Not from what I heard," Kern said. "He's so puffed up, got such a swellheaded opinion of himself, the poor fool actually thinks he's gonna win."

Moran resumed shouting. "Come out, Cross! You don't want folks to think you've gone yellow, do you?" To his fellows, he said, "That ought to bring him out."

No one exited the saloon.

"Hell, maybe he *is* yellow," Moran said after a brief wait. "Not that that'll save him." He started in again. "Don't make me come in after you, Cross. I wouldn't want any innocent folks to get hurt!"

"Ain't no innocents in Hangtown," Haycox growled.

"That's okay. Even if there was, I don't mind hurting them, anyhow," Moran confided. He shouted some more. "What's the matter, Cross? You gone yellow? You can't hide! Come out or I come inside after you!"

"You sure he's in there, Slug?" Moran asked, frowning.

"Sure I'm sure!" Haycox said, indignant. "Fly gimme the high sign no more than five minutes ago and we've been watching the front ever since."

"Maybe he sneaked out the back."

"Fly would have tipped us."

"Go check with Fly to make sure Cross didn't pull a sneak," Moran said.

"He'd have to be almighty shifty to get past Fly," Haycox said.

"Go look anyhow."

"You're the boss." Haycox went to the nearest cross street west of the saloon.

It was empty. Haycox paused, looking around, uncertain. He glanced back at Moran and Kern, then walked forward and turned on Commerce Street, following it to the far end. He looked right—looked left—looked right again—looked up and down. He was looking for Fly but couldn't find him. Puzzled, Haycox scratched his head and ass with equal lack of result. After a moment, he turned, hurrying back down the cross street, emerging on Trail Street. "Fly's gone," he told the others, mystified.

"What do you mean, gone?" Moran demanded.

"He ain't there," Haycox said. "I thought he might be behind the back of the building, but he ain't there, either."

"He must be somewhere."

"Well, he ain't there."

"Maybe he went into the Spur to keep a closer watch on Cross," Moran suggested.

"Went in for a drink, more likely," Kern said.

"If he did, I'll peel the hide off him," Moran said feelingly.

The stall was starting to get on the Randle brothers' nerves.

"Something's going on," Cort Randle said, standing at the window of the café.

"What?" Devon demanded, more short-tempered than his brother.

"I don't know. Terry and the other two are standing around jawing," Cort said.

"Never mind that, what's Cross doing?" Devon asked.

"He's not showing," Cort said definitely.

"Smart," Devon said. "Maybe he means to have Terry go in after him. Being the defender would give Cross the advantage."

"Reckon he tumbled that you and me are laying for him?"

"He's not that smart, Cort."

Moran wasn't handling the frustration well, not one for taking in stride being balked. His face swelled, darkening to a deeper shade of red. His pop eyes seemed on the verge of starting from their sockets. Still standing in the middle of the street, he yelled, "Cross! Come out, ya yellow bastid!"

"Howdy, gents," a voice called to Moran, Kern, and Haycox. The speaker was a young stranger wearing twin belted .45s. He stepped into view from the mouth of the northbound cross street west of the one Haycox had explored, taking Moran and his two sidemen by surprise.

From inside the café, Luke had been surreptitiously monitoring the doings on Trail Street. *That give 'em a jolt. Derned near jumped out of their skins.* He could have laughed out loud but didn't want to draw attention to himself.

In the street, the three gunmen spun around to confront the newcomer. Moran started to go for his gun but thought better of it and held his hand. Totally flummoxed, Haycox and Kern made no move to reach at all.

The easy-walking stranger came to a halt a stone's throw away from them. His arms were at his sides, hands hanging easily over his guns. "I'm Cross." He smiled. "Looking for me?"

SEVEN

Marshal Mack Barton stood around jawing with smithy Hobson at the Hangtree livery stable passing the time. They were sharing a big jug of corn liquor, too.

Hobson cooked the home brew himself and it wasn't called White Lightning for nothing. He and the marshal were looking a bit thunderstruck.

Livery stable owner Hobson was a blacksmith, too, and looked the part. He stood six feet plus and 250 pounds of gnarly bone and muscle. He was bareheaded with tight-cropped brick-red hair and beard.

Marshal Barton was about the same size, maybe thirty pounds less, but was not in the same rock-hard physical condition. He had a spade-shaped face, long narrow eyes, and an iron-gray paintbrush mustache. A tin star was pinned to his vest over his left breast.

His face looked like it was cut into a permanent scowl, tight lips with the corners turned down, deep vertical lines bracketing his mouth. Dour, but not without a gleam in his eyes, put there perhaps by Hobson's home brew.

Nothing illegal about it because there was no law against making it. There might have been some law on the books about taxing it, but that was the kind of law Barton ignored.

He and Hobson stood inside the front of the stable barn to one side of the open double doors. A four-sided wedge of warm afternoon sunlight shone into the structure, though they stood in the shade. An open window let in light and air. Against the wall stood a wooden plank table where Hobson did what little paperwork his business required.

"Good brew," Barton said, smacking wet lips.

"Mebbe you think I don't know it," Hobson said, chuckling. He reached for the jug, hooking a meaty sausage-link finger through the bottle neck loop. Expertly balancing the jug in the crook of a brawny upraised arm, he raised it to his mouth, uptilted it, and drank deep.

His face was red, flushed, a permanent condition brought on by countless hours spent basking in the heat of a smith's forge. When he lowered the jug, a fresh new red tinge blossomed out on his weathered face, that part of it not masked by his scraggly brick-red beard.

His hair and beard were kept close-cropped by necessity to keep from setting them afire as he hammered white-hot iron and steel into shape at the anvil. Even so, parts of his eyebrows had been singed away, and his beard was mottled with scorch marks where red-hot embers had landed.

Forge fires were banked down low. It was lunchtime.

Barton and Hobson were enjoying their midday break. If they wanted to spend their lunch hour drinking instead of eating, it was their business, and who to say them nay?

It was a warm midday. The stable barn was thick with the smell of horseflesh, manure, hay, and oats. They didn't even notice it. Horses were omnipresent in Hangtree and everywhere else, town and country. No one gave it a second thought.

The wide-open center space was bordered on both sides by a rows of stable stalls that stretched the length of the building. Most of the horses were outside in the corral, Hobson preferring to let then run free under the sun.

A mood of easiness generated a laid-back aura. Even the horses seemed to partake of it.

The only discordant note came from somewhere on Trail Street a few blocks north and out of sight. From that direction emanated a kind of braying or yammering that could have come from an ornery jackass.

They paid the noise no never mind. It was something to be ignored, like the buzzing of flies around a manure pile. No matter how clean a stable was kept—and Hobson kept his clean—there was no shortage of manure and flies.

It was the same way with a town, Marshal Barton thought when he put his mind to it. But at the moment, he had better things to occupy his attentions, like the jug of wicked sharp corn liquor.

Hobson's Livery barn fronted north, occupying the south edge of a five-sided dirt—well, *square* wasn't the word, not when the intersection had five sides. Call it a *pentangle* if you must, but to Barton it was just a tricky five-sided intersection.

The easygoing mood was disturbed by the sight of a figure who came running into view south along the street connecting with Trail Street. The blurred antlike figure made its way toward the stable barn at the far end of the street.

Marshal Barton sighed. *This can't be good.*

Hobson finished his turn and reached to hand off the jug to Barton.

"You better hold on to it," the marshal said.

Hobson's eyebrows—what was left of them—lifted in surprise. "Something wrong with it, Mack?"

"Hell no, Hob. It's good as ever. You cook an almighty fine batch of home brew."

"What then? You off your feed or something?"

"Duty calls." Barton indicated the fast approaching figure.

Hobson squinted, eyeing the runner. "Why, I do believe that's Junior Lau."

"So it is," Barton said.

"Wonder what that punk kid's in such an all-fired hurry about?"

"Looking for me, probably," Barton said, sighing.

"What makes you say that?"

"Experience. When folks hereabouts get stirred up enough to get off their lazy asses and get to hustling double quick, they're usually looking for the law."

The figure neared, making a beeline for the livery stable.

"That's Junior Lau, all right," Hobson confirmed.

Junior Lau was a freckle-faced teen who clerked at the feed store. He slowed as he neared the livery stable, looking all around as though in search of someone.

Barton stepped to the open entrance where the youngster could see him.

Junior did a take, starting forward. He had a bowl-shaped haircut, bulging eyes, jug-handle ears, and an oversized Adam's apple that looked like a walnut stuck in his throat.

Hobson set the jug down on the table and moved alongside Barton so he could follow the byplay. Junior rushed up, stopping short a few paces away, breathing hard.

"Looking for me, Junior?" Barton asked.

"Yes, *sir*!"

Barton glanced quickly at Hobson as if to say *told you so*. "How'd you know where to find me?"

"I went to the jailhouse first but it was locked up, nobody there," Junior Lau said. "Fenton from the feed store said he saw you going this way and figgered that's where you might be headed. Better come quick, Marshal—there's trouble!"

"There always is," Barton said more to himself than to the youngster. "What kind of trouble?"

"Bad trouble, Marshal Mack! Shooting trouble, looks like," Junior rushed on excitedly. "There's some strangers in town kicking up a fuss outside the Golden Spur! Ornery looking fellows, too, real mean ones—hardcases!"

"Nothing new there. Only they're starting earlier than usual," Barton said in an aside to Hobson.

"The leader calls himself Moran," Junior Lau went on.

"Moran?" Barton said, his interest piqued. "Terry Moran?"

"That's the one!"

"Know him, Mack?" Hobson asked.

"I know of him. Him and his bunch have been cutting up a swath in Parker County."

"That Moran fellow's calling out Johnny Cross!" Junior Lau blurted out.

"He better be careful. He just might find Cross." Hobson chuckled.

"That's a break." Barton relaxed. "Cross is out at his ranch."

"No, sir, he's not," Junior Lau said. "Him and Luke Pettigrew rode into town this morning."

"Johnny Cross can take care of himself," Hobson declared.

Barton frowned. "It ain't him I'm worried about. I don't want any of the townsfolk to get hurt. You say Moran's got some fellows stringing with him, Junior?"

"Yes sir. Looked like five of them in all. Mean-looking hombres, too."

"I'll take care of it, Junior. Thanks for letting me know."

"Oh, pshaw! Nothing to it. Glad to help out, Marshal." Junior didn't leave but stood around waiting.

"Got a shotgun I can borrow, Hob?" Barton asked.

"Sure do," the smith said. A big-bore double-barreled shotgun stood leaning against the front wall. He broke it to make sure it was loaded. It was. He handed it to the marshal.

"Thanks. That'll save me the time of fetching mine from the jailhouse," Barton said.

Hobson handed him an open box of cartridges.

Barton grabbed a handful, stuffing them into a vest pocket while Junior Lau watched goggle-eyed.

Hobson reached into a table desk drawer, pulling out a six-gun and sticking it into the top of his belt.

"What do you think you're doing?" Barton asked. "As if I didn't know."

"I don't want to miss the fun," Hobson said.

Barton shook his head. "I get paid for keeping the peace. You don't."

"I ain't gonna horn in. I just aim to tag along," Hobson said. "Can't go to a gunfight without packing one myself. I'd feel undressed . . . nekkid."

"I reckon so," the marshal allowed.

"Gonna send for Smalls?" Hobson asked. Smalls was Barton's deputy.

"He's out of town serving writs for nonpayment of taxes. Reckon I'll just have to handle this myself."

"I got your back." Hobson stuck a cork in the mouth of the jug, palm-heeling it into place. He stowed the jug out of sight under the table behind some boxes. "Now we can go." Mock-serious, he looked at the teenager. "That jug better be there untouched when I get back, Junior."

"Aw, Mr. Hobson! You know I wouldn't steal nothing or sneak a taste—"

"Why not? I'd have done it when I was your age."

"Don't go giving the lad ideas, Hob," Barton said.

Junior Lau looked from one to other, face coloring, head swiveling on top of a pipe stem neck. "I would never—"

"We're just funning you, boy," Barton said.

He and Hobson started across the dirt yard and up the street to Trail Street, Junior Lau following at their heels. The men hustled along in quick time as gunfire sounded ahead.

"Looks like we're late to the ball," Barton said, quickening his pace, the others matching it. He wasn't much of a one for running. He double-timed, something between jogging and hustling, as aging big men were wont to do.

Excited, Junior started running ahead of them.

"Wait up, Junior! I don't want you running into something you can't handle."

"Aw, Marshal—"

"You stay well behind me and Hob and get under cover before we reach Trail Street."

Johnny Cross's advent in the street had also taken the Randle brothers by surprise, giving them a jolt they tried not to show to the customers in the café.

"Why, that slippery son of a gun! How'd he get there?" Cort swore.

"I'm going to take a look," Devon said. "Keep these folks covered. Don't want to tempt them into any foolishness. It would be the death of them."

Cort stood with his back to the front wall, swinging the rifle barrel around to point at the diners.

Luke thought that his chance might have come, but he was doomed to disappointment. He might have been able to get under or around Cort's rifle, but Devon was advancing with gun in hand, putting Luke directly in the line of fire. It would be suicide to make a play, but time was running out.

Devon joined Cort at the front window. He turned his back on the crowd to look outside. "No mystery here. Cross must have sneaked out the back of the saloon and ducked down a side street."

"Lucky for Terry and the boys that Cross didn't come out shooting from behind. He might have bagged them all shooting them in the back."

"I'd have shot him first and that would have been the end of the High and Mighty Mr. Cross," Cort said.

"Terry'd be powerful sore. He's got his heart set on adding Johnny Cross's notch to his gun," Devon pointed out.

"So he's sore. That's better than being dead."

Devon had no reply to that one.

"Where's Fly?" Cort asked. "He was posted behind the back of the Spur to set up a holler if he saw Cross making a sneak."

Devon peered through the window. "I don't see him."

"Reckon Cross got him."

"We'd have heard the shooting, Cort."

"Not if he used a knife. Let me see, Devon."

"All right. I'll cover them." Devon turned to cover the assembled customers.

Cort shifted positions at the window. He'd had his rifle pointed at the Golden Spur entrance, but he had to swing it around toward Johnny at the far left of the trio.

"Got a clear shot?" Devon asked.

"I've got him right square in my gun sights," Cort said.

Luke tensed, ready to make his move.

Devon had more to say. "Well, don't shoot until Terry gives you the signal. He wants this to look like a fair draw."

EIGHT

Standing in the street in front of the Golden Spur, Moran, Haycox, and Kern tried not to show their complete surprise.

Moran was the first to recover. "Johnny Cross?"

"That's right," Johnny said.

"So that's Cross? He don't look like much," Haycox said low-voiced to Kern.

"He looks like a kid, wet behind the ears," Kern said.

"Yeah, well, he ain't gonna get any older after today," Haycox said.

Johnny Cross looked like the young man he was, barely a shade past twenty-one years of age. He had gone to Missouri at the start of the war and had spent the four long years of the conflict as one of Quantrill's guerrillas. The year after Appomattox was no picnic, either, but that's a tale for another time.

Johnny handled himself with an assurance far beyond his years. He was medium-sized, trim, and compactly knit. He was black-haired and clean-shaven, adding to the impression of youth.

Lack of facial hair of some sort was a rarity for most

men, but he had his reasons. Too many old-time foemen might remember the wild-haired, scruffily bearded pistol-fighter who had spread such death and destruction in the border states during the war years. He had a new life now and wanted to keep the door to the past firmly shut . . . but was that possible?

Johnny wore a flat-crowned black hat, lightweight brown jacket, gray shirt with black ribbon tie knotted in a bow, and black denims worn over custom-made leather boots. He looked prosperous, another rarity in that time and place. Twin walnut-handled Colt .45s were worn low on lean hips. Nobody was going to take anything of his without a fight.

His lips were curved in a sort of half smile.

The three gunmen changed their grouping. All turned to face Johnny, Haycox and Kern fanning out to bracket Moran on the sides.

Moran stood with fists on hips in a posture of dominance. "Cross!"

"That's right."

"You deaf or something? You must have heard me calling you out!"

Johnny nodded. "The way you were bawling, they must have heard you clear over to the next county."

"You took your own sweet time showing your face," Moran accused.

"I was finishing my drink."

"Hope you enjoyed it, because it's going to be your last!"

"So it's like that, is it?" Johnny said after a pause, looking Moran up and down as though noticing him for the first time. "I didn't catch your name, friend."

"Terry Moran," the other said smugly, relishing the sound of his own name.

"Who?" Johnny asked, trying to get Moran's goat.

"Terry Moran," the other repeated, nettled. "Don't make out you didn't hear me."

"I heard you. I just never heard *of* you."

Johnny had heard of Moran but said otherwise to rile him. It was a ploy to irritate the man, get under his skin, and make him lose his temper. An angry man was at a disadvantage in a fight.

Turned out it didn't take much to get Moran mad. He was hot-tempered, with a short fuse. His face swelled with indignation. "Like hell!" he spat out, red-faced, eyes flashing dangerously. "Don't give me that! You know who I am. Everybody does! I'm Terrible Terry Moran, the bull of the woods in these parts!"

"That so?" Johnny drawled mildly, underplaying. "What can I do you for, Moran?"

Finally, they were getting to the heart of it.

"They say you're fast on the draw," Moran said.

"They do say that," Johnny allowed.

"I say I'm faster!" Moran said belligerently, putting some teeth in it.

"There's one way to find out."

Moran gave a short nod. "That's what I'm fixing to do."

"Ask him about Fly first, Boss," Kern prompted Moran.

"Good point. What'd you do to my man Fly?"

"Fly? That the little fellow with the big pop eyes playing lookout in the alley?" Johnny asked.

"He's the one. As if you didn't know!"

Earlier, when Moran was calling him out, Johnny had slipped out the back door of the saloon. Peeking around a corner of the building, he'd spotted Fly planted in the alley. He gave quick thought to what had happened and what to tell Moran.

Fly was looking for him, but Johnny saw him first. He stepped into view, gun leveled on the gunman. Fly was a dead man and he knew it.

With his free hand—the one not holding a gun—Johnny held a finger upright against his lips, motioning for silence. Fly realized he might have a chance of coming out of it alive if he cooperated.

Johnny motioned to Fly to come to him. Fly started forward up the alley, walking stiff-legged like a man trying to make his way against gale-force winds.

Johnny waited patiently for Fly to reach him, then herded Fly behind the back of the building, out of sight of anyone looking into the alley. "You want to live?" *Johnny asked soft-voiced.*

"Y-yes!" *Fly nodded so vigorously his hat almost fell off his head.*

Johnny again motioned for silence. "Shh. Turn around, facing the wall."

Fly did as he was told.

"Take off your hat."

Fly obeyed. Johnny clipped him, laying the gun barrel across the back of his head, a short savage blow. Fly's eyes rolled up and he went down, out cold.

Johnny holstered his gun and shucked Fly's gun from its holster, breaking it, swinging out the cylinder, and spilling the rounds into his open palm. He threw them away and returned the gun to its holster.

Grabbing Fly by the collar, he dragged him to the back of the building, propping him up in a sitting position. He arranged him so he looked like he was taking a nap or, more likely in Hangtree, sleeping off a drunk.

Fly's head was bowed, chin resting on his chest. Johnny

put Fly's hat on top of the little man's head, pulling it down tight so it would stay in place.

"Have a nice siesta," Johnny said, going down the alley. He peeked around the corner of the saloon to make sure no one else was laying for him.

No one besides Moran and the other two facing the front of the Golden Spur and watching for him. Satisfied, he stepped out into Trail Street to confront them.

"What'd you do to Fly?" Moran again demanded.

Johnny shrugged. He didn't bother to go into the whole scenario. Moran wasn't worth it. "He's having a little siesta behind the saloon. You'll have to get along without him."

"I can take care of myself, mister, as you'll soon find out."

"What're those two for, to hold your coat?" Johnny indicated Haycox and Kern.

"Insurance in case any of your pals tries to butt in."

"You don't know Hangtown very well. Here, a man fights his own battles."

"That suits me fine."

"Yeah, I can see that."

"You got a big rep, Cross. I rode all the way from Weatherford to try you out," Moran said.

"You came a long way to die," Johnny told him.

Ranchers Andy and Jed came out of the Feed and Grain store on the south side of Trail Street. They were arguing the merits of different types of oats and grains for feeding thoroughbred horses, not that they owned any. They'd been in the back room with the store's owner and were unaware of the trouble brewing on the street.

They were halfway to the cross street before realizing that they'd walked right into the middle of a showdown. Cal grabbed Jed's arm so hard that the other winced in pain.

Jed halted, face contorted. "Let go my arm Cal. You're hurting me. What the hell's the matter with you?" He caught sight of Johnny confronting three tough-looking hombres in the middle of Trail Street, and the implications sank in. "Let's get out of here!" he said, low-voiced and urgent.

The two glanced around, looking for a hole to hide in. The nearest refuge was Mabel's Café.

Cal ducked into a crouch, lunging for the café door with Jed close behind.

Cal grabbed the door handle, tearing at it. To his surprise and dismay it refused to open.

Jed crowded up against Cal in his eagerness to be off the street before the shooting started. "Get in there Cal, why don't you—?"

"Can't! Door's stuck. Won't open."

Cal rattled the doorknob of the immovable door, alternating with quick glances over his shoulder at the gunmen squaring off in the street. "It's locked!" he moaned.

"Blamed fools!" Jed agonized.

Cal made a fist, thumping it on the door, pounding away. "Open up, ya blasted idjits!"

"Who's that on t'other side of the door?" Jed said, trying to see inside.

"Yuh got me. Don't know him from Adam."

It was Devon Randle peering out from behind the flap of a lifted shade. He wanted no attention attracted to the café for fear of tipping Johnny Cross's notice to the planned ambuscade at Mabel's.

"Open up. Unlock the door and let us in!" Cal demanded.

"We're full up. Keep moving," Devon growled.

Cal kept pounding away with the bottom of a ham-like fist, shaking the door, rattling it in its frame. "Quit your foolishness and open up that danged door before I bust it open!"

Frantic hammering knocked a square pane of glass clean out of the window frame. It fell to the café floor, shattering.

Cal was intent on reaching through the hole to unlock and open the door, but before he could do so Devon raised a gun to the open square where the glass had been. He pointed it at Cal, who froze.

The hombre meant business!

"My momma didn't raise no damn fools!" Cal said, choking.

Looking over Cal's shoulder, Jed could see the gun, too. "What's going on here?"

"Get out of here before I put a bullet in you!" Devon said. "Go on, git!"

Cal and Jed didn't need to be shot to convince them to move along. They got out of there, scurrying west to the next cross street, turning left around the corner, down the street, and out of sight.

"Opportunity knocks," or so they say. In this case, literally.

Distraction and diversion. It was more than Luke had dared hope for. He planned to make a move no matter what—he *had* to—come what may at whatever cost to himself. Then Cal and Jed had blundered along, scared witless and thinking only of getting off the street before the shooting started. Their timely interruption broke the concentration of Cort and Devon Randle.

Standing at the far end of the three windows near where Luke was sitting on the edge of his seat, Cort's attention was focused on the Trail Street face-off, waiting for the signal from Moran.

Moran wanted the showdown to look like a fair fight, but he was taking no chances. The plan was to signal Cort to shoot Johnny at the same time Moran drew and fired his gun. It would look like Moran outgunned Johnny fair and square, so long as nobody examined the corpse too closely and found the bullet from Cort's rifle in Johnny's back.

Moran and his crew would stage-manage the aftermath of the killing to make sure their secret was protected. They had worked the dirty dodge before in other gunfights, or so Luke understood from picking up on the veiled hints and references in the conversations of the Randle brothers.

"Wait till Terry pushes his hat back on his head. That's the go-ahead to shoot," Devon coached his brother.

"I know, I know," Cort said, impatient and dismissive. "I'll put the first one in Cross's belly right above the gun belt. That'll take the starch out of him!"

Such must not be, Luke told himself.

Devon stood at the front door watching Cal and Jed scuttle away. He chuckled. "That got them going. Put them on the hop like a couple frightened rabbits."

Cort couldn't help but glance away from the street to his brother. "Good! Can't have them tipping Cross that something's not right with the café."

Luke grabbed his crutch, holding it in both hands,

right hand uppermost, with its upper end (curved and padded) pointed at Cort's middle. Using a crutch constantly had endowed Luke with tremendous upper-body strength. He struck suddenly, savagely, without warning, thrusting the crutch at Cort's crotch, right square above where his legs forked. It was a wicked blow, vicious, and he didn't spare the horses any.

He'd been a champion first-class bayonet fighter back in the war, wielding the bayonetted musket with authority to club, smash, and spear. He hadn't lost his touch, he was happy to discover.

Luke slammed a wicked butt-stroke home into Cort's middle, right where it hurt the most. No man born of woman can withstand that kind of punishment.

Cort folded up, imploding. The impact rocked him back on his heels. He pancaked, folding at the knees. Breath whooshed out in a shocked gasp.

His face deathly pale, eyes bulging, mouth a black sucking O, Cort let the rifle fall from nerveless fingers and grabbed himself between both legs as he folded up.

The rifle clattered to the floor but didn't go off. Too bad. It would have tipped Johnny to the lay of the land.

It was all happening so fast there was no time for thought and to stall would be fatal.

Devon whipped around, guns in hand. He held death in each hand, but for a few fateful heartbeats he had no shot. Brother Cort was in the way.

Pushing off with his good right foot, Luke lurched forward and down, grabbing hold of the butt of his sawed-off shotgun where it sat fixed in the leather carrying strap across the back of the empty chair at the table. All came tumbling down with him. Luke, weapon, and chair crashed to the floor.

Luke flopped prone across the floorboards. He snatched at the sawed-off's pistol grip handle, hauling away at it to get it clear of the fallen chair. For a heart-stopping instant, it fought him, the looped leather sling tangled in the top of the back of the chair, which lay on its side.

Gunfire exploded from Devon's guns. He was firing wildly above and around Cort, who was down on his knees. "Get out the way, Cort. Get down!—"

Bullets tore the air above Luke's head, scoring the wall behind him. Screams and shouts sounded from café patrons.

Luke heaved at the sawed-off shotgun, its sling coming free and clear from the fallen chair.

Bullets from Devon's gun tore floor planking inches from Luke's head, spraying his face with stinging needlelike splinters, his eyes slitted against them.

Cort Randle was temporarily neutralized, but for how long? He was a double-edged sword that cuts both ways. While blocking Devon from a clear shot at Luke, he blocked Luke from a clear shot at Devon.

Another instant and Devon could step to the side clear of Cort, bringing his guns to bear directly at Luke's prone form sprawled across the planking. Easy then to nail him to the boards with a few well-placed shots.

Luke clutched the sawed-off shotgun with one hand on the pistol grip, the other cradling the underside of twin barrels. He thumbed back twin hammers, clicking them into readiness.

No clear shot at Devon. All Luke could see of him was the bottom of one booted leg, the rest blocked by the overturned table and white-faced Cort on his knees holding himself between the legs.

One good thing about a shotgun was a fellow didn't have to be too careful about placing his shots.

Luke pointed the sawed-off at Devon's leg and foot and squeezed one of the twin triggers. The sawed-off roared, belching smoke and fire. The blast was deafening but not so much as to drown out the gunman's piercing shriek.

His foot exploded in a grisly blood burst. Cut off at one leg, he pitched sideways down to the floor.

Luke caught a quick glimpse of Devon's face that was a mask of agony. He still held his guns and Luke was minded to do something quick before Devon remembered he was doubly armed.

Luke pulled the second trigger of the sawed-off, loosing a blast that caught Devon square in the middle, leaving a ghastly wet red crater blackened at the edges where his belly had been.

His corpse came crashing down.

Cort tried to call out his brother's name, but he still lacked the breath. His horrified hating face was lead gray, misted with a sheen of cold sweat. He seemed a fraction of his former self, all collapsed and shriveled up, but he still had big hate to keep him going.

Holding himself down below with his left hand, he freed his right hand to reach for the gun holstered on his right hip. His claw-like hand scrabbled at the gun butt.

Luke's sawed-off was spent, both barrels empty.

He let it fall from his fingers, leaving him without a weapon. Or did it?

Luke grabbed at his crutch laying flat on the floor beside him, snatching it up and swinging it high, hard, and to the left. No thrust this time but rather a wicked right hook aimed at and closing fast on Cort's head.

The gunman couldn't draw his gun and block Luke's strike at the same time. Too late, he tried to ward off the blow with his left arm.

Crack! The flailing crutch impacted his head and left arm at mid-center. It broke in two pieces, the upper half flying off somewhere into space. The remaining lower half with its jagged splintered spearpoint tips was clutched in Luke's white-knuckled hand.

Cort pitched sideways, joining Luke on the floor.

Cort had gotten his left arm up in time to absorb much of the force of the blow which otherwise would have cracked his skull if not busted it wide open. His dull glazed eyes could not hide the hate blazing inside. He'd battle all the way to death, no quarter asked or given, by any means necessary.

He rolled over to meet Luke, to destroy him if he could. He pulled his gun, clearing it from the holster. Snakelike, Luke wriggled toward him, reaching him at the same time but striking first, stabbing overhand and down with the splintered end of the crutch as his striking point. He drove the sharp stake-like crutch below Cort's chin, spearing his neck.

Cort spasmed, thrashing. Luke squirmed atop him, pinning him down, using his weight to drive the spearpoint tips home.

Cort writhed, booted heels drumming against the floor. He choked, heaving and wriggling. A final shudder and he was done. All life fled.

Luke collapsed on top of him, spent, panting for breath.

Outside, gunfire erupted.

NINE

Showing no signs, Johnny was aware that some kind of commotion had broken out at the café where Luke had gone earlier to grab some chow while he had hastened to the Golden Spur to get an early start on drinking himself up a skinful.

He tracked the fracas out of the corner of an eye and by ear. His primary focus was on Moran and company but not too tight a focus. He had to be aware of all that was going on around him, for danger could come at any time from any direction.

He guessed that some of Moran's bunch was somehow entangled with Luke, in which case, they'd soon find out they had a wildcat by the tail.

But Johnny couldn't afford to bear down too hard on one factor to the exclusion of all others.

That could be fatal. On the other hand, he dare not become distracted from the issue at hand. He had to keep his balance while walking a fine line. A tightrope. A razor's edge.

That was the way of it as a professional gun.

But he sure wished he knew what was happening in the café.

If Luke had come to harm, Johnny would peel the hide off the guilty an inch at a time.

But not now. Revenge was for later. At the moment, thoughts of it were it a distraction—*dangerous.*

No sign of inner turmoil ruffled the surface of Johnny's bland smiling face.

"I came all the way from Weatherford to try you out," Moran said again.

"What are you waiting for?" Johnny asked.

With his left hand, Moran pushed his hat back on his head, tilting the brim upward at a sharp angle. It was the prearranged signal alerting Cort to shoot Johnny Cross dead. Moran took no chances with his foes. His rifleman would shoot Johnny first, then Moran would draw and fire. In the confusion, it would seem as though Moran had beaten his opponent in a fair draw.

Gunfire broke out in the café but not the kind Moran was expecting. To his consternation, Johnny remained upright and unhurt.

Johnny filled his hands with guns.

Haycox outdrew Moran, pulling his gun while Moran was still reaching. But Johnny's guns were firing before the others' weapons cleared holsters.

Johnny crouched, blazing away with a Colt in each fist. It was not his usual fighting stance, but one he'd taken in hopes of thwarting any ambushers in the café. He fired two shots into Haycox's chest, the reports coming so close together that they sounded as one. Haycox was thrown down.

Moran's gun finally sprung from holster to hand. His bullets cut the air to Johnny's left, close.

Johnny dropped two slugs into Moran's middle.

Moran was hit so hard that for an instant it felt like an express train had churned its way through his guts. His gun fell silent as he stopped shooting. Almost immediately, he ceased to feel anything at all, his upper body seemingly disconnected from its lower half.

A slug tugged at the right-hand flap of Johnny's coat. Kern was doggedly plugging away at him, his eyes wild above a snarling mouth full of bared yellow teeth.

The gun in Johnny's left hand barked, pumping slugs into Kern. One hit him high in the side, knocking him off balance and spinning him around.

Kern stumbled, still shooting blindly, breaking a window across the street. More slugs ripped through him. He fell to the ground, joining Haycox, who already lay crumpled in the street.

From the café came the reassuring boom of a shotgun blast, followed by another. Reassuring to Johnny because it meant that Luke was not only alive but taking an active hand in the game.

Strangely enough, Moran was still on his feet while his henchmen were down. He stood upright and reeling between Haycox and Kern sprawled in the dirt on either side of him.

Johnny stood opposite him, eyes slit in a hard-lined face, guns held level hip-high. A cloud of gun smoke partly veiled him.

Moran looked at his gun hand, peering blearily at it. His vision was hazy, fading in and out.

For a flash, his vision cleared and he saw that his gun hand was empty. He stared at it, unable to remember letting go of the gun. Where was it?

He looked down. It was laying on its side in the street.

The last effort of looking down was too much for him. Moran reeled, swaying back and forth. He lifted a foot to take a step and crashed down, the scene dizzyingly shifting from vertical to horizontal. He didn't feel a thing when he hit the ground. He saw Haycox stretched out beside him, still moving, trying to raise the gun in his hand.

Haycox shook with the strain of his effort as though trying to lift not a shooting iron but an anvil. His mouth gaped open, black blood spilling from it. He got the gun barrel some ten or twelve inches up from the dirt but was unable to hold it steady, muzzle wavering every which way.

A gunshot sounded as Johnny finished off Haycox at point-blank range. Haycox's hand fell back into the dirt, raising a small cloud of dust.

Moran would have liked to see more but blackness engulfed him, swallowing him up. Nightfall, he thought. Odd, he'd thought it was the middle of the day.

His heart beat its last and he thought no more because he was dead.

Johnny swung around, shifting position. He stepped back and to the side so he could cover the trio sprawled in the dirt while covering the café at the same time. It took only a moment to realize Moran and sidemen were done. Johnny warily turned his attention toward the café and quickly reloaded.

The café was silent, no more shots or shrieks, but motion showed behind the windows. From within came a shout. "Don't shoot, Johnny boy!"

"Luke? That you?" Johnny called.

"Sure 'nuff!" came the reply.

"Show yourself!"

"Can't!"

"Why not? You hit?"

"Nope!"

"You okay, Luke?"

"Yup! But my crutch is busted!"

Johnny smiled to himself. "Everything squared away in there?"

"I hope to tell you! And I will. *Yee-haw!*" Luke's wild outcry seemed part coyote howl, part wolf call, and part banshee shriek. Rising to earsplitting heights, it was a sound to send shivers along a brave man's spine.

It was a battle cry well-known during the late war, heard from Bull Run to the border states, from Gettysburg to Goleta Pass, from the Louisiana bayous to the Tennessee mountains.

It was the rebel yell of the fighting men of the Confederacy. A wild, skirling war cry that had curdled the blood of countless brave foemen when they heard it preparatory to a cavalry charge or infantry advance by gray-clad Sons of Dixie.

The rebel yell! Hearing it, Johnny Cross knew that he and Luke had yet again won through another life-and-death struggle.

TEN

The shooting had stopped. The last echoes of the last shot faded away on Trail Street.

On the veranda of the Cattleman Hotel, the man called Top stood up after being hunched over the wheelchair-bound Mallory, serving as a human shield to stop any stray bullets that might come Mallory's way. Top was Mallory's man. His name was a nickname for Top Sergeant, a rank he'd held during the war. His real name was A. C. Quarles. When pronounced correctly, it rhymed with *Charles.*

Kale Dancer, dandified and gun-toting, had moved to protect Ashley Mallory, rushing her into the entryway of the hotel and out of the line of fire.

Piney hadn't done anything. He'd just stood in place on the big front porch watching the show, a thin line of drool clinging to the corner of his open mouth.

Dancer held Ashley backed against a wall, pressing close, face-to-face, his body against hers. She'd quivered anew as each shot rang out, whether out of fear or excitement Dancer couldn't tell. Knowing Ashley, he guessed it was the latter. She was not one to shrink from a little gunplay.

It was exciting for him to feel her high-breasted, long-legged form squirming in his embrace. Her mouth was close to his ear, so close her warm breath tickled his flesh. Her breath was warm and sweet but not her words. "You can let me go now, Mr. Dancer."

"I hate to do so. This is the closest I've been to you in days," he murmured.

"I don't need protection, and I can take care of myself. Now, please release me. I don't appreciate being pawed in public, thank you very much."

Reluctantly, Dancer broke contact, stepping back to let her go.

She was in a state of high excitement. Her eyes sparkled and red dots of color showed on her cheeks. Her moist lips were parted, breath coming fast. She brushed past Dancer without a second glance and went out the doorway to the veranda.

He watched her go, smiling ruefully to himself, yet not without sincere admiration for her feminine charms.

Ashley went to Mallory, making a show of fussing over him. "Thank the Lord you're safe, Father!"

"I was never in any danger, my dear. Thanks to Top." Mallory turned to his manservant. "Thank you, Top, but in the future, please take no unnecessary risks on my behalf. After all, I've been under fire before, as we both have reason to know, eh?"

"No harm must come to the commanding officer, sir," Quarles said.

"The war is over, Top. I appreciate your concern and your valor, but small loss to the world should any harm befall an aging invalid such as I. I trust you understand."

Quarles nodded. "Yes, sir."

Mallory smiled thinly and started to wheel his chair around. Quarles moved to help, but Mallory forestalled him by raising a warding hand. "I can do for myself, Top."

"Very well, sir."

Mallory worked the wheels to turn his chair to face east, appraising the carnage on Trail Street with a cold, shrewd expert's eye. Johnny Cross stood over the three sprawled bodies of men he'd shot down while an unseen party vented a rebel yell.

The sound thrilled along Mallory's nerves, prompting an involuntary shiver. "By heaven, there's a sound to warm a Southern heart!"

"That it is, sir," Quarles agreed almost reverently.

Other folks were beginning to stir along the street. Faces showed behind windows, peering out. Heads peeked out from behind walls, doorways, and corners.

Dancer went to Mallory, standing beside him, eyeing the victor of the gunfight on Trail Street. "These Texans know how to put on a show."

"The gunfighter looks familiar somehow. I can't get over the feeling that I've seen him before," Mallory said. "Do you know him? Ever seen him before?"

"He's a stranger to me. I know his type, though. A gunslick. A killer."

"A rare breed, a fighting man!" Mallory enthused.

"Not so rare in Texas," Dancer said as if tasting something sour.

"Many have the spirit, but few have the ability to shoot like that." Mallory lowered his voice. "That's the kind of man we need."

"It could be that we'll have to go up against him," Dancer said, doubtful. "His allegiance might be to the town."

"It's been my experience that gunmen generally owe their allegiance to the dollar. Find out who he is."

"All right."

People were starting to come out of doors. A number of them emerged from the hotel lobby, where they'd taken cover during the shooting.

Ashley took her place at Mallory's side. Looking long and hard at Johnny Cross, she decided she liked what she saw. "Quite a man, whoever he is."

Dancer was irked, not liking the throbbing tone of admiration in her voice.

"Damn it, you killed those men!" Marshal Barton said, standing in the middle of Trail Street.

"They came to kill me," Johnny Cross said cheerfully enough.

And why not? They were dead and he was alive and unharmed. Luke, too.

"A clear-cut case of self-defense," Johnny said.

"I reckon so," Barton said grudgingly.

Johnny smiled obligingly, holstering his guns,

"Go ahead. I'll take care of these three," Barton said wearily. "It won't be the first time I've had to clean up one of your messes."

"In case you don't recognize him, Marshal, that's Moran from Weatherford. A killer and robber many times over. They don't—didn't—call him Terrible Terry for nothing. I reckon his sidekicks are no better. Hell, I'm doing you a favor cleaning up on them."

"Yeah, well, they wouldn't have been here if not for you," Barton said. "Moran was looking to build a reputation. The Man Who Killed Johnny Cross."

"His epitaph. Now if you don't mind, I'd like to check up on my partner."

"I'll get things squared away here," Barton said, sighing. "I want to talk to you later. Not about this. Something different. You and Luke stop by my office."

"Will do," Johnny said. "By the way, Terrible Terry is—was—a wanted man. Wouldn't be surprised if there's a reward on him, maybe some of his gang, too. I know I can count on you to see that I get what's coming to me . . . me and Luke."

"A silver lining to every cloud, huh?" Barton scowled.

"I'll take mine in gold, thanks. Now if you'll excuse me, I'll be on my way."

"I ain't stopping you," Barton said gruffly.

Johnny nodded, starting toward the café. "See you later, Marshal."

"Make it sooner rather than later."

Now that they were free to come and go as they pleased, most of the patrons of Mabel's Café made a mass exodus out the door and into the street. Some wanted to get away from the sight and smells of blood and violent death.

Others sought to slip away without paying their bills. Only something as severe as the concussing of owner McGurk could have put them out of his watchful reach. He was coming around but still groggy.

Those who left were brought up short by the spectacle of three more corpses sprawled in the street out front. Of those who stayed behind, some were friends or associates of McGurk and were helping him out, as well as helping themselves to what snacks they could lay their hands on. Others were still too stunned or in shock to move.

And there was Luke Pettigrew, a one-legged man with a broken crutch. He wasn't going anywhere, at least not until he could scare up a replacement crutch.

Also not going anywhere, at least not under their own power, were Devon and Cort, the Randle brothers— *deceased.*

Johnny Cross picked his way carefully through the café, avoiding the dead men and the pools of blood surrounding them. The blood drew flies, of which the café already had more than its share. The space was hazed by clouds of gun smoke that were slow to break up.

Luke sat upright, having managed to haul himself up on a chair at a table which hadn't been overturned in the melee. His sawed-off shotgun rested on its side on the tabletop, near at hand.

He had reloaded it with a pair of fresh shells. Also in view was a knife with which he had cut the chaw of tobacco bulging in the pocket of one cheek.

Owner McGurk, too, sat upright, having been helped into a chair by some solicitous citizens. Helpful hands braced him on either side, keeping him from falling off the chair, still somewhat dazed as he was.

"So filled with piss and vinegar, he's too ornery to stay down," old-timer Pete Conklin said of McGurk.

"You think he's ornery now, wait till he finds out

how many customers beat him for the check," one of Conklin's cronies cracked.

The words seemed to rouse McGurk from stunned confusion into some semblance of his fighting self. "I'll get 'em, each and every one. I know who was in here and what grub they et . . ."

Johnny pulled up a chair and sat down at Luke's table. "Howdy, Luke."

"Mr. Cross," Luke said, nodding.

"Tsk-tsk. Seems I can't leave you on your lonesome without you getting into mischief." Johnny shook his head in mock sorrow.

"Funny, I was thinking the same about you," Luke said.

"Who were they?" Johnny asked, indicating the corpses.

"Called themselves the Randle brothers. I never heard of 'em."

"Me neither."

"They was laying for you, hoss. Cort there—the one wearing what's left of my crutch in his neck—was fixing to bushwhack you with his rifle before you could draw on Moran."

"Hardly seems sporting, does it?" Johnny said sadly.

"Not hardly," Luke agreed. "And you know what a stickler I am for fighting fair."

"I can see that," Johnny said, looking around.

"The other one, Devon, was covering the customers."

"Both of them Moran's creatures, eh?"

"Uh-huh."

"I'm beholden to you, amigo. That were a close one," Johnny said. "I owe you."

"You'd have done the same for me." Luke made light of the sentiment with a disparaging gesture.

"Lucky for me you came in here for chow."

"That's me. I'm a fool for luck," Luke said, not without bitterness. "All this fuss and I didn't even get to finish my lunch!"

"That's a damned shame. Still, I reckon Mr. Morrissey over to the Golden Spur can fry up a couple steaks for you. McGurk doesn't look like he'll be doing much cooking for a while."

"I heard that," McGurk said groggily. "I'll be fine, just gimme a minute—"

Thump! His head hit the table. He was unconscious. Conklin and some others moved to help him up.

"He needs a doctor," Johnny said.

"We already sent for Doc Spillsbury. He ought to be here any minute," Conklin said.

"Nothing we can do here now, Luke. Let's mosey over to the saloon for a drink or ten."

"I ain't going nowhere, Johnny. I busted my crutch on Cort Randle's hard head."

"Doc Spillsbury should be able to rustle up a crutch for you, pard. If not, we'll send over to the apothecary for one."

"You do that, hoss. Meanwhile, you could make yourself useful by turning out the Randle brothers' pockets and lifting their pokes," Luke said. "I done all the work here so I might as well profit by it. Let them pay for my new crutch and whatnot."

Johnny didn't move.

"Time's a-wasting, hoss! Get to the plundering before the law sticks its horns in and claims the loot for burial money."

"I'm surprised that none of the other customers has set to pilfering from the deceased yet, this being Hangtown and all," Johnny said.

Luke frowned. "What do you think I've been doing? Whistling Dixie? I've been holding them off with this here sawed-off shotgun! So git to it, hoss."

Johnny got to it.

ELEVEN

Fly Norvine awoke. His head hurt and he had a splitting headache.

He opened his eyes. Darkness surrounded him. He was struck by a bolt of panic. Was he blind?

Memory came flooding back. *He was on the lookout for Johnny Cross but Cross found him first, getting the drop on him and marching him quietly to the back of the saloon, He hit him on the head with a gun, knocking him out— Had he been hit so hard he'd gone blind? Good Lord, what a dire fate!*

Blind on the frontier—and penniless, too!

Fly jumped up, upsetting some trash cans standing at the back of the building. The action dislodged the hat jammed down tight on his head, the hat he'd been unaware of, the hat covering his eyes and keeping out the light, leaving him in darkness.

Light struck him. He could see!

Fly put a hand against the rear wall of the saloon, bracing himself to keep from falling down. His mouth was dry, his heart pounded, and his hair was standing on end. He looked around. He was in a weedy dirt alley between the backs of two buildings. He staggered out of the alley into the open.

A couple passersby a hundred feet away didn't so much as spare him a second glance as they hurried past, going south on a cross street to Trail Street.

"What's your hurry?" Fly called after them.

One bothered to reply, not slackening his pace. "Big gunfight on Trail Street. Johnny Cross killed three men!"

Fly bent down to pick up his hat, triggering a return of his immense headache. Fighting dizziness, he snatched his hat off the ground. Before putting it on, he gingerly felt around the back of his head, discovering a goose-egg-size lump.

He put the hat on his head, avoiding the lump as best he could. *What next?*

His instinct was to run, putting as much distance between himself and Hangtree as possible. Fear of Moran held him back. Fear and hatred. They didn't call him Terrible Terry for nothing. He'd take a life as easily as snuffing out a candle.

Fly was no killer. He lacked the nerve to even shoot a man in the back. He hated and feared Moran. He felt the same about the Randle brothers, Haycox, and Kern, though not to the same degree.

They didn't have much use for him. They kept him around as a lookout and to hold the horses while they were pulling a job. And to run errands and just generally stooge for them.

Fly lacked the nerve to run out on Moran but thought perhaps things had changed. The passerby had said something about Johnny Cross killing three men. Who could those three be if not Moran, Haycox, and Kern?

Fly knew all about Moran's trick of having Cort Randle bushwhack the opponents in Moran's so-called gunfights and figured something must have happened to keep Cort from interceding. Had Cross somehow tumbled to the setup and moved to eliminate the Randles before the showdown? Or had the brothers decided to step aside and let Fate take its course . . . Fate in the form of Johnny Cross?

That seemed unlikely. Terrible Terry Moran was on the threshold of the biggest job of his life, part of a crime whose scope was so bold and audacious that it scared Fly well beyond the limits of his normally fear-filled life. Moran had a big part in the scheme, heading a force far greater than his core group of the Randles, Haycox, Kern, and yes, Fly. Moran had rounded up two dozen hardcases from Weatherford, Parker County, and surrounding areas to gather in Hangtree on the eve of a raid of such size and ambition that nothing like it had been seen since the war.

Not counting Red Hand's raid, of course, but that was different. He was Comanche, and the same standards didn't apply to Indians as they did to whites. Bandit chief Brock Harbin had made a bold thrust against Hangtree but not of the magnitude and brutality of the forthcoming event. With all that was in the works, Moran should have had better ways to occupy his time than rigging a fixed shoot-out with Johnny Cross.

You'd think that, if you didn't know Moran, Fly thought.

Moran was a glory hound, ever eager to fill the minds of men and women with his name, fame, and exploits. Moran had argued that the way things were falling out, he'd inevitably have to buck Johnny Cross. What better way than to take him out as a factor in the upcoming struggle by burning him down in a time and place of Moran's choosing?

Except it seemed like things hadn't worked out that way. Best for Fly to see exactly how things lay before making any moves he couldn't take back.

Pulling his hat brim down low to partially conceal his face, Fly slunk over to Trail Street, where a crowd had gathered. It didn't take much snooping around to learn what had happened. A curious trick of fate had put the Randles in the same café where Johnny Cross's friend and partner was having lunch.

Moran and his key sidemen were dead, leaving Fly alive. How would that affect the Big Job?

Two dozen gunmen recruited by Moran for the undertaking were already in Hangtree or would be there in a matter of hours, certainly before sundown. Moran or not, the enterprise would soon take place. He was just a cog in the machinery, one easily replaced.

Fly knew some but not all of the owlhoots Moran had tapped for his part of the job. Fly had no wish to encounter any of them.

Fly turned away from Commerce Street and retraced his route up the alley to the street behind the Golden Spur, where the gang had tied up their horses to a hitching post. *Well, at least the horses are all still there,* he thought.

He was more than eager to get out of town, but not so much as to leave behind perfectly good loot, ripe for the taking. Loot in the form of the gang's horses, not to mention saddles and outfits and whatever else might be stowed in their saddlebags.

Damn good horseflesh, too. Moran and the Randles rode thoroughbreds for fast getaways. Better mounts than Fly's nag, but it was no time to switch horses. He was in the proverbial middle of the stream and not supposed to switch horses—especially because thoroughbreds were high-strung, nervy critters, like to balk under a strange rider. Fly wanted nothing to interfere with a hasty getaway.

Not with Johnny Cross and Moran's marauders on the loose and maybe looking for him.

Fly took the time to rig his lariat into a lead rope, tying one end to his saddle horn and using the rest as a lead line to arrange the other horses into a string, filing one by one behind him.

That done, all knots checked and secure, Fly stepped up into the saddle and took a last look around Hangtree town. All clear!

He rode east out of town, angling southeast toward the stone bridge spanning the north-south-running Swift Creek bounding Hangtree on the east.

He felt a little better once he and the string of horses were across the bridge and on Hangtree Trail eastbound.

Not until he was over the next ridge and Hangtree was hidden behind it did he allow himself a sigh of relief. He headed someplace far enough away for him to rifle the contents of the saddlebags in undisturbed peace and comfort. Next order of business was to unload the horses and rigs to a buyer who wasn't too particular about their source or things like a bill of

TWELVE

"Have a drink." Marshal Mack Barton sat behind the desk in his office in the Hangtree jailhouse, a one-story flat-roofed stone block building at the east end of Trail Street.

Johnny Cross and Luke Pettigrew stood facing Barton across the desk. Luke was supported by a sturdy brand-new crutch fresh-bought from the town pharmacist.

There was no shortage of crutches, canes, and the like available in any town, North or South. The recent war had left so many men maimed and missing a limb or more.

Luke stood a mite uneasy on his new perch, trying to get used to the fit and feel of the new crutch not yet broken in to his personal specifications. For all that, he was steady enough.

"Pull up some chairs and make yourself comfortable," Barton said.

Johnny went to a table along the left-side wall around which were several chairs. He set up one for himself and one for Luke, facing Barton at his desk.

sale. Fly's line of work put him in the know of many such persons.

After that—well, he wasn't sure what his next move would be. He'd have to study on it.

That was Fly Norvine—the Man Who Learned Better.

Luke unslung his sawed-off shotgun from his shoulder, hanging it by the strap over the top of the back of the chair, but Johnny hung back, waiting for Luke to sit down. He let out the breath he'd been holding after Luke had successfully managed to sit down without upsetting himself or the chair.

Above all, Luke wanted others to avoid fussing over the handicap of his missing limb. He wasn't looking for pity, compassion, or special treatment. He just wanted to be treated "like everybody else." He could get around pretty good on a wooden leg and a crutch, considering. But he had a brand-new crutch and might not have mastered the unique "feel" of it in the short time he'd had it.

Johnny sat down, too.

Barton uncorked the full bottle of red whiskey which he'd taken from a drawer in his desk. He slid it across the desktop to Johnny. "Have a jolt. No cups or glasses so we won't stand on ceremony,"

"Thanks." Johnny took a small swallow, brightening with surprise. He rolled the taste around on his tongue and smacked his lips. "Hmm, not bad." He up-tilted the bottle and took a good long pull, his face reddening with warmth. "Pretty good," he said, sighing with pleasure.

"That's my own personal private stock," Barton bragged.

Johnny grinned. "Not the rotgut you usually reserve for visitors, eh?"

"Hell no!" Barton was genial, unabashed. He seemed to radiate good feeling.

Johnny knew that was the time to be most wary of the old lawdog. Barton wanted something. What?

"Most folks I see in the line of duty are prisoners

or citizens looking to lodge a complaint," Barton said. "The jailbirds got nothing coming, but I don't like to send an honest upright citizen off without a taste."

"Especially if he's a voter."

"That's right! Besides, it ain't sociable." The marshal grinned.

Luke put out a hand for the bottle, but it was out of reach. Johnny took another drink, a big one.

"Leggo of that bottle, hoss, and let me have some," Luke said, not shy about letting his feelings be known. He took possession of the bottle and drank deep, making a sizeable dent in its contents.

Watching the whiskey vanish, Barton manfully fought to keep from wincing, his toothy grin wilting at the edges.

Luke set down the bottle at last, a bit breathless. "Good!"

Barton was quick to take advantage of the opportunity to reclaim the bottle, ruefully eyeing what little contents was left. "Careless of you," he remarked pleasantly. "You left a mouthful."

"I ain't no hog," Luke said. "It wasn't easy, though, Mr. Cross here not leaving me much to work with."

"Heh heh heh," Barton said, unamused. "You boys worked up a pretty big thirst."

"Killing will do that," Johnny said. "It's thirsty work."

"Well, you're certainly good at your job." Barton drank what remained in the bottle, finishing it off. He set the empty down in a wastebasket behind the desk. "Don't want to leave it out in plain sight. Outsiders might get the wrong idea."

"That you're drinking on the job?" Luke asked, working the prod a little bit.

Johnny spoke quickly to head off any bickering

between Luke and Barton. "You said you wanted to see us, Marshal. What can we do you for?"

"I want to ask you a favor, both of you."

"Whew! That's a relief."

"How so?"

"I knew you weren't buying us a drink out of the goodness of your heart," Johnny said. "I was getting anxious waiting for the other shoe to drop."

"Set your mind at ease," Barton said. "I've got no complaint about you boys cleaning up on Moran and his bunch. Quite the contrary. That was a damn fine piece of work you did."

Johnny and Luke exchanged glances.

"That's a surprise," Johnny said. "Here I thought you were gonna heap hot coals on our heads on account of us ventilating those sidewinders."

"Nothing could be further from my mind," Barton said, smiling blandly. "The way I see it, Moran came here to kill and got killed for his troubles, him and the rest of his bunch. A clear-cut case of self-defense, say I. The law says so, too."

"So there won't be any problems then?" Johnny asked.

"Nothing to speak of," Barton said, gesturing as though banishing away all legal squabbles. "Of course there'll have to be an inquest, but that's purely a formality. We've got to go through the motions to satisfy the machinery of the law. It won't amount to a hill of beans.

"That Yankee commander Harrison being out in the field with his troops helps, too. He won't be around to stick his nose into Hangtree business."

"Glad you feel that way, Marshal. To tell the truth, I wasn't sure which way you'd jump on that showdown.

Didn't know but that you might get salty about it."
Johnny was soft-spoken and polite, the way he almost
always was. But his throwaway tone implied he really
didn't give much of a good damn whether the marshal
got salty or not.

"You know me, Johnny. You and Luke can trust me.
Just like I know I can trust you. We're all friends here
in Hangtree," Barton said expansively. "Better than
friends—pards, you might say," he added.

"*You* might," Johnny allowed, putting the emphasis
on *you*. He didn't crack to much.

"That brings us to a delicate matter, but one that
has got be considered," Barton said, getting to the
point after going the long way around the barn. "That
is, I presume our usual arrangement applies, providing there's any reward on Moran and his gang." He
was referring to the arrangement by which Johnny
and Luke kicked back to the marshal a percentage of
any reward on the men they killed.

It was a lucrative deal for the lawman, considering
the high body count the duo had managed to rack up
in the relatively short time since coming home after
the war.

And for any number of reasons, it was useful to
Johnny and Luke to keep Barton sweetened up. Not
the least, it motivated him to speedily process the legal
paperwork needed to claim the rewards, a lengthy
business at best, especially where out-of-town law enforcement agencies were involved.

"A friendly lawman is a useful thing to have," was
how Johnny had explained it to Luke when they'd
first returned to Hangtree.

Poker-faced, Johnny said to the marshal, "It's my
understanding that our agreement stays the same. I

don't see any reason for changing it." He turned to his partner. "That how you see it, Luke?"

"I ain't given it much thought but, yeah, I'm for it if you are." Luke was a canny sort in his own way but preferred Johnny to do the thinking where strategy was involved.

Johnny nodded

Barton's somewhat wintry smile warmed up, widening. "Well! That's fine, just fine."

Johnny smiled pleasantly. He'd been steeling himself against a Barton demand for an increase in his cut, but apparently the marshal was content for things to keep on as is.

Possibly the most recent display of their formidable gunplay was a factor in keeping Barton's no less formidable greed in check.

"Soon as we're done here, I'll send a wire to Weatherford to find out what's posted on Moran and the gang," Barton said.

"From what I've heard, Moran threw a wide loop," Johnny said. "Couldn't hurt to contact Dallas, Austin, and a few of the other big towns to see if the gang's got a price on their heads there."

"Now you're telling me my job," Barton said agreeably enough, cheered by the prospect of a future payday. He rubbed his palms together in a brisk washing motion, indicating anticipation. "Hell yes. I'll check all over as soon as I've got a minute to call my own."

"Let's drink on it," Luke suggested.

Barton shook his head. "Sorry, son, but the whizz has already been drunk."

"Maybe you've got some of that rotgut left, the kind

reserved for just plain ordinary folks who drop in," Luke said. "I ain't particular."

"You don't want to drink that stuff," Barton said, making a face.

"You don't know Luke," Johnny said dryly.

"If you insist," Barton shrugged.

"At least you didn't say, 'it's your funeral,'" Luke said.

"That comes after you take a drink." Barton ducked below desktop level to haul a bottle out of a bottom drawer. It was significant perhaps that the drawer was unlocked, indicating he didn't feel the need to protect that whiskey from pilfering. He set the bottle on the desk, a brown bottle with murky contents and no label. "Don't say I didn't warn you."

Luke waved off the warning, uncorking the bottle and taking a long swallow. He sat back, keeping a straight face, smiling with his lips. His guise of seeming unflappability was undone by choking on the last gulp.

His features swelled from the effort of trying to keep from coughing. He couldn't maintain it and broke out into a wheezing, barking coughing fit that brought tears to his eyes. When the spasm passed, he set the bottle down on the desk, hands trembling slightly. "I've had worse," he said, game. "Try some, Johnny."

"I'll pass, thanks," Johnny said quickly. Not without some good-natured malice, he added, "Have another, Luke."

"I'll let that one settle," Luke said, trying not to gasp.

"History has been made," Johnny announced with mock solemnity, looking to heaven. "Luke Pettigrew has refused a drink." He gathered himself up as if making ready to go. "If we're done here . . ."

"One or two small matters before you go," Barton said.

Johnny eased back into his seat, once more guarded and wary.

"Moran ain't the first red-hot to come gunning for you, hoping to make himself a reputation as a fast gun," Barton said. "He won't be the last, either. You can't help it. It's not your fault. That's just the way of things."

"I don't look for trouble, but I don't run from it, either. Not ever," Johnny said quietly, something ominous in his deadly calm.

"I know that. But it would make my job a lot easier if you and Luke would get out of town and stay out for a few days. We've got a lot of wagon trains passing through and camping down on the south flat this week. I don't want to encourage any would-be red-hots to try their luck against you, Johnny.

"I know you can handle yourself, but that's not what I'm worried about. It's the folks, the townsfolk. I'd hate to see any innocent parties—men, maybe even women and kids—catch a bullet that some bush-whacker meant for you."

"I'd hate that, too, but I'd hate even more for me to catch one of those bullets you're talking about," Johnny said.

"You're joshing, right?" the marshal asked.

"Yes and no," Johnny said. "You're saying you want me—and brother Luke here—to find a hole to hide in."

"That's not the way I'd put it."

"Well and good."

"I'm not asking you to duck a challenge," Barton said quickly, "but if you're not around nobody can take a shot at you."

"I'm not minded to jump in a hole and hide out," Johnny said.

"I'm not asking you to. I'm just requesting that you stay out of town for a few days until this Moran business blows over," Barton said, trying to sound eminently reasonable and fair-minded. "The wagon trains'll be moving on in a day or two. There'll be trouble enough having them in town Friday and Saturday night. They've been on the trail for weeks and they'll be looking to blow off some steam. This is the last place to do it short of El Paso.

"You can do what you want, Johnny—hell, *you will.* I'm just saying that you'd be doing me and Hangtree a kindness by absenting yourselves for a few days."

"What about Damon Bolt? You gonna ask him to get out of town, too?" Luke demanded.

Damon Bolt, owner of the Golden Spur, was a well-respected gambler and gunfighter.

"I can't hardly do that, Luke, what with Damon living here in town," Barton said, sheepish.

Thoughtful, Johnny decided to throw the marshal a bone. "We've got some chores at the ranch that need doing and could keep us busy for a few days."

"That makes for a mighty dull Saturday," Luke fretted.

"Good Lord!" Barton said feelingly. "Haven't you had enough excitement for one day?"

"I'm talking about whiskey and women, not gunfighting," Luke said.

"Maybe we'll stick to the ranch this one weekend," Johnny said. "That okay with you, Luke?"

"I reckon," Luke said grudgingly. "If that's what it takes to keep Hangtown from being swamped with all them poor dead bushwhacked innocent women and children. All I can say is, there'll be a passel of heart-broken ladies in town when ol' Luke fails to make the rounds come Saturday night."

"Thanks, men. I appreciate it. I really do," Barton said, pouring on the sincerity. "There's been enough killing today to last Hangtree for a while. I'm looking forward to a nice peaceful weekend."

"Good luck with that," Johnny said.

"Well, you know what I mean. No killings."

"Like I said."

Johnny and Luke stood up, ready to go.

"By the way, I ain't seen your Yankee pal lately," Barton said almost as an afterthought, but too casual.

"Sam Heller?" Johnny replied, matching the marshal's seeming nonchalance with some of his own.

"Ain't any other Northerners in town," Barton said, "At least none that'll admit to it."

"They would if they could shoot like Sam Heller."

"Maybe so, maybe so. I ain't denying he's done some good for the town, in his way."

"Why do you ask about him?"

"Seems he rode out of town three weeks ago and nobody's seen him since. Thought you might know something about it," Barton said offhandedly.

"Don't ask me. I'm not his keeper," Johnny snapped.

"That's what Cain said, too," Barton reminded him.

"That's right. I guess you'd call ol' Cain the founder of our profession, yours and mine, Marshal."

"And what profession would that be, Johnny?"

"Killing."

Barton let that pass without comment. "I asked you

about Heller because you're one of the few in town who has a good word to say about him."

"He's not such a bad sort . . . for a Yankee," Johnny said.

"Good man to have siding you in a fight," Luke chimed in, a rare concession for him, who had no love for the North. "Sam's got a lot more sand than some Texans I could name."

"Well, that's neither here nor there," Barton said. "You knowing Heller better than most, I thought he might have mentioned what he was up to."

"Sam Heller doesn't keep me posted on his comings and goings. It's a mystery to me," Johnny said. And it was.

"Maybe he left town because he was tired of seeing so many unfriendly faces," Luke suggested.

"Why do you ask?" Johnny pressed. "What's it to you, what Sam Heller is up to? He ain't bothering nobody."

"No reason in particular," Barton said with the air of a man about to pull a rabbit out of his hat. "I was just wondering if he'd joined the hunt for Jimbo Turlock."

THIRTEEN

"Jimbo Turlock! There's a name I haven't heard for a coon's age," Johnny said, genuinely taken aback. "You mean nobody's killed him yet?"

"Apparently not," Barton said too matter-of-factly.

"Too bad," Johnny said. "He's the kind that needs killing."

"You say that like you know him."

"I know *of* him, Marshal," Johnny said, carefully correcting the other.

"You don't tell me!"

"Hell, Johnny don't tell nobody nothing." Luke went to Barton's desk and sat down on a corner of it. "Since y'all ain't done jawing, I'll just set myself down. I ain't used to this new crutch yet and I don't want to do a lot of standing."

"I crossed trails with Turlock once or twice," Johnny said. "Toward the last days of the war he wanted to throw in with Quantrill, but Quantrill wouldn't have nothing to do with him. Told him to take his outfit and move on quick or he'd clean up on them himself. He would have, too, and I would have joined in. It would have been a pleasure."

"Too bad you didn't. You would have saved some folks a lot of grief," Barton said. "That must have been before his Free Company days."

"That was when he was still making out like he was a loyal son of Dixie," Johnny said.

"Who's Turlock?" Luke asked.

"Ah, such innocence," Barton said sardonically. "Never heard of Jimbo Turlock and his Free Company? Man, you must have really been out in the boondocks!"

"Boondocks like Antietam, Gettysburg, and Chickamauga!" Luke was indignant. "I reckon maybe you heard of them—"

"Don't get yourself in an uproar, Luke," Johnny said, playing the peacemaker. "The marshal ain't making light of your war record."

"Hell no!" Barton said quickly. "It's just a manner of speaking."

"You fought the war in the big battles east of the Mississippi, Luke, so a lot of what happened west of the river might be new to you," Johnny explained. "Jimbo Turlock was one of those bottom-feeders turned big fish by the war in the border states. Before Sumter, he was just another ruffian tearing up Kansas and Missouri, taking advantage of the fight between pro-slavery and abolitionist forces to rob and kill folks on both sides.

"When war broke out, Turlock and his gang declared themselves guerrilla fighters for the South. He gave himself the rank of commander. He had no commission from the Confederacy, but nobody gave

that no never mind. What was important was that he
was fighting the Yanks."

Quantrill pretty much started the same way, Barton
thought, but kept silent.

Johnny went on, "Turlock's bunch was made up of
his old outlaw band. At first, they hid behind the flag
of the Stars and Bars but soon showed their true
colors. Before too long his standard attracted all
kinds—deserters, renegades, cutthroats—all scum.
He figured, why fight blue-belly soldiers who could
shoot back when there were so many defenseless
civilians?

"Turlock's marauders raided farmers and ranchers,
merchants and storekeeps. They killed the men,
abused the women, stole anything they could carry
away, and burned the rest. They drew no distinction
between North and South. Anyone who had something they wanted and couldn't keep them from
taking it was fair game.

"Quantrill wouldn't have anything to do with Jimbo's
marauders. Bloody Bill Anderson was none too particular about who he sided with, but even he shunned
Turlock. Kirby Smith, in charge of the whole Confederate Trans-Mississippi district, put a price on Turlock's head. General Sterling Price ordered his troops
to shoot the marauders on sight.

"Long before war's end Jimbo saw which way the
wind was blowing. You can't really say he turned his
coat because he never did much for the South to start
with. He burned the Confederate flag, renamed his
outfit the Free Company, and opened it to anyone
who wanted to join. That way, he swelled the ranks
with the dregs of the Union army, too. It also picked
up the rabble that followed in the wake of the armies.

The camp followers who preyed on the troops—rotgut whiskey peddlers, tinhorn gamblers, pimps, and robbers.

"Turlock had always preyed on Confederate settlers just as much as Yankees but tried to do it when no one was looking, to maintain the lie that the marauders were all loyal Southerners. Once he formed up as the Free Company, all bets were off and they went after the loyalists with a vengeance.

"With the Confederacy fading fast—armies in retreat and falling apart—Turlock saw his chance to make one last big kill. His outfit was *unleashed* on those poor folks who didn't have much to start with. The Free Company ran wild on them. It was pretty bad.

"Things started to get better when the blue-belly troops moved in to occupy Missouri—which should tell you something about how bad things were when the Free Company was running loose. Turlock turned tail and ran at the first whiff of Yankee grapeshot. The last I heard, the Free Company ran out to the Oklahoma Territory. But that was more than a year and a half ago.

"I couldn't tell you what's happened to them since then," Johnny concluded.

"I can," Barton said, picking up the narrative thread. "Turlock hid out in the Indian Nations in the Territory. Federal troops are prohibited from going in there by treaty, so Jimbo found himself a safe haven for a while. He and the Free Company set about doing what they do best—robbing, raping, and killing.

"They were helped by the fact that the tribes don't get along too good there in the Indian Nations and couldn't agree to work together to get shut of Turlock. Until finally they got themselves a bellyful and took action. Some half-breed Cherokee ex-soldier name of Sixkiller* formed up a militia of what they call the Six Civilized Tribes. They not only ran Turlock out of the Nations, they ran him clear out of the territory.

"The Free Company turned up in Arkansas where there was a nice, hot, little war going on at the state's southern border between the Moderators and the Regulators—whoever in the hell they are. Since the big war ended, there's been so many small wars breaking out all over it's hard to keep track of them."

"I know what you mean. We've had a couple right here in Hangtree," Johnny said.

"Like today."

"Shucks, Marshal, that was no war," Luke said. "That was just a little ol' dustup. Cost me a good crutch, though. Ain't sure I can trust myself to this store-bought job."

"We'll get Joe Delagoa to make you a new one, custom-made," Johnny said.

Delagoa was the town's coffin-maker, dabbling in a line of carpentry on the side.

"That'll be fine, mighty fine," Luke said, pleased.

"Of course he might be busy for a while fitting out those five Moran rannies in their pine box suits," Johnny pointed out.

"What's the hurry?" Luke demanded. "Let 'em wait. They ain't going nowhere."

"Never know when there'll be another hot spell," Barton said. "Best get them in the ground, planted fast."

*See the later adventures of Sixkiller in his own big series!

"I reckon they're already feeling the heat where they're going . . . and will be feeling it for some considerable time," Johnny said.

"But what about this Turlock fellow? What happened to him? Where's he got to?" Luke asked.

"Turlock moved out of Arkansas before federal troops moved in," Barton continued. "The army stayed on the border to squat on the homegrown belligerents. They had their hands full trying to ride herd on them feuding Razorbacks. They couldn't spare the men to go chasing after the Free Company. Jimbo and the marauders took off west along the Red River."

"Where are they now?" Johnny asked, striking to the heart of the matter.

"Well now, that's the big question, ain't it?" Barton replied, nearing the end of his little game of cat and mouse. He'd been feeding Johnny and Luke his line, pulling them along preparatory to landing them on his hook.

Yet when dealing with such men, the matter of who was the cat and who the mouse was very much in doubt.

"Where are they now?" Barton echoed. "A lot of folks would like to know the answer to that one—the army, every law enforcement agency between St. Louis and Santa Fe . . . and me. Maybe you, too," he added, meaning Johnny and Luke both. "That's why I asked about the whereabouts of your pal Heller."

"*Pal* is a mite strong, but I'll let it pass," Johnny said.

Barton took a guess. "He's in good with Captain Harrison, the commanding officer of Fort Pardee."

"If you say so." Johnny was giving away nothing.

Barton laughed in disbelief. "Hell, he talked Harrison into getting you your pardon."

Johnny shrugged. "Could be. I don't know what he said to the Yank captain about me and I never asked. I had a deal with Heller—if I helped him bust up the Harbin gang, I'd get a clean bill of health with the law.*

"And by God, I've got it, too," he added curtly, signaling that the subject was closed as far as he was concerned. If Barton didn't like it, that was too damn bad.

"Now don't get your feathers ruffled. What's past is past," Barton said. "Fact is, I'm aiming to do you boys a favor."

"Which means you want us to do you one," Johnny countered.

"That's how it works. But this time you'll be doing yourselves a favor, too."

"You're too good to us, Marshal."

"And you won't even have to kill anybody," Barton deadpanned, straight-faced.

"Too bad," Johnny said.

"Don't be too disappointed. Who knows? Maybe things will work out differently," the marshal said. "Now let's get down to brass tacks."

"You're telling it."

"Not yet, but I will. I'm gonna let you two in on some highly confidential information that just may be of interest to you. This is just between the three of us, mind. It wouldn't do for it to get out to the public. Might cause a panic."

"I'm a closed book," Johnny said.

"I ain't heard nothing yet," Luke said.

*See *Savage Texas*.

"Well, you will," Barton said, all business. "Harrison took most of the fort's company into the field two weeks ago. They went out on maneuvers to take advantage of the weather while it's good. That's what they *said*, but I know better. They went out looking for the Free Company."

"Interesting, if true," Johnny said.

"It's true, all right, and more than *interesting*. Harrison ain't the only one out looking. Most of the cavalry troops in this part of the state are beating the bushes searching for Turlock and the marauders."

"They shouldn't be too hard to find. How many men does Turlock have riding with him?" Johnny asked.

"It's hard to say. There's a hard core of Free Company red hots and a rabble horde of camp followers that trails along with them. Let's say about 150 frontline marauders and twice that for the camp followers," Barton said.

"A force that size could do some damage," Johnny allowed.

"They *have*."

"Jimbo always was a slippery cuss, back in the day in Missouri, I'll give him that. But it shouldn't be too hard to get a line on an outfit that size. It's a small army."

"That's the trouble. It is a small army," Barton said. "The federals have got a rough idea of their locale from what they're not hearing. Turlock's keeping his crew to the back trails, that's for sure, but even there a group of that size is sure to be seen.

"Turlock takes no prisoners. Every small town, ranch, farm, way station, freight or stagecoach stop, trading post—you name it—everything along their route is burned out. No one is left alive."

"That's pretty much how Turlock operated during the war," Johnny said, nodding. His eyes were hooded, thoughtful, as memories from that not-so-long-ago time came pressing in.

"The result is that no one's reporting," Barton went on. "When word precedes his coming, everybody in his way clears out and heads for the hills. If they even suspect they might be on his route, they up and git."

"He casts a long shadow before him," Johnny murmured.

"Eh? What's that?" Barton said sharply, probing.

"That's what they used to say about Jimbo back in the war. He casts a long shadow before him," Johnny explained. "When folks heard he was on the march, they lit out fast. Can't blame them. Why risk your life and your family's on the chance he might not pass by?"

"It's a tactic that works," Barton said. "Hard to get a fix on the Free Company because the refugees come in from all over the map creating confusion. What's known is that there's a broad swath a couple miles wide stretching east to west all the way back to Baxter Springs. Everything in it has gone dark. Deserted, abandoned, burned out. That's how we know where Turlock's been."

"Who's 'we?'" Johnny prodded.

"We lawmen," Barton said offhandedly. "Oh, we're all working together to run the Free Company down."

"How's that working out for you? Where's Turlock? Where's he going?"

"I'll tell you this, and it's to be held strictly in confidence," Barton said, looking owlish. "Captain Harrison took his cavalry northeast into the Uplands to scout for the Free Company."

"Says who?" Johnny asked.

"Harrison himself," Barton said, smug. "We're co-operating, though I never thought I'd say it. You know me. I wouldn't give a blue-belly the time of day, but when it comes to the safety of the town, I set aside my prejudices, no matter how justified."

"Mighty big of you," Luke said.

Barton wasn't sure how to take that, so he ignored it and went on. "Harrison put the word out that they were going on routine maneuvers to avoid stamped-ing the townsfolk. We don't want to clear out the county if it turns out the Free Company's headed somewhere else. That's why I asked you about Heller, Johnny. He left town about the same time as Harrison moved the troops out, so I was wondering if they were working together, and if Heller had told you anything about it."

"Here's some sure enough straight talk so there won't be any mistake between you and me, Marshal," Johnny said, hard-nosed. "What Sam Heller does is his business. What I do is my business. I don't tell him my business and he don't tell me his. That's how we get along."

"Sure. I just thought maybe he let slip something about his plans or what they're cooking up at the fort—"

"I'll tell you this. Heller's not the man to let any-thing slip that he don't want to get around. If he says something it's because he wants you to hear it or don't care if you do. He don't talk much to start with. He's a closemouthed man—which ain't such a bad thing. He's a most mysterious man, too."

"Deep," Luke agreed, nodding.

"Figure it out for yourself," Johnny told Barton. "Sam Heller rode out three weeks ago and Harrison took the troops out two weeks ago, so it don't seem likely they're working together."

"Still, Heller's done some scouting for the army before, so it could be he went out ahead of Harrison to see what he could scare up," Barton pointed out.

"Could be, but now you're just guessing. Never mind about guessing. Let's talk about what you know. Is Hangtree in danger of being hit by Turlock?"

"There's always a chance, Johnny. I wish I knew how much of a chance." Barton said feelingly. "Harrison told me what he wants me to know, not necessarily what *I want* to know."

"He must have thought it was pretty serious to take most of his outfit into the field to go scouting for the Free Company."

"That was orders from General Phil Sheridan, who's in charge of the Texas district," Barton said. "Damn his Yankee eyes! But that's neither here nor there . . . Anyhow, he posted all forts in North Central Texas to be on the lookout for the marauders."

"That covers a lot of territory," Johnny said.

"I don't care where he goes as long as it ain't here," said Luke.

"At this point, Turlock could go any number of ways," Barton cautioned. "He could reverse direction and go back into Arkansas. There's not much north to interest him, though he might raid the railhead that's making for Abilene. Hit the camp at End of Track on a payday and it might make a worthwhile haul. He could strike deep into the Black Earth district of Dallas but lots of forts and cavalry troops are there.

"That dustup we had with Red Hand works to his advantage. The usual war parties found between the Red River and the Canadian won't be so troublesome since we cut them down to size. That gives the Free Company a pass to travel along the corridor until they hit the Llano. That'd stop them cold. The Quesadas are in full force there, full of piss and vinegar and spoiling for a fight. Or they could go west along the trail to the edge of the Uplands and strike south—which would put them on a collision course with Hangtree."

"What are the odds they'll head this way?" Johnny asked.

"Who knows?" Barton said, perplexed. "Who knows what kind of wild hair Jimbo Turlock's got up his four quarters? From what I hear, he's more than a little bit cracked, tetched in the head. No telling what he'll do!"

"He ain't as cracked as he's made out to be. He trades on that loco thang to throw folks off their guard—especially lawmen," Johnny said. "When it comes right down to it, Jimbo can tell a hawk from a handsaw well enough.

"Hangtree is enjoying a boom of sorts, thanks to the demand for beef. It ain't no bed of roses here, but we're doing better than some. There's a lot here worth raiding—a bank with money in it, stores full of goods, saloons awash with liquor, ranches with plenty of livestock.

"Women and girls, too," Johnny added after a pause. "Boys, if he gets them young enough, are worth selling as slaves south of the border. Comanches'll buy or trade for them, too. To adopt the youngsters into the tribe to make up for the loss of manpower we've been hitting them with.

"Jimbo hits us, he can run south all the way to Mexico, or cross the Pecos and head west for California."

Barton's brow was furrowed like a new-plowed field. Thinking had that effect on him. "Hell! I let you in on the secret because you two get around to places where a lawman can't go, and I figured if you dug out any information about the Free Company you could pass it along to me. Now you've got me more than half-convinced that they'll hit us for sure!"

"Not much we can do but watch and wait. See if they show," Johnny said.

"And if they do, we'll kill them," Luke said gleefully, bloodthirsty.

"Well, that's the situation in a nut," Barton said. "Could be Turlock won't come within a hundred miles of Hangtree. I don't know. For now, mum's the word. Considering some of the trigger-happy characters we got in town, if they get a whiff of the Free Company in their nostrils, there won't be a stranger safe on the trail. Not a traveler, freight-hauling teamster, wagon train pilgrim, drifter. Nobody!"

"You wouldn't have told us nothing if you didn't think we can keep our traps shut," Luke said.

"And we will," Johnny said, "unless there's something to shout about."

"You can do the town and yourself some good," Barton said. "Your ranch is in the lee of the Breaks. If the Free Company comes down off the Uplands, they can hide west of the hills. It's an old outlaw trail."

"Not to worry, Marshal, we got an old outlaw

working at the ranch for us, too," Johnny said, smiling with his lips.

"Yeah, and I hope you keep him there. I get tired of having to lock up that reprobate Coot Dooley," Barton said sourly.

"He's on the straight and narrow now, Marshal," Luke said, mock-solemn.

"Hmmph!"

"By the way," Johnny said. "There must be a reward on Jimbo and friends, eh?"

"A big one!" Barton said. "Shoot first and you might live to collect it!"

FOURTEEN

Sam Heller lost two days. He also lost track of the surviving Hog Ranch gunrunners he'd been trailing. What was important was that he not lose his scalp.

In pursuit of the gunrunners, Sam Heller was riding north from the Bench of Bones in early afternoon the day after the massacre, when he caught sight of an Indian band of riders. That they were Indians could be no doubt, even at so far a distance. Something telltale about their outline on horseback said "Indian." And being Indians, they could only be Comanches.

The eastern edge of the Llano was Comanche territory. To the west, somewhere in the heart of the empty quarter, lay the secret Quesada homeland, its location unknown to any living white man . . . except perhaps for a handful of highly trusted Comancheros who had been adopted into the tribe as blood brothers . . . and maybe not even them. No outsider knew the locale.

The band was at the edge of Sam's vision, little more than black specks under the sun. A group of a dozen or more, a long way off in the west, riding east. Too many to be the few Comanche survivors of the Boneyard unless they had added their tattered remnants to a larger group.

Sam had a pair of field glasses in one of his saddlebags, but he didn't bother to reach for them. The position of the sun in the sky ensured that highlights would be reflected off the binocular lenses. That would surely betray his position . . . if the unknowns hadn't seen him already.

It was unlikely that they *hadn't* seen him. Comanches didn't miss much.

Hunting party? he wondered then ruled it out. Little enough game on the flat after the buffalo had run elsewhere, what was left of them. The once-expansive herds of the southwest range had been greatly thinned in recent years, a sore point with the Comanche who lived on them.

Some deer and elk roamed the prairie but not so much where water and grazing grass was sparse. No, he decided, the Comanches were sure to be raiders, maybe even fellow tribesmen of the band at the Boneyard.

"If so, they're liable to be mighty sore," Sam mumbled. He turned Dusty's head to the right, pointing him northeast. His heels dug into the horse's flanks, urging him forward at an easy lope. Only a damned fool would urge the horse into an all-out run.

The flat vast tableland sprawled to all four quarters of the horizon. Only a handful of widely scattered low boulders, a shallow dry streambed, and a gentle hollow offered cover, but they were not places that could be held.

With adequate cover, Sam could have made a credible

stand holding off the hostiles with his scoped long gun. He'd converted his mule's-leg Winchester to a long gun before riding out. It lay near at hand sheathed in its saddle scabbard. He'd be needing it soon.

Nothing to do but run for it, he decided. It would be a long run, a long chase. He was a far piece from where he had to be to stay alive.

Northeast, somewhere beyond the horizon, lay the Broken Hills—the Breaks as they were known—the mountain range running north-south to the west of the Uplands and surrounding plains.

Mountain is a relative term. In Colorado, home of the towering Rocky Mountains, the Breaks would be considered little more than foothills and barely that. Even by comparison with the rugged ranges of the Big Bend region of the Trans-Pecos—Texas's only real mountainous area—the Breaks were held to be puny indeed. But to the folk of North Central Texas, they were something to behold.

Sam longed for the sight of them. A long hard ride lay between him and them—if he was able enough and lucky enough to keep ahead of his pursuers.

Off he went, and the chase was on!

Chase it was, for the raiding party was coming after him, as Sam saw the first time he looked over his shoulder to the west. A plume of dust rising from the antlike blur of distant riders proved they were pushing their mounts to greater speed. Maybe it was a Comanche hunting party after all, with Sam the prey. Well, it wasn't the first time. He just hoped it wouldn't be the last.

Dusty went into an easy lilting trot, gliding across the flat, making a beeline to the northeast. The landscape rolled by, unchanging. No, not exactly unchanging, for there were variants, but they were subtle—a gentle slope tilting by nearly imperceptible degrees, trending into a vast miles-long shallow basin. The colors changed from dull greens and browns, to buff and tan, to dun gray, all shot through with the first fading touch of fall. Occasional sweet scents of prairie sage struck a jarring pastoral note to the grim chase.

The seemingly endless hollow finally uptilted, spilling into a long gentle slope that delivered him out of the basin and on to the next flat.

Sam looked back rarely. He didn't have to. He knew what he would see—his pursuers crowding behind, doing their damnedest to cut the distance between them. When he did chance a look, that is what he saw.

The Comanches were closing the gap between them and their quarry. They were running their horses faster, a trick to provoke Sam into panicking and running his horse full-tilt at a grueling pace that would fatigue his mount sooner and bring the chase to an end.

Sam was not one to be panicked. "Not yet," he told himself. Fast but not too fast would win the race.

Proving his hunch before too long, the pursuers were forced to slacken their blistering pace to spare their own mounts from playing out. They realized they were up against no greenhorn but a veteran frontiersman and were in it for the long pull.

So much the better. The greater the challenge, the greater the sport.

On they rode through the long hours of afternoon. Dusty forged ahead, black mane streaming, nostrils flaring, lungs huffing bellows-like as he coursed ahead, his Steel Dust hide glossy under a sheen of sweat.

Sam was doing some sweating himself and not just from the heat. Random breezes from the west were welcome, seeming to hurry man and mount ahead a bit faster.

Strands of scrubby mesquite trees with low-hanging boughs stretched shadows eastward, shadows that grew ever longer as the day stretched on.

The blurry haze of oncoming evening blanketed the plains when Sam first glimpsed a scrum of blue-gray shadows in the northeast quadrant.

More time passed, the scrum resolving itself into the flat outline of a low wall stretching to the north.

As if to herald the Breaks, the ground began to come apart, shot through with cracks, rills, and fissures that netted the flat in a spidery web. Sparse rock outcroppings began to thrust upward from the turf, spiking jagged fangs of gray-black stone. Lonely sentinels, they were grim mileposts on the race for survival.

Sentinels? They might be tombstones.

The farther Sam advanced the more the flat uniformity of the plain was shattered. The welcome herald of changing terrain brought with it not only the lure of safety, but also the threat of danger underfoot, for if Dusty should make a single misstep, the result could be a stumbling fall endangering horse and rider. At worst, the horse might sustain a broken leg, but even throwing a horseshoe could be fatal to Sam.

His course began to weave around the rocks, which were becoming more numerous. Northeast lay the wall of rock that was the outlying bulwark of the Breaks.

War whoops, battle cries, yips, and yaps came louder behind him as the Comanches whipped their horses to greater speed. Perhaps they sensed the possibility of Sam making good his escape.

Shots crackled, bullets whipping the air in his vicinity. The Comanches were ace marksman even on galloping horseback, but his lead was still too wide for the shots to score. The braves knew it and ceased firing, bending their energies to the chase.

Rock scallops reared up out of the landscape like petrified spines of long-dead armored dragons. Some were head-high and more. He was encountering the outliers, the ribs and spurs of the central formation. West of the hills, they ran roughly north-south for several miles, increasing in size and length the closer he got to the main range.

Sam kept a keen eye on the rocks, looking for a likely spot to rein in and make a stand. It was best done before the Comanches also had the advantage of the rocks for cover.

A long stringy chest-high scallop of rock ahead seemed to bode well. Sam leaned far forward in the saddle, so that his upper body was bent almost double over the horse's croup, his straining thighs gripping its surging flanks. His mouth near one of the horse's pinned-back ears, he urged, "Dig dirt, Dusty! Give it all you got, boy!"

Scenery flashed by in a blur of speed. The Comanches once more opened fire, a heavier volley peppering the air. A number of rounds whipped by Sam, too close for comfort.

At the near end of the outcropping he reined in the horse, sacrificing precious split seconds of speed to slow the animal to swing around a tight curve.

Once behind the rock, he reined Dusty to a halt, the horse stopping wonderfully short and nimble, showing the surefootedness of his mustang blood.

Hands gripping the saddle horn, Sam alighted to the turf. The ground was not so springy as elsewhere but featured thin soil on rocky ground. The soles of his boots skidded on loose pebbles.

He shucked the rifle from out of the saddle sheath and guided Dusty to an area screened by the covering rocks and out of the line of fire. The horse had been in similar scrapes before and knew what to do, quickly following Sam's order to lie down on his side, head down.

No need to attach the rifle's telescopic sight. The Comanches were so close.

Sam pushed back his hat brim, tilting it upward out of the way. The rifle's heft, its cool machined steel and polished wooden stock, felt good in his hands. He took up a stance, positioning himself near a notch in the rock, facing southwest. That was a break. He wasn't looking directly into the orange disc of the setting sun, and the Comanches wouldn't be charging straight out of it.

The braves came on full-tilt, a furious intimidating spectacle. Their fighting blood was up. The end of the chase was at hand. Prestige for the brave who made the kill, greater prestige still for he who took the white man alive, a captive for the torture. War whoops sounded and resounded. Hoofbeats pounded, drumming hard-packed ground. They were so close that individual details could be made out—a shrieking brave in a red shirt, a lance hung with feathers, a wild-eyed charging horse.

Paradoxically, a great stillness came over Sam, a

deep calm. He had done this many times before. It was what he did.

Shouldering the Winchester, he sighted on the brave in the lead. Kill the leader and sometimes it would take the heart out of a Comanche attack. Sam squeezed the trigger.

The brave went down, falling off his horse. The horse kept coming for a while before breaking off to the side.

Sam didn't pause to watch his target go down. In tight spots, it was vital not to freeze on one target but to keep in continuous motion, constantly moving to the next target. Besides, he knew that when he pointed his rifle at a target and pulled the trigger, he hit the mark in all but the most extraordinary situations.

He went for the braves at the spearhead of the charge. They were bunched up tighter and the ones farther back on the flanks could see the others going down, a demoralizing experience.

Five shots in rapid succession, five downed braves. The others knew they had a wildcat by the tail.

Their forward motion arrested, they fanned out at the wings, the right flank swinging farther right, the left flank farther left. The straight-on charge was broken for now.

Sam freed Dusty's reins, gathering them up in one fist, rifle in the other. He urged the horse up, Dusty quickly scrambling upright on all fours.

Grabbing the top of the saddle horn with his left hand, Sam boosted himself up into the saddle and rode diagonally northeast deeper into the Breaks.

He slammed the still-smoking rifle home into the scabbard.

The rock wall was at his back for protection, shielding him from Comanche bullets as he rode bent low, leaning far forward. Dusty hit the gallop.

A lull developed as the surviving Comanches regrouped.

Not all the downed braves were dead, but those who weren't were mortally wounded and would not ride again, not alive. They had taken their last ride in this world. The next would be in the Invisible World of the Spirits.

Glowering and dark looks, muttering and shaking of heads occurred between the survivors. Their prey had proved a most formidable marksman, cutting their numbers almost in half in one quick exchange. Could he be *El Solitario*, The Man with the Devil Gun?

A great prize, if he could be taken. But the braves' ambition for glory was countered by the superstitious half-mystical aura that had come to envelop the shooter. A man of power, he was not to be reckoned lightly.

Meanwhile, stray riderless horses must be rounded up. Pride won out over awe and the chase resumed.

The quarry had vanished behind a curtain of brittle rock outthrusting from the earth at an angle. The broken land provided welcome cover for Sam.

The elements of the chase had changed dramatically for the hunters. Possible death lurked around every blind corner, every scrim and scrum of rock. The Comanches advanced cautiously, sending scouts ahead in places of potential ambush—and they were many. It was a landscape of heights and depths, for the broken land counterpointed needle pinnacles and rocky ridges with washes, arroyos, and man-deep cuts. The pursuers began to lose sight of Sam for long stretches at a time.

Sam was unable to shake them. His horse left tracks the trail-wise Comanches were able to follow even in the gathering gloom of oncoming night. To his right, the central range of the Breaks rose up, climbing higher into the darkling sky.

He smelled fresh water from a long way off and soon came to a trickling creek. Pausing at the thin stream, he stepped down from the saddle. The water smelled good and tasted better. He tasted first rather than the horse for fear of alkali or foulness.

Dusty's head dipped to the rivulet and he began to drink. Sam allowed only a taste. All too soon he hauled the horse's head up and away from the water. He couldn't risk having Dusty slowed by drinking too much.

Sam took advantage of the break to reload the rifle, then mounted up and rode on.

Just like the Comanches lost sight of him, he lost sight of the Comanches—a double-edged sword, for he was unable to see if they had split their force and were stalking him from more than one direction.

Rocky ridges flanking the central range grew in height and width, forming a sort of maze fronting the high hills. The skyline of the Breaks was gilded by the setting sun. The foothills were dark with thickening shadows. Sam rode a winding course through the rocky ridges. More and more often he came to a choice between paths.

If he chose wrong, the route might lead him to a blind alley, a dead end penning and trapping him. In such a case, the Comanches could play a waiting game, sealing him in the passage with no escape and staging the assault of their time and choosing.

But it was North Central Texas, not the Rocky Mountains; the pathways remained open as he followed his course.

Sunlight narrowed at the hilltops as the sun went down. Sam came to a long, low, stony shelf that spread out for some distance from the foothills. It was slightly rounded at the top, an expanse of rock.

It could be the break he'd been hoping and waiting for. A godsend, for the hard rock surface would help mask his trail. Not erase it. The Comanches would be on the lookout for signs—the telltale white scuff mark a horseshoe made on stone, an overturned rock with its dark underside exposed, a trampled thatch of weeds and broken twigs.

But such sign would be hard if not impossible to find in the gathering dark.

Sam followed the stone ground in close to the foothills, then way out to the edge. Horseshoes clip-clopping on stone as Dusty picked out his steps sounded uncomfortably loud, like a pounding drumbeat.

The shelf played out all too soon and he was off the rocks with a pang of regret. Had the shelf ended too soon for him to hide his trail and shake his pursuers?

Once more, turf lay beneath the horse's hooves, muffling sound. No sign nor sound of the hunters, but Sam was uncomfortably aware of their looming presence. It was like not seeing the wind, but knowing it was there.

He rode up a long lane between two rocky ridges, a slot pooled with gloomy shadow. Bad place to be

caught. A cleft opened on the left, a gap slanting
northwest toward the flat. He followed it, breaking
out into a wider expanse. Water came down from the
hills and greenery speckled the landscape. Ahead lay
a shallow creek, its banks lined with a fringe of brush.

Sam rode Dusty into the center of the creek, following it upstream for a distance in hopes of hiding his
trail. The last traces of light were gone from the peaks.
A thin hazy mist rose from the ground.

In the west, the evening star twinkled in a purple-
blue sky.

Nightfall.

Sam rode on, the horse moving at a quick walk.
Darkness deepened the sky to star-dusted black.

Comanches preferred to fight in daylight, but they
would do what they had to during the hours of darkness. They'd stay on the trail as long as they could.

Sam unknotted the bandanna from his neck, wet-
ting it with water from his canteen. He leaned far
forward to rub the moist cloth against Dusty's snout,
the horse grateful for the coolness of welcome moisture. Now and then, Sam fortified himself with a bite
of jerky.

The hours wound toward midnight, the stars slowly
wheeling their courses through the heavens.

Sam halted atop a sugarloaf-shaped hill topped by
a stand of trees. He stopped to rest the horse; he
could have kept going and would have preferred it,
but the horse's needs came first. He wanted Dusty to
rest and refresh to have some reserves of strength and
endurance for what the coming hours might bring.

Man and horse were positioned on the north slope
below the crest to avoid skylining.

Sam emptied the better part of a canteen into his upturned hat, holding it under Dusty's mouth. The horse lapped it up, slurping greedily, while Sam stroked the animal's long head, murmuring soft words of encouragement.

Sweet fresh grass on the hillside furnished Dusty with grazing fodder. The horse had the mustang's ability to live off and thrive on grass and hay versus the thoroughbred's limiting need for oats and grain.

Sam stretched, pacing around, trying to work out the kinks of stiffness. Jerky, parched corn, and canteen water provided cold comfort but were most welcome.

He went to the hilltop to watch the moonrise. Bats flew out of the trees at his approach, cutting their wild skittering capers against the starry sky. He lay prone, peering over the crest at the flat, screened by brush and weeds.

A waning moon rose above the eastern hills into the heights, flooding cold pale golden light down on the nightscape. The glow etched the edges of rocky ridges, moonbeams slanting through banks of mist on the ground.

No sign of the Comanches. That didn't mean they weren't there. He probably wouldn't see them if they were there. The first warning of a Comanche attack would be a bullet or arrow coming his way, providing it didn't kill him. Satisfied, he returned to Dusty.

They were back on the trail hours before sunrise. It was a lonesome trek; Sam hoped like hell it would stay lonesome, because the only company he was likely to encounter was Comanches.

Moonset brought a predawn lightening of the sky showing above the hilltops. Purple-black night sky faded to purple, then purple-blue, stars paling.

Daybreak and till no sign of the Comanches. The pressure at the back of Sam's neck like the onset of heavy weather was gone, a kind of instinct hinting that he'd lost his pursuers. He seemed to be in the clear as far as he could tell.

Somehow during the night he had shaken the Comanches.

He continued to proceed as though they were hot on his trail. The sky turned a soft blue and a tad hazy. The early morning air was cool and fresh in the long shadows of the Breaks. Shadows that would be there for a long time until the sun crested the skyline.

Mist lay over the flat, leaving dew on the grass. Small birds fluttered under thin-leafed tree boughs. The few trees were stunted and dwarfed.

The day grew warm long before the sun topped the ridgeline. The heat was welcome, soaking into Sam's taut muscles and sore limbs.

On he trekked, finally entering familiar territory. To the right, the line of hills began to dip, sloping downward, opening up more of the eastern sky. A forerunner of the Notch.

The Breaks ended temporarily. Ahead lay the distinctive outline of Buffalo Hump, a butte-like landform rising several hundred feet high with curved sloping sides and rounded summit. A significant landmark.

Here was the Notch, a gap several miles wide in the Breaks, opening into Hangtree County. It divided the range into the North Breaks and South Breaks.

Through the gap running east-west lay the Hangtree

Trail; east it ran to Hangtree town and beyond. West it took three branchings—south toward San Antonio and the Pecos Trail to New Mexico; north to Fort Pardee, the Canadian River, and Comancheria; and far west into the heart of the Llano.

The south fork was well traveled, the north lightly traveled, and the west hardly traveled at all. West of the Notch lay Anvil Flats, gateway to the Llano, the landscape dominated by Buffalo Hump. The landform was once a Comanche campsite on the Long Trail connecting Comancheria through Texas to Mexico.

The North Fork ran west of the Breaks, clear of all but a few sparsely scattered rocky outcroppings. Sam followed it, pointing Dusty north. The hulking bulk of Buffalo Hump lay behind him. His destination was Fort Pardee, some long miles away. He wanted a parley with Captain Ted Harrison, commanding officer of the post. Sam had some important information he wanted to pass along and some questions he wanted answered.

He was unaware that during his three-week absence from Hangtree dogging the Comancheros and Hog Ranch gunrunners, Harrison had led most of his cavalry company far northeast into the Uplands in search of Jimbo Turlock and the Free Company.

By mid-morning Sam was sufficiently confident of his escape from the Comanches to allow himself the luxury of a pipe. And luxury it was. He tamped down a rough-cut tobacco blend into the bowl of his corncob pipe, its bowl yellow-brown from age and use, broken in the way he liked it. Pipe stem clenched

between strong white teeth, he fired up the bowl,
drawing deep and sighing with contentment.

His destination was Fort Pardee.

But not before making an important detour to the
Hog Ranch.

FIFTEEN

Sam reached the Hog Ranch at twilight. The lowdown dive was a phenomenon of the frontier. Just as dogs have fleas, army bases have places like the Hog Ranch.

Soldiers have needs to fill off-duty hours—women, whiskey, and gambling, in no particular order. They require a place to blow off steam lest they blow their stacks or blow their brains out.

Garrison life is hard, never more so than out on the wasteland. Long hours of hard work and boring stretches of inactivity were periodically punctuated by explosive outbursts of action and violence.

The military brass often tolerated such deadfall dives as the Hog Ranch so long as they didn't transgress certain rules of behavior or detrimentally affect the performance of the unit.

Fort Pardee's Captain Harrison would have taken swift and decisive action against the site had he known that its crowd was running guns to the Comanches, a fact of which he was unaware but of which Sam Heller intended to apprise him.

The Hog Ranch lay in a valley a half mile west of the north fork of the Hangtree Trail and several miles south of Fort Pardee, which lay out of sight beyond the far side of the valley's north ridge. A forlorn locale, made squalid by the Hog Ranch.

Sam left the trail, angling northwest. He approached the Hog Ranch at a tangent, using the valley's south ridge as a screen.

Black V shapes—buzzards—circled not-so-high above the valley. This in itself was not necessarily unusual. The birds were scavengers, carrion feeders thriving on dead things. Dead things were liable to be found around the Hog Ranch.

But what kind of dead things and how many?

A fair number of buzzards circled the site, more than the usual handful of opportunistic scouts. Sam was already on his guard, so this detail merely ratcheted up the tension a turn higher.

He dismounted at the foot of the south ridge, tied Dusty's reins to a low scrub bush, and drew his rifle from the saddle sheath. He surveyed the scene from a distance through a pair of field glasses, sighting no sign of lookouts posted on the south ridge. That meant little if they were hunkered down on the far side below the crest, hidden from view.

Still they'd have to stick their heads above the ridgeline to see what was on the other side. Sam watched for a long time as the dusky gloom deepened, but no lookouts showed themselves.

He knew from past experience that Hog Ranch folk generally weren't in the habit of posting sentries. They were too shiftless, lazy, and uncaring. But survivors of the Boneyard massacre might have put their fellows on guard.

More direct action was required. Sam climbed the low south slope. Lying prone just below the crest, he looked over the ridge. Beyond lay a dismal valley, a brown creek snaking across the bottom of the valley floor. Squatting on the far side of the creek was the Hog Ranch itself, a broken-down ranch house surrounded by a handful of rickety outbuildings, sheds, and shacks. No grass grew around the site. The ground was bare and muddy.

Well, not entirely bare. A couple of bodies lay in the yard. Two bodies almost obscured by the flock of vultures feeding on them. The vultures were the only signs of life.

The Hog Ranch seemed deserted, abandoned. The corral was empty. No horses were tied to the hitching post in front of the main building, no smoke rose from the chimney.

A quarter-hour's watch detected no lurking skulkers, no movement save for the hordes of big black birds hot at their grisly work on the corpses.

The scene required a closer look.

Sam returned to Dusty, stowing the binoculars safely away in a reinforced leather carrying case which he put in a saddlebag. He mounted up, rifle in one hand, reins gathered in the other.

He rode over the ridge, down the other side into the valley toward the ranch house. The site stank and not only of death. Its inhabitants set no high priority . . . or any priority at all . . . on hygiene and sanitation.

"Hog Ranch? No self-respecting hog would be caught dead in this filth," Sam muttered.

Dusty was untouched by the smell of death. He was a warhorse familiar with battlefield carnage.

The muddy ground bore heavy sign of much recent traffic, a maze of footprints and hoofprints.

Hardly a straight line was to be seen in the ranch house, a low one-story building whose long façade fronted the yard. It was aproned by a hazardous plank board veranda, many boards loose, sagging, or broken. The flat roof sank in the middle, its four corners leaning inward. A ramshackle stone chimney seemed in imminent danger of collapsing, leaning at a perilous angle.

It was hard to make out any details of the two bodies sprawled in the muddy yard, the dead all but hidden by the vultures feeding on them. The buzzards were unimpressed by Sam's advent, few bothering to do more than glance up from their grisly repast.

Buzzards are nasty-looking creatures, Sam thought. *Fowl indeed!*

Their beaky heads were bare of feathers, a caricature of hateful old men—bald, wizened, beady-eyed, and bad-tempered. How those eyes glittered! Sharp-eyed and watchful that none of their fellows snatched a morsel they regarded as rightfully theirs.

"A lot like people," Sam told himself.

They worked close! Like nothing so much as human chowhounds crowding the free lunch table at a saloon.

They were a noisy bunch. Ill-tempered, too, constantly nudging and shoving each other with massive folded wings. Sharp-pointed predatory beaks stabbed, dug, and tore at the cadavers and each other.

It was standing room only around the bodies. Latecomers and less assertive members of the flock walked around on ungainly taloned feet, circling the corpse-mounds, angling for an opening.

Sam climbed down, hitching Dusty to the top rail of a fence post. He advanced, stepping carefully through ankle-deep mud, Winchester leveled hip-high.

He wanted a closer look at the bodies, a feat not so easily accomplished. No way the buzzards were relinquishing their place at the feast. They weren't giving an inch for him to satisfy his curiosity. The feeders couldn't have been less intimidated by Sam.

He charged, shouting and waving his arms around, halting a few paces away. They ignored him.

If that didn't beat all! A bunch of scavenger birds making him feel like a damn fool!

Firing a few shots might get their attention, but he didn't want to risk the sound of gunfire to call attention to his presence to any who might be lurking unseen on the far side of the ridge.

He picked up some rocks and threw them at the buzzards. That got some reaction, some positive results from the ones who were hit. He didn't throw too hard, not wanting to do any real damage. He held no brief for buzzards but had nothing against them. They had their place in the web of wildlife as a kind of cleaning crew.

Sam drove some of them away from one body, enough for him to get a quick look at the corpse. It was the cadaver of an adult white male on which the birds had really gone to town, making serious inroads.

The man had been clad in red flannel long underwear. The rest of his clothes were gone. So were his boots. He was barefoot. Not much meat or offal left and what there was going fast. A curved white rib cage gleamed through the bloody carcass.

Impossible to tell the cause of death—had he been

shot, stabbed, or bludgeoned? Only the buzzards knew and they weren't talking. They rushed back in to reclaim their places or chisel a new one, setting off a round of short savage infighting until the pecking order—literally—was restored.

Throwing well-aimed rocks temporarily cleared a space around the second corpse. Feathers flew and beady vulture eyes glared at Sam, hating but not enough to attack.

The second body told him as little as the first except that they both had been left in the same condition, stripped down to their underwear and robbed of their boots.

Stealing the boots, Sam could understand. That was a fairly common practice on the frontier and in the savage slums of the big cities, too. The clothes theft gave him pause. One would have to be mighty hard up to steal the garments off a dead man to sell or wear.

Some of the Hog Ranch crowd were pretty low. Sam wouldn't put it past them to eke out a little gain from dead men's clothes. Hell, some of those characters would steal the shroud off their mother's corpse if they could turn a few copper pennies on it.

Another reason came to mind—to conceal the dead men's identities. A dead cavalry trooper in his drawers looks the same as a civilian. But it would take more than the death of two troopers to stampede the Hog Ranch crowd into abandoning their home base. Better than most, they knew how to make a couple dead bodies disappear. Yet they hadn't even bothered.

Could be the Boneyard massacre had panicked them into clearing out . . . maybe. But desert their headquarters for where?

A mystery here, Sam thought, scratching his head.

Hungry, greedy vultures thronged back around the body even before he began to move away.

The ranch house door gaped open, hanging heavily on strained leather hinges. Through the doorway Sam could see a dim cave-like interior.

Carefully stepping over loose planks of the veranda, he went inside. The ranch house was set up along the lines of a trading post. One that dealt in rotgut whiskey, women, gambling, and stolen goods. The place stank of tobacco smoke, raw whiskey fumes, human sweat and stink, and other less pleasant smells.

A big, open, rectangular center space took up most of the floor space. Opposite the open doorway, a long slab table stood against the long rear wall—the bar where whiskey was served.

The floor was covered with sawdust and littered with wooden cups and shards of broken brown jugs and glass bottles. Wooden kegs and barrels of six-snake whiskey stood drained and empty of all but the six rattlesnake heads placed in each container to put a further kick into the mix.

In the back of the space lay a row of partitioned wooden stalls where the women did their business. Each was narrow and closet-like, featuring a coffin-like wooden bed topped by a thin stained pallet serving as a mattress and covered by a filthy, tangled, threadbare blanket.

One bed was occupied by a corpse, that of a woman. Hard-used, from the look of her—skin yellow and wrinkled like old newspaper. Her throat had been cut from ear to ear, with a massive amount of blood drenching body, pallet, and bed.

What had her offense been to earn her a death

sentence? Perhaps no more than being inconvenient and in the way.

Sam went back outside. By comparison, even the fetid air smelled good . . . or at least, better.

He prowled around the rest of the site. A fourth body lay facedown in the muck behind the back of the building. A woman—the birds had left that much of her. Mouse-brown hair streamed out from her head in all directions like a sunburst. She wore a thin, color-less, shift-like dress. Her small bare feet were white as tree roots, the soles heavily callused.

Had she been shot down trying to run away? No way to tell for sure, though the place where she was found might suggest it. The Hog Ranch crowd had surely held a kind of housecleaning before quitting the site, one which included four casual murders.

The other outbuildings—shacks, really—were simi-larly abandoned.

Sam thought it over but could reach no final con-clusion. Between a dozen and fifteen people had ridden out, judging from the tracks, which all angled off to the northwest on a course which would eventu-ally put them abreast of Fort Pardee and several miles west of it.

What lay out there? Nothing but empty prairie, as far as Sam knew. Strange destination!

When did they leave? The condition of the tracks said that it was a matter not of days but of hours.

Sam mounted up, riding toward the valley's north ridge. On the other side hidden behind it lay Fort Pardee.

Sixteen

Sundown in Hangtree.

Getting on toward the dinner hour, Marshal Mack Barton had been fixing to get himself some chow when an excited youngster burst into his office at the jailhouse to tell him he was needed.

"There's been a shooting over to the campgrounds, Marshal," the freckle-faced kid piped. "A man is dead!"

Barton grumbled heavily. He hated missing or delaying his meals. But it was best to move fast to nip trouble in the bud before it got out of hand. He was in a hurry but not so much that he neglected to take a shotgun down off the wall rack. He loaded the twelve-gauge double-barrel and slipped a handful of buckshot shells into a vest pocket. "Let's go, Deputy."

Smalls was a medium-sized man with a long mournful basset-hound face. He followed Barton out the jailhouse door onto Trail Street. They turned right, going south on a cross street.

The campground was southwest of town, a vast rolling meadow cut by a stream that ran southeast to eventually join Swift Creek. It was far enough away that Barton would have liked to ride, but he didn't have a horse saddled and ready. He moved at a steady deliberate pace, Smalls falling into step beside him. Now that he was out and about Barton showed no great haste. No sense in getting all sweaty and out of breath prior to horning in to a situation.

Hangtree was a jumping-off point for westbound wagon trains. The town picked up a lot of traffic especially during the warm weather months before early snows closed the mountain passes in the California Sierras. It was good business, too, with pilgrims and wayfarers stocking up on supplies of all kinds, from horses, oxen, and cattle to foodstuff, seed, tools, firearms, and whatnot.

Wagon trains stayed at the campground, with its open unused space, grass for grazing, and fresh water. At any time, one or more wagon trains would make camp on the grounds—which could lead to trouble, people being people.

That's how lawman Barton saw it. Hell, he *knew!*

"Lots of Southrons pulling out and moving farther west nowadays," Barton remarked to Smalls as they walked toward the campground. "Specially the diehards and bitter-enders."

"Seems like more every day," Smalls agreed.

"They ain't too keen on living under the Yankee yoke."

"Can't say as I blame them."

"Who knows? If the blue-belly yoke gets too heavy, anybody might be minded to do the same," Barton said. "Me, you, anybody!"

"Leave Texas?!" The deputy stiffened, halting.

"You should see your face," Barton chuckled. "You look like I insulted your momma or something."

"B-but leave Texas?" Smalls all but wailed. "Leave Hangtree, home, the Big Sky country?"

"Quit waving the Lone Star flag at me, Deputy. I'm as loyal as the next Texan. Just thinking out loud, that's all."

They walked some more.

"Reckon we'll stick for a while longer at that," Barton said.

"Amen!" sounded Smalls.

Reaching the campground, the lawmen nosed out the situation. Three separate wagon trains were encamped on the site. They were camped on both sides of the creek, fresh water being a priority. Space was a priority, too, so they were well apart from each other. It cut down on personal friction.

In time-honored fashion the wagons were formed up in circles. Campfires burned, thrusting long thin lines of smoke into the air. In the west, the sun was setting in a splash of orange, yellow, and red.

Barton and Smalls quietly prowled the edges of the camps, walking soft, keeping a low profile while they got the lay of things.

The conflict was centered around the Hughes and Brooks outfits. The latter group was led by wagon master Preston Brooks. Twelve wagons were full with families from the Deep South, mostly Georgia, moving to California.

They'd clashed with the Hughes outfit, which numbered six wagons—freight wagons and a couple Conestogas, shoddy vehicles showing signs of ill-use and low maintenance, topped by dirty off-white canvas coverings—and about two dozen men. No families, no women and children. They were camped on the south side of the creek.

A big crowd had collected outside the semicircle arc of the Hughes wagons.

A smaller group, angry and vocal, were from the Brooks outfit. They stood apart from the mass, clustered at the forefront where they were confronting the Hughes bunch almost nose to nose. The Hughes wagoneers were giving no ground, standing resolute and foursquare in opposition.

The bulk of the crowd was made up of spectators from the Baca party, the third and largest convoy— twenty wagons, Santa Fe–bound. They didn't have a dog in the fight. They just wanted to see what it was all about.

More people arrowed into the scene by the minute, hastening the onset of a crisis.

Barton noted the presence of wagon master Preston Brooks and his ramrod Tim Hurley. He knew Brooks to be a well-respected leader and organizer who'd conducted a number of successful trips west, stopping in Hangtree several times.

Brooks was a big solemn bearlike man in a dark suit. Silver-haired with a bushy iron-gray mustache, he wore a flat-brimmed black hat with a round-topped crown popularly called a "parson's hat" though he was no preacher. The big Colt in his well-worn hip holster tended to counter any ecclesiastical impressions.

More dangerous by far was the skinny galoot at Brooks's side, a tall gaunt man with a wizened face and scruffy ginger-colored beard. He was Tim Hurley, the wagon master's top scout, ramrod, and enforcer. Not a trouble-hunter, but he was fast on the draw and had killed several men in gunfights.

They hovered over a knot of three young men,

angry, outraged, and showing it. A distinct family resemblance was visible among the trio.

Standing opposite them were the Hughes men, rowdy, belligerent, and well-armed.

"Pretty tough-looking bunch, Marshal," Smalls said of the Hughes group.

Barton grunted in assent. "Teamsters can be a wild and woolly bunch, but they're packing a lot of heavy artillery for wagoneers. Looks more like hardcases and troublemakers."

At their head were two big hulking figures several inches over six feet tall and built like lumberjacks.

Barton's eyes narrowed at the sight of them. He bared yellow teeth in a mirthless grin that was more of a grimace. "What do you know! The Hughes in the Hughes bunch is Denton Dick Hughes from Denton, Texas," he marveled. "What's more, he's sided by none other than Leo Plattner—Leo Plattner!"

"Which one's Denton Dick?" Smalls asked.

"The one on the left with the big hat."

Denton Dick Hughes had wide sloping shoulders and a pear-shaped torso. He wore an oversized hat with a brim three feet wide and a baggy gray suit. He looked like a heavyweight gone to seed. Big oversized hands with swollen knuckles hung at his sides. His gun was worn high on the hip, holstered cavalry style, butt-out.

"That's Denton Dick? He's supposed to be a real fire-eater," Smalls said. "Huh! Looks like he's been eating everything but. He's been exercising them dinner table muscles."

"Dinner table, hell! He got that way from the whizz—whiskey—the old redeye," Barton said.

"That Plattner's sure got a mean face on him."

"He's a killer."

Leo Plattner was a heavyset brute, thick in the shoulders and torso. He had small round glaring eyes, a lot of stubbornly set blue-stubbled jaw and a belligerently outthrust chin. The sleeves of his plaid shirt were rolled up past the elbows, baring brawny hairy forearms folded across a massive chest. His gun was worn way down low, gunfighter style.

"Something's wrong here," Barton said knowingly. "Denton Dick honchoing a freight-hauling outfit? It don't add up! He never did an honest day's work in his life."

"He's got a bad name, all right," Smalls agreed. "He wanted for anything?"

"Not right now. He's been wanted for plenty in the past—banditry, rustling, horse stealing—but they never pinned nothing on him in court. He's pretty slick at staying one step ahead of the law, I'll grant him that.

"Plattner's been taking lessons from him. Leo was charged in a couple killings, but they couldn't get anybody to testify against him. The witnesses were either dead or so scared that they 'forgot' the facts," Barton said. "Come on. Let's ease in closer."

They circled the edges of the crowd, Barton holding the shotgun pointed down along his side to render it more unobtrusive.

"You know, Leo and Terry Moran were great pals," Barton said to Smalls.

"You don't tell me! That's quite a coincidence, the two of them being in town at the same time."

"Is it? I wonder . . ."

The lawmen hugged the darkness for cover, swinging right until they neared the disputants, then

edging in sideways to get closer. They eased their way
to the spearhead of the conflict where wagon master
Brooks, Hurley, and the three young men faced
Hughes and Plattner, quickly noticing a dead man
sprawled on the ground between them.

Barton sidled up alongside a white-mustached man
with a weathered high-crowned hat who stood with
the Brooks group. "Say, old-timer, who're those three
young fellows with Brooks?" he asked in an easy con-
versational tone.

"Cal Lane and Pete and Stan Burgess," the oldster
said. He was watching the argument and didn't bother
to glance at the man who was addressing him. If he
had he might have seen the tin star pinned on
Barton's vest over his left breast.

"It was Cal's brother Bob who got kilt. Pete and
Stan are Cal's cousins," the oldster said.

"Much obliged," said Barton.

Young Cal Lane was lean and rawboned, jutting
cheekbones and sunken cheeks giving him a half-
starved look. Unkempt inky-black hair stuck out
under a hat worn with sides pinned to the crown.

Prematurely balding, Pete Burgess had a wicked
squint that was fixed on Hughes and Plattner. Stan
Burgess was thin-haired, square-jawed, brown-bearded.

Cal Lane was making most of the noise, shouting.
He was red in the face, neck muscles corded, hands
balled into fists. The two Burgesses seemed equally
upset but were less vocal.

Young Lane said something to which Plattner took
offense. Barton couldn't make out what it was. Plattner bridled, neck swelling, starting forward.

Denton Dick Hughes stopped him, laying a big

hand flat across Plattner's chest. He put his head close to Plattner, saying something to him. Plattner shook his head angrily but backed off.

Barton took note of that. Not many men could stop a stampeder like Plattner when he was minded to raise a ruckus.

Barton edged closer to hear what was being said.

Denton Dick moved a step closer to Cal Lane, saying, "Slow down, sonny, before you bust a blood vessel."

"Best watch out I don't bust more than that!" Cal fired back.

Again Plattner stuck his oar in, demanding, "What's that supposed to mean, little man?"

"Big enough, mister, big enough," Cal said.

Barton decided it was time to take a hand. He passed the shotgun over to Smalls, saying, "You know what to do. Wait till I get into position and make sure you've got Denton Dick and Leo covered."

Smalls made a small tight nod, his face grim.

Barton pushed himself to the fore, shouldering aside all who stood in his way. It was a well-practiced move and he had the confidence to pull it off, confidence so vital in crowd control when it comes to taking charge of a situation.

He was a big man, yes, but Texas was a land of big men, many of whom would be ordinarily inclined to dispute his passage.

Barton moved with the ready tread of authority. Who knows? The tin star pinned to his vest might have had some effect, too.

Plattner was getting into it again. "Keep sounding off and you'll wind up like your pal here," he said, meaning the dead man.

"My brother! He was my brother! Now he's dead and one of you killed him!"

When Smalls was in place, Barton made his move. He horned in, mindful of the lawman's cautionary proverb, Hapless are the peacemakers for they're sure to get both sides mad at them.

"Careful how you go about making accusations, boy, especially when you can't prove them," Denton Dick said, trying to cool things down, perhaps taking notice of the lawman's approach.

Barton got between the two knots of men, putting himself to the left of Denton Dick. Now that he was closer, he recognized more familiar faces among the Hughes bunch—the weaselly Henshaw, swampman Moss Roberts, and the ox-like lunk Plonk—all Texas guns and very bad native sons.

Cal Lane didn't like being called "boy," a word with loaded connotations south of the Mason-Dixon line. He blustered, "You see a boy here, knock him down!"

"I aim to do just that." Plattner started forward, but Denton Dick stopped him again.

Plattner moved to shake off the restraining hand on his arm. Denton Dick indicated Barton by a curt nod of his head. Again Plattner backed off, not liking it, but stepping back all the same.

"I'm Marshal Barton, the law in Hangtree," Barton announced, making it clear from the start who he was and where he stood. He nodded to Brooks and Hurley, with whom he had friendly relations, acknowledging their presence. He also nodded to Denton Dick and Plattner. He'd crossed paths with both several times in the past, though they'd never tangled. "What happened here?" the marshal demanded.

"Why, looks like somebody got his self kilt, Marshal!"

That came from Henshaw, trying to be funny, touching off a few snickers from the Hughes men.

Firelight made Barton's eyes narrow to glittering slits in a dour spade-shaped face. He gave Henshaw a hard look, which said, *I've got you marked down in my bad book.*

Henshaw slipped back into the press of his fellows, making himself scarce.

"There's nothing funny about a killing." Barton nudged the dead man, looking down at him.

The deceased lay on his side, face a mask-like grimace, a line of blood hanging down from a corner of his mouth. He was bareheaded, his hat laying upside down on the ground nearby. He was about thirty, with wavy black hair and a bearded rough-hewn face. He looked like a decent-enough fellow, but veteran lawman that he was, Barton knew looks could be deceiving.

On the other hand, being on the opposite side of a tilt with Denton Dick's bunch spoke in the dead man's favor, for what that was worth. The Hughes men were a bad bunch.

The victim's eyes were open, staring. He wore a brown-and-green flannel shirt and baggy brown pants. He was armed with a gun holstered at his side, undrawn.

Barton hunkered down beside him, putting a hand on his shoulder and turning him over on his back so he lay chest-up. Even in the unsteady mix of flickering firelight and deepening darkness, Barton had no trouble making out that the deceased's middle was pretty well shot to pieces, pierced by a line of bullet holes—three in the belly, two in the chest. One in his left breast killed him fast; the other wounds were all mortal but he might have lingered on in agony for some hours.

Barton straightened up, stifling a groan caused by his aching knees. His joints weren't as flexible as in the golden days of youth. "Who was he?" Barton addressed his question to Brooks, whom he knew he could trust for a straight answer.

"Bob Lane, Marshal," Brooks said somberly. "He's with the group I'm taking to California. Regular fellow, minded his own business, did his share of the work and more, so far as I could tell. Not a troublemaker." He cut off his words with a sharp finality that suggested he could name a few troublemakers on the other side, but he wasn't going to.

"He was all right," Hurley said, a pretty fair compliment coming from the tight-lipped scout, a man of few words.

"See what happened?" Barton asked.

"It was over when I got here, Marshal," Brooks said, glum.

Scout Hurley shook his head no.

Barton looked at Cal Lane. "You see it?"

"No, but—"

"Hold your horses, mister. I want to find out a few facts," the marshal said, not unkindly but firm.

"I didn't see it," Cal said, falling silent, unhappy, fidgeting with unease.

Barton established that neither Pete nor Stan Burgess had witnessed the shooting, either.

"They killed him!" Cal Lane said, starting up again, meaning the Hughes bunch.

"We didn't kill anyone, sonny," Denton Dick said coldly.

"One of you did!"

"Who? Show him to me if you can," Denton Dick challenged.

Cal Lane looked ready to burst. He looked around wild-eyed, staring in the hard unfriendly faces of the Hughes bunch.

"Well?" Denton Dick prodded.

"I-I can't!" Cal blurted.

Denton Dick turned to Barton. "You see how it is, Marshal. Nothing to it. The kid got himself crossed up. Just because his brother got killed over here don't mean any of us did it. Anyone could have done it. Even someone from his own outfit."

"That ain't so!" Cal said.

"The youngster saw smoke and figured it for fire," Denton Dick concluded.

"Sometimes that ain't a bad way to figure it," Barton said noncommittally. "The dead man didn't kill himself, Dick."

"Well no, he didn't, Marshal, and that's a fact—"

"Who did?" Barton demanded, turning on Denton Dick, pinning him.

The other seemed thrown for an instant but quickly recovered. "Derned if I know. I didn't see it myself . . ."

"Uh-huh," Barton murmured.

Cal Lane got his feelings under control enough to continue. "The killer rode out after the shooting!"

"I seed someone ride out a minute after the gunfire," Tim Hurley volunteered. "Rode out of their camp."

"That's what you say," Plattner spat.

Hurley stepped forward, deceptively casual, hand hanging loose over the butt of his holstered gun. "I do say so, mister."

"Listen, you—"

"Pull your horns in, men. We already got one dead man here," Barton barked. "I don't aim to get caught in a crossfire, neither."

Denton Dick stepped in front of Plattner, effectively blocking him out of the exchange. "Could be the shooter stole one of our horses, that son of a gun," he said reasonably.

Barton nodded, smiling with his lips, a cynical twist at the corners of his mouth, as if saying, *That's a good one.*

"I'll tell you who done it, Marshal," a high-pitched voice crackled, brittle but strong. The speaker was a small, spry, bird-like, white-haired old woman. Cal Lane and the Burgesses clustered protectively around her.

The oldster's advent provoked some mocking laughter from the Hughes bunch.

"Shut your mouths," Barton snapped, not even bothering to look their way. The snickering was stilled.

"Who might you be, ma'am?" Barton asked the elder.

"My name is Alberta Stonecypher," she said. Her hooded eyes glittered, hard, bright, unforgiving. "Bob—Bob Lane—that's him lying there shot dead. He's my son-in-law, married to my daughter Katy."

"You saw it, ma'am?"

"I know something," Alberta said, not answering directly. "One of them-all"—she pointed to the Hughes bunch—"was messing with Cherry, my granddaughter. She's all of fourteen."

Barton nodded, indicating for Alberta to continue.

"Cherry went to the creek by herself to fetch a pail of water. We didn't think nothing of it. It's only a stone's throw from camp. Some no-good caught the

girl alone, tried to . . . well, tried to interfere with her."
She paused, almost speechless with indignation but
managing to choke it back.

"Randy! The one named Randy. That's his name.
He done it. He messed with Cherry and kilt poor
Bob!" Alberta accused shrilly.

"How do you know that, ma'am?" Barton pressed.

"He told her, the no-good horndog! He was trying
to make up to her at first, sweet-talking her with that
serpent's tongue, that Old Serpent the Devil, but
Cherry was raised up right. She's a good girl. She
seen through his honeyed words, his lies, and tried to
get away.

"He grabbed aholt of her, wouldn't let her go, but
she scratched his face, clawed him up good! She got
shreds of his skin under her fingernails and marks on
her face where he hit her with his fist, but she got
away from him, Praise the Lord!

"Look for Randy. Randy with the clawed-up face
and you'll have your man, Marshal!"

"Where's the girl now?"

"She's in our wagon with her mother, trying to
comfort each other. They're all tore up," Alberta said.
"Cherry came back crying her eyes out, the side of her
face all bruised and swole up where that dog hit her.
She's crying and carrying on.

"Bob—her pa—Bob got the name from her and
went looking for this Randy, only Randy got him first,"
Alberta concluded. "Now what you aim to do about it,
Mr. Lawman?" she demanded.

Long years as a lawman had taught Barton that the
truth is an elusive thing, yet he had no doubt that no
matter how the matter had actually fallen out, Alberta

Stonecypher believed in the absolute truth of the story she told.

He also tended to take any version coming out of the Hughes bunch not with a grain of salt but with a pound of it. More, the name *Randy* stirred up memories. . . . "This Randy got a last name, ma'am?"

"He must, but I don't know it," Alberta said.

"Does the girl know?"

"Cherry didn't say nothing 'bout no last name. All she said was, 'Randy, Randy.' That's all I got from her. But she might know," the woman added hopefully.

Barton shifted position so that while he was looking at Alberta he could also see Denton Dick and Plattner. "The name wouldn't be *Randy Breeze*, would it?" he asked, watching the two bad men out of the corner of his eye.

Plattner stiffened. Denton Dick had better control of himself. He started at the mention of the name but remained poker-faced.

"'Randy Breeze?'" the old woman said, studying on it, thinking it over. "Sorry, Marshal, it don't ring no bells. I ain't saying Cherry heard a last name or no, but she might have."

"Thanks. I'll talk to her later." Barton turned toward Denton Dick and Plattner, moving within arm's length of them.

Denton Dick looked shifty, evasive; Plattner openly hostile.

"What about you, Leo? You know Randy Breeze?" Barton asked.

"Never heard of him!"

"Tsk, tsk. Now you know it ain't polite to lie, Leo. Especially not to an officer of the law."

"You calling me a liar?"

"I just did."

"That tin star don't give you the right to insult me to my face, lawman—"

"Keep your head, Leo!" Denton Dick said sharply. "Remember where you are and don't start nothing now."

"Nobody calls me a liar, Dick, lawdog or no."

"*Leo*—" The icy chill in Denton Dick's voice got through to Plattner, forcing him to break off.

He muttered something under his breath.

"So you don't know Randy Breeze, huh?" Barton pressed, returning to the subject.

"I may have heard of him," Plattner allowed at last, grudgingly as if the words were being dragged out of him.

"May have heard?" Barton echoed, incredulous. "You ain't talking to no pilgrim now, Leo. I know, *know*, that Randy Breeze is one of your main bowers."

"All right, I know him," Plattner admitted. "So what?"

"Seems to me I recollect him spending a two-year stretch behind those big stone prison walls for rape not too long ago."

"That was a frame-up."

"The way I heard it, the only reason he skipped a date with the hangman was because the gal was a woman of the town, a soiled dove, as they say, and not part of the respectable element."

"She lied. They all do. He went off with another gal and she wanted to get him in trouble so made up a story about him."

"Way I heard it, Leo, your old pard Randy was lucky to get out of town without a neck-stretching. Seems some of the concerned citizens wanted to elevate him with a grand necktie party. But the Parker County sheriff sneaked him out of town in time for him to cheat the noose."

"I don't know nothing about it."

"Here in Hangtree we're not so easygoing. We hang rapists," Barton said, which wasn't exactly true. It wasn't possible to always know which way a judge and jury were going to jump. But they had hanged men for rape, more than a few in Barton's time.

"Good for you," Plattner sneered.

"If memory serves and I believe it does, Randy Breeze served his term and got out of the hoosegow not more than a month or two ago. He went home to his old haunts in Weatherford."

"I wouldn't know."

"No? You're from Weatherford, Leo."

"What of it?"

Barton stepped back. Standing with hands on hips, he slowly surveyed the solid wall of stony, stubborn, unyielding faces of the Hughes bunch. There were exceptions, of course. Plattner sneered, Henshaw smirked, and Denton Dick looked like he wished he were elsewhere.

"Come to think of it, a lot of you boys hail from Weatherford," Barton said as if mulling it over. "Weatherford and Parker County. Leo, Henshaw, Swampman Ross, Plonk . . . A couple more of you rascals look familiar, though I can't quite put the names together with the faces just yet. Oh yes, and one more. Randy Breeze. He's one of the old hometown crowd, too."

"I tell you, Randy Breeze ain't with us!" Plattner exploded.

Denton Dick cast him a warning glance.

"I believe you . . . now," Barton mocked. "As for the rest, it remains to be seen."

He turned his attention to the leader. "Now we come to you, Denton Dick. Funny that with all these Parker County fellows around, they bring in an hombre from Denton, Texas, to honcho them. Why's that?"

"You know how it is, Marshal—cream always rises to the top," Denton Dick said, trying to make a joke out of it.

"Scum, too," Barton shot back, his tone jocular, but meaning it, too.

"That ain't right. You got no call to talk to me like that, Marshal, no call at all," Denton Dick said, his face clouding.

Barton shrugged. "Never figured to see you ramrodding a line of freight wagons, Dick. What're you hauling?"

"A wagonload or two of supplies for ourselves, that's all. The rest of the wagons are empty," Denton Dick said through clenched teeth, sullen. "You don't believe me, take a look for yourself."

"Since you offered so nicely, it must be so. I'll let it pass."

"Nice of you to take it on account, Marshal."

"A curious business. Can't make much on empty wagons."

"We're going down to Midvale."

Midvale was a town south of Hangtree in Long Valley that had been sacked and burned by the Harbin gang the last spring.

"We're going down there to salvage some scrap lumber," Denton Dick continued, trying to regain his poise. "Good money in scrap lumber—planks, boards, and beams. Should be plenty in what's left of the town."

Barton smiled, making no secret of his disbelief. "Whew! Sounds like hard work. It's like to ruin some of you boys."

"We're not afraid of a little hard work."

"That ain't how I heard it."

Leo Plattner had been on a slow burn. He was a man with a low boiling point and he was fuming. His eyes blazed, nostrils flaring. He breathed hard like he was running a race. He did everything but paw the ground with his feet.

Barton resumed working on him. "Been quite a day here for the Parker County set, Leo. You and the boys must be in mourning for Terry Moran and friends."

"We don't like it," Plattner said through clenched teeth.

"Tell me about it. I'm the official Hangtree Jail Complaints Department."

"What kind of law you running in this two-bit cow patty of a town, Barton? Here you are picking on us for trying to make an honest dollar while you let Terry Moran's killers run around free as air!"

"Moran and his two guardsmen got beat in a fair draw. A fair draw, Leo! Johnny Cross burned them down one-two-three, that's what I heard. Must've been some show," Barton said, wistful. "Wish I'd seen it!"

"What about the Randle brothers?" Plattner demanded. He took a step forward, big fists clenching and unclenching. "Butchered in an eatery for trying to eat their lunch!"

"That ain't exactly the way it went down, Leo. They put the café under the gun to do a little bushwhacking, but it blew up in their faces. Poetic justice, I'd say."

"Bah! This ain't no town, it's a slaughterhouse!"

"Some say yes and some say absolutely. You all might want to keep it in mind while you're in Hangtree."

"We ain't forgetting," Leo said ominously.

"Good," Barton said. "Seeing as you're so broken up about the passing of the Moran gang, maybe you want to take up a collection to pay for the funeral. Them being part of the old hometown crowd and all."

"That ain't the funeral I'd like to buy!"

"No? Whose funeral might that be, I wonder."

"*Guess*," Leo said with heavy breathing and teeth-gnashing menace.

Denton Dick intervened once more. "Leo."

"Back off, Dick, I've stood as much guff as I can stand off this lawdog!"

"Leo," Denton Dick repeated.

"Let it go, let it go," Barton said, chuckling with false good humor. "By the way, Leo, don't worry about the funeral. We'll give the boys a real nice send-off—one-way to Boot Hill."

"You're prodding me, Marshal, and I don't like that!"

"Well, you let me know when you've had enough," Barton said, his smile widening.

"I've had me a bellyful now!" Leo cried as he lunged for Barton, hands coming up, reaching for the lawman's throat.

There was only one way to deal with hardcases, Barton knew. Stop them before they get started—and stop them *hard*. In one smooth continuous movement he sidestepped Leo's lunge, drew his gun, and clubbed the back of Leo's skull with the long heavy barrel. A sound like a woodchopper's axe taking the first bite out of a tree trunk was heard by all.

Leo dropped to his knees, stunned. He clawed reflexively at his holstered gun.

Barton pistol-whipped him again, harder.

Leo fell forward, facedown.

Barton leveled his gun on the Hughes bunch.

It all happened in a couple heartbeats.

The crowd of spectators arrowed away from the scene like a flock of spooked starlings, vanishing within seconds.

Deputy Smalls was ready and waiting for the fracas. When Leo charged, he shouldered the big double-barreled shotgun, pointing it at Denton Dick and the center of the knot of bad men.

Some of the Hughes bunch started reaching—mostly those on the flanks of the shotgun's line of fire. But they were late to the party, uncertain.

"Stand down, you fools!" Denton Dick's shout rang out loud and clear, spurred no doubt by the prospect of being the prime target of Smalls's ready shotgun.

"I'll kill the first man whose gun clears the holster," Barton said.

"You know what I'll do," Smalls said.

"*Stand down!*" Denton Dick repeated, louder and with more urgency. "What kind of dumb clucks have I got working for me? Anybody pulls a gun and if I get out of this, I promise I'll kill him myself!"

"I'm with you, Marshal," said the voice of Scout Hurley standing with his hand on his gun butt somewhere behind Barton

"Me, too," Wagon master Brooks said gruffly, also at the ready.

"That's fine," Barton said, not looking away from the Hughes bunch. "I'd be obliged if you'd keep your folks from cutting in; we're hanging by a mighty fine wire now and I'd hate for it to break."

"Will do, Marshal," Brooks said, moving between Cal Lane, the Burgesses, and the Hughes bunch. "Don't shuck those guns from the holsters, men, lest you start a free-for-all that nobody can win."

Stan and Pete Burgess eased off a bit, but not Cal Lane, who all but trembled with the urge to slap leather.

"Don't do it, son," the wagon master said. "You don't want Miz Alberta to maybe get hurt."

Cal shuddered, dropping his hand away from his gun.

"Get those hands away from your guns," Denton Dick urged his men.

After a timeless few minutes, the moment of truth passed. The Hughes bunch lacked the stomach for a blazing gunfight. By slow degrees, the bad men straightened up, exhaling held breaths with a sigh, carefully moving hands away from six-guns.

All but Leo Plattner. The irrepressible strength of the man kept him going, forcing him to hands and knees. Glazed eyes peering out of the tops of his eyes, he moved a hand toward his holstered gun.

Barton stepped forward, kicking Plattner in the chin. "Leo, you dumb son of a—!"

Plattner flopped facedown, out like a light. A couple bad men standing nearby involuntarily winced from the force of the kick. Plattner lay with his hands at the sides of his head.

Barton had to fight to repress a powerful urge to stomp and break Leo's gun hand with his boot heel. "Well . . . maybe next time."

"We'll be done here in a minute. In the meantime, be good and you've got nothing to worry about."

"I'll hold on the mark as long as you want, Mack!" Smalls said, still covering the Hughes bunch in general and Denton Dick in particular.

"We understand each other better now," Barton said to the bunch. "Y'all are guests in Hangtree, mind. Any more trouble from you and I'll be down here fast with a posse to clean up on you. If I do, won't be many of you going home to Parker County, I promise you that. Savvy?" he demanded harshly.

"We savvy, Marshal," Denton Dick said, not much liking it but liking the alternative a whole lot less.

"Good. See that you do." Barton turned to Brooks. "Get your people out of here, wagon master, and we'll be moving along to your camp."

"Right, Marshal," Brooks said, gallantly offering his steady arm as a support to Miz Alberta, who fastened a claw-like hand on it. He began escorting her away from the scene.

Over his shoulder, he called to Cal Lane and the Burgesses. "Come on, you three. Get out of here while the getting's good. It'll never be better," he said under his breath.

"Eh? What's that you say, wagon master?" Miz Alberta asked.

"Nothing, ma'am. Nothing."

"Go on, Brooks. Get them out of here," Scout Hurley said. "I'll lay behind for a bit."

"Okay." Brooks hurried his charges off, hampered by having to move at the pace of the slowest, Miz Alberta. But she was spry and stepped along quite lightly.

Scout Hurley moved closer to Barton and Smalls,

neither of whom had lowered their weapons leveled on the Hughes bunch. The scout's hand was empty but rested on his holstered gun. He didn't pull it to avoid ratcheting up the tension. "They're clear, Marshal," he said when Brooks and the others were out of the line of fire.

"Good. We're going now." Barton started to back away.

"Good riddance," Denton Dick said sourly.

"And a good night to you, Dick," the marshal said. "And to Leo, too, when he wakes up."

"I expect he'll have something he wants to say to you personally."

"I'll be waiting."

Barton, Smalls, and Hurley edged sideways away from the bunch in crabwise style caused by the need to watch the gunmen and retreat from their camp.

"Careful with that twelve-gauge, Deputy. It's got a hair trigger," Barton said, joshing, but meaning it, too. He wanted the bunch to hear it as a reminder not to cut up capers.

"G'wan, git!" a voice ragged from the enemy camp.

Barton laughed. It's what the Hughes bunch heard once he and the others had moved out of the circle of firelight and out of sight into the darkness.

They made no move to pursue.

The withdrawal had been accomplished.

"Much obliged, Hurley."

"Nothing to it, Marshal."

"All the same, thanks."

Hurley nodded. "You're welcome."

"You, too, Deputy."

"All in a day's work, Marshal."

"Yeah," Barton said, chuckling. "That's the trouble. And the day's far from over, even though it's night."

They were inside the campfire-lit circle of Brooks wagons. The wagon master had posted plenty of sentries and guards and most of the male emigrants went about armed. Barton noted the precautions with approval.

"That's sure a heap of no-goods," Hurley pointed out needlessly. "Wonder what they're doin' here."

"I wonder," Barton said. "Nobody would buy that cock-and-bull story about them going down to Midvale to salvage scrap lumber."

"The very idea!" Smalls said, indignant at the affront to common sense. "They's robbers and killers in the first place because they's too shiftless and mean to do a lick of work."

Cal Lane and Pete and Stan Burgess came crowding in.

"What's next, Marshal?" Cal demanded grimly.

"Not much," Barton said. "I want to talk to the girl. Best leave your brother's body where it is until daybreak when I can arrange a way to pick it up."

"Leave Bob uncovered all night where the animals can get at him? That's awful raw," Pete protested.

"The real animals are inside the Hughes camp, not outside," Barton said. "Four-legged scavengers won't go near that camp tonight. They'll leave the body alone."

"Still, that's awful raw," Pete repeated.

"It's worth your life and anybody else's who goes to that camp tonight. Stay away until I say different," Barton said harshly. "That's an order. Break it and you won't get arrested, you'll be lying there beside Bob Lane."

"Hard words," Stan said.

"That's how it's got to be," the marshal concluded.

"What about Randy?" Cal Lane demanded.

"What about him?" Barton asked.

"Ain't you going after him?"

"I wish I could, but I can't leave the town without a lawman—especially now."

"What about your deputy? Can't he lead a posse?"

"I need him," Barton said. "Sorry, Lane. I know it's cold comfort, but that's the best I can do for you tonight. Come daybreak it'll be a different story. For now, I've got to stay put and I recommend you do the same. In case you and your kinfolk ain't noticed, we're all in a pretty tight spot here. You, me, your outfit, all the decent folks on the campgrounds, and the town itself."

"So you ain't gonna do nothing to catch the killer," Cal Lane said, mouth full of bitterness.

"See me at dawn. I'll be at the jailhouse. Things'll move then," Barton said.

"It'll be too late by then, the killer'll be clear out of the territory," Cal said, vexed, worked up.

"Could be," Barton admitted.

"If you won't go after him, I will!"

"I had a feeling that's what you'd do. I ain't saying I wouldn't do the same if I was in your shoes," the marshal said. "If you want to wait till the deputy and me go back to town, I'll make the rounds with you, see if we can scare up a posse. A lot of the boys don't rightly care for those who go messing with the womenfolk, with decent young gals."

"I've had all the stall I can take," Cal said. "I'm done waiting. I'll do what needs to be done myself."

"I'm with you, Cal," Pete said emotionally.

"Me, too!" Stan offered.

They started off.

"Hold it!" the marshal barked, stopping them in their tracks. He had the voice for it when he wanted to use it. "A word of advice before you go, Lane."

"I ain't asked for none," Cal said.

"It might save your life and your cousins', too."

"Might not hurt to listen, Cal," Stan said, frowning, upset.

Pete shrugged.

"Make it short, then," Cal said. "I'm in an almighty hurry!"

"Any trail-wise owlhoot's gonna be looking for someone to come dogging his trail," Barton began. "If it's Randy Breeze, he'll sure 'nuff be looking. Look out for spots where he might be laying up to bushwhack you, is what I'm saying."

"I'll keep it in mind, Marshal," Cal said shortly.

"See that you do. Might keep you alive."

"Thanks! Thanks for nothing," Cal spat, stalking off, Pete following. Stan acknowledged Barton with a tight nod, then hurried off to catch up with the other two.

"Kid's got sand," Hurley said after a moment.

"But not much sense," Barton shot back.

"Would you do any different?"

"Hell, no!"

Within a short time Cal Lane and the Burgesses were mounted up on three fast horses.

Wagon master Brooks organized a group of men at one of the wagons on the west side of the wagon train circle. Gathering around the extended wooden wagon tongue to which the team was hitched while traveling, they lifted it, using it as a handle to swing the wagon outward like a hinged door, breaking the circle to make an exit for the trio.

Cal Lane, Pete Burgess, and Stan Burgess rode outside the ring to the accompaniment of much waving and cries of "Good luck!" and "Good hunting!"

The trio angled northwest to the Hangtree Trail, following it west out of town, the direction taken by the fugitive "Randy."

When they were out of sight, the work gang hefted the ox-tongue handle, levering the wagon back into place, closing the circle.

In the Hughes camp, a spy came running to Denton Dick to tell him of the three men riding in pursuit of Randy. Denton Dick scared up a couple capable henchmen, since Leo Plattner continued to be of no use to him, still unconscious from Barton's titanic front kick.

Denton Dick started barking orders. "Slim! Brown! Get a couple of the boys and go after those three. See that they don't come back! No, wait!" he said, immediately countermanding his first orders. "It won't do to be seen chasing them. Let them get out of sight, then leave. Go north till you're out of sight, then cut west after them. Get them. You know what to do."

"We sure do," someone said, chuckling evilly.

"Don't bring back their horses. They might be recognized!"

"Okay, Dick!" a enthusiastic henchman cried as he and a few others moved to obey.

"Make sure you dump the bodies where they won't be found," Denton Dick called after them.

"Right!"

Denton Dick rounded up another stooge. "Go to the Cattleman Hotel and tell Kale Dancer what happened here, about the killing and Barton and all. No," he reversed instantly. "No, wait. Never mind. This is important. I'll do it myself."

SEVENTEEN

The Hog Ranch was merely a prelude to the horror of Fort Pardee.

"Not so many buzzards this time," Sam Heller said to himself as he reached the fort at sunset. That helped, somehow.

It sat on a flat, a stone rectangle with walls ten feet high and three feet wide. Cube-shaped turrets rose at the four corners of the oblong. The hollow rectangle enclosed lines of buildings bordering an open parade ground and barracks square.

Set in the middle of nowhere, the man-made geometric structure lay a quarter mile west of the northbound Comancheria Trail, beyond the shadow of the Breaks. The walls were made of stones quarried and gathered from the west face of the Breaks. It was grueling, backbreaking work, but that's what peacetime garrison troops were for. Not that peace was so peaceful in Hangtree County, or Greater Texas, either, for that matter.

A dirt road ran west from the trail to the front gates of the fort. A stream ran a hundred yards north of the structure, behind the back of the north wall. A working artesian well lay inside the walls, supplying an independent water source.

Fort Pardee had been built a few years after the successful (for the United States, that is) conclusion of the Mexican War. It was part of a string of such forts the federal government had built along the frontier line of the hundredth meridian to check and suppress the Comanche and lesser hostile tribes. Its high thick stone walls had been proof against the tribes, who had never been able to overcome it. Many a blistering Comanche charge had broken under withering rifle fire from those ramparts. When the War Between the States broke out, the government in Washington, D.C., closed the forts, pulling the troops out in preparation to fight the big battles east of the Mississippi.

Fort Pardee had been reopened after the war's end in the summer of 1865. It was undermanned and had never been at full strength since commencing operations.

As Sam approached, it was obvious the fort had fallen, the manner of its undoing as yet a mystery to him. But that it had fallen, of that there could be no doubt.

A handful of buzzards circled high overhead. A few stray horses roamed aimlessly in the middle ground outside the walls. They looked up with curiosity from their grazing to take note of his arrival. A few thin gray lines of smoke rose from within the walls.

New tracks crisscrossed the land, the ground churned up by many hoofprints. A hundred and fifty horses or more, like a cavalry column. Nothing unusual there. It was a cavalry fort. But the direction of the line of march was surprising.

It came out of the Breaks via the nearest path north of the fort, cutting diagonally southwest, then circling around to the southern front gate. The assembly massed, some entering and then leaving the fort, the entire column moving south beyond the horizon.

Damnedest sequence of troop maneuvers at Fort Pardee Sam Heller had ever seen! The question was, Whose troops?

The front gate was open, its massive portals flung wide. The walls were stone but the gate door was wrought of fire-hardened timber reinforced with iron bands. Fire-resistant and unbroken it remained.

A couple of bodies lay on the ground in front of the open gate. Unlike at the Hog Ranch, the dead men were decently clothed, for all the comfort they could take from that. They were soldiers, cavalry troopers.

Dusty sidled uneasily just outside the gate. The warhorse was used to battlefields, blood, smoke, and mass death, but something about the scene got to him, working on his nerves.

Sam knew the feeling. He felt it, too.

From where he sat on Dusty, he could see the central area. The courtyard was littered with corpses of men and animals, even corpses of buzzards. There had been massive violence.

Sam unknotted the bandanna around his neck, re-tying it so it covered the lower half of his face. That helped against the smell, a little.

He rode through the gate into the fort. The foot of the walls was flooded with purple-blue pools of dusky shadow gloom. The rifle was in his hand before he knew it, unaware of having drawn it from the saddle scabbard. Its heft and solidity was a comforting thing.

Even more so was its death-dealing potential. He slowly rode the perimeter.

Fort Pardee had been built according to the usual army plan.

A quadrangular courtyard, a large open center space, served as a parade-drilling ground and assembly area. Buildings stood with their backs to the stone walls, their fronts edging the four sides of the quad.

Opposite the front gate on the far side of the quad, against the inside of the north wall, stood the administrative building, a two-story structure. Staff offices lay on the ground floor and the officers' quarters on the second floor.

Along the inner east stone wall were the stables, storehouses, and the guardhouse. The stables had been looted, the horses were gone. The quad bore the tracks of their hoofprints, where they had been cleared out of the stables and herded off the barracks square, out the gate and on the road in a mass exodus.

The west wall was lined by barracks for the enlisted men, and a mess hall shared by officers and enlistees.

The administrative building had been trashed, ransacked, vandalized. Windows were all broken, with barely a shard of glass remaining in the frames.

Files lay strewn about in haphazard disorder. Papers—documents, heaping double armfuls of them—had been tossed out the windows, littering the barracks square. They'd been torn, shredded, and trampled under many hooves.

An attempt had been made to burn the building but it had been a flop. Ground-floor offices were burned out, gaping windows outlined by smeary soot and scorch marks. But the flames had failed to take hold and the structure remained relatively undamaged.

On a low mound bordered by a circle of paving stones was a flag stand. The flagpole was broken off near the base. The flag was torn, trampled, and partly burned, all but a tattered scrap of white stars on a blue field and red and white stripes.

Sam dismounted and picked it up, folding it and stashing it inside his shirt for safekeeping. He continued his observation on foot.

To one side stood a wellhead, a surface-level vent for the artesian well. The circular stone wellhead was topped by a peaked roof supported by four upright pillars. The rope attached to turn handles at one end and a bucket at the other had been cut. Sam peered into the well. The upper part of a dead man stood floating vertically upright in the water.

Shocking as the number of dead was, it could have been far worse. Sam judged that the complement of soldiers was way understrength, one-third or even a fourth of its usual complement of between 150 and 175 troops.

All the troopers showed signs of having died hard. Death was rarely pretty, violent death less so.

The bodies showed a strange divide. Some had died by conventional means—shot, mostly, with a few stabbings and bludgeonings. Most had died without a mark on them, yet paradoxically died hard. Those bodies lay twisted and contorted, their hands like claws, their faces agonized masks. Some showed streaks of dried blood that had run from mouth and nose or discolored foam covering nostrils and mouths. Heaps of vomit pooled everywhere.

Those corpses, which were in the vast majority, showed no marks of violence—no bullet holes or stab wounds. Nothing. *Nada.*

A mystery, a sinister mystery. Sam's nerves were rock steady, but the macabre scene of mass death was starting to get to him.

The buzzards—ah yes, the buzzards. Their presence, such as it was, added to the mystery.

Sam sensed they made up a significant piece of the puzzle. He looked up and noticed more had joined the party. It appeared there were scavenger birds airborne, circling their wheels without number, ever-alert for carrion. Predators they were not. They took no live prey. They never killed. They fed on table scraps of carcasses killed by others. They were specialists, eating only dead things, a needful part of the wasteland's self-cleansing cycle.

Most folks thought the birds found their carrion by sense of smell, but that was a misconception. Their famously keen eyesight was the secret of their success. They could spot a dead desert mouse from a quarter mile or more straight up.

Seeing dead bodies in the fort, the buzzard flock had no doubt eagerly swooped down for the feast. The forerunners, the first in line, set about their grisly task of scavenging. Taloned claws ripped and tore, wickedly sharp beaks pierced and shredded. Something went wrong then.

The seemingly bountiful banquet had proved fatal to them.

A number of buzzards lay strewn about the dirt of the sandy courtyard of the quad. Their forms were weirdly contorted, stiff-legged. Dead.

Other still-more opportunistic buzzards had attempted to feed on their fallen fellows. They, too, had succumbed.

Somewhere along the way, the buzzards had

gotten the idea that the dead of Fort Pardee were bad medicine—tainted—their flesh lethal to taste. So the remainder left them alone, shunning them. That patrol wheeling ceaselessly overhead in the sky kept vigil, but they had ruled Fort Pardee off-limits.

Sam tried to put the pieces together. What could have done it? Plague? But no epidemic was that virulent, acting with such speed as to take out so many all at once.

Also to consider was the evidence of violent death, looting, vandalism, and pillaging. A number of dead soldiers lay barefoot, their boots having been stolen. Men sick or dying of plague don't do that.

Poison?

That seemed the most likely solution. It fit the facts, the evidence of twisted unmarked bodies, and the greenish froth surrounding noses and mouths of so many dead.

Yes, poison would explain much. Who had administered the fatal dose?

Not the Comanches. Mass poisoning wasn't their style. Under exceptional circumstances such as relentless hot pursuit, they might poison a waterhole to halt a cavalry patrol, but never at this level.

While Sam was deep in thought, the sky began bleaching, losing its blue hue. Shadows grew, darkening. He went into the enlisted men's barracks. Only a few dead there and all by violence—shot.

Any familiar faces among them? Friends, comrades? He tried not to look. He didn't want to know. Later, yes, but not now. It was a sore trial for him to keep going, but did he owe the dead any less?

The quarters had been hastily looted, plundered. Soldiers' wooden chests were shattered into scraps and splinters to get at their contents. Blankets were stripped and stolen from beds, mattresses overturned and slashed, stuffing ripped out like spilled entrails.

Anyone who knew the army must know that the enlisted barracks would provide mighty slim pickings and the officer's quarters little better. Army pay was little enough to start with, barely a pittance. Most troopers drank up, whored, or gambled away their pay almost as soon as they had it.

Sam went out, glad to be quitting the barracks. He caught sight of the mess hall standing beside it, a long low single-story shed-like building with a long wall at the front. The kitchen was in an annex on the right-hand side to minimize heat of cooking in the eating hall during hot weather.

Here lay the height of horror, the black heart of the whole deadly business.

A handful of bodies lay in a fan-shaped display outside the mess hall's front entrance. They all lay with their heads farthermost from the entryway as though they had been fleeing the building when the poison took them.

A hazy miasma hung floating about the open door and windows. Sam stood in the doorway looking in, a sign of how unsettled he was. Trail craft had long schooled him in the folly of standing outlined in a doorway where a man made a particularly inviting target.

But he was rooted to the spot.

About three dozen dead men were heaped on the mess hall floor. Tables and benches lay overturned amid piles of corpses. Plates, tableware, and spilled food were strewn about everywhere.

"An unholy mess," he mumbled.

The stench was a physical thing, a yellowish haze that stung Sam's eyes, making them burn. The bandanna covering his nose and mouth might as well not have been there for all the good it did.

Unholy mess.

Luckily he was holding his breath; in the shock of revelation he had forgotten for a moment to breathe. Bile rose in the back of his throat, his gorge rising.

Unholy.

Sam had seen enough, too much. He had seen all he needed to see, all he needed to know:

The men had been poisoned at their meal!

He stepped back, stumbling, coughing, and choking. By accident, he stepped on a dead man's limb, nearly losing his footing. He staggered a dozen paces away, gasping for breath. Tearing away the bandanna, he sucked great heaving breaths of air.

Blessed relief. Bad as the air was in the fort, it was far better than that of the miasmic mess hall.

Sam swore aloud, cursing the race of poisoners, damning them to eternity—

A voice came then, a weak shout. Had he imagined it?

No, there it was again!

"Help! . . . Help!"

A voice crying for help in the fortress of the dead.

Eighteen

The voice crying out for help was raw, weak, and cracking with strain. It came from behind Sam. He turned and looked around, scanning for the source of the sound.

A flicker of motion showed on the far side of the square, in a small barred window of the guardhouse.

Sam made his way to it, glad to quit the hell of the mess hall. His rifle was held hip-high, leveled and ready for trouble. The cries increased in volume and frequency as he neared the army jail.

Discipline must be maintained on post. Infractions of the rules brought about forfeited pay, fines, punishment work details, and forced marches. More serious violations put the offender behind the bars of a detention cell in the guardhouse. Major crimes resulted in the offender being sentenced to a period of hard labor at such military prisons as the one at Fort Leavenworth, Kansas.

The motion which had caught Sam's eye was that of an arm waving through the bars of a small window in the upper left-hand corner of the guardhouse. It was a squat, stubby, flat-roofed, single-story blockhouse set in the northwest corner of the rampart walls. It was made of stone quarried from the foothills of the Breaks, timber being rare on the plains and too expensive to cart overland, especially with all that potential free labor of the garrison troops on tap. The gray-brown limestone blocks were dressed, fitted, and held together by mortar at the joins.

The guardhouse wasn't big on windows, held to be a security risk. Their use was limited to the minimum needed for health and hygiene of guards and secondarily, prisoners. There were enough windows to let in sunlight and fresh air. Cell windows were small square slits placed high in the walls, with iron bars set in the casements.

The guardhouse door gaped open and uninviting. Sam entered, stepping into a large space. The interior was damp, dank, and gloomy, heavily shadowed at the hour of near-dusk.

The front space was taken up by a small office area with a desk, chair, and several filing cabinets. A wall rack with rows of hooks held forbidding-looking sets of restraints—fetters, manacles, handcuffs, and suchlike devices. It held, too, whips, quirts, and truncheons.

A dead man lay on the office floor beside an overturned wooden stool. His uniform identified him as a guard. He was a soldier, big, solid, and stolid with a squat thug-like face. Prison guards needed to be tough and army prison guards that much more so.

A black leather belt four inches wide circled the dead man's waist. Fastened to it were a leather club the size of a belaying pin, a set of handcuffs, an oversized ring of keys, and a holstered gun.

Details of the scene told a tale, revealing the great hidden in the small.

On the floor near the guard lay a metal cafeteria-style tray and an overturned wooden bowl containing some stew-like mess of meat and liquid, most of it spilled. Beside a puddle of the slop lay a dead rat. It lay on its back, glazed beady eyes sightless and staring. Its four legs stuck out stiffly from its body at right angles, twisted claw-like paws clutching empty air.

The stuff in the bowl—some stew-like concoction from the look of it—was *poisoned*.

The toxin must be strong stuff. The mass puddled on the floor, showing that the guard hadn't taken more than a few bites before being struck down dead. His paw-like hand still held a tablespoon, clutching it in a death grip.

The dead soldier's face held an expression of outrage, as though indignant at being slain by poison rather than by some more martial means.

Sam reckoned that the rat must have come out of hiding to sample the spilled chow, and the poison killed it. "So much for the dead guard, dead rat, and poisoned meal," he told himself, moving on to the survivor.

Apart from the central office area, the rest of the space was partitioned off into cells. Six in all, they were minimal cage-like affairs made of gridded iron bars with inset hinged locking doors. Each cell came furnished with a crude wooden bed, thin mattress pallet, and a wooden bucket for sanitary necessities.

All of the cells but one were empty, untenanted. It held a prisoner, a live one. Sam found it somehow heartening to find another living being in the fort of death. He went to the cell for a closer look at the caged wonder man.

The prisoner was big, hulking, built like a circus strongman. He was a no-neck monster with a head perched atop broad slab shoulders. He wore a red flannel shirt and blue cavalryman's pants with yellow stripes running down the sides.

He was bald, his shaved skull looking like a melon rind, so scored was it with scars, creases, dents, and lines. He sported a big black mustache under an eagle-beak nose and above a lantern jaw.

The prisoner seemed somewhat out of sorts, judging by his appearance. His eyes bulged and veins stood out like baby snakes writhing atop his hairless skull dome. He was sweat-soaked, gnashing his teeth. The wooden frame bed in his cell had been smashed to pieces.

His distress was understandable, considering the circumstances.

"Let me out of here, friend," the prisoner rasped, voice coarse and husky, the result perhaps of having shouted for help until his throat was raw.

"Friend?" Was he friend, or foe? Sam wondered, thinking the prisoner looked familiar. He might have seen him around the fort on previous visits. Recognition tugged, nagging Sam with a sense of familiarity. The prisoner was a distinct type, not easily forgotten once seen.

"When I first saw you, I wasn't sure if you was one of them or not," the inmate said. "But when I heard you come out of the mess hall cussing a blue streak, calling down hell's fire on the ones who did this, I knew you were okay.

"I thought I was never going to get out of here. I had some crazy idea of using the bedframe as a battering ram to bust the bars out of the window," he went on, looking sheepish. "All I did was bust the bed into splinters."

"You never would have fit out the window anyway," Sam said.

"Maybe not, but I sure would have tried," the prisoner said, showing signs of agitation. "Come on, mister, let me out of here!"

"The keys?" Sam asked.

"On a ring hanging on a hook on the wall near the door."

"Be right back." Sam turned and went back into the office. He found the key ring where the prisoner had said, an oversized metal hoop as wide across as a cake plate. It held a long solid blue steel key that seemed made for opening cell door locks, and a lot of little lesser keys.

Sam took it and returned to the cell. "A word of advice. I'm not the trusting type. What I've seen here in the fort so far sets my teeth on edge. So don't make any sudden or suspicious moves. I might shoot. I'm the nervous type."

"You look it," the prisoner said sarcastically. "Do what you like, but for Pete's sake let me out of here. I've been going crazy since dinnertime last night when the troops started screaming and dropping like flies—" He fell silent, shuddering.

Sam handed him the key ring. "Here, let yourself out," Sam said, stepping back a few paces. He held the rifle level at hip height, pointing not at the prisoner but in his general direction.

The prisoner gripped the key, reaching through

and around the bars to fit it into the keyhole of the cell door lock. He turned it, metal squeaking as tumblers turned and the bolt slid back. He opened the door and stepped out of the cage, shambling down the aisle into the front office.

He paused, looking down at the dead guard, studying on him. "Thanks, Fritz," he said at last. "You dirty, rotten, no-good son of a—!"

"He's dead, soldier," Sam Heller said dryly.

The trooper looked up with a crooked, broken-toothed, jack-o'-lantern grin. "Fritz here was having some fun with me last night, making me wait for my dinner while he ate his first. Turned out, he saved my life. He took a couple spoonfuls of that chili, then jumped up like he'd been struck by lightning. He grabbed his throat, let out a holler, and dropped to the floor like a poleaxed steer, *dead*."

The cavalryman took a close look as if seeing Sam for the first time. He frowned furiously, ridged brow furrowing, thick black brows knitting in concentration. Some of the fierceness faded as dawning recognition flickered in his eyes. "Hey, I know you."

"Do you?" Sam said.

"Yes, I do—you're the bounty killer, a friend of Captain Harrison's," the trooper said. "The one who cleaned up on the Harbin bunch. I've seen you come in to the fort a couple times."

"That's right," Sam said, seeing no harm and some possible benefit in admitting the obvious truth.

"I knew it!" the trooper crowed. "Thought I recognized you before like I said. Figured I'd take a chance you wasn't one of *them*. I was going crazy in here, scared nobody would come to let me out." His voice was thick with emotion.

"I've seen you around here," Sam said, certain now. "You're a corporal."

"Private now. I got busted down in rank for drinking on duty," the trooper said. "That's why I'm in here, doing a stretch in the calaboose. Hell, I used to be a sergeant, but I lost my stripes for brawling." He wasn't bragging exactly but not ashamed, either. "I'm Berg, Otto Berg—Private First Class Otto Berg now. What's your handle?"

"The name's Heller, Sam Heller."

"Glad to know you, Heller, I owe you for getting me out of that cell," Otto Berg said, thrusting out an over-sized hand. "Shake!"

Sam decided to take a chance, shifting his rifle to the other hand and reaching out to the trooper. Otto had big strong hands, a powerful grip. Sam tightened his own grip. If this was to be a test of strength, he'd be damned if he'd come out second best.

It was and he didn't. Sam stepped up the pressure, causing Otto Berg to break off the handshake first.

"That's a strong grip you've got there, brother," the trooper said, trying not to wince.

"Is it? I hadn't noticed," Sam said nonchalantly, smiling to himself a moment later when he saw Otto surreptitiously trying to massage some feeling back into his hand.

"Got any water?" Otto asked. "I'm parched. The last of my waters ran out this morning and I ain't had a drink all day."

"There's a body floating in the well," Sam began.

"Mister, I ain't eating or drinking nothing inside this fort," Otto said feelingly. "No telling what's been poisoned!"

"Good thinking," Sam said. "I've got a canteen out on my horse by the gate."

"Let's get out of here. I've had enough of this guardhouse to last me nine lifetimes!"

Sam and Otto went outside, the trooper moving unsteadily.

"I'm a little shaky on my pins," Otto said, grinning weakly.

"Need a hand?" Sam asked.

"No, I can make it. You said something about water?"

"Canteen on my saddle. Wait here, I'll get it." Sam crossed the quad to where Dusty was tethered near the front gate.

"Damnation!" Otto whispered, looking around in shocked awe. He went to the storehouse next to the guardhouse, weaving and staggering.

When Sam returned, Otto was sitting on the shallow wooden steps, elbows on knees, head in hands hanging down. He didn't look up when Sam stood over him.

Sam put a hand on Otto's shoulder, which felt like a big round rock under the shirt, and shook him.

Otto started, looking up groggily, bleary eyes coming into focus. "Huh! I must have drifted off."

"Here," Sam said, passing him the canteen.

The trooper drank greedily, throat working. Sam had a passing thought about cautioning the other to drink slowly but kept silent. Otto could take care of himself. As for resupplying, there was fresh water in the creek beyond the fort's north wall.

"Thanks," Otto croaked gratefully, lowering the canteen. His voice was still harsh and rasping. He wiped his wet mouth with the back of a ham-sized hand.

Sam unsheathed his knife, cutting off a chunk of beef jerky. He'd eaten the last of the parched corn earlier that day. "Here. It ain't much, but it's all I got."

"It looks like plenty to me. It ain't poisoned neither and I thank you for that," Otto said.

There was no way to eat beef jerky fast. It was too tough. Otto stuffed a chunk into a corner of his mouth and began working on it between his jaws, methodically grinding it. Several mouthfuls of water helped moisten it up. "I'm starting to feel better already."

"More?" Sam asked.

"I could use a chunk for later if you could spare it," Otto said.

Sam cut another piece of jerky, then slipped the blade back in its sheath.

"That's some pigsticker you got there," Otto said appreciatively, his mouth full.

"Gets the job done. Otto, what the hell happened here?"

"We got hit by the Free Company."

"The Free Company! I didn't think they were this far west."

"Well," Otto Berg said heavily, "they are. Two weeks ago, Captain Harrison took most of the company into the Uplands and beyond to look for them. General Phil Sheridan figured Turlock might try making a sneak through South Comancheria."

"So that's where most of the unit is! I was wondering," Sam said.

"While the troops are out on a wild goose chase up on the Canadian River looking for Turlock, the Free

Company came here." Otto was thoughtful, brooding. "I should have been with them, but I got written up for drinking on duty. Hell, I wasn't drunk. I'm never drunk . . . but rules are rules. They busted me down to private and gave me thirty days in the guardhouse."

"And . . . the poisoning?" Sam prompted.

"Fort Pardee has never been taken by force or siege, never! So how did it get took? They had a Judas on the inside, a she-Judas." Otto shook his head over the infamy of it all.

"Who?" Sam Heller asked

"Malvina. Malvina the cook."

"A civilian cook?" Sam said, somewhat taken aback. The Army made a practice of using its own to get the work done, not farming it out to outsiders. "What's wrong with army cooking?"

"What ain't?" Otto fired back, mustering up a halfway grin to show he was joking. "I take that back, though, Army cooks don't poison you. Not on purpose, that is."

"Who's this Malvina?" Sam demanded. "I never heard of her."

"Malvina the Gypsy, the old witch. Malvina the *Bruja*, the Mexicans call her. She may not be a Gypsy, but she sure as hell is a witch," Otto said. "A devil! One of the Hog Ranch crowd."

"Ah," Sam said, beginning to understand. The Hog Ranch! They'd been at the heart of this murky business from the start.

"They were shorthanded in the kitchen," Otto explained. "One of Cookie's helpers went over the hill, deserted. Another got beat up so bad one night when he was off-post that they had to send him back East to recover. They never did find the one who did it or even a motive for the attack."

"The motive was to get him out of the kitchen and Malvina in," Sam offered.

"It's easy to see the pattern now that everything's gone down the way it has, but nobody had a clue that it was all part of a plot. I had a lot of time alone in my cell since last night to think things out, so I can see how it all came together."

"It was a setup. I'll wager that the other cook's helper was no deserter, either. His body's probably buried in an unmarked grave somewhere in the hills around the Hog Ranch," Sam said grimly.

"No bet. That's a sure thing," Otto agreed. "The post laundry was already using Malvina as a laundress so she was right in place to promote herself for the kitchen job."

Sam nodded. It made sense. In frontier posts, laundress was one of the few jobs traditionally filled by civilian women.

"The hell of it is that Malvina was a pretty good cook," Otto said. "Better than Cookie, the Army chef. Poor Cookie! I wonder what happened to him?"

"He was probably one of the first to go once the poisoning got underway. Being headman in the kitchen put him in place to see too much, know too much," Sam said.

"It'd be a mercy if he died before he could see his mess hall turned into a slaughterhouse," Otto said sadly.

"How did it go down?"

"One of boys bagged a deer while out hunting, so Malvina offered to make venison chili. A real treat for the troops, right?" Otto's laughter was harsh, mirthless. Merciless.

"Everybody was looking forward to it," he went on. "She even mixed up a special batch for the officers at the staff building. You know how the troops are. A bunch of chowhounds, always hungry. When that chili was served out, they must have dug right in.

"Then pure hell broke loose in the mess hall. Shouts, screams, all kinds of carryings-on. I never heard anything like it before—and I've been in the wars. Civil and Indian. I hope to God I never hear anything like it again. I was in the guardhouse on the opposite side of the fort from the mess hall and I could hear it clearly, too clearly."

A shiver ran through Otto Berg, causing him to quake for an instant, though the early evening air was still warm. "Remember, some of this I saw, some I heard and some of the blanks I got to fill in by guessing."

"Go on, Otto. You're doing fine. Tell it," Sam said.

"The Hog Ranch crowd must have been outside the fort, hiding and waiting. A couple got inside the fort. I don't know how. The front gate was guarded and there were guards on the walls. But the Hogs got inside. I know this, though. The first band were wearing cavalry uniforms. Once they were inside, they were able to approach the guards and get close enough to kill them quietly, probably with knives."

"That clears up something that's been puzzling me." Sam told Otto how he had earlier prowled the deserted Hog Ranch, discovering several male bodies that had been stripped of their garments down to their drawers. "They must have been troopers from the fort, killed for their uniforms so the infiltrators could disguise themselves as cavalrymen and have the free run of the fort. As for the dead women at the ranch— maybe they got cold feet and couldn't be trusted, maybe they were too drunk to ride a horse, maybe they were just in the way . . . Who knows?"

Otto continued his tale. "When mass poisoning pandemonium broke out, the disguised Hog Ranchers rushed the front gate, gunning down the sentries. They opened the gate, letting the rest of their fellows in. Troy Madison was there, Hump Colway, Kinney Scopes, Half-Shot, and some others from the Ranch I know in passing. I've spent plenty of time off duty there. None were what you'd call friends, but you could have a drink or ten and some laughs with them, as long as you kept your eyes open and your wits about you. I've gotten drunk with them many a time, bought them drinks, and cadged drinks from them . . . Hell! Let it go . . .

"While they were killing my brothers in arms, where was I? Locked in my cell! My window looked out on the quad, so I had a pretty good view of what was happening. But first, Fritz the turnkey went to the kitchen to pick up my dinner and his ahead of the rush. He thought it was funny to make me wait for my chow. He dug a spoon into my bowl of chili and started digging in, eating it in front of me. Then the thunderbolt hit. I didn't know what was happening. I thought maybe he was choking on a bone stuck in his throat or throwing a fit, until he fell to the floor dead.

"When the Hog Ranch rode in and started killing everybody, I finally figured out what was happening. I kept out of sight as best I could, peeking out of the bottom of the window, not showing myself.

"There were some troops who hadn't eaten because

they weren't hungry or were on duty and planned to eat later or maybe they just plain didn't like venison chili. Hog Ranch men hunted them down and killed them, then set to robbing and tearing the place apart.

"They were almighty thorough. A couple came in here to make sure of a clean sweep. I saw them coming and climbed the bars to the top of the cell. I wedged myself out of sight, hanging on to the rafter beams running under the ceiling. I was out of sight as long as nobody looked up. Two came in. Luckily, they didn't stay long. They made sure Fritz was dead and the cells were empty. From what they could see, the cells *were* empty. They were in a hurry. Guess they didn't want to miss out on their share of the looting.

"I was just about finished, played out by the time they left. I thought my arms would tear out of their sockets. Nobody came back though, and it's a good thing. I don't think I could have done it again.

"The Hog Ranch was real big on tearing up the staff building. They took all the paperwork and threw it out the windows, burning big piles of it," Otto said.

"Probably wanted to destroy any records about themselves," Sam suggested. "Captain Harrison must have had his intelligence officer keep files on Hog Ranch, a pack of suspicious characters to any commanding officer."

"About two hours after the Hog Ranch came in, the Free Company rolled in—talk about your suspicious characters! A robber bandit army of marauders that makes the Hogs look like a Sunday school picnic by comparison."

"Was Jimbo Turlock with them?" Sam asked.

"Not so's I could tell."

"Big heavyset fellow about fifty. Looks more like a banker than a bandit chief."

"I've seen pictures of him on Wanted posters, but I didn't see anybody that looked like him."

"With Free Company around, Jimbo must be near."

"Not that I could see. Maybe he's keeping out of sight for some reason of his own."

"Could be," Sam allowed. "Turlock is a deep player, wheels within wheels."

Otto shrugged. "If he was here, I didn't see him. That doesn't mean he wasn't here, just that I didn't see him. All I saw was what I could see from my jail cell window.

"When Free Company arrived, they put things on a businesslike basis. They picked the fort clean like a plague of locusts. They cleared horses out of the stables, broke into the armory, and stole all the guns and ammunition. They loaded the loot into wagons, stole food and supplies out of the storehouse, blankets, too. Hell, they even stole our cannon. Hitched a team of horses to the howitzer and rolled it out of here. They're loaded for bear now!

"On the way out a couple of them threw some torches into the staff building. One of their handlers gave them hell for it. For a while, I thought he was gonna shoot a couple as an object lesson to the rest. He didn't, but he reamed them out good. Said it was stupid to burn down the fort because they were the masters of it. They could hold it against the rest of the cavalry unit when they returned from patrol and ambush them. So the fort stayed unburnt after all."

"But they didn't stay to occupy it. Didn't even leave behind a platoon to secure it," Sam pointed out.

"Maybe they didn't feel like setting up housekeeping

with a pile of freshly poisoned corpses," Otto said sourly. "I'm minded to get out of here myself!"

"We'll be gone soon."

"I got the impression that Free Company had something pretty important to do, some mission yet to accomplish. It's just a feeling, but I've been Army long enough to know when a unit is moving out for more action."

"I trust your instincts, Otto."

"When Free Company rolled out, the Hog Ranch went with them. They're part of Free Company now."

"Easier to get into than out of," Sam said.

"Yeah—like the cavalry," Otto retorted. He sagged with fatigue and emotional strain, slumping. "Well, that's it. The rest you know."

"Let's get out of here." Sam said.

He ran to Dusty and rode outside the fort, quickly rounding up a horse for Otto—one with a saddle still strapped to its back. While he was gone, Otto managed to find a rifle, a couple of pistols, and some ammunition. He wasted no time arming himself.

Sam returned with the horse for Otto, and he mounted up. A quick discussion followed, and they decided to water the horses and fill their canteens at the creek behind the fort since they didn't trust the food or the water supply inside. They discovered a set of scaling ropes rigged with three-pronged grappling hooks at the ends, hung from the rear wall of the fort. Standing outside at the foot of the wall, the infiltrators had grappled the hooks to the top of the wall, climbing up the outer wall and down the other side. That was how they'd breached the fort's outer defenses.

Tasks completed, Sam and Otto hastened away.

NINETEEN

Johnny Cross and Coot Dooley were up early in the morning doing some hunting. Manhunting? Maybe, depending on how things fell out. Or in.

It was morning of the third day since Johnny and Luke had returned from Hangtree and morning of the day after Sam Heller rode into Fort Pardee. But of what had transpired to turn the fort into a charnel house, the occupants of Cross Ranch were as yet blissfully unaware.

Johnny and Coot roamed the north section of the Cross ranch. The ranch was the westernmost such habitation in Hangtree County, the better part of a half-day's ride west of town. It lay north of the Hangtree Trail at the foot of the eastern range of the Breaks. The land was well-watered by a stream that took its source in the hills, winding a snakelike course southeast for many a mile before feeding into the north branch of the Liberty River.

It had been claimed and settled by Pa Cross some years before the war, when Johnny was just a lad. He was the last of the family still alive. Frontier life was hard and took its toll through natural causes and violence alike.

Johnny and Coot were breakfasted and mounted up on horseback, making the rounds of the range. The sun was just edging the eastern horizon, slanting long yellow shafts of brilliance across the landscape.

Johnny rode a fine chestnut horse with Arabian and North African blood from some distant equine forebears before the line came to the New World with the conquistadors. The animal was the kind of mount he favored from back in the war days when he rode with Quantrill in Missouri, a horse fast, sleek, with plenty of endurance.

Coot Dooley rode a brown and white pinto cow pony. Swift and nimble, it was a cutting horse.

A half mile north of the ranch house, they rode up a flat-topped knoll that commanded a good view of the surroundings. Knots of cattle wandered, grazing across the range. Looking south from the knoll, the duo could see the north slope of the mound that was an integral part of the old Cross ranch house.

When the family had first staked out the claimed land, Pa Cross dug into the south slope of the mound to build a dugout. He had excavated several rooms, shoring up walls and ceiling with laboriously hand-hewn timber beams, rafters, and braces. The front was walled off by stones cemented with mortar. The front door was made of thick fire-hardened oak planks and beams. The few windows were protected by fire-hardened wooden shutters fitted with loopholes for shooting out of in case of attack. And attacks there were, from Indians and outlaws.

Some improvements had been made to the ranch in the months since Johnny had come home. The stable barn had been rebuilt and refurbished, as had the corral and some of the outbuildings. New wooden wings, square rooms, had been added on to the east and west sides of the dugout to provide elbow room for the new tenants.

Johnny and Luke were partners in the ranch, as well as in several other enterprises including mustanging, cattle raising, and selling their guns for hire. Thus far gun work paid best, though the cattle ranching was starting to come into its own.

The ranch's nearness to Wild Horse Canyon with its numerous herd of mustangs had inspired Johnny to go mustanging—catching wild horses, breaking them to bridle, saddle, and riders, and selling them at market. He had a contract with the procurement officer at Fort Pardee to sell horses to the Army. It paid pretty well.

Being a Texas rancher, Johnny just couldn't help but get involved in the cattle-raising business. During the war, countless longhorn cattle had gone into the brush untended and unclaimed. Thriving there, they were fruitful and multiplied so that at war's end hundreds of thousands of cattle were running wild and free throughout the Lone Star state.

The livestock surplus coincided with a great hunger for beef in the industrial cities of the North. A beef worth five dollars in Texas was worth ten times that much at the railhead in Sedalia, Missouri. Entrepreneurial, ever-hungry, the ranchers of Hangtree County had gotten into the cattle business in a big way.

So great was the demand that visionary entrepreneurs were raising a town in Abilene, Kansas, to meet the transcontinental railroad surging west. But in the summer of 1867, the dawning of Abilene's day lay ahead in the future.

With no neighbors near, the Cross spread and surroundings were thick with wild longhorn cattle. Johnny and Luke often went into the brush, rounding up the ornery maverick critters and branding them. Their brand was the "Cross Bow," consisting of two arrows crisscrossed in an X shape on a rocker. Their herd had been part of a big cattle drive by the Hangtree County ranchers to Sedalia the past summer. Johnny and Luke had come out of it pretty well.

They had added two ranch hands to their outfit, Coot Dooley and Vic Vargas.

Coot was an old-timer, white-haired and white-bearded with the energy of a much younger man. Tough, sinewy, and leathery, he'd been many things in his day—a day he boasted was far from done. He'd been an explorer, mountain man, Army scout, hunter, trapper, Indian fighter, and soldier. He'd fought in the War for Texas Independence, the Mexican-American War, the War Between the States, and countless "little wars without a name," as he called them.

Vic Vargas was a powerfully built young man with curly black hair and a fierce mustachio. He was from Mextown in Hangtree, an ace ranch hand with a vested interest and percentage of the profits and a ready fast gun with plenty of guts. His résumé was far shorter than Coot Dooley's, but he'd been alive a lot shorter time. He burned to make his mark on the frontier and his fame fill the minds of men and women.

Luke and Vic had stayed behind to guard the ranch. It was agreed that both pairs not wander off by themselves where they could be picked off more easily by old enemies or new—the Free Company or whomever.

Johnny and Coot hadn't ridden out to admire the view. They had dismounted and were looking around with a purpose and a particular point of view.

The grass of the knoll had recently been trampled down by a number of horses. Discarded butts of hand-rolled cigarettes littered the turf. Hoofprints were thicker at the foot of the knoll on the north side, where they would have been screened from sight from those at the ranch house. Grass and leaves had been heavily browsed where the horses had grazed.

"Like I said when I come in from riding trail yesterday, somebody's been sure 'nuff dogging us."

Johnny agreed. "You were right, Coot."

"That's what I like to hear!" Coot said, slapping his thigh to enthusiastically underline his words.

"Why not? It don't cost me nothing to say so."

"That's what you think. Jest wait till I hit you up for a raise, boss."

"You wait," Johnny said. "And do me a favor—wait a long time."

"Why so tightfisted? You got plenty of money," Coot said.

"I've got a lot of expenses, including a lazy, no-working, no-account son of a gun on the payroll, not to mention eating me out of house and home."

Coot tsk-tsked, shaking his head sadly. "Oh, young Vic ain't all that bad."

"Who's talking about Vic?" Johnny asked.

"Surely you don't mean pore ol' hardworking Luke!" Coot exclaimed. "He does drink too much, though Lord knows he's got reason to."

"No, I don't mean Luke, and I'm sure not low-rating myself. You figure out who's the party in question."

"I resent those remarks, so I'll jest pass over them with silence," Coot said, assuming an attitude of sorely tried dignity.

"A refreshing change, especially the silence part. I'm looking forward to it." Johnny eyed the horse tracks at the knoll, studying on them. "Three or four watchers, from the look of things. Those are marks of iron horseshoes, so they're not Indians. That and the cigarette butts pretty well prove that. Could they be rustlers, maybe?"

"No sign that any of the stock's been run off, Johnny. And rustlers are more likely to stay away from the ranch house, not close to it. They been watching us!"

"Dry-gulchers, maybe. Ambushers." Johnny sounded undisturbed by the prospect.

"There's more," Coot continued. "T'other night while you and Luke was in town, I seed lights in the cut. Torches, I'd say. Been meaning to mention it to you, but I plumb forgot."

"Better late than never." Unconsciously, Johnny ran his hands over the omnipresent twin Colts in hip holsters, but for him, it was only the beginning. A veteran pistol fighter in the Missouri Long Rider tradition, he had armed himself with several other revolvers—one worn in the top of his waistband and a smaller caliber gun tucked in his pants at the small of his back.

Coot Dooley had a well-worn .44 at his right hip, a tomahawk-style war hatchet and knife at his belt, and a Spencer carbine in his saddle scabbard.

"The tracks lead over to the Breaks. Let's follow them and see where they lead," Johnny said.

They mounted up, pointing their horses west toward the hills. No rain had fallen for the last few days, so the tracks remained intact. Sunlight at the riders' backs threw a golden glow on the foothills, the light climbing ever higher on the range as the sun rose.

Johnny and Coot threw long shadows as they neared the vertical rock walls looming ahead. A keen-eyed search unearthed another spot that the unknown watchers had used as an observation post to spy on the ranch. Sets of tracks indicated that the Unseen had made more than one such visit in the past few days.

All the tracks came from the cut—Cross's Cut, as it was called—and returned there. It was a pass running east-west through the Breaks into Wild Horse Canyon, which ran west of and parallel to the north-south range of hills.

They rode into the cut. It was several hundred yards wide and a half mile long. Purple-blue shadows lay at the far end of the passage where the sunlight had not yet reached. The two rode to the cut's western mouth at the opposite end.

The Breaks was not a single range but a group of several ranges of high rocky limestone hills and ridges running north-south. Wild Horse Canyon lay between the eastern range and the next long parallel ridge of the Breaks. It was well-watered with good grazing land. Hundreds of free-roving mustangs lived there, using it as a corridor to access a wide expanse of grassy valleys nestled in the hills. The terrain featured lots of side-pockets, draws, and gaps—good hiding places.

As a place of refuge for the hunted, it attracted

not only wild horses but wild men. Indians, outlaws, fugitives, hermits, half-crazed solitary wayfarers, and such had all made the canyon their home at one time or another.

The canyon was cool and hazy, the grass dewy. Chuckling, purling sounds of streams and rivulets could be heard throughout the canyon.

"No mustangs to be seen hereabouts today, Johnny."

"Could be they were scared off by strangers, Coot. Plenty of comings and goings here lately," Johnny said, indicating tracks on the turf.

It was easy to tell the difference between the hoof-prints of wild horses and those of mounted men. Mustangs went unshod. The horses of men bore the unmistakable imprint of iron horseshoes. Indian ponies were often unshod, but the hoofprints of mounted men dug deeper into the ground due to their heavier weight.

Any number of tracks were laid down over the springy turf. The strangers never traveled alone, always riding in groups of no fewer than three men at one time, and often as many as a half dozen. They not only went back and forth to the cut but south toward the Notch and Buffalo Hump, too far distant to be seen.

"Most of them tracks lead farther north," Coot said.

"Let's follow them," said Johnny.

Follow them they did.

The cool morning air was freshened with moisture from the many streams of the canyon. Ghostly fleeting images of horses in the distance flitted in and out of sight, quick and elusive as cloud shadows.

Johnny and Coot rode on for several miles. They were watchful, talking little. Tracks of intruders curved to the left going from Wild Horse Canyon into the pass that ran through the western spine of the Breaks to the plains and the limitless Llano beyond.

A massive rock buttress shouldered deep into the western pass, forcing Johnny and Coot to go around it to proceed farther.

"Looks like that's where them rascals have been coming from," Coot said, leaning to one side in the saddle for a better look at the horse tracks.

"And here they are," Johnny declared flatly, his soft-spoken voice quivering with implicit menace. Menace that radiated, not menace felt.

Rounding the blind corner of the rock limb, Johnny and Coot suddenly saw a group of riders coming from the west end of the pass. Johnny's thumbs stealthily slipped the rawhide thong loops at the tops of his twin holstered Colts, readying them for action. He and Coot were confronted by five well-armed strangers.

A stir went through the others at the sight of the duo. Low mean laughter sounded.

Johnny and Coot looked cool, unflappable. And why not? Both had made a longtime habit of riding into trouble and, what's more important, riding out of it. They might have been out for a pleasant Sunday ride, so calm and unaffected did they seem. Unruffled as a clear pond surface on a windless day.

A close observer might have noticed a peculiar change come over Johnny's eyes. Ordinarily, they were hazel in color, a kind of yellow-brownish hue. They were changeable by nature, sometimes shading more yellow than brown, other times more brown than yellow. Their color could depend on many things of the moment—the season, time of day or night, the light or lack of it and, especially, Johnny's mercurial moods.

When he was heading into trouble, the yellow hue predominated, giving his eyes a catlike glow as if shining with an eerie inner light. For more than a few men, those shiny yellow orbs were the last thing they saw in this life.

Johnny and Coot advanced their horses at a walk.

The strangers were little more than a stone's throw away. They looked like—were—hardcases. Some were recognizable. Troy Madison and Kinney Scopes were part of the Hog Ranch crowd, an important part. Troy was the outfit's resident fast gun and Kinney was a versatile, devious crook-of-all-trades. All lawless trades, that is.

Also present was Buck Thornton, a sometime scout for wagon trains passing through Hangtree. Apparently the wagon trains had passed through, but Buck remained.

The other two were strangers to Johnny. One was a youngster who looked barely out of his mid-teens, if that. He had a mop of sandy hair, round blue eyes, a snub nose, and a shiny-smooth pink face. Draped on his undersized frame, the big-caliber gun in his hip holster looked like an oversized horse pistol, almost too big for his neat small hands.

The other man had a lion's mane of unkempt wiry iron-gray hair and long narrow eyes. His weather-beaten face was a mass of wrinkles where it wasn't covered by a long straggly salt-and-pepper beard.

"Psst! That baby-faced kid is Brat Sisely," Coot said in a stage whisper only Johnny could hear. "Don't let his looks fool you. He's lightning fast—killed twelve men in gunfights that I know of. Take him first. I'll take Troy."

"Uh-huh," Johnny murmured, letting the oldster know he'd gotten the message.

"Howdy, boys," Kinney Scopes said, smirking. He'd just commenced the endgame whether he knew it or not. A tough, rowdy loudmouth, he wore a battered high-crowned hat, tufts of hair sticking out the sides over a jowly face whose receding chin sprouted a mass of billy goat whiskers.

"This here's Johnny Cross, a big man in these parts and fast with a gun," Scopes announced to his partners. It was his way of alerting those who didn't know who Johnny Cross was that he could shoot.

"Never heard of him," Sisely piped up in a high-pitched boyish voice.

"You should have," Madison said, looking a bit sullen around eyes and mouth. "He ain't no green-horn."

"And I am?" Sisely challenged. Something in his voice, some note or tone evocative of a whiny, smart-alecky kid sassing off raised the hackles of every grown man within hearing distance.

"Don't take offense where none is offered, boy," Madison said, his sullenness increasing. It was clear there was no love lost between him and the youngster.

"Don't tell me what to do!" Sisely shrilled, bridling. "And don't call me *boy*, I don't like it!"

"Now, now lad. Don't go picking fights with your friends," soothed the prune-faced man with the lion's mane of hair and wild beard.

"I don't want none of your advice, Titus Gow. You ain't my pa!" Sisley retorted.

"It's good advice. Pretty soon you won't have no

friends left to pick fights with," Gow said with seeming good cheer. "'Specially not with that quick trigger finger of yours," he added with a laugh.

"Dog my cats if it ain't Buck Thornton," Coot said conversationally across the narrow gap between him and Johnny and the oncoming riders. When they were facing each other, he went on as if merely passing the time of day. "Hardly expected to see you in these parts, Buck." In reality, so much more than that was going on beneath the surface of the chance encounter. The undercurrents were running deep.

Buck Thornton wore a fringed buckskin jacket and a flat-crowned hat with a snakeskin hatband. His six-gun was worn in a soft, rawhide, Mexican-style buscadero holster rig.

"Last I seed of you, Buck, you was scouting for Major Adams and a wagon train of pilgrims headed for Califor-nye-ay."

"The major and I came to a parting of the ways, Coot," Thornton said easily.

"Haw!" Scopes's laughter was explosive, raw, and taunting, provoking a glare from Buck Thornton. "Major Adams fired his ass off the wagon train after ol' Buck got somebody's unmarried daughter in the family way!"

"Shut up, Scopes," Thornton said tightly, his face coloring red from the neck up.

Scopes's broad grin radiated undimmed.

"Nothing to be ashamed of, Buck. You was just doing what comes natural." Gow made a show of looking around at his fellows. "Ain't a one of us here that ain't made a slip one time or another."

"I'll say!" Scopes said, laughing his loud jack-ass bray.

"And done worse than getting some pore little Sunbonnet Sue with a child," Gow added.

"Ain't that the truth!" Scopes chimed in.

Madison kept aloof from the horseplay, remaining serious and unsmiling. He was watching Johnny's hands and eyes. Watching closely.

Resting folded hands on top of the saddle horn, Gow leaned forward, eyes nearly swallowed up in a nest of wrinkled creases as he squinted at Coot, studying him. "I know you," he said with the preoccupied air of one struggling to recall a memory. "I know you from someplace. Wish I could recollect where . . . Well, it'll come to me."

"Everybody knows Coot Dooley. He's been around forever and he's older than the hills," Scopes said. "Older than the dust on Moses's sandals!"

Coot didn't bat an eye. "You said it, not me, but I'll second the motion." To Gow he said, "You might remember me from a long time ago, a long long time ago. I was at Fort Tanner when the McKie rescue party came in."

Gow never lost his smile, showing a mouthful of the blackened stumps of rotten teeth.

"Then again you might not recall me. You was in mighty sad shape when they brung you in," Coot went on. "Being snowed in at that mining camp in the mountains all winter with no food and just them seven other miners must have been mighty rough."

"It surely was," Gow said, eyes getting a fixed faraway look. "Surely was." If there had been a risk of him losing his composure, it was gone. The moment had passed.

"You was the onliest one to survive, as I recollect," Coot said. "Mighty lucky!"

Gow nodded. "I'm a lucky fellow. Reckon I've always been lucky that way."

"Not today," Coot said with a ring of finality. That dropped a heavy stone into the pond, ripples spreading outward.

"We gonna stand here jawing all morning?" Sisely demanded, breaking the stillness.

"That's youngsters for you, al'us in a hurry to git somewhere," Gow said, chuckling. "They don't appreciate the satisfaction a man takes in talking over old times."

"Kind of a surprise running into you out here, Johnny," Scopes said. "Off your home range, ain't ya?"

"You know what they say about the early bird catching the worm," Johnny pointed out.

Gow laughed. "They do say that! The question is, who's the bird and who's the worm?"

"You know how you can find out," Johnny said. Mindful of Coot's warning, he threw down first on Brat Sisely.

The kid *was* fast. Johnny moved first, but Sisely's gun cleared the holster before his did. That big, oversized horse pistol was clutched in both hands at the same time and began firing away. Overanxious, his opening shots missed, the rounds thrumming so close by that Johnny felt the wind of their passage.

The kid missed his target, but Johnny didn't. The Colt in his right fist put two in Sisely's middle, blowing him out of the saddle.

As Johnny and Sisley traded shots, Coot dug his boot heels sharp into the pinto's flanks, hauling back hard on the reins at the same time.

Nickering in protest at the unaccustomed hard use, the pinto upreared, rising on its hind legs, forelegs off the ground. Coot held himself in the saddle by the viselike grip of his long, bowed thighs.

The draw between Johnny and Sisely gave Madison a lightning-like but very real jolt, throwing him off a hair by its surprise. He'd expected to be Johnny's prime target.

Madison drew without thinking, snaking his gun out of the holster. Johnny was still his intended target, but Coot's horse going up on its hind legs and rising to a height of eight feet and more blocked his line of fire. He balked for an instant in the deadly contest where life and death were measured in instants and split seconds.

Madison had no clear shot at Coot, either, shielded by the horse's bulk as he was. To the outlaw's way of thinking shooting a horse was a waste of bullets, especially in a gunfight, so Madison was temporarily put in check for a critical interval during the moment of truth.

Coot was not. Using his right hand, he shucked his short-barreled carbine out of the saddle scabbard. The reins were wrapped around his left hand and wrist.

Coot leaned forward and down along the right-hand side of the pinto's magnificently muscled neck to shield himself behind the body of his horse, clutching the saddle horn for support with his left hand. It was a classic maneuver of the kind used by mounted Comanche warriors. He thrust the carbine under the horse's head and around its massive neck. Not making a fuss about aiming, he simply pointed the weapon at its target—Troy Madison.

Wielding the piece one-handedly, Coot squeezed off a shot, the carbine barking.

A black dot blossomed in the middle of Madison's forehead where the round drilled it neatly. He died instantly, like a frog pierced through the brain by a hatpin. Blood so dark it seemed almost black jetted from the bullet hole.

Madison flew backward off his saddle and horse so violently and abruptly it was as if he'd been lassoed by an invisible rope and yanked to the ground.

Of the five Hog Ranch riders, only two were gunfighters—Troy Madison and Brat Sisely. They were both stone dead before the others went for their guns.

The other three were gunmen, killers, but not gunfighters. They lacked the keen eye and razor-sharp instincts of the professional gun. The veteran scout and sometime Indian fighter Buck Thornton was quickest of them, his six-gun leaping into his hand and swinging toward Johnny Cross. He glimpsed the gun in Johnny's hand pointing at him.

Gunfire flared from Johnny's Colt, three quick rounds tearing Buck's chest to pieces.

Buck jerked and twisted in the saddle under the impact. The gun in his hand suddenly felt like it was a million miles away. Unfired, it dropped from his nerveless fingers. He didn't care. He was beyond caring. He pitched out of the saddle and a black abyss opened to swallow him up.

He knew it was the blackness of death and then he ceased to know anything.

Titus Gow had a gun in each hand, and he was shooting at Coot. Shouting, and roaring, his voice seemed louder than the gunfire. If it was words, they were in a language no mortal man could understand, an unintelligible primal shriek.

The pinto's forelegs came down, dropping all four hooves on the ground.

Coot worked the reins wrapped around his hand and wrist, turning the pinto to the left, wheeling it around to bring the carbine in line with Gow. It spat, making a sharp, flat cracking sound. The bullet tagged Gow in the belly, a puff of dust springing up from his incredibly filthy shirt. He spasmed, then collapsed, jackknifing.

Coot's next shot took the top of Gow's head off.

It all happened so fast that Kinney Scopes was in a dilemma. He didn't know whether to pull his gun or turn tail and run, so he tried to do both. One hand tugged out his gun while the other tried to turn the horse to flee in the opposite direction.

Johnny Cross had always disliked Scopes, with his face seemingly frozen in a permanent expression of sneering contempt. He wiped off Scopes's smirk . . . with bullets.

"You okay, Coot?" Johnny asked, not even breathing hard.

"Fit as a fiddle." Coot put his carbine back into the sheath. Catching sight of Johnny, he frowned. "Looks like you got tagged, though, son."

Johnny lifted an eyebrow in question. Coot motioned, touching a hand to the right side of his neck. Johnny put a hand to the same place on his own neck, surprised to see his fingers come away bloody. He quickly became aware of a burning, stinging sensation in the affected area. Blood droplets stained the right shoulder of his lightweight denim jacket. His fingertips traced out the path of a shallow groove a half inch wide and several inches long running diagonally along the side of his neck.

A flesh wound—one of Brat Sisely's bullets had creased him. "Well I'll be a son of a—!"

"Told you Brat was fast," Coot said, not smugly but righteously, a man justified.

"Fast but not accurate," Johnny countered.

"Lucky for you!"

It was lucky, Johnny knew. But as the saying goes, A miss is as good as a mile. He wasn't going to get upset about what *could* have happened. That was no way to go through life. Not his kind of life.

Johnny unknotted his bandanna, folding it and pressing it against the wound. It was still bleeding but not much. No veins or arteries severed, else he'd be spurting a stream of blood three feet long with every heartbeat.

Uncapping his canteen, he wet the bandanna and used it to mop up the blood, wiping it clean.

In the intense physical excitement of the kill, he'd been unaware of the wound. Now that he was aware, it discomforted him. Nothing he couldn't handle, though. Hell, he'd been shot for real, not once but a few times during his wild youth. This wound was only a scratch by comparison.

Coot rode up so that he was alongside Johnny and turned in the saddle to face him. Lifting the flap of a saddlebag, Coot took out a quart bottle of whiskey. "Here, try some of this. It's good for what ails you."

"Thank you kindly," Johnny said, uncorking the bottle "It's a little early for me—"

"Since when?" Coot scoffed, snorting.

"Considering the circumstances, I'll join the jubilee." Johnny took a long pull, liquid heat trickling down his throat into his belly, only to shoot back up to the top of his head to deliver a much-needed blast. "Ahhhhh . . ."

He wet a corner of the bandanna with the whiskey and swabbed it against the grooved crease in his neck, cleansing it. It burned wicked good, throwing a wave of delicious weakness through him that passed as quickly as it came.

"Drink it. Don't take a bath in it," Coot said impatiently.

"No worry about that. It ain't even Saturday night." Johnny started to hand the bottle back, thought better of it, and took another pull before returning it.

Coot raised the bottle in a kind of toast. "Seeing as how I do hate to see a man drink alone, I believe I'll join you." He drank deep, corked the bottle, and dropped it into the saddlebag.

Johnny eyed the body of Brat Sisely sprawled on the ground, a skinny galoot under five feet tall with pipe stem limbs. "I felt kind of bad about burning down that punk kid, but since he almost got me, I don't feel so bad."

"Kid, eh?" Coot said, a corner of his mouth twisted cynically upward. "How old you reckon he was anyway, Johnny?"

"Fourteen . . . fifteen, maybe."

Coot's laughter was mocking. "Fourteen? Not hardly! Brat Sisely is—he *was*—bout as old as you."

"The hell you say," Johnny scoffed.

"It's the gospel truth," Coot maintained. "He was raised in an orphanage where they fed the kids hardly ever and never. Brat wasn't able to get his growth after that, though he could pack away the grub like a lumberjack.

"He was just naturally born lightning fast with a

gun, but that baby face and undersized stick-figure body was his real ace in the hole. Brat fooled a lot of bad hombres into underestimating him as a punk kid so that he could get close enough to kill them. I seed him at End of Track railroad camp in Kansas last year. That's how I knowed who he was. Brat was working for a ring of tinhorn gamblers, wiping out the competition one kill at a time. Killed twelve men in all, like I said.

"Reckon you was the unlucky thirteenth . . . unlucky for him."

Johnny pushed back his hat, scratching his head. "If that don't beat all! Kid looks like he barely got out of knee pants."

"You'd change your tune if you ever seed the way he could soak up the redeye. He was pure hell on the saloon gals, too."

"Now you're just joshing me, Coot." Johnny said, putting his foot down.

"Like hell! He used to take 'em on—two, three a night. Some of the ladies told me he worked 'em almighty hard, too," the elder man insisted.

"It's a wonderment," Johnny said, shaking his head. "Just goes to show that sometimes things ain't what they seem. . . ."

"Sometimes? More often than not, I'd say," Coot crowed, cackling with glee.

"You really are a crazy old bast—"

Coot's laughter drowned out the tail end of Johnny's remark. Mirth subsiding, he looked around at the bodies littering the sandy soil of the pass. "What to do with the bodies, son?"

"Leave them where they fell. I don't give a good damn who finds them and I ain't minded to go to the time and trouble of hauling them to the sinkhole to hide them," Johnny said.

"Maybe we should go make ourselves scarce, instead," Coot said.

"Now I know you ain't that drunk, old-timer," Johnny said, eyeing the other doubtfully, "so where'd that loco notion come from? The law don't care about a bunch of dead Hog Ranchers. Ol' Barton'll be so tickled that a sizeable vacancy has opened up in the gang that he'll probably make us special deputies."

"T'ain't the law I'm worried about, Johnny."

"You can't be talking about the Hog Ranch. Not that bunch of pimps, chicken thieves, and six-snake whiskey vendors!"

"No, no," Coot said, making warding gestures as if trying to shoo away Johnny's mistaken notions.

Johnny wondered, not for the first time, whether the wizened but still spry oldster might not be a bit cracked upstairs.

"Let you in on a little secret, son," Coot began. "Back before the war, and I mean *way* back, Titus Gow was partnered up in a slave-stealing ring with Jimbo Turlock."

"I know Jimbo was a slave stealer back in the day. He was a lot of things . . . all bad." Johnny was interested despite his misgivings that Coot was going off on a wild tear. "Titus Gow is new to me. Never heard of him."

"That was before your time up in the border states," Coot said.

"Things being what they are, I don't reckon I'll be getting to know him any better," Johnny noted dryly, indicating Gow's corpse with a tilt of his head.

"Think so? You might be surprised. Anyhow, Titus

and Jimbo was thick as thieves in the early days—hell, they *was* thieves. Worse—they posed as abolitionists in Missouri, feeding slaves a line to run away from their masters so's they could smuggle them across the river to freedom in Kansas. Instead they took them into Arkansas and sold them to new masters."

"I've heard how it works," Johnny said, "and it's no surprise to me that you know how it works. Such devilments! I reckon there ain't no scoundrels on the frontier you don't know, old-timer."

"I been around," Coot Dooley said, self-satisfied. "And I mean to be around a whole lot longer. So listen to me when I tell you this and listen good. There's an old saw about big fleas having little fleas that live off'n them, and so on and so forth. Think of Jimbo Turlock as the big flea and Titus Gow as the little flea. Titus surely did admire Jimbo and fastened on to him whenever he could. He followed him down into the Nations in Oklahoma and rode with the Free Company, savvy?"

"What're you trying to say, Coot?" Johnny asked. "Spit it out."

"Titus Gow wasn't no Hog Rancher. He ran with the big dogs. I suspicion that with Titus here in the Breaks, Jimbo Turlock can't be too far off."

TWENTY

The Mallory family and friends ate dinner in a private room off the dining room of the Cattleman Hotel. Present were Gordon Mallory, the gray-bearded patriarch; his lovely daughter Ashley; family advisor Kale Dancer, and the senior Mallory's manservant and confidant, Sgt. Quarles.

The private room had ornate red-and-gold wallpaper and its own fireplace, where a crackling blaze shed light. The table was set with a shining white linen tablecloth, fine china, and glittering silverware.

The Cattleman Hotel was the best hotel in Hangtree town—best in the county, not that that was saying much. It featured a good chef, offered a varied bill of fare, featuring many courses, and received a fair amount of trade from the businessmen of the district, the promoters, cattle buyers, and speculators, and the handful of well-to-do ranchers and farmers.

The Mallory group was served by a long-faced, tight-lipped waiter in a white jacket and dark slacks. He served the various courses off a wheeled cart, periodically perambulating back and forth to the kitchen as needed.

Gordon Mallory and Kale Dancer began with a big drink of whiskey or three. Quarles declined, being an abstainer. Miss Ashley sipped sherry from a delicately thin, dainty glass, which saw more than a few refills.

Gordon Mallory sat in a chair at the head of the table, his wheelchair set off to one side out of the way. The diners consumed various courses of chicken, veal, ham, and beef—lots of beef. Ribs, roasts, cutlets, chops. Baked potatoes, corn fritters, hush puppies, biscuits with gravy, and dinner rolls with butter were part of the meal.

Each course was washed down with a bottle of wine, each bottle being of a different vintage. The Cattleman boasted a pretty fair wine cellar, considering its location on the hundredth meridian, which marked the westernmost advance of civilization.

Miss Ashley kept up the wine-bibbing pace with her father and Kale Dancer. Her eyes sparkled and her cheeks were red. As the wine kept coming, Mallory cast ever more anxious glances at the bubbly, vivacious Ashley, who had begun to laugh and chatter a bit more animatedly and louder than might be thought entirely proper for a young lady of refinement and breeding, even on the rim of civilization.

"I do believe you've had enough, dear," he said after a bit of throat-clearing and ah-hemming.

"I'm fine, Father," Ashley said, not without sighing and raising her eyes to heaven as if calling on the Divine to mark her long-suffering forbearance in the face of such gauche and unwarranted parental tyranny.

The meal continued to unroll, course by course,

bottle by bottle. After Mallory refreshed and refilled his own glass of wine, he positioned the bottle so it was out of Ashley's reach.

She chattered on about some pleasant triviality or another between swallows, soon draining the last. Noticing her empty crystal goblet, she proffered it to Kale Dancer, seated within ready reach of the wine bottle. "If you would be so kind, Kale," she said, smiling.

Dancer reached for the bottle, ready to oblige.

"Er, I think not," Mallory said gently, with more throat-clearing.

Dancer's face fell for an instant, but he recovered his blandly assured self-confidence in a heartbeat and withdrew his hand from the wine bottle. A gentle smile was accompanied by a shrug which said, *I know it's ridiculous, but what can I do?*

"Father, please! I'm not a child," Ashley said, downcast and pouting.

"How much more do you need, Ashley? Haven't you had enough?" Mallory softly chided.

"What do you expect me to do, *Father*, drink the water?"

"That would be a lot to ask," Kale Dancer said lightly in a sortie to forestall the darkening mood. He showed a mouthful of splendid white teeth in a shiny smile.

"Have some coffee," Mallory suggested

"I don't want coffee. It keeps me awake," Ashley snapped.

"Not with all the wine you've been drinking."

"How often do I get to eat a decent meal in a real restaurant? Why do you have to spoil it for me?"

"Oh, all right," Mallory said, breaking first. He

sighed, his face troubled. "Kale, if you'll do the honors . . ."

"My pleasure, sir," Dancer said cheerfully, pouring fresh wine into Ashley's glass, filling it halfway.

"Don't be a piker, Mr. Dancer," Ashley said. "Fill it."

Dancer looked at Mallory, who shrugged, a tiny nervous tic twitching away at a corner of his mouth. Dancer resumed pouring, filling the glass nearly to the brim.

"Thank you!" Ashley said pettishly. She drank deeply, her face reddening. After that first long thirsty swallow, she slowed down, making a show of taking small, delicate sips.

The meal continued without further incident. The waiter returned as needed, clearing away dirty dishes and setting out clean ones for subsequent courses. Empty bottles were replaced by full ones, those soon emptied.

Finally came dessert and coffee. Mallory and Dancer had an after-dinner drink, a brandy. Ashley had a brandy, too, though not without displaying a flash of temper when her father initially made a foredoomed attempt to deny her request.

The meal was done.

"Thank you for dinner, sir," Quarles said quietly.

"Quite all right, Quarles," Mallory said. He suggested Dancer join him outside for a cigar.

"Shall I get Piney?" Quarles asked.

"That won't be necessary. You and Kale can put me in my chair."

"Yes, sir."

Quarles positioned the wheelchair nearer Mallory, then pulled back the chair with Mallory in it, away from the table. Dancer and Quarles stood on each side of him and reached under one of Mallory's arms, lifting him out of the chair to a standing position. A blanket slid off Mallory's legs, falling to the floor. Supporting Mallory's weight, they hefted him to the wheelchair, easing him into it.

Quarles picked up the blanket, brushed it off, and unfolded it, covering Mallory's legs.

Kale Dancer stood behind the wheelchair, pushing it slowly across the floor with Mallory in it, while Quarles crossed quickly to the connecting door between the private room and the public dining room, the latter unoccupied save for a table or two of late diners.

Dancer wheeled Mallory through the dining room into a hallway. Ashley traipsed alongside, with Quarles bringing up the rear a few paces behind.

Through the lobby and out the front entrance to the veranda fronting Trail Street they went. The men lit up cigars. Ashley Mallory sat a few paces away in a porch swing, fanning herself, looking unutterably bored and making no attempt to hide it.

When he finished smoking his cigar, Quarles went off to fetch Piney, returning with him a few minutes later. They found Mallory in his wheelchair at the foot of the stairs leading to the second floor where the group had their rooms.

Piney leaned over Mallory, scooping him up in his arms. The hulking manservant held him like a child, showing no sign of strain or muscular exertion. With equal facility, he carried Mallory upstairs, Quarles hurrying on ahead to open the hotel room door.

Dancer and Ashley stood together at the foot of the stairs, chatting away, She was doing most of the talking.

Piney paused for a moment at the top of the landing

to catch his breath. Mallory turned his head to glance downstairs, Ashley and Dancer's words inaudible to him. He watched his daughter. She displayed the most spark and verve she had shown all evening, while the handsome Dancer seemed to be feeling no pain.

Piney moved on, carrying Mallory into his suite of rooms.

"That's something you don't see much any more, not since the war," the hotel manager said to the night clerk as they stood at the front desk in the hotel lobby watching the goings-on at the staircase to the second floor. It was slack time in the hotel, quiet.

The clerk turned. "What might that be?"

"A distinguished gentleman like Mr. Mallory. Exquisite manners, the real gentry." The manager beamed as though basking in the glow shed by that luminary.

"He's got a good-looking daughter," the night clerk noted approvingly.

The manager's frown made the clerk defensive. "What're you giving me that look for? All I said was that Mallory has a good-looking daughter. Well, he does. She's a stylish piece of goods."

Following a brief internal struggle, the manager decided the remark was nothing to take offense at, though he had noticed that the night clerk tended to be a bit flip at times, a bit fresh. It was why he was working the desk at night instead of in the daytime.

Still, the manager resolved to let it pass. "Charming girl," he agreed.

"Looks like she might be something of a handful, though," the night clerk ventured.

"Eh? Why do you say that?"

"Dyll the waiter said she put away quite a bit of wine tonight. *Quite*," the night clerk emphasized, making quick hand movements to pantomime someone tossing back a glass of wine.

"Tell Dyll he shouldn't go around discussing the guests," the manager said, sniffing. "Never mind. I'll tell him myself."

TWENTY-ONE

It was easy to follow the Free Company's trail; even a blind man could have found it. Their track was like a gigantic scar ripped across the countryside.

The marauders moved en masse down Wild Horse Canyon in a column that Sam estimated had about 150 or more mounted men, twenty wagons and other wheeled vehicles, and a trailing body of foot soldiers and camp followers that could have numbered somewhere around 250 people. Whatever their plans, they were making no attempt to conceal their presence.

Sam and Otto followed.

"Mind if I ask you a question?" Sam ventured after a while on the trail.

"I don't mind. Ask away," Otto said.

"Ordinarily I keep to myself, minding my own business, but I can't help wondering what's the shaven skull all about? Scared of being scalped by Indians?"

"That's a good one! Lice—that's what I'm scared of, head lice. The barracks are full of them. It's better to go bald than be picking the blasted little critters out of your hair all the time, night and day. They itch something fierce, too."

"You've got a mustache. Don't they get into that?"

"They do, but I've got to have it. Without a mustache, my head looks like a giant thumb."

Sam cut the other a quick side glance, looking to see if Otto was pulling his leg. The trooper seemed serious enough, though. "Oh. Just wondering."

"Now you know," Otto said.

On they rode.

"Cross! Johnny Cross!"

It was nighttime at the Cross ranch, about ten o'clock, a late hour in the countryside where most folks rose with the sun and went to bed not long after nightfall.

But Johnny Cross was no ordinary citizen. He kept odd hours and numbered many a strange breed of cat among his acquaintances. Two of them were in the front room of the ranch house with him. Vic Vargas was somewhere outside, but it wasn't he who was doing the shouting.

Coot sat by the stone fireplace, where a low fire burned, fine-tuning the action on one of his rifles. "Got me a feeling I'll be needing it before too long," he had said earlier.

Luke sat on the other side of the fireplace. His left pant leg was rolled up past the knee, and his wooden leg was off. It tended to chafe and discomfort him. He was kneading the stump below the knee, trying to relieve the tension knotted there.

Johnny sat on a chair at a long table, cleaning the guns he'd used earlier in the fracas. They lay on a square of cloth spread on the tabletop. Some stiff metal-bristle brushes, gauze cotton patches, ramrods, and other instruments lay near at hand. The scent of gun-cleaning oil was in the air.

A lamp on the table shed a cone of light on the business at hand.

"*Come out, Johnny!*" the voice in the night rang out, coming from somewhere in the darkness surrounding the ranch house.

"Now who in tarnation do you suppose that is?" Coot wondered aloud.

"Beats me," Johnny said, shrugging. "This must be my week for getting called out."

"The last time that happened, I missed lunch," Luke said, sounding sore about it.

Johnny grinned. "Good thing you already ate dinner tonight."

"He et enough for two dinners," Coot complained.

"I'd have had three, if it wasn't your cooking," Luke returned.

"I didn't hear no complaints while you was shoveling that grub down your maw," Coot grumbled.

"I was hungry. Hungry enough to eat even that slop," Luke said cheerfully. "Besides, it ain't polite to talk with your mouth full."

"When did that ever stop you?" Coot asked. "I don't know what you got to be so all-fired hungry about anyways. You ain't hardly done a lick of work around here since you come back home from gallivanting in town."

"Some gallivanting! I damn near got myself killed trying to eat a nice peaceful lunch."

Coot groaned. "You ain't gonna tell us about it again, is you, Luke? You already boasted your big brags about it so much it's coming out of my ears."

Once more the call came out of the night. *"Johnny Cross! Come out! We need to talk!"*

"Persistent cuss," Coot remarked.

"Whoever it is, he ain't from the Free Company. They don't bother to announce themselves when they go night riding," Johnny said. "A shot in the dark's more their style."

"Maybe he'll go away if you don't answer," Luke said hopefully. "Then we can go back to our drinking."

"I don't see you slacking off none. Quit hogging that bottle and pass it to me," Coot said.

"Get it yourself. You got two good legs."

"See if I don't," Coot said, rising.

"Cross, this is Sam Heller. Sam Heller! Come on out. I want to talk to you! It's important!"

"Well, what do you know, Johnny. Your pet Yankee's back in town," Coot said, not sounding particularly pleased.

"Thought he sounded familiar," Luke said.

"Then why didn't you say so?" Coot demanded.

"Because I wasn't sure, you cantankerous old mossback."

Johnny pushed back his chair and stood up. He was barefoot and his shirtsleeves were rolled up to the elbows. A six-gun was stuck in the top of his pants over his right hip. He didn't feel right without a loaded gun close to hand especially now that trouble hunters were abroad in Wild Horse Canyon, not to mention poking around the ranch.

He turned a knob at the base of the lamp, dimming the light in the room already thick with shadows. He padded to a front window, standing to one side so as not to outline himself. "That you, Sam?" he called out into the night.

"*Yup!*"

"What about it, Vic?" Johnny asked loudly.

"It's Sam," Vic Vargas replied. He was taking his turn at sentry duty.

Between Terrible Terry in town and the canyon dustup, Johnny wasn't taking any chances on being caught unawares. He and the others were taking turns pulling guard duty outside, keeping an eye on things so nobody could sneak up on them.

The situation must be under control or Vic would have started shooting by now, Johnny thought. It'd take a mighty soft-walking hombre to sneak up on Vargas and get the drop on him. From what Johnny had seen of Sam in action, he might well have been such an hombre, but the Yankee gunman had apparently approached openly, without subterfuge.

"Sam's alone," Vic Vargas went on. "But four other fellows are down in the hollow on the road to the Trail. He's also got one of the dangedest contraptions you ever seen."

"Huh!" Johnny said, thinking it over.

"I ain't funning," Vargas said. "You want to see this. It's something to see!"

Johnny would have gone out anyway, but his interest was piqued. "I'll be right out."

He sat down on a chair and pulled his boots on. No way he was walking around barefoot outside—rattlesnakes! The land was full of them. They weren't as active by night as they were by day, but they were active enough. Johnny and friends had mostly cleaned out the ones who made their dens around the ranch house, but they could never tell for sure.

He went outside, Coot following. Luke would be along once he'd strapped on his wooden leg, Johnny reckoned.

The front of the ranch house looked out on a broad dirt yard—the dooryard, where nothing grew. It was ringed by various outbuildings—stable barn with tack room, toolshed, and corral.

The moon was up, an amber half moon hanging midway between the eastern horizon and the zenith. The night air was cool and pleasant. Moonlight shone down into the dooryard, picking out the forms of Sam Heller and his horse. Sam stood beside Dusty, holding the reins.

Sam's mule's leg was worn on his right-hand side. It seemed kind of clumsy to Johnny, who was a fast-draw artist with a regulation-sized Colt six-gun in a hip holster, but Sam could get that mule's leg into action pretty damn fast. Its cut-down size was more practical for wielding the piece in close quarters in towns—saloons, alleys, and such.

Off to one side in dark shadows under the eaves of the stable barn stood Vic, holding a leveled rifle pointed in Sam's general direction.

"It's all right, Vic," Johnny said.

Vic lowered the rifle. "I'll stick. He's got one of the biggest damn guns I ever saw down in the hollow with the others."

"They're Army from Fort Pardee," Sam said.

"That ain't exactly a recommendation in these parts," Johnny said.

"Don't I know it! You and the good folks of Hangtree might change your tune when you hear the news."

"What news?"

"Fort Pardee's a tad below fighting strength right now. The four men with me are the only effectives alive right now," Sam said grimly.

"You lost me," Johnny said, frankly mystified. "What's it all about?"

"I'll tell you in a minute, but I figured it might be wiser for my four friends to keep their distance until you know what's what."

"What's all this about some contraption, some big gun?" Johnny craned his neck to see down into the hollow. It was dark where the moonlight did not reach, making it difficult for him to discern what it was exactly that was down there. "What've you got?"

"A howitzer," Sam said.

"Say again?" Johnny queried.

"A howitzer. It's a kind of cannon."

"I know what a howitzer is. That's what you've got down there? I can't hardly make it out from here. A howitzer, eh? What're you doing with it?"

"That's part of the story."

"This I've got to see," Johnny said, starting forward.

"Careful, Johnny." That was Coot speaking, standing in the yard near the house.

"It's all right, Coot. I trust him," Johnny said. "Mostly."

"Thanks," Sam said, his tone neutral, giving away nothing. He hitched Dusty's reins to a top rail of the corral fence.

Johnny walked to the opposite end of the yard, Sam falling into step beside him. Johnny looked south where a dirt road extended from the ranch house to the Hangtree Trail, meeting it at right angles somewhere in the middle distance.

In a dip in the dirt road a hundred yards away were four men, a wheeled cannon—howitzer, Johnny silently corrected himself—and what looked like a freight wagon.

Three of the men were on horseback, and a fourth sat up high in the driver's seat of the wagon. The howitzer was mounted on a wheeled carriage hitched to a six-horse team, horses yoked two-by-two. The wagon was hitched to a separate team of horses similarly yoked.

"Whatever it's all about, you sure don't do things by halves," Johnny said, shaking his head. "Come on in and tell me about it. Your friends can stay down there while you tell me about it."

"All right," Sam said. "A fair hearing, that's all I ask."

"I doubt it, knowing you. One thing's certain though, whatever it is, it's a sure bet that I'll wind up getting shot at sooner or later. Probably sooner."

"Maybe so," Sam said.

Johnny laughed. "Well at least you don't deny it! Come on in."

"Let me tell the others first, so they don't get worried."

"Go ahead. It's your deal."

Sam walked partway down the slope toward the men in the hollow. "I'm going in for a parley, so sit tight till I come back."

"See if you can wrangle us some coffee," one called back.

"To hell with that. See if you can wangle us a drink," another said.

"I'm not making any promises, but I'll see what I can do," Sam said.

He and Johnny started back toward the ranch house.

Vic called out, "I'll stay out here for a while and keep an eye on things, Johnny."

"Okay, Vic."

Johnny, Sam, and Coot went into the ranch house.

"Howdy, Sam." Luke had finished strapping on his wooden leg. He and Sam had worked together in the past and got along pretty well.

"Howdy," Sam said.

"Pull up a chair and take a load off," Johnny said.

"I'll stand if that's all right with you. I've been in the saddle for so long that if I sit down I'm afraid I'll stiffen up and be unable to stand."

"Suit yourself. Coffee?" Johnny asked, indicating a battered coffeepot set out beside the hearth.

"I'd rather have some redeye," Sam said.

"Who wouldn't? Believe I'll join you." Johnny went to the cupboard filled with bottles of whiskey, mostly. He took out a fresh bottle, uncorked it, and handed it to Sam. "We don't stand on ceremony here, help yourself.'

"Thanks." Sam took a long pull of the whiskey. It put some color in his face, which was drawn and haggard with fatigue. "Much obliged." He took another, longer drink.

After Sam had sufficiently refreshed himself by consuming a fair amount of the bottle, he went into his story, telling Johnny and company about the abandonment of the Hog Ranch, the massacre-by-poison at Fort Pardee, and the advent into Hangtree County by the Free Company.

"After we left the fort, we encountered three riders coming from the west, out of the Llano.

"They were hidden behind a ridge but showed themselves at the crest when we unsuspectingly drew abreast of their position. I could tell by their outline that they were not Comanches. Otto thought maybe they were strayed marauders who got lost on the plains. That being the case, they could have caught us out in the open and picked us off and they could have seen his Army uniform. If they were Free Company, we knew what to do," Sam said grimly.

"The trio rode downslope to meet us. Turned out, they were friendlies—three civilian trackers who were working as scouts for Fort Pardee. I'd done some scouting for the Army and to my surprise, I recognized them. Friendly acquaintances, all three. An Indian and two white men. They're the men in the hollow.

"The Indian is named Tonk, short for Tonkawah. The Tonkawah were a tribe of Texas Indians who have been pretty well wiped out by the Comanches over the last half century. The last few survivors have a big hate on for Comanches, as well as being ace trackers and manhunters.

"The white scouts are Noel Maddox and Steve Dirkes. Maddox was born on Christmas Day, hence the name 'Noel.' Oddly enough, he and his folks pronounced the name so it rhymes with *mole*. He's better known as Mad Dog Maddox, a veteran mountain man and trapper who'd been with Pathfinder Fremont and Kit Carson on one of their last expeditions into the wilderness before the war.

"Dirkes is ten years younger than Maddox but trail-wise and trouble-savvy. He scouted throughout the Southwest for the Army's Surveying and Topographical Corps, mapping and exploring lands acquired from Mexico by war and treaty.

"They joined us in our mission.

"The marauders' tracks told many a story for those of us who knew how to read sign. One of the most intriguing was the progress or rather lack of progress of the stolen howitzer and munitions wagon.

"The howitzer was heavy and so was its accompanying wagon filled with powder and shot. From the beginning of the trek from Fort Pardee, they traveled well behind the rest of the column, even behind the last of the horde of camp followers making the march on foot. I think it was not only because they were weighty and traveled slow but because of fears of an explosion in the munitions wagon." Sam stopped speaking for a moment, thinking of the disastrous explosion at the Boneyard meet between the Hog Ranch gunrunners and Comanches. He knew such fears could take on a real threat.

"In any case, as the caravan wound its way farther and farther south, the howitzer and wagon steadily fell back more and more, eventually dropping out of sight several miles behind the rear of the column. As we represented Fort Pardee, we resolved to attack the laggard artillery transport should the opportunity present itself.

"Several hours passed and the transport crew lost sight of the column and vice versa. I assume the marauders and auxiliary irregulars got impatient. The Free Company and its trailing rabble horde wanted to get to their main camp so they could get to the all-important task of dividing up the loot. Then they could get on with such all-important matters as drinking, gambling, and wenching.

"The artillery transport crew was out of luck. They'd get to camp as soon as they could but nobody was going to wait for them. They grumbled. All the good shares of loot would be gathered up long before they finally reached camp. The crew whipped and cursed the horses, trying to get more speed out of them. The result was that the animals became over-tired and needed ever more frequent rest breaks.

"The twelve-member crew halted at sundown and decided to have some food and drink before complet-ing the rest of their trip. They built a fire and broke out some bottles of whiskey, the last few left undrunk during the long trip south.

"They didn't bother to unhitch the horses but left them in place in harness and yoke. According to the bits and pieces of conversations we overheard, it was the horses' fault—the dumb brutes—for not hauling the heavy load faster, so let them wait while the crew looked after their own needs." Sam shook his head. Not a way to treat a horse.

"The transporters sat around the fire, eating and drinking, having as good a time as they could without being in camp. No loot and no women tended to put a damper on the festivities, but they carried on, carousing as best they could. But they were not en-tirely stupid. They set out sentries before starting to eat and drink. One swiftly fell asleep and the other was soon drunk.

"We attacked at nightfall.

"Tonk crept up to them one by one, quietly cutting their throats, then joined the rest of us as we got into position just outside the circle of light shed by the campfire. We opened fire without warning. It was not a game with rules. It was serious business—*war*. Any impulse of restraint was erased by thoughts of the mass poisoning at Fort Pardee. What followed was more of a firing squad than a fight.

"It was over very quickly. Two marauders remained

alive when the shooting stopped. I wanted them taken alive for questioning.

"The first wouldn't talk. Otto blew his brains out. The second talked plenty.

"According to him, the Free Company is camped at Sidepocket Canyon, a box canyon west of Wild Horse Canyon. The company was massed in advance of a planned attack on Hangtree town, which would be taken, looted, and burned. The plan is to then roam the countryside, picking off the ranches along the Liberty River in the county's Long Valley.

"That's what we needed to know. Maddox slit the prisoner's throat so Otto didn't have to waste a bullet.

"We gave the artillery transport horses enough water to refresh them but not so much that they would be sluggish and slowed. Tonk and Dirkes got the howitzer team back on the trail and moving. Otto climbed up into the driver's seat of the munitions wagon, took up the reins, and followed.

"I set their course for Cross's Cut, following an evasive path to throw off pursuit, first plunging west to clear the outer range of the Breaks, then going south where plains footed the western range. The hills screened us from being seen by Free Company lookouts. We continued south for some miles before turning left into a pass that wound through the Western Breaks and into Wild Horse Canyon, emerging well below and out of sight of Sidepocket Canyon. Eventually, we were on the Wild Horse Canyon trail.

"Two hours later, we arrived at the western opening of Cross's Cut. We followed the pass to its eastern end, coming out on Cross ranch land, and took the dirt road between the ranch house and Hangtree Trail, following it until the ranch was in view, laid out under the moonlight.

"I rode alone the rest of the way to the ranch house, leaving the others in the hollow with the howitzer and powder wagon.

"That's all of it," Sam concluded.

Johnny went to the cupboard and took out a couple bottles of whiskey. "Take these to your men. They've earned it. Coot'll fix up some grub so y'all can chow down."

"How come I got to cook?" Coot complained.

"After that poisoned chili, even your cooking won't taste so bad," Luke said.

With many a groan and grumble, Coot rustled up some grub.

Sam delivered it to his men. While they ate, Steve Dirkes volunteered to ride to Hangtree to warn Marshal Barton and the others in town to spread the alarm. Sam approved the choice. Steve was a level-headed young fellow and a Texan whose word would carry weight with the townsfolk.

When he was finished eating, Dirkes rode off into the night, east toward Hangtree.

Sam and the others sat around drinking and making plans.

TWENTY-TWO

The hour was late. The second-floor corridor of the Cattleman Hotel was empty when Ashley Mallory slipped out of the suite of rooms she shared with her father.

The suite had two bedrooms, one for her, one for him. They were connected by a drawing room whose outer door opened into the hallway. Gordon Mallory had retired for the night an hour or two earlier, behind his closed bedroom door.

"What he doesn't know won't hurt him," Ashley told herself, smiling a secret smile. She wore a robe over a nightdress and a pair of slippers. Her hair was unpinned, hanging loose and free over slim shoulders. Her face was a pale oval in the wan light shed by corridor wall lamps.

Her eyes shone; red dots of color burned in her cheeks. She looked left and right to make sure that the hallway was empty and no one was watching.

All clear.

She crossed the hall on silent feet to the door opposite her suite, the door to the room occupied by

Kale Dancer. Pressing a shoulder against the door, she rapped a knuckle softly on the panel.

No response.

Ashley knocked again, a bit more forcefully. Still no response.

She frowned. Men fortunate enough to be graced by a midnight visit from her were always ready, eager, and waiting. Perhaps Kale hadn't heard her. She knocked again.

Nothing. She put an ear to the door panel, hearing no sounds from within. Was it actually possible that he had fallen asleep while waiting for her?

That would really be too much, intolerable! But she doubted it. Kale was a most ardent suitor, bold to the point of rashness.

He might have been called away on some late errand. Kale Dancer was a very important man, subject to all kinds of unusual appointments and mysterious meetings night and day. It was something she got used to when acting as a traveling companion of her father.

Ashley almost giggled at the thought, but the reality of her position firmed up her self-control. She really couldn't afford to be caught doing what she was doing. She played a dangerous game.

Still, a lady can only stand for so much. She knocked again, a bit more sharply, softly calling out, "Kale? Kale?"

He must have been called away on unexpected business. Of all the damn inconvenient times! Her opportunities for nighttime rambles were few and far between and could not, must not, be wasted.

Light shone through the narrow slit at the bottom of the door where it failed to meet the floor. On impulse, Ashley gripped the doorknob, turning it. The door was unlocked. She opened it, stepping inside.

Kale Dancer's suite, smaller than hers and Mallory's, had an outer drawing room, inner bedroom, and bath. A globe lamp sat on a drum table in the drawing room. The light was low, the room dim and shadowy.

Kale Dancer sat slumped in an overstuffed armchair beside the table. He wore dark pants and a maroon velvet smoking jacket with quilted golden lapels and collar over a white ruffled shirt. His bare feet were tucked into a pair of expensive backless Moroccan leather slippers. His head was bowed, chin resting on chest, face hidden by shadows.

So . . . he was sleeping after all!

"Well, he will have to exert himself to extra efforts before I allow him back into my good graces," Ashley whispered. But she must not play too hard to get. Time was precious. Time was fleeting!

Standing over him, she gripped his shoulder, giving him a good shake to waken him. Kale failed to rouse. Not even a murmur came from him.

Was he drunk? He had certainly consumed enough whiskey after dinner.

But that was impossible. He was all man. A real man. She had never known him to be unable to hold his liquor.

She shook him again.

Dancer's upper body slumped to the side, sagging against a cushioned chair arm. His head tilted, rolling to the side, exposing his face and neck.

He was dead. His eyes were open in horror, staring, sightless. His face was a gray, corpselike pallor. A gaping wound showed below his chin where his throat had been cut from ear to ear.

Ashley would have screamed, but she lacked the breath. Her heart lurched in her chest, skipping a beat. Dizziness crashed over her. She feared she might faint—but of course she could not, must not!

Deep down she was a survivor, and her well-practiced instincts came rushing to the fore. Raising a hand to her open gaping mouth, she bit a knuckle to keep from shrieking.

She must not be found in Kale's room alone with his dead body. Dead—murdered! How would she explain her presence?

She had to get out. She staggered to the door, throwing it open.

Standing on the other side of the doorway, blocking her way, was Gordon Mallory. She was surprised to see him, but not surprised that he could stand.

Their eyes met and she knew, *knew*! His was the face of death.

Mallory advanced, crossing the threshold. Ashley stepped back, retreating. He closed the door behind him, sealing them in together, off from the rest of the hotel, the world.

His eyes shone, no longer seeing her as a daughter. Little flecks of saliva clung to his lips. "I fear your lover is in no condition to receive you," Mallory said, husky-voiced. He spoke slowly, relishing the sound of each word. "I paid him a visit first. So sorry, my dear.

"Well, not really," he added, his hands coming up. They were large hands, thick-fingered and steady. Not a tremor disturbed them.

His hands fastened on her long swanlike neck, squeezing with great strength, strength born of mania and mad love thwarted. He lifted her into the air, holding her at arm's length with her feet off the floor.

His hands were strangler's hands. He did what had to be done. . . .

When Mallory was finished, he set her down gently on the floor, quite dead. He looked down, studying her. "Faithless slut!" he whispered almost tenderly.

Quarles found them later. The perfect manservant, quick-witted, efficient, he stepped inside, locking the door from within.

Mallory stood in the same place he had been when he lowered her to the floor.

"Good Lord, Commander, what have you done?" Quarles asked.

The comedy was finished, the masquerade done. Gordon Mallory was really Jimbo Turlock, Supreme Commander of the Free Company.

Kale Dancer was Turlock's second in command.

Ashley Mallory was Osage Sally Potts, only recently the prettiest kept woman in the Oklahoma Territory.

Turlock had been on a secret mission concerning the upcoming Hangtree venture. He'd taken the role of Mallory, pretending to be a wheelchair-bound war veteran so none would suspect his real identity.

Sally Potts, Turlock's woman, impersonated his daughter, while Kale Dancer took the role of family advisor.

All would have gone well, but Sally and Dancer had a secret plot of their own. Just not so secret that Turlock hadn't found out about it.

He looked up, eyes focusing on Quarles, noticing him for the first time. "I had to do it, Quarles. They were conspiring against me. They were conspiring against me and, what is worse, against the Company. That is unforgiveable."

"Certainly, sir," Quarles agreed. He set about arranging their getaway.

Within the hour, Turlock, Quarles, and Piney were mounted on fast horses, riding west out of town on the Hangtree Trail.

TWENTY-THREE

Marshal Mack Barton and Deputy Smalls were on late-night duty at the jailhouse, standing by for action. They got it.

At eleven-thirty, a runner burst in from the Cattleman Hotel to report a double murder.

The marshal went to investigate, leaving Smalls to hold down the office.

Barton found two corpses in the suite of rooms registered to Kale Dancer. The hotel manager and the night clerk identified them as Dancer and Ashley Mallory, daughter of Gordon Mallory, who held the suite across the hall. They were strangers in town.

Quick questioning revealed that Mallory was gone, along with his personal manservant Quarles and a second servant named Piney. Mallory's wheelchair had been left behind in his hastily abandoned suite.

"Either he made a miraculous recovery or he didn't need the chair in the first place," Barton said.

"Why would a man pretend to need a wheelchair if he could walk?" the manager wondered.

"That's a real head-scratcher, ain't it? To fool somebody, maybe."

"Who would he fool?"

"Us," Barton said. "You, me, the whole town."

The manager couldn't figure the reasoning. "Why would he want to do that?"

"That's the question." Barton didn't have the answer, but he was working on a few ideas.

Had the trio exited through the front entrance, they would have been spotted by the night clerk. Therefore they had not exited via the front entrance. They had made a sneak exit from the hotel, most likely down the back stairs and out the rear door.

Barton left instructions to call the undertaker and left the hotel. Only two liveries were open all night. Hangtree was the kind of place where any number of individuals might find it necessary to leave town in a hurry at any hour of the day or night, so the twenty-four-hour service was a well-appreciated convenience. Of the two, Hobson's was bigger and better and was within easy walking distance of the hotel, so Barton tried it first.

Hobson had gone home for the night, but his kid assistant was on duty. He'd been napping and was sleepy-eyed and yawning when Barton roused him. The kid told the marshal that a man answering Piney's description had come in sometime after ten o'clock and had bought three fast horses, complete with saddles. No questions asked.

"Paid top dollar with no dickering over the price," the kid said. "In gold, too!"

"Better hold on to it. I'll want a look at it later,"

Barton said. Sometimes coins could furnish valuable clues to the bearer's identity by their denomination, date, place of coinage, and even the condition they were in—new, used, or old.

Barton was not going to work up a posse for a manhunt in the middle of the night. He wouldn't do it under ordinary circumstances, and certainly not with the extraordinarily strong undercurrents of murder and mystery roiling the town. He judged it best to stick to Hangtree where he could stay on top of breaking developments, if any.

Back at the office, Barton and Smalls kicked around the case.

"Seems open and shut to me," the deputy opined. "It was a matter of honor. The father discovers his unmarried daughter laying up on the sly with this fellow Dancer and kills both of them in a fury. You know how some fathers are about the honor of the family, especially if they're Southern gentlemen of the old school as you say this Mallory jasper was described as being."

"Southern gentlemen of the old school don't pretend to be wheelchair-bound when they're not," Barton pointed out, his tone sardonic.

"You got me there," Smalls said. "How do you figure it?"

"I don't . . . yet. I'm still working on it."

A little after one in the morning, two riders halted in front of the jailhouse.

One was Steve Dirkes, the Army scout who'd volunteered to notify Barton of the coming of the Free Company. He dismounted and called out for help.

Barton and Smalls hurried out of the jail and

helped carry the second rider into the office, laying him faceup on a long, wooden side table, which had been quickly cleared by the deputy. He then left to fetch a doctor.

After introducing himself, Dirkes explained how he came to have picked up the other rider. "An hour's ride outside of town, I came across a number of bodies laying strewn about the Hangtree Trail. A couple saddled horses that had belonged to the dead men roamed around anxiously nearby, upset by the violence and bloodshed but unsure what to do and not wanting to leave the nearness of the men."

He pointed at the man on the table. "He was still alive, though badly wounded. His name is Cal Lane, and he's been shot twice. I used my knife to cut some squares off my saddle blanket, forming them into bandages, and put them on his wounds, hoping they would keep him from bleeding out before I could get him to a doctor.

"He insisted he could stay on a horse and ride it, so I lassoed one of the horses and helped him into the saddle. I rigged the lariat as a lead rope to Cal's mount and tied the other end to my saddle horn. I didn't want to chase a runaway horse."

Marshal Barton examined Cal Lane's wounds, gingerly probing at the edges of them, but not fussing with the bandages for fear of starting the wounds bleeding again.

One shot had blown a chunk of flesh out of the top of Cal's left shoulder, and the other had tagged him in the right side about a hand's-width above his beltline. Barton couldn't tell if the slug had gone into the innards. He was no doctor.

Cal wanted to talk. He wanted to tell his story while

he could so that if he didn't pull through, the marshal would still have the facts to act on.

"Me and Stan and Pete Burgess were barely an hour's ride out of town when we were jumped by five bushwhackers. Stan and Pete were killed, but not before we gunned down all the attackers. I recognized some of the Hughes bunch but don't know their names."

Dirkes offered, "The moon was high overhead, moonlight shining down on their faces. I recognized two of them, Swampman Moss Roberts and Nails Doig." They were known bad men and frequenters of the Hog Ranch.

"Swampman and Doig are two of Denton Dick's henchmen," Barton said, smacking a meaty fist into his palm. "That's all I need to shut down that crowd!"

Cal forced a weak smile, deathly pale and looking green around the edges.

Deputy Smalls returned with Doc Ferguson in tow, black leather medical bag in hand. One of Hangtree's leading physicians and a former Confederate Army medic, the doc was by necessity and practice an expert on treating gunshot wounds. He wasted no time getting the others to move the table under the pull-down ceiling lamp so he'd have better light.

Steve Dirkes took the opportunity to bring Barton up to speed on the whirlwind vortex of calamities which had hit the country west of the Breaks like a tornado—mass murder by poisoning at Fort Pardee, the onslaught of the Free Company and its rabble horde of camp followers, the stealing of the howitzer and munitions wagon from the marauders and its deliverance to the Cross Ranch, and the Free Company's encampment at Sidepocket Canyon west of Wild Horse Canyon.

Long before Steve had finished his account, Barton sent Deputy Smalls to make the rounds of the Golden Spur, Alamo Bar, and Doghouse Bar to round up a posse ready for action as soon as possible.

Doc Ferguson removed the bullet from Cal's side; luckily it had not hit any vital organs. He cleaned the wounds, sewing them up and patching them with bandages. "He's lost a lot of blood, but he's got youth and strength on his side. With that and a little bit of luck, he should pull through." Doc mopped the sweat from his brow with a handkerchief already soaked with the stuff.

"Nice work, Doc," Barton said appreciatively.

"From what I've heard tonight, my work is only beginning."

"Mine, too."

Three a.m. found the Hughes camp sound asleep save for a handful of night watchmen. Denton Dick slept under a canvas top on a cot in one of two Conestoga wagons, a prerogative of his rank as leader. Second in command Leo Plattner slept in the other prairie schooner.

The rest of the men slept out in the open under the stars and around the campfires. Some slept on bedroll blankets, others on the grassy ground where they had passed out dead drunk.

Half an hour later, they suffered a rude awakening, rousted from their slumbers by well-armed Hangtree posse men. Numbered about forty in all, the posse was mostly hardcases of the type one would expect to find lingering into the wee hours in the town's saloons and dives. They bristled with rifles, shotguns, six-guns, and an excess of ill will toward the outsider bad men.

That the Hughes bunch had literally been caught napping was no accident. The handful of armed guards who weren't snoring away noisily in drunken slumbers had been surprised and knocked out cold by a select band of veteran Indian fighters chosen by Marshal Barton for the task. Those who have hunted the Comanche and lived to tell the tale were not the type to be thwarted by the likes of Denton Dick's backshooting renegades.

As the main force of posse men moved in to subdue and disarm the sleeping outlaws, gunfire erupted over the scene. A couple outlaws with good reflexes and little common sense jumped up, shooting. They downed several of the posse before being shot to pieces by the concentrated firepower of massed Hangtree shooters.

It was an object lesson that took out what little fight the remaining bad men had in them.

Denton Dick Hughes from Denton, Texas, tried to flee, climbing down from the rear of his wagon only to find himself looking down the barrel of the gun.

The waiting Marshal Barton thrust it into his face the instant the bandit chief's boot soles touched ground. "I knew you'd take it on the run, Dick. That was a sure-thing bet."

He disarmed Denton Dick, pulling first one gun then the other from their holsters and tossing them away. He patted him down, searching him none too gently, discovering a covert sleeve gun, pocket pistol, folding knife, and set of brass knuckles.

He also discovered Denton Dick's sizeable bill-roll,

which he dropped into a vest pocket. "I'm confiscating this money in the name of the law, Dick."

"But you're keeping it for yourself," Denton Dick said after mouthing a few obscenities.

"I *am* the law in Hangtree," Barton said.

The bandit chief mouthed a few more obscenities until a well-placed meaty fist in the belly abruptly silenced him.

"Don't take any chances with these rannies, men!" Barton shouted, with a hand cupped to the side of his mouth to amplify the volume of his words so they'd be sure to be heard. "Be sure to search for concealed weapons and be careful. These men are slippery cusses!"

The posse men set to with a will in carrying out Barton's commands, all but tearing the clothes off the bad men and tenderizing their flesh with many well-placed punches and kicks. It was a melee, an out-and-out rout of the outlaws.

A squad of searchers ransacked the wagons to make sure that no outlaws were hiding in them. They were surprised and delighted to find Leo Plattner in the other Conestoga wagon, bound hand and foot the way his fellows had left him after subduing him from his whiskey-fueled hell-raising.

The bandit chief stood hunched over, hugging his middle with both arms and leaning against the wagon for support. He was hatless, his face bruised, his nose bloodied.

Barton raised a hand, causing Denton Dick to flinch, cowering with both hands raised to protect himself.

"Why Dick, I was just brushing away a bug to keep it from flying in my eye. You don't think I was going to hit you?" Barton asked, mildly soft-spoken. "Remember our town motto. 'We're all friends here in Hangtree.'"

"I ain't from Hangtree," Denton Dick gasped.

"Oops, there is that. Hard luck for you, I reckon," Barton said. "Now suppose you leave off slinging the horse manure like you been doing all day and tell me what you know about Jimbo Turlock and the Free Company."

TWENTY-FOUR

Sunrise came to the Cross ranch.

"Ready?" Otto Berg asked.

"Ready as I'll ever be," Sam Heller said. "I've got my ducks all lined up in a row."

"Yeah, but that ain't birdshot you're using."

"Not hardly."

Sam was preparing to use canister shot, the artillery equivalent of double-ought twelve-gauge buckshot. In close combat, it was the anti-personnel weapon supreme. "We'll make it hot for the marauders."

Sam had the howitzer from Fort Pardee set up on top of a knoll facing the eastern mouth of Cross's Cut and about 150 yards away from it. He was no artilleryman, but he'd picked up enough tradecraft in that line during the war to be able to effectively aim and fire the weapon. He couldn't do it without a gun crew. Otto Berg had some knowledge of the piece's working arrangements. The three scouts had also been recruited for the crew.

Surprisingly, Luke had volunteered to help out. He couldn't get around too quickly, so he was in charge of the care, maintenance, and disbursement of the howitzer's gunpowder loads. Premeasured and self-contained within their own bagged containers, a supply of the charged loads had been found in the munitions wagon accompanying the stolen howitzer, along with various types of shot and shell, ramrod swabbing sticks, fuse cord, and other items needed for turning the piece into a working engine of destruction.

Luke had volunteered for the chore because, as he said, it would put him in the front lines of the action.

As darkness had shaded into dawn, Sam had trained and practiced with his crew to prepare them for the coming clash. He'd schooled them in the basics of reloading and tending the piece.

He reckoned they were as ready as they could be in the time allotted. Of one thing he was sure—men like these would withstand anything the foe threw at them, or die trying. Such men would not run.

Luke stood to one side leaning on his crutch, eyeing the howitzer, and scowling.

"What's got your back up, Luke?" Sam asked.

"One of these devil's tools took off my left leg below the knee. You can't expect me to like it."

"Well, here's a way to get your own back," Sam said cheerfully.

Luke smiled tightly.

"Be careful not to get in front of the piece while it's firing or you might lose the other leg," Otto Berg said seriously, not joking.

"Don't you worry about me, Yankee boy. I'll be safe behind that cannon when the shooting starts, tending the powder charges. You're the one who'd best look out," Luke said.

Otto laughed without humor. "Think you've got a soft job? Think again, Reb. If one spark or ember touches the charges, it'll blow you sky-high."

"You and me both, mister, and don't think that won't be a comfort."

"Save the fight for the enemy, men," Sam said, knowing how easily such back-and-forth needling could degenerate into harsh words and quick guns. "We've got to pull together."

"Don't worry. I've got enough scrap to go around," Luke assured him.

"I believe it!" Sam said. He did, too.

"For a civilian, you sure can make noises like an officer," Otto said to Sam.

"I'm no officer and you can walk off anytime. Nothing's keeping you here. Nothing but yourself."

"I was at the fort when the poisoning went down, remember? I'll stick till the last Free Company dog dies," Otto said.

"Then we're all squared away," Sam said.

"All we need is somebody to fight," Luke said.

"We won't have long to wait for that," said Sam.

The gun crew was the tip of the spear blade of Hangtree's fighting forces. Two hundred men or more were massed in the area opposite the cut. The county militia was assembled for the fray.

Mack Barton had organized a formidable fighting force in the hours since Cal Lane had ridden into Hangtree. The marshal had been aided by the movers and shakers of the town and county—the Big Men of Hangtree. They'd clawed and scraped and schemed for everything they had and no one was going to take it from them without a fight.

Chief among them were the three biggest ranchers

in the county, Wade Hutto, Don Eduardo del Castillo, and Clay Stafford.

Wade Hutto was town boss, a rich rancher and power broker who pulled the strings of the mayor and town council. He'd helped Barton win office as marshal, but Barton had made it painfully clear to his overbearing patron that he was his own man when it came to laying down the law in town. He'd secured his own following among the small ranchers, farmers, and storekeepers, anxious to avoid being gobbled up by Hutto and his moneyed clique.

Hutto held a controlling interest in the town bank, not to mention its president Banker Willoughby. He owned much of the choicest real estate on Trail Street and its surroundings and owned a piece of or held the mortgage on many more buildings, lots, and small ranches and farms. He was also the owner of a prosperous and sprawling ranch on the south fork of the Liberty River. Impressive as it was, it was not the biggest ranch in the county.

That honor was reserved for Rancho Grande on the Liberty's north fork, whose master and patron was Don Eduardo del Castillo. The spread had been owned by his family a hundred years and more before the first English-speaking Texicans had settled in the area. His relations with his Anglo neighbors were prickly at best, fueled by his vast distrust of all Tejanos and his passionately held belief that they were out to steal his land and property.

In this assumption, he was one hundred percent correct. His small army of hard-shooting, hard-riding vaqueros and the high, thick adobe walls protecting his magnificent hacienda and home grounds ensured that the rancho remained securely in his possession.

The third member of this power trio was Clay Stafford, a recent newcomer to Hangtree who'd come up hard, fast, and strong. A relatively young man, he was a ruthless, ambitious rancher and landholder who had survived a murderous family blood feud to become sole master of the Ramrod ranch.*

The Ramrod land lay along the Liberty's south fork, butting up against Wade Hutto's extensive holdings. Stafford and Hutto's volatile relationship proved the truth of the saying, *Well-armed neighbors make good neighbors until the shooting starts.*

Clay Stafford was well-prepared for the inevitable confrontation. A number of his hired men were handier with guns than they were with livestock. His foreman Jord Hall was a hard man and Tom Lord, another hire, was a well-respected triggerman. He was also known as "Tom the Lord" for his aloof, standoffish ways. More than a few other fast guns were in his employ.

The Ramrod forces were held in check by Hutto and his top gun Boone Lassiter, who headed a crew of fast-shooting hardcases.

Hutto and Stafford maintained an uneasy peace, but it was only a matter of time before their simmering mutual antagonisms burst into flame.

But this day the two of them and Don Eduardo were united in bucking the Free Company horde massed on the far side of the Breaks. All three had sent sizeable groups of their best fighters to the Cross Ranch.

*For the doings of the murderous Stafford clan, see *Savage Texas: A Good Day to Die.*

A semi-invalid, Don Eduardo had remained behind at the Rancho, sending his son Diego, foreman Hector Vasquez, and a cadre of pistoleros. Wade Hutto and Clay Stafford rode in at the head of their flying squads of gunmen.

Fewer in number but second to none in heart and nerve were the small ranchers and farmers of Hangtree, represented at the Cross Ranch by a solid contingent of up-on-their-hind-legs-and-fighting militiamen.

The townsmen were no less represented, with shopkeepers, store clerks, artisans, stable hands, bartenders, and a score of other occupations appearing in the form of well-armed, rough-and-ready fighting men.

Several notable Hangtree personalities had come out for the fight. There was Damon Bolt, scion of a Louisiana plantation dynasty and onetime riverboat gambler, now turned co-owner with the redoubtable Mrs. Frye of the Golden Spur Saloon. His was a deadly gun.

Also present was Dan Oxblood; the raffish, red-headed, left-handed gun for hire was donating his formidable professional services for free.

Squint McCray was there, owner and proprietor of the rowdy Doghouse Bar. He headed a crowd of Doghouse regulars, those who sobered up in time to get in on the scrap. They were drifters, saddle tramps, petty gunmen, and smalltime crooks, a rough bunch, but most of them basically decent and goodhearted at bottom, if not the most scrupulously law-abiding element in the community.

But they could fight like wildcats and were always ready to tie into a tussle. In fact, when there was no fight to be had, they'd often start one, which frequently brought them the unwelcome official attentions of Marshal Barton.

The denizens of Mextown formed up a band of pistoleros and vaqueros, seconded by a following of hardworking campesinos of modest means armed with shotguns, muskets, machetes, scythes, and whatever else might come in handy in a close-quarters fight to the finish.

Together the defenders made up a cross-section of Hangtree society high and low, from prosperous businessmen to penniless, hard-bitten drifters.

Their numbers were increased by the addition of fighting men from the Brooks and Baca wagon trains who'd offered to pitch in and help out. They were frontiersmen who'd battled the perils of pitiless Nature and their fellow man in the form of warlike Indians, bandits, and renegades.

Most had served in the Confederate army during the war. They came loaded for bear and spoiling for a good fight.

Organizer and key man Marshal Barton had more volunteers than he could use. He detailed a large group to stay behind to guard the town, including the wagon trains out on the campgrounds.

He was wary of Hangtree being taken by surprise by Free Company gunmen making a sneak on the town while most of the defenders were massed at the Cross ranch, guarding the eastern portal of the cut.

The howitzer was positioned on the knoll and aimed so as to have a clear field of fire deep into the corridor of the pass.

Riflemen, marksmen all, were posted high up on

the rocky summit of both sides of the hills bordering the cut.

A large number of foot soldiers originally formed up in a military-style square between knoll and pass dispersed to take cover in the rocks and rills of the flat at the base of a gently uptilting slope accessing the pass.

On the flanks of this infantry force were two groups of mounted men, the cavalry. They waited in the wings in anticipation of the moment when they would be called to deliver the decisive killing stroke.

The dawning sun began picking out countless reflected glints and highlights from weapons in the hands of the defenders of the pass, the blue steel of a six-gun barrel, the razor edge of a sharpened machete.

All the defenders could do was wait, wait for the enemy to engage them.

But they couldn't be sure the Free Company would come through Cross's Cut, rather than going east through the Notch and along Hangtree Trail. If the attackers went that way they could swing north and hit the defenders hard on their south flank.

Or the Free Company could strike farther north, traversing a different pass to advance east of the Breaks before moving south to hit the defenders on their north flank.

The defenders had no guarantees that the Free Company would come by way of Cross's Cut, especially if they learned that a counterforce was massed there to resist them. The presence of the Hangtree militia could not be kept secret for long.

What was needed was some irritant, some gadfly to sting Free Company and sting it so hard the marauders would come charging full-tilt after its tormentors, with no thought to the consequences of such a headlong rush. Just as a man may be driven temporarily mad by the sting of a persistent horsefly, some aggravating factor would enrage the Free Company into insensate fury, causing it to charge blindly into the cut.

When he was so minded, Johnny Cross could be such a gadfly.

Johnny Cross, the Kid from Texas who during the war shot his way into the inner circle of Quantrill's Raiders. . . .

TWENTY-FIVE

Johnny Cross led a group of fifteen mounted men on the mission to maraud the marauders.

Among the band of gunfighting skirmishers were Lone Star notables. Tom Lord from the Ramrod wore a fancy brocaded vest and black sombrero with silver filigree embroidery. His weapons were a pair of elaborately engraved silver-plated revolvers.

Kev Huddy was an up-and-coming young gunfighter who also rode for the Ramrod. Long straight brown hair framed a pleasantly ugly horse-face with a massive overbite. His pale gray eyes were keen, alert, intelligent. He wore no holsters, instead keeping a pair of guns stuck in the top of his pants. He could get them into action fast and shot straight.

From the Cross ranch, Vic Vargas wore a holstered gun on each hip and two more guns holstered butt-out under brawny arms. He'd learned the technique of forting up with many readily available six-guns from Johnny Cross.

El Indio Negro, a mysterious gunman of mixed blood, had gotten his name from his penchant for wearing all-black outfits, including a black hat and a fringed black buckskin jacket.

Fritz Carrados, half German and half Mexican, had long thin straw-colored hair, bulging watery blue eyes, and a long thin face. He wore a planter's broad-brimmed hat and white suit. He didn't care that the white suit made him a better target. He was something of a dandy. A dandy shot, too.

Wiley Crabbe was disreputable and oafish, and a no-account brother-in-law of Squint McCray. But he was earning a mark on the plus side of the ledger by putting himself on the line in defense of Hangtree. He wore a big floppy shapeless hillbilly hat, a pair of blue denim bib overalls, and thick-soled, lace-up, brown "farm boy" boots. He was armed with his notorious "shotgun revolver," a custom-made four-barreled shotgun featuring two barrels over two barrels, all clustered around a long central axis that could be rotated 360 degrees. He wore a bag of shotgun shells hanging from a cord worn over his neck.

The others were mighty men of renown, each whose exploits and adventures could fill a book.

Luke Pettigrew had demanded to be included in the group, but the hard truth of the matter was that his left leg ending with its stump below the knee would prevent him from doing the all-out hard riding that the mission required. He'd argued, protested, and wheedled to go along but all in vain. In the end, he'd had to admit to himself—if to no one else—that his handicap might endanger others of the band, not the least Johnny, who would try to protect his friend and partner at the risk of endangering himself.

Luke had consoled himself by staking out a role in

the howitzer's gun crew, which was sure to put him in the thick of the action.

As dawn was breaking over the knoll, he thought back to that conversation.

"Only one of us can go, and I'm the logical choice," Johnny said. *"Besides, one of us partners has to stay behind. If I don't come back, I want to know that the ranch will be in good hands—yours."*

"If I get the ranch, the first thing I'm gonna do is rename it the Pettigrew Ranch," Luke groused.

"Hmm . . . Wonder if it's too late for me to bequeath my half to Coot."

"And have it renamed the Coot Ranch?"

"Ouch! No, that don't sound right. Reckon I better come back alive after all."

"You'd best, hoss."

About the same time, the band of Hangtree gun-hawks was in a secret passage in Sidepocket Canyon where the Free Company was camped.

Sidepocket was commonly held to be a cul-de-sac with only one way in or out, but Johnny knew better. He had grown up in these parts. In a sense, they were his own backyard.

As a boy, he had explored and hunted extensively in the backcountry west of the Breaks, in Wild Horse Canyon and the flats stretching out to the Llano. He'd ferreted out all its hidden and secret ways, its little-known and almost unknown byways, its gulches, draws, coverts, caves, ledges, benches, fans, and slides.

Jimbo Turlock and Free Company must surely adhere to the common wisdom that Sidepocket had one way in and out—one way only—and therefore would take precautions to ensure that the portal was well-guarded.

But like much that passed for common wisdom, the belief in a lone entryway was wrong.

Johnny knew of a long winding gorge, so narrow in some places that a well-girthed horse could barely proceed through it without scraping its flanks on rock walls. It entered the canyon from the northwest, worming its way through seemingly solid stone bulwarks to spill into a hollow under a cavernous rock overhang inside Sidepocket. The outer entrance was screened by a wall of trees at the base of a limb of towering rock.

Johnny had taken the point and led the skirmisher band into the gorge in black predawn darkness. The riders had been forced to proceed single file. With no room for a horse to turn around and reverse position, once in the gorge there was no turning back.

It was no place for those with a dislike for tight confining spaces, as Johnny had made clear to the others when first outlining his plan. To a man, they were determined to take the hard ride.

"The better to smite the Philistines," fancy-talking Mick Sabbath put it.

Dawn was breaking when the riders could see the enemy. The scene in Sidepocket looked like something out of the Middle Ages, when mounted bands of robber knights were followed by a locust-like horde of predatory rabble eager to feast on the leavings of a warlike wolf pack.

The main force of Free Company was a nomadic group of riders, not unlike Plains Indians, mounted tribes, or an army unit out in the field. The base camp partook of elements both mobile and martial.

The hard core of the Company numbered about two hundred mounted fighting men. Their camp followers, who squatted apart in an encampment of their own, were somewhere in the number of three hundred men and women and more than a few children.

Free Company had several dozen wagons of all types—wagons to carry water barrels, food supplies, weapons, loot, personnel, and personal belongings. Like the Company itself, the transport vehicles were a ragtag crazy-quilt assemblage.

The variety of wheeled carriers included teamster freight wagons, covered wagons of the Conestoga type, rancher's flatbed wagons, buckboard carriages, chuck wagons, and tall, high-sided gypsy-style homes on wheels.

There was also a motley collection of lesser vehicles—coaches, gigs, two-wheeled dog and fly carts, and even some man-powered wooden push carts.

As with all nomads, horses were a prime necessity. A section at the rear of the canyon had been penned off into a corral enclosed by a semicircle of wagons laid end to end. A gap in the middle was eliminated by a plank-and-beam wooden gate. Several hundred horses were penned in the big corral, but knots and clusters of the animals were picketed around the many smaller campsites scattered about.

A second, similar corral held several score of rustled cattle. The hapless beasts were tightly penned, crowded together with little room to move. The stock provided the Free Company with its own traveling commissary of "meat on the hoof." What wasn't eaten could be sold later.

The canyon floor was covered by a mosaic of homemade hand-crafted structures, lightweight and portable, designed with traveling in mind. A number of canvas tents dotted the scene, having been looted from army stores and mining camps.

The better tents were gathered together in a separate section set off by themselves, away from the more primitive and squalid living areas. Other shelters included lean-tos, several tipi-like constructions, and many foxholes roofed with blankets, sheets, or rags.

The mass of people had had an immediate damaging effect on the surroundings. Grass, weeds, and the leafy brush of the canyon had pretty well been grazed down to the nub by horses and cattle. Branches were picked clean of leaves, trees and bushes had been torn up by the roots to be used for firewood. The ground underfoot had been trampled into a muddy morass.

At the early morning hour, the camp was as quiet as it ever got, coming alive with activity as the more sober denizens began to rouse themselves for the day's ill deeds ahead—which were eagerly anticipated by all and sure to be bloody, horrendous, and profitable.

Bedlam was astir as groups of drunks shouted at each other, argued, sang, laughed, cried, and fought over cackling, slatternly women and trollops. Occasional shots and screams rang out, ignored by all but those who were immediately concerned.

In the hidden cave, the Hangtree skirmishers prepared to make their wild ride. They were on foot, holding the reins of their mounts, the cavern ceiling being too low for them to sit their horses beneath it.

Vic Vargas was a *dynamitero*, a dynamiter. An open-mouthed canvas sack slung over his neck and shoulders was filled with bundles of dynamite. Each bundle contained several sticks of TNT tied together with a short fuse sticking out of the top. Vic had been helped by Sam Heller, himself an experienced hand in the bomb-making line, in preparing the explosive packages the night before.

Vic was making a few last-minute adjustments, trimming the tips of some fuse cords with a penknife blade, his face a study in concentration.

"Dynamite is tricky. Sure you know what you're doing with that stuff, Vargas?" Tom Lord asked dubiously.

"If he don't, it's too late to do anything about it now." Wiley Crabbe snickered.

"You want to do it, Tom?" Vic Vargas said, looking up from his chores.

"Not me!" Lord said quickly, holding his hands up, palms-out in a warding gesture. "All I know about gunpowder is that it shoots a bullet!"

"And it's served you very well, Tom," Fritz Carrados said, smiling thinly.

"Thanks, Fritz . . . I think." Lord was unsure how to take the other's comment. Was it a compliment or a sly dig? He didn't know; the elusive Carrados was a hard man to read.

Vic finished what he was doing, folded his jackknife, and put it away. "My folks died when I was a kid. I got taken in by miners at a mining camp. They raised me to be a powder monkey. I'd put the gunpowder charges in the holes for blasting. You've got to know what you're doing in that job to keep all ten fingers." He held out his hands with fingers extended. "I've got mine. That satisfy your concerns, Tom?"

"The proof is in the blasting," Lord said stubbornly.

"So it is. We'll all find out soon enough, eh? Me first of all," Vic said.

"We ready to go then?" Johnny asked.

"Let me light up this cigar first and we'll be on our way," Vic said.

"Light it when we're in the open," Lord said. "I don't see the sense in playing with fire with that sack full of dynamite in here."

"Vic knows what he's doing," Cross said.

"Sure, but does the TNT?" Lord countered.

For reply, Johnny flicked a thumbnail against the white phosphorous tip of a self-igniting wooden lucifer. The flame sputtered, underlighting Johnny's face, casting weird flickering highlights and shadows in the cave under the ledge.

A hiss sounded. Possibly a sharply indrawn breath from anxious Tom Lord, maybe from somebody else. It was too dark to tell who'd made the sound.

Johnny reached over, holding the match flame to the tip of the long thick cigar held clenched between Vic's teeth.

Vic puffed it alight. "*Gracias.*"

"*De nada,*" Johnny said. "You ready?"

"Yes," Vic said.

"The rest of you?" Johnny asked the others.

All signaled their eager readiness, with no dissenters.

"Let's go." Johnny took the lead, holding the reins of his chestnut horse. He went up a gentle dirt slope, stepping onto the canyon floor and out from under the overhang. Parting the screen of brush with an arm, he stepped out into the open, the horse following.

The other skirmishers followed one by one until all men and horses were under open skies, clear of the brush. They stepped into the saddles, mounting up in a ranked line side by side, facing the Free Company camp and the gap in the far side of the canyon that was the exit.

The canyon floor was covered with a haze of smoke from the many campfires and cooking fires scattered around the site. The gray pall was so thick in some places that it stung the eyes of those nearby. The canyon walls held the smoke, forming a protective bulwark against cleansing winds. Through only two vents could the smoke escape—straight up into the sky and by drifting east out of the mouth of the canyon.

Baldy Vance pointed at a clump of well-ordered, well-kept tents clustered off to one side at the north of the canyon. "Reckon them tents is for the high muckety-mucks in this crowd?"

"That's how to bet it," Fritz Carrados said.

"Let's be sure to take care of them," Kev Huddy chimed in.

"Hear that, Vic?" Johnny Cross asked.

"Yes I do. Strikes me as a property that's ripe for demolition."

"That means he aims to blow it up, Wiley," Hilton George condescended to remark to the man seated astride a horse to his left.

"I know what it means, dang you," Wiley said, irritated.

The area with the greatest concentration of people was in the center of the canyon, but the space was relatively small. Free Company and its tattered auxiliaries were many, so several dozen ragtag foot soldiers and followers were camped farther away, closer to where the Hangtree raiders suddenly emerged as if they were phantoms who could mysteriously appear at will.

A line of smoke rose from a low campfire. Around it, men stretched out on bedrolls or wrapped in blankets. A few early risers stood around the fire, smoking and passing around a half-gallon brown jug. A pretty sorry-looking bunch, dirty, unkempt, raggedy-assed, they turned to stare at the newcomers.

Johnny Cross had something to say before the skirmishers went into action. "Remember, men, our job is to take a club and whack it against the hornet's nest. So hit it hard!"

One of the gawkers separated himself from the others, starting toward the strangers. His gait was unsteady, weaving. "Hey! Hey, you! What you doing over there?" he shouted while still some distance away. He was loud, causing heads to turn to see what the fuss was all about. Men sat up on their bedrolls, rubbing sleep out of their eyes, blankets falling to their waists.

Vic Vargas puffed away steadily at his cigar.

Some of the men standing around the campfire straggled after the loudmouth shouting at the skirmishers. Had he known they were skirmishers, he'd never have gone so much as a country mile near them.

The stragglers began buzzing, talking among themselves.

"Who's making all that noise?

"It's Fred. He's got the wind up about something . . ."

"Whatcha hollering about, Fred? My head hurts from the hangover I got, and your bellowing ain't doing it no good."

"Something about them jaspers ain't right," Fred said darkly. Speaking directly to the newcomers as he lurched toward them, he demanded, "Who're you? Where'd you come from, anyway?"

"Hangtown, friend," Johnny said. "We come from Hangtown."

Fred stood there thinking it over, mouth gaping open.

One of the stragglers figured it out first. "Hell, they're from Hangtree. *Git 'em!*" he cried, going for his gun.

Johnny Cross reached, his gun seeming to spring into his hand in less than an eye blink, shooting the straggler down.

Fred finally got it and clawed for his gun. Johnny burned him down, too. For good measure, he put some slugs into a couple men rushing forward, tugging at their guns. They spun as they were hit, crying out and falling down.

Shouts of outrage came from the cluster of camp followers, some women screaming. The scramble was on. Men on the ground threw aside blankets and jumped up, pulling their guns and firing wildly at the skirmishers.

Vic touched the hot tip of his cigar to the end of a fuse sticking out of a bundle of dynamite. The fuse began sizzling, alive and burning fast. "Short fuse, boys. Let's ride!"

The Hangtree raiders charged forward, shooting and shouting. Some ripped loose with a ringing rebel yell, a high howling cry full of fight and defiance.

Horses' hooves dug dirt, kicking up clods of earth in the force of their surging rush.

Men grouped around the campfire fired away, more guns joining in.

Enemy gunmen were black outlines against the campfire's red glare. Johnny leaned over to one side of his horse, letting loose with a few ripping rounds.

The shooters screamed, throwing up their arms over their heads, whirling, and falling.

The skirmishers' line parted in the middle, going around the campfire on both sides, riding down those too slow and luckless to get out of the way.

Vic dropped the bundle of TNT into the flames as he raced by. Leaning forward, he touched spurs to his horse's flanks to get more speed and outdistance the upcoming blast.

The Hangtree raiders pointed their horses at the opposite end of the canyon and raced full-tilt for it, resolved to do as much damage as they could along the way, and woe to anyone who tried to bar the way. Making full use of the advantage of surprise, they tore through the crowds like a whirlwind, irresistible!

A few heartbeats later, the dynamite exploded. A dazzling flare of incandescence burst into the air, accompanied by a roaring torrent of noise and force. The light was at once orange, red, and yellow. Bodies were tossed high in a pillar of smoke and fire.

The Free Company and its followers were shocked, unable to imagine that anyone would have the audacity to attack *them*!

The hard-core main fighting force of the Company were hardcase killers, used to taking risks and being paid for it. The yellowbellies and cowards were in the larger group of hangers-on and camp followers—a choice crew. They were tinhorns, pimps, thugs, slavers, six-snake whiskey vendors, renegades who sold liquor and guns to the Indians, and still worse malefactors whose unnatural lust for cruelty and depravity had made them outcasts even among the freewheeling owlhoot fraternity.

The women who trailed the Free Company from

town to town on its cross-country cavalcade of robbery and murder were the dregs and drabs, mattress-backs who'd lay for any man with the price of a drink. Sunbonnet Sues and Good Time Annies, they were often called.

Some of the younger ones still had their looks and figures, others were shapeless slatterns. Most were gutter-tough. More than a few were murderesses. They had to be or they would have gone down for the last time a long while ago.

Theirs was not the way of the gun but of the stiletto, knockout drops or poison in a drink, a hatpin or knitting needle through the ear and piercing the brain of a sleeping victim—male or female, adult or child.

Yes, it took a certain kind of woman to follow the Free Company. They accepted a life of hardship, privation, starvation, and disease. But they hadn't joined the horde of camp followers to get shot at. That was for the men.

When the raid opened, most of the women did what they'd learned to do in a hundred, a thousand barroom fights, knifings, and shootings—they ran for cover. But little cover was to be found in Sidepocket's box canyon.

The attack loosed a floodtide of chaos. The raiders split into a center group and two wings. The left flank made for the cluster of tents where the inner circle of the Company was thought to be. Johnny, Huddy, and Carrados rode ahead of Vic, clearing a path for him. Vic galloped along, reaching into the sack of bundled dynamite sticks, pulling one out, lighting the fuse, and tossing the package where he thought it would do the most good.

Johnny swerved his horse to charge a line of gunmen guarding an unhorsed wagon housed with provisions, water barrels, and food stocks. Carrados and Huddy followed his lead. Ten gunmen fired at them, red lines of flame licking out from their gun barrels.

Johnny kept going, reins clenched between his teeth to free both hands to work his guns. He squeezed out shots, first from one gun, then from the other. He heard the guns of Huddy and Carrados firing along with his as the line of shooters began to melt away under the rain of bullets.

A shooter screamed, dropping in front of the supply wagon. Another went down as Johnny closed in. The line had been cut by half. The others suddenly lost their nerve. They broke, scrambling for the sidelines, getting out of the way of the gun-wielding fury and his sidemen. Johnny shot some down as they ran.

He swerved away from the wagon. The gun in his right hand clicked on an empty chamber. He holstered it, hauling out another pistol stuck in his belt, one of many. It was a tactic of a veteran pistol-fighter to not waste precious time reloading. He took as many loaded guns to a fight as he could.

Such was part of the gospel as preached by Quantrill, and Johnny had learned his lessons well. He had three spare guns tucked into his belt and a saddlebag full of extras. He didn't believe in doing things by halves, and making war was no exception.

Vic reined in at the supply wagon, stopping suddenly. He tossed a lit bundle of TNT into the wagon and quickly spurred his horse away from it.

Johnny had already changed course, making for

the cluster of tan canvas tents that boasted the most military look of the sprawling camp. Vic followed.

A few beats later, the dynamite blew up, demolishing the supply wagon. In its place rose a new pillar of fire.

The tents were laid out orderly in classic grid style, with regularly spaced intervals between each one. A cart called a water buffalo held a big hogshead barrel of fresh drinking water. Rifles were stacked upright in cone-shaped arrangements in open squares fronting the tents.

Here was where the elite of the Free Company was sheltered, the all-important leadership cadre by which elusive Jimbo Turlock exercised his authority over the rank-and-file troops.

With the alert sounded and the attack well-launched, men rushed out of the tents in varying states of undress. Their women either screamed and ran or stayed behind, huddled on the ground inside the tents.

Reaching the squares, men grabbed rifles, shouldering, pointing, and firing them at the raiders.

Huddy charged, coming on strong. He was hit twice and went down, falling off his horse. A soft patch of muddy ground cushioned his fall, but he hit hard enough to knock the wind out of him and make him see stars. He was down but not yet out.

One shot hit him high on the left side of his chest, just below the collarbone. The round had missed heart and lung—lucky! He'd also been shot through the bicep of his left arm.

He was in a tight spot, plenty tight, but rose to his knees in the mud wallow, hands on the ground. His left arm wasn't working too well. He shook his head to clear it, to wipe away the shower of little colored lights that floated in front of his eyes, veiling the scene.

More Free Company men were running out of the tents, guns in hand. Three gunmen saw Huddy and ran toward him.

He pulled a revolver—fast, like lightning—from the top of his waistband and started banging away.

The man in the lead of the charge went down, falling on his face and dropping his gun. As he dragged himself up on his hands and knees, he and Huddy eyed each other for an instant.

The outlaw grabbed the gun on the ground in front of him and pointed it at Huddy, but Huddy fired first, blowing the top of the other's head off.

The other two gunmen fired. The bullets passed over Huddy's head.

Huddy slammed the gunner moving in on the left side with two shots. He stopped suddenly, hitting an invisible wall.

The third man was at point-blank range. Huddy swung the gun at him and fired. Momentum carried him forward until he came to a halt, dead. The hand of his outstretched arm was only inches away from where Huddy stood on his knees.

The tent area continued to yield Free Company men running along the aisles between the tents looking to get in the fight. Women stuck their heads out from between tent flaps to see what was happening. In the early morning light, their painted and rouged faces looked like unnatural fright masks.

A fat woman with frizzy brown hair in a bun, wearing a soiled white shift, ran back and forth in front of the tents shrieking and waving her hands in the air. Yet she seemed unhurt, not a mark on her.

On every side, the camp was in an uproar. Free Company members were on their feet, some grouping together, others standing alone. The canyon floor seethed, a cauldron boiling with angry desperate men—armed men.

The fast-moving figures of mounted horsemen, the Hangtree raiders, darted this way and that, plowing through the mass.

The racket of gunfire rising to a steady roar was periodically punctuated by earth-shattering booms as Vic detonated a succession of dynamite blasts.

Huddy was still kneeling in the muck, isolated and alone. He lurched upright, rising to his feet, unsteady. He'd taken quite a blow when he fell. His left arm hung down at his side, numb, useless. He clenched his fingers, making a fist. The hand worked, but he couldn't raise it past his waist. The wound in his upper arm had impaired some key tendon or muscle.

His right hand was still good and that was his shooting hand. He'd make it count.

He looked around. His horse was nowhere in sight. Fled, long gone.

Staggering to one side, he came into view of a group of men grabbing stacked rifles. He fired at them, dropping a man with one shot. Another in the group pointed a rifle and fired at Huddy, missing.

Huddy's gun clicked on empty. He let it fall, his hand streaking to the next gun in his belt and hauling it out. The motion threw him off balance.

That saved his life. Rifle bullets tore through the place where Huddy had been standing. Lurching sideways, gun in hand, he threw down at the riflemen, pumping out lead.

One man went down, then another until Huddy's gun was empty and the riflemen were no more.

A fierce black-bearded man hovered on the sidelines,

rifle in hands. Holding the weapon hip-high, he swung the barrel toward Huddy.

Huddy shouted something inarticulate, charging the other barehanded, set to sell his life dearly.

The black-bearded man's face vanished in a red wet blur as a bullet smashed into it.

A massive shape loomed over Huddy, the figure of a rider on horseback. Johnny Cross.

Wiley Crabbe rode up behind him, clutching his outlandish four-barreled revolving shotgun. He was not a big man. In fact, he was a scrawny undersized whelp who looked to weigh about a hundred and ten pounds soaking wet. In his hands, the outsized weapon looked like a genuine hand cannon.

Wiley tossed Johnny a half salute with a free hand. "I'll cover ya!"

Johnny holstered his gun, freeing his hands, and turned his horse toward Huddy.

Huddy reached out with his right arm, left arm hanging down limply at his side.

Johnny got the idea. Approaching Huddy, he leaned out of the saddle and grabbed Huddy's forearm. In one sweeping motion, he hauled Huddy up, lifting him clear off the ground and setting him behind the saddle on the horse.

"Thanks!" Huddy said.

"Hold on!" said Johnny.

While the rescue was in progress, a fresh batch of Free Company men came into view. They'd been hanging back, held at bay by the volume of firepower Johnny had been pumping out of those twin Colts. The lethally streaming lead had come to a halt when he'd moved to save Huddy.

A rush of a dozen or more men with guns blazing came pouring out from a lane behind a row of tents.

"Git going, boys. I got you covered!" Wiley Crabbe called out.

Johnny turned the chestnut horse toward the canyon exit and put heels to the animal's sides, surging forward. Huddy hooked his good right arm around Johnny's middle, holding on tight to keep from falling off as the horse leaped forward.

A vigilant observer might have noticed something unusual about Wiley's attire. The jacket was similar to a hunting jacket in that it had a heavily padded quilted cushion sewn into the right chest and shoulder area, where the shotgun butt would be snugged up against it when shooting. The padding absorbed much of the impact from the piece's jolting recoil.

His saddle was custom-fitted with a special high cantle in back. Its curved inner wall, also reinforced and padded with cushioning, supported his lower back.

Not a wealthy or well-to-do man, Wiley lived hand-to-mouth. It was the best he could do on the scant wages paid him for laboring at the Doghouse Bar. He was a middling worker, at best. The drinks he sneaked behind the bar probably cost more than he was worth.

The point being that while Wiley rarely had a coin to his name, he'd managed to scrape up enough cash to pay for certain vital accessories to complement his fearsome weapon and maximize its striking power. When it came to killing, this proud son of Hangtree, Texas, spared no expense.

Bracing himself against the paddled cantle at the back of the saddle, Wiley shouldered the stubby short-barreled revolving shotgun and cut loose with a double-barreled blast into the charging Free Company frontline marauders. Yellow flame and clouds of gun smoke stabbed from twin-mouthed big barrels on the upper side of the weapon.

A handful of gunmen at the head of the charge ran full-on into a devastating double-barreled blast of 12-gauge double-ought buckshot. For each of them it was like catching the full-force blow of a lumberman's double-bladed axe square in the midriff. They went down like sheaves of wheat chopped by a scythe—the Grim Reaper's scythe—falling in a heap of bodies, clothes, and flesh charred and smoking from the close-range blast.

Some of those behind or to the side of the frontliners were caught in the broad fan-shaped spray of the shotgun burst. Even to catch one of the white-hot metal shot pellets in the flesh was a hurting for he who was hit.

"That'll learn yez!" Wiley chortled.

A marauder held both hands to his ruined face, blood streaming out between his fingers. He tripped and fell over the pile of corpses in front of him. He did not rise again. Others fell down at the flanks of the group, staggering and crying out.

The Company's inner circle, its ruling cadre or officer class, the smartest and most ruthless killers of the crew came to fill the gap in the ranks.

The bantamweight figure of Wiley Crabbe sat on horseback, wrapped in an ash-gray cloud of gun smoke. His right shoulder and chest were numb, his bones ached, his back was pressed hard and deep into the pads cushioning the built-up cantle. Undaunted, his blood hot and raging for battle, he braced the gun butt against a bony hip and thumbed the central axis release, allowing the barrels to revolve in a circle.

Gripping the stock with one hand, he turned the four-barrel assembly in a counterclockwise direction with the other. A metallic click sounded each time the rear of a barrel came under the freed locking plate. As each smoking barrel came clear, he fed in a fresh cartridge.

Two clicks sounded as Wiley turned the barrel assembly 180 degrees, bringing a pair of fully loaded barrels into place. All four barrels were fully loaded with two previously unfired barrels in place on the high side. He thumbed the release lever back down, locking it into place. "I'm ready for action and loaded for bear!" he crowed.

More of the outlaw cadre popped up in the rows between the tents, shooting and shouting.

Once more settling himself firmly in the saddle, Wiley ripped loose another big double-blast, clearing a significant space in the landscape by mowing down more Company men.

The bone-jarring boom of Vic's TNT blasts came less frequently. The battle was about to turn in favor of the defenders' far greater numbers and firepower. The Hangtree raiders' initial advantage of surprise was gone. The Free Company was starting to get its own back.

The raid was meant to give Turlock's outfit a bloody nose and get them good and mad, and it had certainly done all of that.

"The climate's getting unhealthy," Wiley said to himself. "Too much lead in the air!" He turned his horse toward the east canyon wall, the way out to Wild Horse Canyon and escape.

It looked like most of the Hangtree hometown boys were making for it. A handful of riders, some alone and others in groups of twos and threes, tore eastward across the canyon floor. Bodies sprawled on the turf marked the raiders' single-minded path toward the canyon mouth.

"Time to make tracks. Dig dirt, horse!" Wiley kicked his horse forward, cutting a winding weaving path among the crowding robber bandits.

Of all places in the Sidepocket encampment, the eastern portal was the best guarded. Protected against an attack from without, however unlikely that might seem, it was also secured against deserters from within. From the top-ranked members of the leadership cadre to the lowliest scum of the camp followers, none could be allowed to depart freely and without official approval from the Commander, for fear they might betray some vital intelligence about the Company.

If Jimbo Turlock had wanted stone walls and impenetrable gates he could have held Fort Pardee, but mobility had always served the Free Company well in the past, and he had no intention of sacrificing it, so the entrance was only partially blocked. In the center of the canyon mouth, several wagons had been turned on their sides and reinforced with stacked hay bales to serve as a shooting platform for a twenty-man squad of riflemen on duty. Open areas on both sides were blocked with waist-high ropes and chains that could easily be lowered to offer entrance or exit for duly authorized parties.

When the attack broke, the gate guards were at first unsure what was happening or what to do. They feared the havoc within might be intended to divert them from an attack from without.

The Hangtown Raiders massed under a towering

rock on the south side of the canyon mouth, forcing
the gate guard rifle squad to move to the far side of
the barricade for protection, which put them on the
outside shooting in. Instead of trying to keep hostiles
out, they were trying to keep them in.

The boulder at the south portal was shaped like
an egg standing on its rounder, fatter end. Grouped
under its overhanging curve, the raiders were shielded
from the riflemen's bullets by the curve of the massive, house-high boulder, but not from the guns of the
masses inside Sidepocket Canyon.

Cooler heads among the robber bandits were starting to take control of the situation. The cadre realized
what had happened and were organizing a counter-
attack, getting their men under control.

Working against them was the near-complete chaos
among the main body of the rank and file, who were
confused, angry, and frightened. They had been
stampeded. Being gunmen, they used their guns.
Some shot at each other, mistaking their fellows for
foes. Others shot their guns off in the air just to be
doing something.

As for the horde of camp followers, they were in a
blind panic. An undisciplined horde at the best of
times, they were responding to the violence and brutality. They were being rounded up and herded like
cattle, pushed out of the way so the main body of the
Free Company could get into action.

Johnny Cross, with Kev Huddy riding behind him
on the same horse, reined in, joining other Hangtree
raiders who had gathered under the big boulder.

Seeing them mounted two on a horse, El Indio
Negro started to ride off.

"Wait! Where're you going?" Baldy Vance shouted after him.

"Be right back!" El Indio Negro called over his shoulder as he galloped back into the enemy camp, making a wide curving swing south along the canyon rim, then going north.

"Crazy fool!" Baldy said, shaking his head.

Under the outward-arching rock were Johnny, Huddy, Vic, Baldy Vance, Mick Sabbath, and Fritz Carrados. Of the original sixteen raiders who'd begun the charge, more than half were missing.

Wiley Crabbe came in at a gallop, reining in and taking cover with the others.

"That's the last, I think," Fritz Carrados said, "not counting El Indio."

"He'll come back," Baldy said.

"Is this all of us that won through?" Johnny asked.

"Looks like," Wiley Crabbe said.

"We've got to be sure," Carrados said.

"Look around. You see any of the others?" Wiley demanded.

"What about Lord? Don't tell me they got Tom the Lord!" Vic shouted.

"Gone!" said Mick Sabbath. "I saw it, but was too far away to help out. Lord's horse went down, throwing him into the middle of a mob. They rushed him, swarming all over him. He went down shooting to the last—" He stopped speaking for a moment. "Well, almost to the last. He saved one bullet for himself. He shot himself before they could lay hands on him. He was looking at me over the tops of their heads. He nodded to me before he pulled the trigger."

"Tom the Lord dead! I thought for sure he'd come through," Vic said.

"He died game," Mick Sabbath said. "*Ave atque vale!* Hail and farewell!"

"Why the hell don't you speak English?" Baldy grumbled.

"I said it for Tom Lord, not for you," Mick Sabbath said icily.

"Your way of saying adios, huh?" Vic said, trying to smooth things over.

"If you like," Mick Sabbath said.

"More than half of us gone!" Fritz Carrados exclaimed softly, shaking his head as in disbelief.

"No guarantees on this mission," Johnny Cross said, not unkindly.

Bullets *spang*ed the outthrust curve of the boulder above their heads, spraying them with stone chips.

"It's getting hot!" Vic involuntarily ducked his head.

"We'd best get out of here pronto if we don't want to wind up like the others," Wiley said.

"Wait till El Indio comes back," Baldy said.

"If he wants to get hisself killed that's his business. He must want to, charging back into that mess," Wiley said.

"No, wait. Here he comes," Mick Sabbath said.

The black-clad Indian came in at the gallop, leading a horse in tow, clutching its reins in one black-gloved hand. A swarm of Free Company bullets accompanied his return, none tagging him. He slowed to a halt, joining the others under the bulging rock.

"We were about to give you up for lost," Carrados said.

The corners of El Indio's mouth turned up in what passed for a smile on his generally inexpressive face. He walked his horse over to Johnny and Huddy. "You no get far with two on a horse. Plenty strays around, so I take one. They no miss, I think. If they do, to hell with them."

"You got plenty of sand, mister. You sure showed me something today," Johnny said.

"You showed us all something," Carrados said.

"I owe you more than I can say, but thanks and much obliged," Huddy said.

"Steal me a horse sometime and we call it even," El Indio said.

"I'll steal you a whole string of them, soon as I get patched up proper," Huddy said feelingly.

Some of the others helped Huddy get down off the chestnut horse, assisting him into the saddle of the replacement brought by El Indio.

"Don't worry about me. There ain't a horse I can't handle with one hand," Huddy assured them, holding the reins in his good one.

"You see, Baldy? I come back," El Indio Negro said.

Baldy nodded. "I never doubted it."

"You man of faith, Baldy."

"I put my faith in my gun, and in some folks, too, I reckon. You being one of them. But not many folks. Baldy Vance ain't nobody's fool."

"Time for us to make our breakout, men," Johnny said.

"Glad I saved something for the occasion." Vic reached in the deflated canvas sack hanging from a strap around his neck and pulled out a bundle of dynamite. "Last one. I saved it, figuring it might come in handy."

The others readied for the breakout.

Vic had lost his cigar somewhere en route to the boulder. He struck a match, cupping a hand around

it to shelter the flame and help it grow. When it
burned hot and strong, he applied it to the fuse cord
of the bundled TNT, setting it alight. "Cover me!"

The Hangtree raiders opened fire on the squad of
riflemen behind the barricade, streaming lead at
them in a furious onslaught, forcing them to take
cover.

Riding out and around the curving limb of the
egg-shaped boulder, Vic headed for the barricade.
Reining in just short of it, he pitched the lit dynamite
bundle up and over the tops of the overturned
wagons, tossing it to the far side where the riflemen
were, then quickly turned his horse around and rode
back under the big rock.

The dynamite blew, generating a rushing, swelling
cloud of smoke, glare, heat, and shock waves that
cascaded through the portal.

"Let's ride!" Johnny shouted after the last debris
of wagon fragments and body parts had come rain-
ing down.

The Hangtree raiders charged out from under the
rock, surging toward the canyon mouth.

The dynamite blast had overturned one of the
shattered wagons, pinning some screaming riflemen
beneath. Bodies lay strewn on the ground around the
broken barricade. Some few surviving riflemen had
taken cover in the rocks outside the south portal.

The raiders poured through the wide gaps in the
barricade, jumping their horses over any low-lying
wreckage in the way. They rode out shooting.

A volley of bullets was thrown their way, but by the
time the last few rifle-wielding guards had gotten
enough nerve to start shooting, the raiders were safely
out of range.

The Hangtree gunmen swung around in a tight curve and raced toward the cut in the Breaks. They were grouped pretty much side by side in a loose chevron-shaped formation as they rushed along the middle of wide Wild Horse Canyon.

"Sure gave the hornet's nest a good whomping!" Johnny Cross shouted to those riding alongside him.

And they still had a Sunday punch to deliver.

TWENTY-SIX

For Jimbo Turlock, it had been a black night of betrayals, setbacks, and harsh reversals. First was the faithlessness and infidelity of his lady love Ashley, deceiving him with his trusted second in command. Then came his shameful retreat from Hangtree, fleeing like any thief—murderer, rather—in the night. That was followed by the harsh, grueling hours-long ride west along the Hangtree Trail through the Notch, then north to the Sidepocket camp off Wild Horse Canyon.

Upon arrival at camp, he'd been greeted by the news that his howitzer and the munitions wagon, the crown jewels of his Fort Pardee loot, had gone missing and were presumed stolen.

"I leave the command for a few days, not even a full week, and look what happens!" Turlock complained to his adjutant Phineas "Finny" Clark in the privacy of his big tent in Sidepocket camp a few hours before dawn. "Apparently you all can't get along without me. If I'm not here to do the strategizing, you'd all wind up in front of a firing squad!"

"From what I heard tell, hanging is the preferred method of execution in these parts, Commander," Clark said slyly, taunting Turlock but not in a way that was actionable.

"Never mind about that, Clark," Turlock said huffily, not being one who cared to be contradicted by anyone, especially not a subordinate, having already suffered the supreme betrayal by his second in command Dancer.

How many others? he wondered.

How long had Ashley and Dancer been conducting their illicit affair? Days, weeks, months?

And who else knew about it? Did Finny Clark know? Did Quarles?

Turlock bitterly recalled the age-old maxim that the betrayed party was always the last to know. He was no husband to Ashley. They had never married, but she was his woman. She belonged to him, and no legally wedded married man could have felt any more jealously possessive of what he considered his property.

Then, too, no one was more righteously indignant about being robbed than a thief.

His proud boast had always been that he took what he wanted. Ashley had been simply Osage Sally Potts when he had discovered her while the Free Company was hiding out in the Indian Nations in Oklahoma Territory. She was young, fresh, and relatively unspoiled, the prettiest young harlot in the territory.

He had taken her, made her his woman, and given her a place in his home—an honored position in his household. She'd had a bountiful array of fancy clothes, jewelry, and furs—all looted plunder from Free Company raids. He'd even had her change her

name to hide what he saw as her less than humble
origins, *Ashley* being the name she'd picked for herself.

He frowned, pricked by thorns of bitter memory.
Come to think of it, Sally hadn't chosen the name of
Ashley. It had been suggested to her by Malvina.

Malvina! That sly old witch. She was a procuress,
old and wise in the ways of crime and vice. She had attached herself to the Free Company in Oklahoma,
making herself invaluable to Turlock by providing
him with a steady stream of girls and young women.
Women were not hard to come by in the Territory,
not if you wanted Indian females or those of mixed
blood.

But he had a fancy for pureblooded white women,
young pretty ones, and those were not so easily come
by in the wind-blown, sun-blasted, God-forsaken reser-
vation lands of the Indian Nations.

Malvina was able to supply them, always knowing
where to find families of poor whites willing, if not
eager, to sell off a spare daughter. "One less mouth to
feed," was the hard maxim and harder truth behind
such sordid transactions.

When Turlock tired of them, Malvina would take
them off his hands, selling them to saloon keepers or
brothels whether they liked it or not. And there was
little to like about it.

Osage Sally Potts had been Malvina's prize specimen. Sixteen, with a pretty face, long blond hair, and
blue eyes, she was slim-figured yet roundly curved.

Malvina claimed Sally was an orphan child of good
family. Turlock believed her because he wanted to believe. He was quite taken with the girl, besotted, even.

He had thought briefly of marrying her, but the

thought was short-lived. Jimbo Turlock was a soldier, a man of action, a man of destiny! He had no place in his life for a wife and family.

Not when he still needed the hired guns of the Free Company as the vehicle to win fame and fortune. Later, perhaps, when he had made his pile and retired from the active life and gone somewhere far away, somewhere where he was unknown and courting respectability. Then he would be wed—just not to Osage Sally Potts. She was dead. But she'd been a protégée of Malvina the fortune teller, poisoner, and procuress. No matter how much he'd been taken with Ashley's alluring young charms, he wouldn't have married her after her betrayal.

Even so, he had allowed himself to believe that the girl loved him, which made her flagrant betrayal of him all the more galling.

And with such as Kale Dancer!

Well, the veil had been lifted from Turlock's eyes. He had learned the awful truth and done what had to be done to redeem his honor. It was the unwritten law!

He still had some loose ends to be dealt with, Malvina foremost among them. Hard to believe she had not known of Ashley's infidelities. She was the girl's mentor and confidante . . . and Ashley couldn't keep a secret to save her life.

As was proven.

Perhaps Malvina had even encouraged her to take Dancer for a lover as part of a cunning scheme to get rid of Turlock and take over the Free Company and its loot for themselves!

Poison was Malvina's stock in trade—the mass murder of the troops at Fort Pardee was proof of that. Nothing easier for her than to give Ashley some poison to slip into his food. They could say he died of natural causes—apoplexy or a stroke.

The Free Company needed a leader and would not have questioned too closely when Kale Dancer took Turlock's place, making himself the new commander.

Turlock had had plenty of time to think about it during the long hours of the night ride from Hangtree to Sidepocket. He broke into a cold sweat thinking some more about what a narrow escape he'd had.

Angry all over again, he sent for Malvina, preparatory to doing her in personally, with his own hands, as he'd done for Ashley and Dancer. Traitors must die!

His aides and henchmen came back empty-handed.

"Can't find her, sir."

"Look harder, damn it. She's got to be in camp someplace," Turlock growled. "I want that old hag found!"

He assigned responsibility for locating Malvina to Quarles, his onetime top sergeant long since turned manservant and valet. Quarles had been his indispensible right-hand man for many years, going back to the Missouri-Kansas Border Wars of the 1850s. The one man Turlock *knew* he could trust.

But even the redoubtable Quarles met with no success in his quest, reporting back, "Malvina's gone, Commander."

"Gone? Impossible! We're in the middle of nowhere!" Turlock said, sputtering outrage.

"She's gone, sir."

"Where could she go?!"

"The gate guards report she rode out at eleven

o'clock tonight, in her two-wheeled donkey cart," Quarles said, deadpan, unflappable.

"I gave strict orders that no one was allowed out of camp without my express authorization!" Turlock thundered.

"They say she had a pass written and signed by you, sir."

Turlock was on the verge of roaring that he'd never issued such a pass when the realization struck him that, in fact, in the not-so-distant past he had written many such passes for Malvina. She had been uniquely valuable to him in her capacity of procuress of young women for his bed.

He had given her broad latitude to enable her to fulfill her duties in that role, including the freedom of the camp and the power to come and go as she willed at all hours of the day or night.

The guards knew to let her go, and they would have assumed she was on yet one more mission to furnish fresh young flesh for the Commander.

A chill came over him as another thought struck him. "What time did she leave camp? At eleven o'clock tonight, you say?"

"Yes, Commander, eleven o'clock," Quarles said, poker-faced.

"That's about the time that I—" Turlock stopped himself in mid-sentence, firmly clamping his jaws shut. *That's about the time I cut Kale Dancer's throat and strangled Ashley to death,* he'd been about to say.

He bit down on his lip, stifling himself. He didn't have to say it. Quarles knew what he meant without having to hear it spoken aloud. Quarles had been there for the aftermath. If not for him, Turlock wondered if he would have been able to carry on.

Jimbo Turlock took a deep breath to steady his nerves, but it didn't work. "Send out a search party, Quarles. I want the gypsy woman found and returned to camp."

"Yes sir. I'll get on it right away."

"Don't you go looking for her yourself, Quarles. Put somebody else in charge. I need you here."

"Very well, sir." Quarles went out, leaving Turlock alone in his tent.

Turlock shuddered, his blood running cold.

Malvina was a fortune teller. The Mexican Americans with the Free Company called her *bruja*—witch.

Was it possible that she really was gifted with what some called second sight, clairvoyance, the power to see far-off events without physically being there?

It seemed fantastic, but the hour of Malvina's leave-taking from camp—the same fatal hour when Turlock murdered Ashley and Dancer—surely that must be something more than mere coincidence?

It was as if Malvina had divined Ashley's death by occult powers and, knowing that her own death at Turlock's command must surely follow, she had ridden out in the night to make her escape. . . .

Jimbo Turlock knew that he would not rest easy until he had seen Malvina dead. He was haunted by the sinking feeling that it would not come soon, if ever.

A bottle of brandy helped numb his senses. He fell into a stupor, dozing off at his long conference table, arms folded on the table, pillowing his head.

Sleep, blessed sleep, came, but it was not oblivion or pain-ease. It was nightmare. Evil dreams, shapeless formless images of suffocating horror, tormented him.

He dreamed of entombment, of being buried alive, trapped in the well of a deep grave while dirt was shoveled down on him by Ashley and Kale Dancer, dead-alive. Dancer with his throat cut and Ashley with eyes bulging, face purple, blackened tongue protruding, it was just the way he had left the two of them when he fled Dancer's suite in the Cattleman Hotel.

Malvina leaned over the open grave, leering down at Turlock, laughing.

He was hauled out of the grave head-first, hauled out by a rope noose around his neck, a hangman's noose at the end of a hempen rope. Then he was hanging by the neck in empty air, swinging back and forth pendulum-like, hanging in timeless eternity with the gates of hell gaping wide below to receive him—

Jimbo Turlock awoke.

It was a rude awakening at early dawn. The choking billows of the nightmare were banished by the sounds of battle. He awoke to the reality of gunfire, explosions, and mass chaos. It was no evil dream, no nightmare. It was real, horribly real!

But the Free Company was not in the habit of being raided.

Jimbo Turlock jumped up, overturning the folding camp chair on which he'd sat while falling asleep at the table. The brandy bottle was upset, too, rolling on its side, falling off the table to the ground.

That was okay, it was empty.

He picked up his tunic jacket that had been draped on the back of his chair and put it on, struggling with it. He had a hard time getting his arms inside the sleeves. He'd gained weight recently and the tunic did not fit properly nor comfortably. He didn't bother to button it. This was an emergency, judging from the clamor hammering the camp.

Had a riot broken out?

It was not unthinkable, considering the low nature of many of the men in the ranks under his command, the scum. It wouldn't be the first time one of their drunken brawls had raged out of control until the squad leaders had broken a few heads and beaten the troublemakers into submission.

Impatient, Turlock fumbled with the button snap securing the top flap of his shiny, black, patent leather holster. He finally drew his big-caliber revolver, taking strength from the empowering sensation of it in his hand.

He looked for his hat but couldn't find it. He'd lost his hat somewhere. It seemed important to remember what he'd done with it. Fear gripped him as he struggled to remember where he'd left his hat.

With a shock of piercing clarity, he recalled that he'd left his hat in Kale Dancer's suite when Quarles had hustled him out of there, away from the dead bodies of the two people he had murdered, his woman and his second in command. He'd made the long night ride bareheaded through dark windswept plains to Wild Horse Canyon and the Sidepocket camp.

Turlock stumbled to the tent entrance, pawing at the flaps, opening them and bulling his way through to the outside.

Then he truly did step into chaos, for the raid was on, the camp a scene of pandemonium. Mobs of men and women ran in all directions at once, crashing into each other, trampling the fallen in their maddened haste to escape the pistol-fighters on horseback tearing through Sidepocket Canyon.

Hangtree gunhawks plowed through the seething horde like sharp knives slicing up suety pudding.

Among the tents where the leadership cadre bunked,

the response was better, more orderly. Not a complete rout like it was on the sandy main floor of the box canyon. The Free Company's inner circle showed fight, running *to* the battle, not from it.

They were members of Turlock's so-called Honor Guard, a platoon of picked men whose primary function was to serve as his personal bodyguards and enforcers. They were professional guns, not the saddle tramps and saloon sweepings that made up most of his following.

Rattling bursts of gunfire grew louder and closer, dangerously close.

Turlock experienced the dim realization that *he* might be in peril. He'd been acting as a spectator, not a participant. He was about to be roundly disabused of that notion.

A gunman rode up to the tents, one of the raiders. He held the reins of his horse between his teeth, had a blazing gun in each hand, and opened up on Turlock's men as they came racing out of the tents. For each shot fired, a man fell down dead. The raider was mowing them down as fast as they came at him.

Turlock got a good look at his face, experiencing the shock of recognition. It was Johnny Cross, the gunfighter who'd slain Terrible Terry Moran and his men several days ago in Hangtree!

Turlock had made a point while in town of finding out the man's name, wondering if he was for hire. He'd been unable to connect the smooth-faced young gunman who'd gunned down Moran and his sidemen with the long-haired, bearded, scruffy, unkempt starveling who'd stood at the shoulder of Colonel William Clarke Quantrill in Clay County, Missouri, when

Turlock had sought in vain to make an alliance with the Confederate guerrilla leader.

He didn't know that the Johnny Cross of those far-off days had taken close notice of *him.*

Johnny's guns were empty. Leaning over, he tucked them into a saddlebag, and for an instant, he was unarmed.

In that same moment, Jimbo Turlock realized that he held a loaded gun in *his* hand.

It was his chance to bring down Johnny Cross, a killing that would send Turlock's prestige soaring sky-high not only among his men but all along the frontier—throughout the West!

Thumbing back the hammer, Turlock swung his gun toward Johnny.

Vic Vargas rode up. Turlock didn't know who he was except that he was one of the raiders and be damned to him. Vic held a lit bundle of TNT in one hand. Grinning hugely, he pitched it among the tents and amid Turlock's Honor Guard.

Johnny and Vic swung their horses around, riding away hard and fast.

Jimbo Turlock had a clear shot at Johnny's back— but there was that bundle of dynamite pitched his way. The package of TNT sticks hit the peaked roof of a tent, sliding down a slanted side and falling off the edge to the ground, dropping into the open square where Turlock stood, the sizzling fuse fast-burning its way to the explosives.

He turned and ran, scrambling to put some distance between himself and the dynamite.

The last thing he heard before the blast was the

piercing yowl of a Rebel yell vented by Johnny Cross as he raced off.

The TNT blew up. An irresistible force, it was a combination of light, heat, and pressure. A shock wave picked up Turlock in an invisible hand and tossed him in the air. The dizzying flight was halted when he crashed into a standing tent, bringing it down.

It acted as a kind of safety net, catching him and cushioning his fall. He tumbled head over heels, taking quite a bruising. He found himself sitting on the ground, dazed, senses stunned. Smoke and dust billowed around him, turning men nearby into phantomlike outlines. His ears rang, and he had a bloody nose.

A couple of his men, Honor Guard stalwarts all, recognized him, helping him to his feet, holding him up.

"It's the Commander! Are you all right, sir?"

Turlock saw the man's mouth moving but couldn't make out his words for the ringing in his ears. "I can stand by myself!" he shouted, unable to judge the volume of what he was saying.

He brushed himself off with his hands, flicking off bits of ember and ash, pieces of straw, weeds, and debris. His hair, eyebrows, and mustache were scorched, his face and hands blackened by sooty smears.

Just when he thought he'd regained his composure, the scene was rocked with another earth-shattering boom.

Vic had loosed another blast of TNT. Luckily for Turlock, the explosion hit a different part of the camp. It was jarring and frightening but inflicted no physical damage to him.

The men tending to Turlock remembered that they were supposed to be his bodyguards and started guarding him. They formed up in a loose knot around him, interposing their bodies between him and those who might mean to do him harm.

The raiders were already far away at the eastern end of Sidepocket, readying for the breakout assault on the exit into Wild Horse Canyon.

The tent city bivouac area was an unholy mess. Canvas, rope, and wooden tent poles were a flimsy hedge against TNT. The same went for flesh and blood.

Men and material had been pulverized by the dynamite blasts. The area looked like a tornado had gone through it. The ground was littered with bodies and rubble.

Jimbo Turlock left the scene, bodyguards escorting him inside a loose security cordon so that he was ringed on all sides. He paused on a slight rise overlooking the shallow basin of the center of the canyon, his escorts pausing with him. Sticking close to the commander beat the hell out of trying to give chase to those fighting devils who had ripped through camp.

Turlock's ears suddenly popped and he could hear again. He all but recoiled at the torrent of noise flooding the encampment—screams, shouts, shots, runaway horses, and running men and women.

The Hangtree raiders dashed out from behind the cover of the rocks to make their breakout, blowing up the barricade and crashing out of Sidepocket Canyon.

Galloping north up Wild Horse Canyon, they whooped and hollered, laying down a mocking chorus of Rebel yells as they raced out of sight.

"Lord, how I hate that sound!" Jimbo Turlock said with quivering emotion.

TWENTY-SEVEN

The Free Company was on the march—not that there was any actual marching being done.

The hard core of the outfit, the two hundred or so mounted marauders, rode out in a massed column ten deep, riding north up the middle of Wild Horse Canyon.

They didn't assemble in any formation or any real semblance of order, with platoons and squads, ranks and files. The Free Company wasn't that kind of outfit. They were robber bandits, a band of horse-mounted barbarians who wandered from town to town, killing, looting, and burning.

You want military-style precision and discipline? Join the army. That was the marauders' sneering attitude toward the basics of drill and all martial routine. The last thing in the world they were interested in was military discipline.

Many of them had been in one army or another, the Union Army or the Confederacy, sometimes both at one time or another. Jailhouse recruits mostly, they had joined the military as a judge-mandated alternative to hanging or going to prison.

They soon learned that the army was a kind of jail itself, with the additional hazard of possibly being shot dead by the other side, and deserted as soon as possible, often taking with them stolen weapons, ammunition, and horses. To their surprise, their time in the army proved not to have been a total loss after all.

In the Free Company, a man was his own man, generally. No snotty chicken-squat officers or bullying noncoms to ride his ass about keeping his person neat, clean, and squared away; no falling out for drill at four in the morning; no guff about not drinking on duty, no women on post, or any other nonsense that made army life a chore and a bore.

No rules against robbing, raping, and killing, either. In fact, it was expected. That was the job of a marauder.

Of course, there were certain obligations and duties. A man had to have his own gun and horse and be fairly proficient in the use of both. He had to be able to take care of himself and not be pushed around. But hey, brother, where didn't those basic facts of life apply?

On went the mounted marauders.

Behind them were the foot soldiers, those too damn lazy or incompetent to steal a horse or just too damn drunk to stay on one of the swaybacked nags without falling off. They were the camp followers, a mob of criminal rabble who trailed along in the wake of the robber army to see what they could glean of the spoils. A horde of renegades, tinhorns, thimble riggers, diddlers, dealers in stolen goods, sharpers, sneak thieves, pickpockets, the sly, the sick, and the damned. Male and female, they made up an entire criminal underworld on the hoof, wandering across the countryside in search of what they could steal with little risk.

They were armed with a spectrum of weapons, from rifles, shotguns and six-guns to derringers, blunderbusses, pocket pistols, axes, machetes, knives, meat cleavers, brass knuckles, and blacksnake whips—every instrument and tool that could be used to put a hurt on another living being.

The Free Company was on the move. The robber bandits were going to demonstrate their power and terrible vengeance. They would avenge the indignity of the vicious and unprovoked assault made on the Sidepocket camp.

Their first objective was Cross Ranch on the other side of the cut. They'd kill all they found and strip the ranch clean of livestock and possessions. They'd have a great feasting at a mighty barbecue of Cross Ranch cattle.

Thus fortified, they would continue onward to their next day's target—Hangtree town. A rich, fat target ripe for plucking!

Most Texas towns hadn't been doing too well even before the war, their inhabitants barely getting by, eking out a hardscrabble living. It was the frontier, after all, where life was hard. Constant attacks by bandits and Comanches didn't help.

Come the war and its aftermath, things got worse. Ranches and farms were left untended during the conflict, livestock running off into the wild, cultivated land being reclaimed by weeds and brush.

Most families had lost male kin to the war—fathers, brothers, sons, husbands, and sweethearts. Privation, famine, and disease had taken their toll on the home front, with many a weary returning veteran finding no living family members to return to.

But Hangtree was different. Hangtree was on the boom, cashing in on the rising cattle market economy and prospering as a jumping-off point for westbound wagon trains. Hangtree was fat and sassy, easy pickings, and the Free Company marauders would do the taking.

Banks were heavy with gold and silver, stores were jammed with goods, taverns and saloons were awash in whiskey—good whiskey, not cheap raw rotgut with six rattlesnake heads added per barrel to give it some bite.

All the Free Company had to do was reach out their good strong hands and take it—first killing any and all who got in their way . . . or just happened to be in the wrong place at the wrong time.

All these dazzling prospects had been laid out by Jimbo Turlock in a short but rousing speech he'd given to the Free Company and its ragtag auxiliary army of foot soldiers and camp followers.

He had been a politician once, and still retained the breed's leather-lunged gift for oratory, exhortation, and exaggeration. Not to mention outright downright lying. He'd taken the horde up on the rhetorical mountaintop, verbally laying out all the riches that would be theirs. No mealy-mouthed pie-in-the-sky preaching, brother, this was the genuine, the real goods. A dazzling vision to fuel the fires of avarice and greed.

What the commander neglected to mention to his shocked troops was that he was in the pay of a foreign power—and the wages were good. For him.

The foreign power was represented by agents of Emperor Maximilian, Archduke of Austria-Hungary, whose greedy ally, scheming colonialist French emperor Louis Napoleon, had put on the throne of Mexico. An Austria-Hungarian Emperor of Mexico, of all places. Mexico!

It was outlandish, improbable, but most incredible, it was true.

It took several French armies, the Foreign Legion, and a traitorous cabal of rich Mexican landholders and aristocrats to depose rightfully elected Benito Juárez from the office of President of the Republic of Mexico.

That and an American civil war. With the Union and Confederacy locked in conflict in the War of Secession, there was no federal authority to enforce the Monroe Doctrine and kick Emperor Maximilian out of Mexico.

Maximilian, his cohorts, and their European style of fighting had pretty well already lost the fight with Juárez's revolutionists.

The War Between the States having been decided in favor of the Union, Washington, D.C., was pressuring the French to get out of Mexico and take Maximilian with them.

The Emperor's inner circle of French generals and Mexican landholders—the so-called Max Men—were fighting back with a variety of plots. Their secret agents had thronged the Southwest, jumping back and forth across the border to stir up trouble to keep Maximilian in power. Gunrunners shipped wagons of illegal arms shipments to Imperial forces.

Max Men worked with Comancheros to supply the Comanches with weapons and whiskey to encourage them to make war in Texas, diverting valuable U.S. government resources to put down the uprising.

The Free Company plot to overthrow Fort Pardee and sack Hangtree was the product of another Max Men plot.

North Central Texas Comanches had received a serious setback the summer before when Hangtree beat back war chief Red Hand's so-called Great Raid. Removing Fort Pardee from the board freed the Llano Comanches to spread their war against the Tejanos far to the east.

Sacking and burning Hangtree would destabilize the region, strengthening the renewed Comanche onslaught and hampering the Army in establishing its power and presence in the territory.

Jimbo Turlock had ventured to Weatherford to finalize the deal with some of Maximilian's secret agents operating in the Lone Star state. He'd been accompanied by his ultimate inner circle—Kale Dancer, Osage Sally Potts, Sgt. Quarles, and Piney.

It was unnecessary for any others in Free Company to know the true purpose of the trip, unnecessary and supremely dangerous. Maximilian's secret agents were paying Turlock a chest full of gold coins to carry out the mission. It was a mission he would have been only too glad to carry out for free on his own hook.

A cache of gold!

Its existence must remain unknown to the Company. There'd be no controlling the greedy gun wolves once they got a whiff of gold in their nostrils. The Free Company would instantly degenerate into total anarchy, with every robber and killer double-crossing each other in their mad lust to win the prize.

Only three had known of the gold—Jimbo Turlock, Kale Dancer, and Quarles.

In light of subsequent events, Turlock assumed Dancer had told the secret to Ashley, probably during some intimate pillow talk following a bout of love play.

They were dead and would tell no tales. But the possibility existed that Ashley had confided the secret to that cunning old witch Malvina.

That chilling likelihood threw its shadow over Turlock's every waking moment. He had no doubt that Malvina would not rest until she had somehow possessed herself of the chest of gold—all of it. Every last glittering gold coin, every speck of gold dust.

To forestall the attempt that he knew was coming, Turlock had taken precautions to secure the gold against Malvina's schemes and machinations. During the wild night ride from Hangtree to the Sidepocket camp, the party of Turlock, Quarles, and Piney had paused to hide the treasure. They had buried the chest in a safe place in the wilderness where it would never be found by anyone else.

Piney knew the chest held something of great value, but no matter. Turlock had knifed him in the back, tumbling him into the hole in the ground and atop the chest of gold which lay at the bottom of the excavation. Then the commander and Quarles had filled in the hole with dirt, burying Piney and the treasure. Turlock had no doubts about Quarles. He was loyal. Through long years, over nearly two decades of robbing and plundering, Quarles had had countless opportunities to do away with Turlock and steal his loot if he'd wanted to do so.

But Quarles was not so minded, always serving his

commander with unquestioning doglike fidelity. It was quite touching, actually, Turlock thought.

He had knowingly turned his back to Quarles a number of times while they were burying the gold. If Quarles had wanted to kill him and keep the gold for himself, he could have easily done so right then and there.

Most would have thought Turlock's ploy a foolish, dangerous gamble, but the commander believed otherwise. He trusted in Quarles's loyalty, but even more, he trusted in his own luck, in the mystical workings of that star of destiny which had never failed him, seeing him through adversity and hardship to ultimate triumph.

Once again, he had been proven right. Quarles had not moved against him, despite having had very real opportunities to do so.

As he rode forward, Turlock hoped he would not have to do away with Quarles in the end, once they had escaped to a safe place with the chest of gold and whatever loot he could plunder from Hangtree.

For loyal though Quarles unquestionably was, the unexpected was always something to worry about. Quarles might take sick and rave about the treasure in a fever delirium. He might become boastful when drunk and give away the secret. Not that he ever had been drunk. The man had never touched a drop of alcoholic spirits in all the years since entering the commander's service . . . but in some unforeseeable future, he might.

Quarles could even get religion someday and decide to reform, endangering his master. Who knew? Stranger things had happened.

Turlock shook his head. But such contingencies

lay somewhere over the hill, tomorrow and tomorrow and tomorrow to come. Or maybe never.

He shook his head again to dislodge his musings. He needed Quarles alive and functioning as never before, denied as he was of the able assistance of Kale Dancer. The Cross ranch was to be taken and burned, Hangtree gutted and plundered.

Turlock led the Free Company robber army north along Wild Horse Canyon road toward the pass at Cross's Cut.

TWENTY-EIGHT

"I ain't done with Jimbo Turlock yet," Johnny Cross said to the surviving Hangtree raiders during a stop along the trail. "We already gave the hornet's nest a hell of a clubbing, getting them good and mad. We lost some good men doing it, but it had to be done. We had to get Jimbo so mad he'll come straight on to the ranch through the cut instead of going the long way through the Notch. You know why."

The others nodded, murmuring agreement. They *did* know why.

"I want to give him one more whomping, just to seal the deal," Johnny continued. "I mean to do it no matter what, by my own self if I have to, but I wanted to ask y'all first to see if you wanted to join me."

When he got no immediate answers he asked, "Well, what's it to be?"

"Quit trying to hog all the fun for yourself. That's what I say," Wiley declared.

"That's a hell of a way to treat your friends," Vic said.

"Maybe he thinks he's too good for us," Baldy grumbled.

The others all said pretty much the same in their own various ways. To a man, they wanted in.

Johnny grinned. "I figured that's what you'd say, but I don't take nothing for granted."

"Just try keeping us out of the play," Fritz Carrados said.

"It's a go," said El Indio Negro.

"I hate leaving something unfinished," Mick Sabbath said.

"Good. Let's get to it," Johnny said.

They were giving their horses a rest, standing around at the western mouth of the pass where Cross's Cut opened on to Wild Horse Canyon. Positioned just inside the pass at its south end, they were out of sight of anyone approaching via the canyon's northbound road. Some of them were smoking.

"All this hoopla, fussing and fighting, bombs exploding—it's enough to scare the mustangs clear to Comancheria," Wiley said.

"Be a long time before Wild Horse Canyon sees wild horses again," El Indio agreed.

"Looks like I got into the cattle business just in time," Johnny said.

Vic rummaged around in his saddlebags. "Hey, look what I found!" He pulled out a stick of TNT. "Turns out I had a spare left. I'll have to put it where it'll do some good."

"I'll tell you where you can put it," Baldy said, all sour-like.

"Yeah? Where's that?" Vic said menacingly, squaring

his broad shoulders, his big hands fists. He loomed over the raider, taking a step forward. "Why don't you tell me just where I can put it, amigo?"

Baldy changed course hastily. "You can stick it up Jimbo Turlock's—"

"Hey men, here they come!" Carrados called out from the end of the pass where he was peeking around the corner to Wild Horse Canyon road. He'd lost his straw hat and his once-white suit was anything but, grimy, soot-smeared, ripped, and torn as it was. His watery pale blue eyes seemed to be bulging even more than usual.

The raiders knew what he meant. They mounted up, turning their horses' heads west toward the end of the cut.

Kev Huddy was pale, but standing on two good legs. The holes in the top of his torso and his upper left arm had been patched up with gauze bandages and tape from a first-aid kit Carrados carried in a saddlebag.

Taking a deep breath, Huddy gripped the saddle horn with his good right hand and put his left foot into the stirrup. With one intense exertion, he stepped up and straddled the saddle, though not without a curse and a stifled groan. Holding the reins in his right fist, he looked paler and more white-faced than before.

"Where do you think you're going?" Johnny asked.

"I bought a ticket to the show and I aim to see it," Huddy said, stubborn and defensive.

"You're buying yourself a ticket to Boot Hill, ya danged fool!" Baldy said. "Hell, you tell him, Johnny. Nobody around here listens to me nohow."

"That's because of your sunny disposition," Mick Sabbath said.

"Huh?"

"Never mind, Baldy." Sabbath gestured as if waving his comment away.

"Don't try talking me out of it. I've still got one good hand," Huddy said.

"You need that to hold the reins. What're you going to shoot with? You can't even throw rocks at them," Johnny pointed out.

"I reckon you could cuss 'em out. Call 'em a lot of dirty names and such. That might get 'em riled up some," Wiley said.

"I know you want to take the ride, Huddy, but face the facts," Sabbath said. "With those holes in you and one wing down, you're more liability than asset. All you can do is get yourself killed or worse, taken alive by the marauders. Then some of us will get killed trying to save your ass, so why not do yourself and us a favor by sitting this one out?"

"Instead of getting yourself or one of us killed—or even worse, *me* killed—you could do some real good by riding back and tipping the others back at the ranch that the Free Company is here," Johnny suggested.

"Johnny talk sense. You listen," El Indio said sternly.

Huddy thought it over, eyes bright, feverish. "Oh hell. Reckon I'll have to play hero some other time." He smiled weakly.

"Go on then. Get to it before it's too late," Johnny said. "The boys back at the ranch are cooking up a powerful surprise for the marauders, and I'd hate to see it spoiled."

"All right," Huddy said. "Good luck and give them hell!"

"Pure hell is what we surely intend to dispense," Sabbath said.

Huddy turned his horse toward the east end of the pass and put heels to its flanks. The horse leaped forward swiftly, speeding along.

"Hope he don't fall off," Baldy said, watching him go.

Wiley scratched himself. "Cheerful cuss, ain'tcha?"

Huddy stayed on the horse, which was soon out of sight.

"Come on. Let's ride!" Johnny urged.

Jimbo Turlock wasn't much for military strategy and tactics, but he knew enough to send out scouts and skirmishers in advance of his main body of troops.

A platoon of forty or so advance gunmen patrolled the Wild Horse Canyon road ahead and out of sight of the rest of the Free Company's long column. Rowdy, sullen, and ill-tempered, they rode bunched together in a mass rather than maintaining a proper distance, sending no single or double teams of scouts ahead to see what lay farther up the road.

Truth be told, the earlier raid had left them demoralized and in low spirits. Each man took comfort in the nearness of his fellows, and no one in the platoon wanted to separate from the group.

Ahead on the right lay the western mouth of Cross's Cut, their destination.

Suddenly without warning, a small party of riders burst out of the pass, turning south to charge straight at the platoon. Riding full tilt, they were the last of the

Hangtree raiders. Whooping wild rebel yells, they came on, shooting into the mass of forty Free Company skirmishers.

Each raider was a crack shot, as deadly accurate charging on galloping steeds as they were standing with both feet planted on solid ground. They rushed the foe as if they were the superior force outnumbering the other side, crashing into the Free Company vanguard.

The robber bandit skirmishers were taken by surprise. An attack was the last thing they expected. The sound of gunfire was a roaring racket as clouds of gun smoke engulfed the combatants.

Johnny Cross was at the fore, both guns blasting, knocking men out of the saddle left and right.

Vic Vargas swung wide to one side of the point of the platoon, sweeping south along their left flank toward the rear. He gripped the last bundle of dynamite and lit the short fuse. With an overhand throw, he tossed the bundle over the heads of the bandits, dropping the TNT into the rear of the platoon, far from his own men.

He turned his horse to the right, peeling off and away.

The TNT blew up, wreaking terrible havoc on the skirmishers. A space was cleared in the center of the blast, the ground littered with the bodies of men and horses heaped in smoking ruins.

That did it! The rest of the platoon broke and ran, turning their horses back the way they came and galloping for their lives, full speed down the road.

From behind them came mocking derisive hoots and hollers, sparked by triumphant rebel yells. The Hangtree gunhawks reined in, leaning forward on their horses and peering through the smoke to watch the flight of what was left of the robber bandits' vanguard.

Johnny grinned, having counted on the success of such a bold attack.

Quantrill and his mounted guerrillas had learned early in the war that the best defense against superior numbers was to go on the offense. Charge straight-on with no hesitation and go in shooting, and more often than not the foe would be so startled by the savagery of an unexpected assault that they would rather run than fight.

Jimbo Turlock just about blew his stack when the advance guard platoon came galloping into view. The fugitives were in a blind panic, whipping and spurring their horses to greater speed in a frenzied effort to escape. The horses were wild-eyed and sleek with sweat, some foaming at the nostrils and mouth from exertion.

When the retreating force reached the Free Company column they didn't bother to stop. They peeled off to the flanks, riding south on the left and right of the line of march and racing past mounted men who stared at them with open-mouthed amazement. They kept on going—past the long snakelike line of foot soldiers and camp followers who brought up the rear—until they were out of sight.

For all that is known, they might have kept going until they reached Mexico.

Recovering from his astonishment, Turlock snapped orders to have some of the fleeing men brought back for questioning.

This was done with difficulty—the platoon was running so fast—but a few at the rear were bagged and taken to the commander. The spooked skirmishers babbled of having been struck by an overwhelming force of fierce fighters who outnumbered them five-to-one. No, ten-to-one!

Turlock knew better. Had there been an enemy force of that size, they surely would have fallen on the Free Company at Sidepocket Canyon like the wrath of God and wiped them out to the last man. More, there was no towering dust cloud on the northern horizon that such a large-sized force would have raised.

From Missouri, Turlock was a product of the vicious guerrilla warfare that wracked the border states for a decade before Fort Sumter. He well knew the tactics of such men as Quantrill and had more than a suspicion that his advance force had fallen prey to some of the same.

He sent more scouts forward. They quickly returned to report that just over the hill lay a group of about a half-dozen riders who mocked and jeered them.

"What I thought," Turlock said grimly. "Inform the troops that we will attack at once and in full force, Sgt. Quarles. We will proceed ahead at full speed through the pass and take the Cross Ranch, killing any and all we encounter who are not of us. Tell the men to raise the Black Flag, Quarles. Take no prisoners—no quarter to the foe!"

Quarles did as ordered and reported back to his commander.

At the head of the column, Turlock stood in his

saddle, pointing his rifle toward Cross's Cut. He would lead. "*Charge!*"

The Free Company marauders put spurs to horses and started forward. The entire column was on the move, surging into action.

Drumming hoofbeats hammered the hard-packed dirt road of Wild Horse Canyon. Long untrimmed manes streamed in the air behind horses like banners. War cries and oaths of death and destruction to the enemy echoed off canyon walls.

Once the marauders saw the insignificance of the foe facing them, they would come back into their own. Their murderous instincts would be stoked when they learned how they had been fooled and run ragged by so few men—men they could easily obliterate once they set themselves to the task.

The column of mounted men pulled away from the foot soldiers. The spearhead of the horse troops crested the hill.

Instead of an opposing army arrayed on the north road, they saw only a handful of riders.

The Free Company charged, venting blood-chilling war cries. Gunfire crackled as they opened fire.

Johnny Cross and the other raiders turned, fleeing into the pass and out of sight.

The marauder column rushed downhill, turning to the right to enter Cross's Cut. Several hundred yards ahead of them, the Hangtree raiders could be seen racing for the east end of the pass.

The robber bandits poured into the cut. The effect was like a stream suddenly entering a narrow channel. They were packed close together in a tight bristling mass that slithered and squirmed its way through the cut like a giant snake. On either side rose the cliffs, some several hundred feet high.

Rocky walls bulged with arches, ledges, and overhangs that blocked off much of the narrow strip of open sky at the top of the cut. At its most narrow, the pass was only about a hundred feet wide.

The Hangtree raiders reached the end of the pass, flashing through it to the open range of the Cross Ranch.

The Free Company column was close behind.

TWENTY-NINE

Jimbo Turlock waved a cavalry saber whose curved gleaming blade struck glints of reflected sunlight. He was at the point of an Honor Guard platoon of his personal bodyguards, hard men riding six riders abreast on either side of him.

The column extended far behind, deep in the pass, marauders crowding and hurrying. They shouted, whooped, and hollered, brandishing pistols and rifles, shooting them off though there were as yet no targets at which to shoot.

Rock walls fell away, flaring outward like the mouth of a trumpet, then ending abruptly as the head of the column broke out of the pass and into the open.

Their speed was great, their momentum well-nigh irresistible. They poured out of the pass, streaming down the gentle slope at the foot of the cut, onto the land of Cross Ranch.

On the knoll across a shallow hollow were Sam Heller, his crew, and the howitzer the Free Company had looted from Fort Pardee and which Sam and friends had stolen back from the marauders. The field piece's barrel was leveled at the charging vanguard of the Free Company column.

Lookouts and snipers posted on top of the summits of both sides of the cliffs bordering the cut spotted the raiders coming home pursued by the Free Company. They waved red flags to signal their fellows below to be ready.

Ready they were.

Johnny Cross and the other raiders galloped hell-bent-for-leather, quickly swinging to the side to get out of the line of fire of the howitzer on the knoll.

The Free Company vanguard streamed out of the pass and were charging down the slope when they realized what they had rushed into.

Jimbo Turlock shouted, "*It's a trap!*"

Sam touched a piece of hot fire cord to the touch hole in the side of the squat blue-black howitzer barrel. A spark ignited the primer in the touch hole, igniting the gunpowder charge loaded in the howitzer. The gunpowder detonated, spewing fire and smoke, hurling a cannonball into the head of the Free Company charge.

The howitzer rocked back on the carriage of its wheeled framework from the mighty recoil. The gun crew were careful not to stand behind it, having been thoroughly schooled by Sam on its dangers.

The blast was deafening. The very air seemed to shimmer and shake from the concussion.

Sam was firing canister shell loads. The disintegrating shell loosed 148 white-hot .69-caliber lead musket balls traveling at ultra-high velocity. It was the artillery equivalent of a giant sawed-off shotgun and served a similar purpose—to inflict maximum damage at close quarters to as many combatants as possible and terrorize the survivors.

It performed both functions superlatively well, stopping the Free Company charge dead in its tracks.

Rows of mounted horsemen were cut down, falling in smoking heaps to the ground. The devastation was awesome.

Combat veterans had learned the maxim *You never hear the shell that kills you.* Truly, Jimbo Turlock heard the shrill shrieking scream of the canister shell as it tore into the ranks. And it didn't kill him. The wide fan spray of sizzling white-hot musket balls missed him. He felt the wind and heat of their passing as they killed and maimed the cream of his frontline cavalry troops.

With cannonballs passing harmlessly over their heads, a platoon-sized group of Hangtree riflemen hid among the weeds and rocks and rills of the hollow fronting the knoll. Veterans and hunters whose aim was true, they opened fire from the prone position. The reports from several dozen rifles firing at once made a great crackling noise . . . like a giant sheet tearing. It tore into the massed ranks of mounted marauders on the slope and in the mouth of the pass, sweeping dozens of Free Company marauders from their saddles.

Other groups of shooters were posted on the left and right flanks of the center group. Their weapons spoke, entering the fray as they opened fire. Streaming sheets of lead ripped through the Free Company ranks like a hailstorm tearing down a field of cornstalks.

Sam Heller and his gun crew were hard at work readying the howitzer for another round. Otto Berg worked a ramrod with an oversized water-saturated swab at the business end, thrusting it down the bore of the howitzer's barrel to extinguish any remaining sparks or embers within, which otherwise might disastrously touch off the fresh charge of gunpowder about to be inserted.

Luke Pettigrew handed off a gunpowder charge bag, pre-mixed, pre-measured, and self-contained, passing it to Tonk. Tonk scrambled up the knoll, loading the charge into the receptacle at the base of the howitzer's barrel, sealing it closed tight.

Once the needful wadding was in place in the bore, Noel Maddox and Otto Berg, with no small amount of heaving and straining, manhandled a canister round into the barrel.

As enemy bullets whizzed past the top of the knoll like a fusillade of vicious metal wasps, the gun crew completed their tasks, dropping flat to the ground at the sides of the howitzer.

The first blast had broken the back of the Free Company's charge, but the pressure of massed cavalry still in the cut and the teeming horde of camp followers and foot soldiers who had followed the mounted marauders into the pass pushed fresh ranks of cavalry to the eastern mouth of the pass and down the slope.

All being in readiness, Sam Heller fitted the lit end of a piece of fire cord to the howitzer's touch hole. The howitzer vented like an erupting volcano, sending canister shot deep into the pass among the dense-packed marauders. It boomed. The shot screamed and the shell exploded. It hit the Free Company cavalry like a wrecking ball.

The slope at the foot of the cut and the pass itself had become one enormous killing ground. Marauders were wedged so tightly in the pass that those at the front were unable to turn and retreat. The western exit was jammed by mobs of foot soldiers who had eagerly rushed into the cut behind the last of the horsemen.

The platoons of Hangtree marksmen no longer fired volleys in unison. They fired at will. Most had repeating rifles, each picking a human target and downing it, adding a particularly vicious personal touch. They fired shot after shot without reloading.

The howitzer boomed again, clearing a wide passage deep into the cut, plowing its way through the Free Company swarms massed shoulder to shoulder.

The slaughter was prodigious. More, it was righteous.

The shock from an exploding shell knocked Jimbo Turlock from his horse. He decided that the better part of valor was to play dead.

Taking advantage of a lull in the hostilities, he stripped off the fancy navy blue tunic with golden horse-comb epaulets and elaborate gold braid and buttons that he wore as a mark of supreme rank as Free Company commander. He buried it in the sand and began crawling away from the battlefield.

He did not get far before being taken prisoner by an alert Hangtree lad of thirteen armed with a .22 squirrel gun "for shooting varmints."

Victory was swiftly seized by the Hangtree defenders.

Most of the Free Company's two hundred mounted marauders were killed outright in the Battle of the Pass. Some at the rear of the column managed to escape, as did a number of foot soldiers and camp followers. A good portion of the floor of Cross's Cut was jammed with dead bodies, male and female, human and horse.

Johnny Cross pushed his hat brim back off his forehead as he surveyed the scene, one hand resting on the upper rim of a howitzer wheel. He and Sam Heller exchanged glances.

Johnny rapped his knuckles on the weapon. "Handy piece to have around, especially in a pinch."

"The Army's going to want it back," Sam said.

Johnny shrugged, a gesture which Sam knew might mean much or nothing at all.

Marshal Mack Barton rode up, reining in beside the knoll. His eyes glittering slits, he smiled a self-satisfied smile.

"Talk about the cat who ate the canary," Sam said.

"Careful—when he smiles like that it usually winds up costing somebody else some money," Johnny cautioned. He greeted the lawman. "Hey, Marshal."

"Some dustup, eh? What a fight!" Barton said.

"Uh-huh," Johnny said noncommittally. "Say, Marshal, me being a taxpaying citizen of Hangtree County, I got a question for you."

"Shoot," Barton said cheerfully.

"Cross's Cut is a valuable piece of property. Useful, too, not just to me and Luke but to lots of other folks who use it. It's a shortcut that saves men and livestock long detours going to and from Wild Horse Canyon."

"If you're trying to sell me some real estate, forget it! I ain't in the market," Barton chuckled. "Don't mind me, I'm just joking."

"Now the cut is filled with about a hundred tons of dirt and rock, not to mention a couple hundred bodies of men, women, and horses," Johnny continued. "What I want to know is, who's gonna clean it up?

Don't seem right that I gotta take a loss after helping save the whole blamed county. I didn't ask to fight a battle in my own background, especially if it puts me out of pocket."

"I'm glad you asked me that question," Barton began, only to be interrupted by a noisy clamor.

Behind him three well-guarded freight wagons came rolling up, halting in a cloud of dust. In addition to a shotgun messenger occupying the front seat of each along with the driver, several rifle-toting escorts rode alongside each wagon.

Blacksmith Hobson held the reins of the lead wagon, Deputy Smalls seated beside him. Smalls held a big shotgun, looking about as happy as his mournful basset hound face allowed him to express.

The freight wagon's hopper held a half-dozen or so men. Chained men. So did the other two wagons.

The men were bruised, battered, dirty, and hatless, their clothes torn and ragged. Each man was fettered with a pair of iron cuffs around the ankles with a thirty-six-inch length of chain joining the cuffs.

Additionally, each set of ankle cuffs had one cuff rigged with an extra-large iron eyebolt, through which a length of stout chain had been passed, the single chain linking all the men together. There was enough slack in it to allow them to sit together and presumably move around in a constricted shuffling gait, but it did not give much in the way of freedom of movement.

"What-all you got there, Marshal?" Luke asked Barton.

"That's an idea from one of our Georgia friends," Barton said. "What you call a chain gang. Keeps the prisoners from wandering off and getting into trouble."

"Sorry-looking bunch," Johnny said. "Who are they?"

"That's what's left of Denton Dick's bunch," Barton said.

"Denton Dick from Denton, Texas?"

"The very same. There he is yonder, sitting in that first wagon. Say howdy to Johnny Cross, Dick," Barton ordered.

One of the prisoners in the lead wagon turned to face the marshal and the others, his chains rattling as he shifted position. Shame and woe had brought him low, so that he seemed shrunken, used-up. He sat forlornly with shoulders hunched, head bowed, droopy eyes rheumy and filmed, mouth so downcast that it looked like a horseshoe with the two ends pointing down. "Howdy," he croaked, his voice flat and dry.

"That's Denton Dick?" Johnny said, surprised.

"None other. He's kind of hard to recognize without his big hat, I reckon," Barton said.

"What're you doing with him and them others?" Luke asked.

"Them rascals was looking to throw in with Jimbo Turlock, but we nipped them in the bud," the marshal said. "Most of them didn't do enough worth hanging for, so we're gonna put them to work for the town to teach them the error of their ways."

"I know a good place for them to start." Johnny said, a gleam in his eye.

"I'm way ahead of you. Who do you think's gonna clear out Cross's Cut?" Barton said, beaming, expansive.

"That a fact?" Johnny was surprised and impressed.

"No lie."

"Well, if that don't beat all! I'm obliged to you,

Marshal, much obliged. Why, shucks, I don't rightly know how to thank you."

"Be sure to vote for me come Election Day. That's all I ask," Barton said, smiling a crocodile smile. "You, too, Luke."

"Hell, Marshal, I'll be proud to vote for you as many times as you like," Luke said enthusiastically.

"Don't say I never did nothing for you boys," Barton said. "Now after them rannies clean out the cut and bury the dead, here and at Fort Pardee, we'll find plenty of chores for them to do in town. Yes, sir. Meet Hangtree County's brand-new, all-purpose chain gang!"

"Generally I don't much hold with chaining a man up, but I got to admit, on them it looks good," Johnny said.

Jimbo Turlock had hoped to go unrecognized, but as chance would have it he was paraded past the men at the howitzer.

Years of living off the fat of the land had increased Turlock's girth, but Johnny had no trouble recognizing the pretender who had once considered himself an equal of the great Quantrill.

"Howdy, Jimbo." Johnny's smile was so warm that you would have thought he was genuinely glad to see the other.

He was. He was genuinely glad that Turlock hadn't gotten away to escape the noose.

THIRTY

In the days that followed, most of the rabble horde of camp followers associated with the marauders were hunted down by the folk of Hangtree. Jimbo Turlock was one of prisoners held for trial. The results were not pretty. All were speedily found guilty and sentenced to death. Swift justice satisfied the law-abiding citizens of the county, who would have been the first to suffer had the Free Company triumphed.

Spread out over a few days so as not to have too much of a good thing, the condemned were executed the old-fashioned way, at the Hanging Tree. Long-dead, lightning-blasted and missing most of its limbs and branches, that grim old towering tree trunk stood sentinel on top of Boot Hill, across from the church and west of Hangtree town. By virtue of his position as the Free Company commander, Turlock was to be hanged last.

Executions were always popular and edifying events with mass attendance. Folks came from all over the

county and even from Weatherford to see Jimbo
Turlock swing.

A festive carnival mood filled the air. The area
around Boot Hill was jam-packed with hundreds of
spectators—men, women, and children—who'd come
to see the show.

Execution hour found Turlock sitting astride a
horse, hands tied behind his back. A length of corded
hempen rope with a noose at one end hung from a
gnarled tree limb overhead.

Marshal Mack Barton asked Turlock if he had any
last words.

Turlock wanted to make a fine bold speech, but
when the time came his throat was bone-dry, and he
was unable to speak.

The hangman fitted the noose over Turlock's head
and around his neck, tightening it. He had a quirt, a
short braided rawhide whip used to lash the horse
holding the condemned man into motion.

Pastor Fulton wielded a Bible, reading aloud the
psalm with the line about the "valley of the shadow
of death."

Among the crowd, Johnny Cross nodded approvingly. He'd always liked that psalm.

The preacher finished. The marshal and the hangman exchanged glances. Barton nodded, signifying
yes, it's time.

The hangman raised the quirt, bringing it down
hard on the horse's rump. The animal was reluctant to
step off.

Professionally embarrassed, the hangman wielded
the lash again, slashing the horse's hindquarters.

The horse lunged forward. Turlock was brought up

short by the noose around his neck. An overexcited spectator in the crowd vented an enthusiastic rebel yell of approval.

Hanging by the neck at the end of a rope, it was the last thing Jimbo Turlock heard in this world before crashing the gates of Hades:

A rebel yell!